# BY J A JOLLEY

## *THE CHRONICLES OF SATERIA*

Book One: A Light of the Lost
Book Two: Mourning Light *

## *THE EYE OF THE DAY SAGA*

Book One: Cataracts

*Forthcoming

# A LIGHT FOR THE LOST

## — THE CHRONICLES OF SATERIA —
### BOOK ONE

### BY

# J A JOLLEY

Cover design by Star Shine Stories in conjunction with Sir Doodle
Art and Jewelry

Edited by Alex Richmond and Constance Price

Second Edition, 2026 ISBN: 979-8-9996651-3-3

Published by Star Shine Stories

Printed in the United States of America

# Dedication

*To those who feel the shadows closing in, remember: Even*
*the smallest spark can ignite a flame.*
*This book is dedicated to those of us standing together to*
*find our way back to the light.*

*Never stop fighting.*

## Special Thanks

I would like to thank my mother, Vivian, and my good friend, Alex, for helping me craft this story into something that can be enjoyed by everyone; and to Constance for being the original inspiration that allowed me to create the first threads in what I hope to be a grand tapestry.

I would also like to extent a special thank you to the Pathfinder group that made this story possible:

*Adam Chandler*
*Alex Richmond*
*Constance Price*
*Jason Pitts*
*Robert Collins*
*Nikki Smith*
*Tyler Smith*

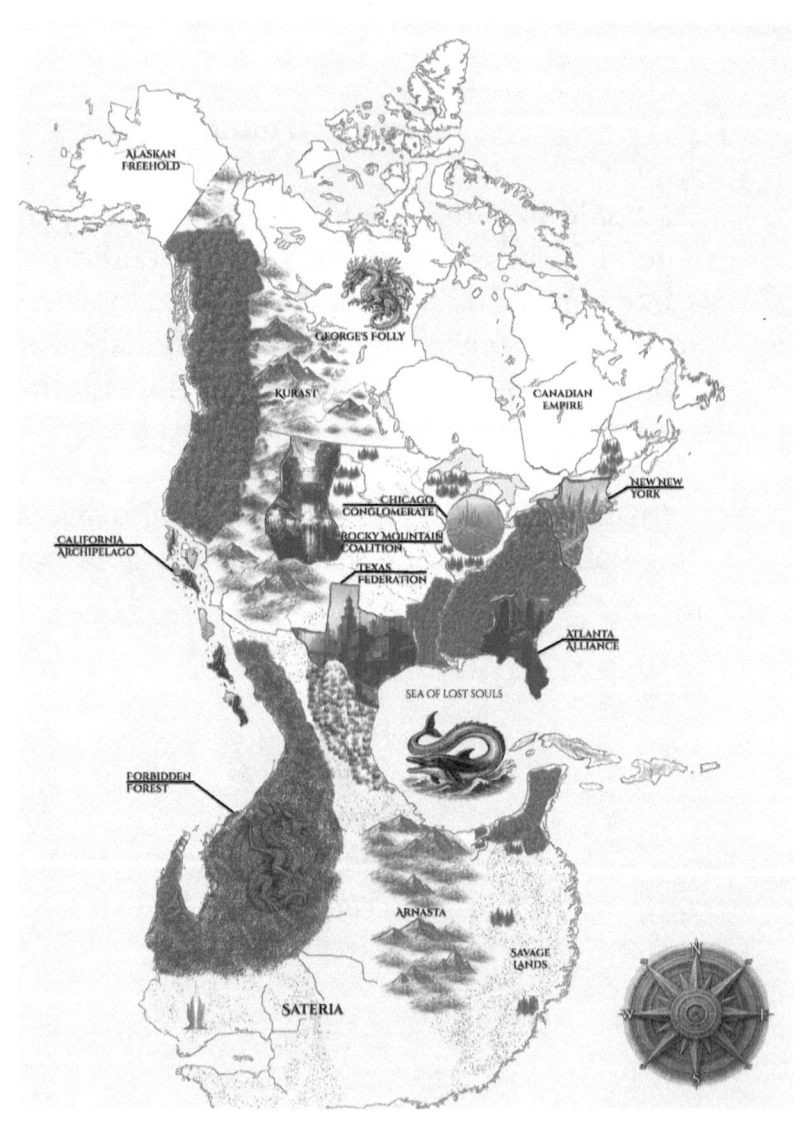

# PROLOGUE

Harold stepped off the bus and a wall of heat hit him—wet and heavy as if opening a barn in August with the doors shut all day. The smell of diesel hung in his nose. The glare from the gravel was blinding and cruel. His legs went slack —rubbery, swaying—something he had to master fast before anyone saw. Wool scratched at his throat as he pulled the duffel strap higher and felt the canvas cut into his shoulder.

"Line up, single file!" The shout cracked across the yard, went through his skull. Blinking hard against the glare, he found the sergeant—square jaw, cap set low—planted in front of a run of cinderblock buildings. There were no sandbags or wire he could see, just paint baked dull by the sun and a few hills rolling soft and green beyond. State of the art? It looked like county property.

"Fort Bradley," he said under his breath, trying the name.

He fell in; gravel shifted under his boots with a dry crunch. Someone ahead coughed—a wet rattle. Harold flinched before he could stop himself, then felt rotten for it. Poor fella sounded beat to ribbons by a cold—or worse. He eased his breath to keep from drawing it in and fixed his eyes on the sergeant's shoulders instead of the back of the man's neck.

The sun needled his eyes, sweat stinging so hard he couldn't wipe it without losing the strap; the heat here had a temper—mean and personal—and while Pennsylvania summers could get ugly, this was like trying to suck air through a damp rag, his chest aching with the work of it. Harold counted the breaths—four in, four out—like toting feed when the mud wants you down.

"Company! Atten—SHUN!" The bark hit his ears. He straightened so fast his spine popped, teeth clicking with his heels. Yes, sir. Eyes front. Shoulders square. His father's voice came soft as prayer: Stand up, be a man, and answer plain. He swallowed and fixed on a point over the sergeant's cap brim, steadying.

There was movement on the far side of the yard: an officer, neat as a new dime, came on with two troopers flanking. They walked like their boots knew the ground. Behind them—wrong as a snowdrift in July—came a man in a white coat with a clipboard. His coat was so clean it threw the dust into relief around him. Not Army. A doctor, maybe? Harold felt a small lift of the skin along his arms, a prickle that made him want to rub at it. Doctors were fine when you chose 'em, but a doctor flanked by soldiers made the back of his mind say specimen. He hated that word.

"All right, maggots," the sergeant—Collins, his name tag said —snarled, and the word made Harold's teeth touch. "This here is Dr. Martin. He'll be conducting your initial health screenings. Don't waste his time, and for God's sake, try not to faint on the man."

A thin laugh rippled and died. Harold kept his face still. Needles flashed in his thoughts—alcohol burn, steel bright as the sun on the gravel. This wasn't Europe. It wasn't beaches and banners and folks cheering from windows. This was a sun-baked yard in West Virginia with that spotless coat and a clipboard with potential orders he hadn't heard the shape of yet. He shifted the duffel to his other shoulder. The strap squeaked against his damp shirt.

He reckoned he'd follow the book until it ran crooked. He could do that. When his turn came he'd say, "Yes, sir," and hold out his arm. He'd look the doctor in the eye like a man looks at another man, not a thing to be handled. And if the handling turned unnatural—if it slid from soldiering into whatever this place kept under its fresh paint—well. He felt his hands ball once and loosen. God help us, he thought, and stepped when the line stepped.

Men went to the white coat one by one and came away stamped on the clipboard, faces tight with relief—as if passing a gate they hadn't known was locked. Sweat ran down Harold's side. When the sergeant called his name, he stepped out because his legs knew to, not because his head felt ready.

Dr. Martin wasn't the hawk Harold had pictured. Older—creases at the mouth, a day's wear behind the eyes. Wire frames low on his nose. The blue of his gaze had a lake-cold clarity Harold hadn't seen on any parade ground. For a second, there was a hitch in the doctor's expression—familiarity or a thought unfinished—then it was gone.

"Head up, chest out, soldier." The voice was even, not the bark of Collins. Harold set his shoulders; the muscle across his back pulled and held.

The doctor moved around him with a calm, practiced look, as if counting boards on a fence. "Miller, was it?"

"Yes, sir." His mouth was dry; the word rasped.

"Mm." A small sound, and then a soft chuckle that didn't quite belong out here in the yard. "You've got your mother's eyes, I'd wager. Strong German stock, wouldn't you say?"

The words landed oddly. Harold blinked. His mother didn't come up with strangers—certainly not here. He felt the heat in his face and couldn't tell if it was the sun. "I… suppose so, sir."

"You remind me of my grandson, Joseph." The doctor's tone thinned, went careful. "Same stubborn chin. He's in the European theater. Good soldier."

Pride tugged at something in Harold—pride for a boy he didn't know—braided with a sour twist. Europe meant fighting Germans; "German stock" lived under his skin and behind his mother's eyes. He couldn't resolve the knot—

"Private Miller!" Collins's voice cracked like a timber under weight. "Step lively—we're not here for story hour."

The moment snapped clean. Dr. Martin's pen ticked the page. "Fit for duty," he said, not unkindly. "Next."

Harold stepped away, the duffel suddenly heavier, as if the canvas had soaked up the sweat pouring off of him. The brief humane warmth of the doctor's gaze made the yard feel harsher by comparison, the white coat brighter, the fatigues darker. Fort Bradley kept adding corners he couldn't see around.

Names were shouted; boots dragged. He let the tide carry him to the barracks. Inside, the light went dim through flyspecked windows. Heat held there too, thick with other notes—wool, damp socks, metal bunks, a chemical tang that stung the back of his nose. The floorboards had a waxed sheen and a scuffed path down the center, like a trail beaten through corn. Bunks stood in ranks, blankets folded to exact edges, footlockers square as tombstones.

He found his tag, let the duffel fall. The thud sounded louder than it should've. He flexed his fingers to bring the blood back and worked at the knot in the strap where it had chewed his shoulder. Around him: boys who weren't boys anymore by their bearing; a freckled kid rubbing at a vaccination mark; a broad-shouldered farmhand with chapped knuckles twisting his cap brim into a rope. Faces began distinct and then blurred into the same drawn look—tired, sleep-hungry. Maybe they all carried the same quiet questions. Or maybe he was the only coward in the room.

"Listen up, shit-stains!" Collins filled the doorway like bad weather. The scowl didn't move, only his mouth. "You'll find your kit and a fresh uniform at the end of your bunk. Mess hall in thirty. Don't be late."

The words hit like a stamp on wet clay—impression made, no room to argue. Harold reached for the tin at his bunk's foot. It was cool and gritty under his fingers. He set it on the blanket, breathed slow through the harsh smell of disinfectant in the air, and made himself stand straight in the narrow space he'd been given. Thirty minutes. He could do thirty minutes. Then the next thirty. Then the next.

Harold fought the buckles with clumsy fingers, webbing stiff as kindling and the brass snaps tacky with new paint. The wool shirt rasped his forearms. At the edges of his vision the room went busy—men down to undershirts, displaying pale skin that

13

would eventually be marked with tattoos which would blue and blur, maybe a future pinup faded to a ghost on a shoulder blade or two. Talk ran sharp and too loud, laughter that broke off a half beat early. Somebody whistled a bar of a song and lost it halfway through.

He felt his chest go hollow for a second, the feeling you get when a ladder shifts under you. Posters and parades had promised something clean; but this wasn't hero work. It was keeping up, day after day.

The mess hall took the sound of a hundred men and made it into a single roar—trays clanging on the rail, benches skidding, the harsh scrape of tin on tin. Steam carried the smell of boiled cabbage, coffee gone bitter, ceiling fans pushed hot air in slow circles. Harold slid his tray along, took his scoop of gray beans and a cut of meat that fought the knife, and found a spot at a long table where no one had yet staked a claim with a cap or a fork.

He was worrying a string of fat loose from the roast when a figure shadowed his tray. Dr. Martin set his own down opposite him with the careful quiet of a man approaching a skittish horse. Up close the coat held a trace of hospital—carbolic and clean—but his smile was easy.

Collins's disapproval carried without him raising his voice. "Doc, surely you've got better places for your meal hour than pestering recruits."

"Just checking on my young friend," Dr. Martin said, the answer even and set. "Can't have him wasting away."

Heat rose in Harold's cheeks, he couldn't blame on the chow line. The doctor sipped coffee, made a face, and, as if to push the taste away, said, "My grandson Joseph—fished the

14

Monongahela with me before he left home." The images came quick and small: a tin pail that smelled of river, a boy's laugh bouncing off water. Harold nodded along before he meant to. The gentleness in the old man's eyes took a thin layer off the hardness of the room.

"You know," the doctor went on, leaning in a fraction, "we used to play chess on Saturdays. Keeps a mind awake. If you ever want a distraction…"

Something jumped in Harold—hope or shame, he couldn't tell. "I've never learned, sir." The admission felt like he'd left a button undone.

"All the better." Dr. Martin's mouth creased. "I'll teach you. Call it a welcome."

A bell clanged somewhere by the serving line, sharp enough to set forks down. Men rose as one. Harold pushed back on unsteady legs. Collins's look found him across the room—a flint spark. Message received: keep your head down. He bused his tray, the metal cold and slick under his fingers, and fell into the current toward the door.

Night made the barracks a different place. The heat leaked off and left a thin draft that threaded under the door and tapped at his ankles. Springs creaked when a man rolled; someone's breath rattled like paper; a far fan ticked out of rhythm. The day replayed in quick cuts—Collins's bark, the white of the doctor's coat, the snap of the pencil at "Fit for duty," the clatter and heat of the hall. Each time he felt himself starting to drop, his legs twitched like he'd missed a step and he was back on the yard squinting into the sun.

He thought of Joseph as a shape more than a person—and of Dr. Martin's voice when he said his name. There was a give to the man that didn't match the rest of this place. A crack in the wall where a little air got through. Harold lay on his back, eyes open to the dark, and counted the fan's ticks until they blurred. When the fan stuttered and caught again, he let his jaw unclench and promised himself: learn the board; keep the steps; watch for what's under the paint.

The chess offer stayed the oddest piece on the board. A doctor in a white coat, with officers for company, seeking out a string-bean recruit? The tiny swell of being chosen didn't last; unease settled in behind it. Maybe it was kindness. Maybe it was a test dressed up to look like one.

Sleep took him in snatches. When it came, Fort Bradley followed. The board he and the doctor had set between them bled into a field, squares turning to muddy plots, pawns to boys with tin tags and torn sleeves. A calm voice—Dr. Martin's, but thin and cool—counted tempos, traded pieces as if they were hours. A knight fell with the soft clack of wood and Harold felt it in his ribs like a boot striking a step he couldn't see.

Nights stacked up like cordwood: slow, bright moons and a fence line that never moved. On guard he learned the sound of his own boots, the rifle's balance across his palms, the way cicadas filled the hollow spaces between thoughts. He counted steps until numbers stopped meaning anything, mouthed a line of his mother's old poem and lost it halfway through, tried to let his mind empty and found it circling back to a checkered board and a white coat.

The game made a small harbor in the weeks that followed. Dr. Martin—Victor, he'd said, "Call me Victor when it's just us"—set out a battered set whose pieces had been handled to a polish. He taught by stories when he didn't teach by names: castles and rivers and bottlenecks where a single bridge decided a march. "Here's your river," he'd say, sliding a file of pawns, "and here's the ford," touching a square with his fingertip. He wove Joseph into it without forcing him—tales of a boy with quick hands and a loud laugh who could pull a radio apart and have it singing again before the coffee went cold. Harold listened and learned when to trade, when to wait, when to walk the king like a farmer taking the long way home. The warmth in the old man's eyes took some of the sting out of the days, but the stories left a burr: Joseph—in the stories—had a river with a real current, while Harold's battles were all wood and rule.

Sometimes the talk fell away. The doctor's hand would rest light on Harold's sleeve, the blue of his eyes gone far off, and he'd say, "It's good to be young," in a tone that held both blessing and weight. Harold never knew where to put that sentence. He stored it with the rest of the base's odd corners.

Back on the fence he shrank to what he could trust: gravel, wire, trees ticking together in a wind that smelled of damp earth and hot metal. The rifle strap cut the same groove into his shoulder every shift. If danger lived out there, it hid well. His worry lived closer in.

Days blurred: measured by whistle, by mess line, by the ache that moved from thighs to shoulders and back again. Collins barked them into the same shapes until Harold's body answered without any need for thought. Letters from home stayed in his footlocker with the corners yellowing; he told himself he'd open them when his hands didn't shake from drill, and the day for that never seemed to come. Still, the games remained—one square of light in the routine.

It was during one of those quiet evenings, the mess hall emptied to scrape and mop, the set between them smelling faintly of old varnish, that the pattern broke. Victor had just lifted a knight from the board—dark wood warm from his palm—and didn't put it down. His easy warmth cooled, not to anger but to something exact.

"Do you know what I do here, Harold?" he asked, eyes on the captured piece, thumb running the carved ear smooth. He asked it again, softer, as if the first time had been to himself.

Harold kept his eyes on the board. "No, sir," he said. "I'm a surface guard. I don't have clearance for that." He meant it to sound steady; the words came out stumbling over each other. A cool run skittered up his back.

Victor studied the pieces like they might confess if he stared long enough. His brow tightened; a breath left him heavy. "Perhaps that's for the best," he said, almost to the knight in his hand.

Silence spread. Somewhere down the hall a door shut and the sound traveled the floorboards. Harold knew how things worked here: do the task, ask nothing, keep your profile narrow. Still, curiosity pressed. Why him? Why a doctor and a scrub recruit with a board between them?

Victor looked up. The blue had gone tired around the edges. "There are things happening here, Harold. Things the world isn't ready for." He seemed to reach for a further sentence and think better of it. A small shake of the head. "Forget I said anything. Knowledge is a dangerous load to shoulder."

The table felt a fraction lower, the shadows deeper. Harold's pulse drummed at his ears. He tried to breathe through his nose and only caught disinfectant and the sweetish ghost of mess-hall coffee. The waving of the spoken thought felt like a backhand, making him feel inadequate. Though, it did pique his curiosity—what kinds of 'things' could a doctor's hands be in? The thought made his skin itch.

"Don't worry that young mind of yours," Victor said after a moment, and bent a smile into place. "Perhaps it will make sense someday. For now—let's keep that king of yours from getting cornered, shall we?"

He set the knight down with a soft click and the game moved again, but the warmth had been usurped by an unnatural chill. Every pawn Harold advanced felt like stepping into tall grass where he couldn't see the ground. Victor's gaze slid past the board now and then, as if checking a clock only he could see. Whatever his work was, it had worn a rut in him. Harold felt a sliver of it settle across his own shoulders—the kind you notice only when you straighten and it pulls.

He drew a slow breath, squared the file, and made the safe move Victor had taught him. Defend first. Learn the shape of danger before you name it.

\*\*\*

Word of Harold's promotion ran the length of Fort Bradley faster than the mess line, helped along by Harold himself—grinning, holding up the paper and tapping the fresh chevron at his sleeve for anyone who'd look. It wasn't much on a ladder that stretched past sight, but it tasted fine after two months of grit. Interior guard duty meant walls instead of wind, a warm hallway instead of frost on his boots, and—God willing—less of Sergeant Collins's looming shadow.

He didn't think about who to tell first; his feet already knew. He found Victor in an unrestricted lab—no guard on the door, just a metal placard and the hum of air through a vent. Ballasts buzzed overhead, flattening everything. Glassware stood in ranks: beakers with taped labels, pipettes in a jar, a scale with its pan polished to a mirror. The room smelled of alcohol and something sweet beneath it—phenol, maybe—over the dry scent of paper. One wall was covered in maps and charts drawn with hair-thin lines in colors Harold couldn't place. Rivers where no rivers ought to be. Rings inside rings like age marks on a tree. He filed it as "Victor's business" and kept his eyes off it.

"Victor!" he blurted, breath high in his chest. "I got promoted. Private first class—interior duty." The last bit came out almost sheepish.

"Private first class," Victor said, and the smile that rose was slow. "Congratulations, Harold. I'm proud of you."

The words landed right. The smile didn't. Not the open grin Harold had pictured, but a small, knowing crease, as if Victor had read the orders yesterday. The thought made Harold feel both taller and a little foolish.

He rushed to fill the space. "No more fence line. You wouldn't believe how the wind cuts out there. Last week a coon went crazed at the wire—eyes like coals. I almost put a round through my boot. Anyway, inside duty—warmer nights. Maybe I'll be able to hear myself think." He heard himself babbling and couldn't stop it. He painted the job rosy without meaning to, held the picture up between them like a tin toy.

Victor nodded at the right spots, but his gaze drifted past Harold's shoulder to some fixed point on the far wall. The smile stayed—tidy and satisfied, not moving with the talk. The mismatch lifted the small hairs at the back of Harold's neck.

Silence came down. Harold's voice ran out; the hum of the lights took over.

"Thank you for telling me," Victor said at last, quieter. "It's good to see your hard work noticed."

He turned with that to the bench—gloved a hand, steadied a test tube, made a small mark on a chart. It wasn't rude, just a dismissal gentle enough to leave no bruise.

Harold backed a step and then another, orders crackling soft in his fist. Out in the corridor the air felt colder, the concrete floor colder still through his soles. He looked once at the chevron stitched on his sleeve. The lift he'd walked in with had already died under that fixed, unreadable smile, and he couldn't say why. He folded the paper carefully, as if neat edges might hold his good news together, and went to learn the halls he'd be guarding.

\*\*\*

The news moved the way everything moved at Fort Bradley— quick, efficient, and hard to escape. First a whisper at the mess line, then two men trading looks outside the latrine, and finally a typed notice pinned to a corkboard and read aloud in a voice that let none of it stick to the reader. Joseph Martin. KIA.

Harold felt the words strike and spread. Shock first. Then guilt, bitter as bad coffee in his gut. Yesterday—had it only been yesterday?—Victor had told the hornet story, laughing at the memory of a boy flailing with his cap, then boasting on a catch that bent a cheap bat. Now all that sound had been pressed flat into a line on a page.

He went looking for Victor with a knot tightening under his ribs. The lab's door gave against his palm. Inside, the noise was missing; no centrifuge, no fans, only the faint tick of electricity. On the bench: a stack of maps with the corners lifted, a pencil rolled to a stop against a glass beaker. Victor sat folded over his desk, shoulders working in small, helpless shudders.

"Victor," Harold said, barely there. He set a hand on the coat's shoulder seam and felt the tremor through the fabric.

Victor started as if waking. He lifted his face. The blue in his eyes had gone watery; the rims were raw. "He's gone," he said, the words catching. "My Joseph."

The room seemed to pull in around that admission. Harold had never seen Victor without the soft control he wore like a habit. Here it had sloughed off, leaving a man hit square in the center. "I'm sorry," Harold managed. It sounded small against the weight in the room, but it was all he had to offer.

Somewhere down the hall a cart wheel squeaked and turned a corner. Harold couldn't make the scale of the loss fit in his own chest. His promotion, his new post, the way the cold stayed off his bones on interior guard—what were those next to a telegram and the devastating news it had carried?

Victor drew a breath that scraped and sat up by inches, forcing order back into himself. "Thank you, Harold," he said, wracked with sorrow. "It means… a lot."

22

Something passed between them that didn't need naming. The war Harold had pictured—clean lines, flags, a purpose you could point to—shed its skin. What stood there instead was a machine that took everything and gave nothing in return.

After that day the lab changed. The chessboard stayed on a shelf and gathered dust. Victor did not sit so much as pace. Charts migrated from the wall to the bench to the floor; strings of figures filled margins; arrows ran over maps in colored inks Harold didn't recognize. The smell of disinfectant was cut by hot metal and the ghost of solder. Papers hissed as Victor slid them under his hands. He talked more, faster, as if the words themselves could keep him upright.

"Telluric currents," he said, eyes fever bright. "Beneath us— veins—conductive paths in the mantle, in the crust. Information rides them as surely as charge rides a wire." He tapped a diagram where rings nested inside rings. "Look— geomagnetic disturbance here, here—see the phase lag? The field sings, Harold. We are deaf to it, but it sings."

Harold nodded because something was required. The terms came in gusts—electromagnetic fields, conductive rare earth minerals, auroral coupling—and then the phrase that set the hair on Harold's arms: "Sea of Souls." Victor said it with care, not sermon, more scientist than mystic and somehow that made it worse. "A medium," he pressed on, "not water, not air—call it the spiritual substrate if you must. Perturb it here," a finger jabbed a circle, "and something answers there."

Harold held the bench edge and listened as a man far out in deep water marks his breaths. He tried to match what he heard to what he knew: wire strung from barn to house; a radio that found voices from nowhere; a compass needle that would not lie. He could not tell if grief had unmoored Victor or if it had stripped something away to reveal the hidden frame beneath. The lab felt smaller by the day. Even the fluorescents seemed to buzz with a different pitch.

When Victor paused, it was only to scratch a new line or yank a drawer for another map. His hands shook when they were still; when they moved, they steadied. Harold fetched pencils, held a straightedge, learned when to be quiet. He thought of the chessboard with its clear rules and sixty-four squares of possible mercy and felt the absence like a pulled tooth.

Inside the lab, the currents Victor named ran underfoot unseen, and Harold kept his balance the way he had learned on the fence: one step, then the next, eyes open for what moved in the corner of sight.

He caught what he could and tried to make a whole from scraps: the Earth as wire, currents running under rock the way sap runs under bark, energy that could be steered if you knew where to put the hand. The ends of it stayed out of reach. Victor's talk veered when it neared purpose, broke into warnings about watchers and rivals and the kind of enemy that didn't wear a uniform.

One night Victor pressed a notebook into his palms hard enough to grind his joints. "Observations," he said, voice sanded raw. "Measurements. Years of work, Harold. Don't lose it. Study it."

The leather had been sweated smooth by other hands. It smelled of oil and graphite and the faint, high tang of old glue. Harold thumbed it open and saw figures marching in tight rows, dates and latitudes, little arrows sketched along curving lines. The margins held words he knew—storm, amplitude—

and others he didn't—phase lag, resonance—woven through with a phrase that showed up like a tide mark: Sea of Souls.

Fear gnawed low in him. Maybe he was a piece being slid without his seeing the board. Or maybe this was a man with a hole punched clean through him asking for help in the only language he had left.

Interior duty put him in halls he'd never had cause to walk. Light pooled on floors buffed to a dull shine. He passed doors that used to be just doors and now hummed at the seams. Through glass panels he saw banks of equipment awake and watchful—oscilloscopes breathing green lines, racks of vacuum tubes glowing like coals, reels turning the way wind turns prayer flags. The phosphor glow of small bulbous glass screens made the technicians' faces pale and flat. Someone laughed, and it died fast, swallowed by the walls. The mess hall, once a noisy mercy, lost its color; men joked like actors who had forgotten the point of the play.

He couldn't tell whether Fort Bradley had changed, or whether he had.

Sleep came in fragments. When it did, the ground in his dreams wasn't ground at all. Roots braided into lit veins, pulsing slow as a heartbeat. Hills rose like sleeping backs and shivered as the field passed through. He woke tangled in the thin blanket, the notebook clutched to his chest like a prayer book, Victor's voice still in his ear—Don't lose it—the tail end of a command or a plea.

By day he read a page, then two, finger tracking the lines like a child, recognizing only enough to be dangerous. He learned the look of storms on paper: neat columns turning ragged; margin notes dark with pressure. He traced rings that nested without touching and tried to feel what Victor claimed—paths underfoot, singing. Sometimes, by a steel door with the strap cutting the same groove in his shoulder, he thought he heard a tone too low for his ears—felt it in his teeth instead. He'd bite down and it would vanish.

Victor moved faster now, a man running downhill because stopping would break him. Charts slid, pencils snapped, and tubes warmed the air with a dusty heat. He spoke as if to a roomful, ignoring that it was only Harold at the edge of the bench. "Coupling," he'd say, rapping the page with his knuckle. "Alignment. You can't force it—you wait for the field to open. You listen." Then he'd go quiet, the silence crowded with all the things not said.

Harold learned when to steady the straightedge and when to get out of the way. He kept the notebook under his mattress or under his shirt—close enough to feel its weight.

The base felt primed for something—like a thunderstorm that never broke. He lived in that pressure, afloat in other people's secrets with one sure tether: a grief-hollowed doctor whose kindness had turned to drive—and whose drive might blaze them both to ash. He ground his teeth against the drag of it, squared his stance, and did what he'd been taught—defend first, keep your king safe, and watch for the moves you can see coming.

***

Victor's hand shook as he slid the folded papers across the bench. "Change of orders," he rasped.

Harold felt the weight before he looked—thick stock, embossed seal cold under his thumb. Dread pooled low, the way it does when a ladder shifts under you. Another post. Another turn of the gear inside the walls of Fort Bradley. He kept his voice even. "Victor—shouldn't this come through channels?"

Bloodshot eyes lifted to him, hollowed by sleepless nights. "The Well of Souls Project," Victor said, his voice catching, then hardening as if bracing into wind. "It's of the utmost importance. Unparalleled military significance."

Harold hesitated.

Victor let the words sit, then met Harold's stare with cutting clarity. "Why do you think you were promoted—reassigned so quickly?"

"You did that?" The question came out accusatory. Pride and shame collided in his throat and went down like bad swill.

"Of course." Impatience flashed. "Collins would have left you to rot on the fence. I saw that you could be more. You could even be—useful."

The word struck harder than any barked order. *Useful.* A piece slid into place by a hand he hadn't seen. He looked at the seal again and felt small in his own sleeves.

"And now?" he asked, something steelier threading the words. "What am I useful for now?"

"I need someone competent enough to grasp the basics and disciplined enough to follow instructions." Victor's gaze traveled over him like a caliper. "Someone impressionable."

"A—an assistant?" Harold heard the foolishness as he said it. "A gopher?"

"This isn't about your scientific aptitude." The calm in Victor's tone chilled more than anger would have. "Your assignment will be split—high-level interior guard and my personal aide."

"I'm hardly qualified for lab work," Harold said, heat rising up his neck. "I barely passed high school chemistry."

"Precisely." No apology. No smile.

Harold's breath hitched. "But you're not an officer."

Victor released a small, weary sigh. "I am not a civilian, Harold. Lieutenant colonel. I don't stand on show. My rank is for generals and paperwork, and generals seldom visit. Couriers carry orders. Progress reports." He touched the corner of the orders with two fingers as if to bless them.

Shock ran through Harold in a wave of icy dread. The board he'd built in his head—sergeants here, doctors there—tilted. Victor the chess partner. Victor the grandfather. And now, Victor the colonel.

"Your service will be rewarded," Victor went on, the old charm ghosting into his voice. "Privileges, access… a place in something extraordinary."

The fluorescents buzzed in his head so loudly the edges of Harold's thoughts went fuzzy. Somewhere in the next room a relay clicked and settled. He looked at the papers and felt their edges bite his skin. The extraordinary opportunity sounded like bait. Even so, curiosity flared despite the sense he might end up like a fish—beheaded, gutted, and roasting over a fire. He pictured the notebook under his mattress, the maps with rings like tree growth, the hum at certain doors when you walked too close.

He folded the orders once, twice, keeping the creases clean. "What exactly do you need me to do," he asked, "that doesn't require my understanding?"

He drew a steady breath. The lab—once a place he enjoyed—pressed in on him. "Sir," Harold said—because he didn't know what else to call a grieving grandfather who also wore a hidden crown. "With respect, I don't… I don't think I'm the right man for this. Shouldn't you find someone more—qualified?"

Victor held him in a flat, unsettling look. "Qualifications are a matter of perspective," he said. "I believe you're uniquely suited."

He let that sink in, then with the ghost of a smile. "A man loyal enough to humor a grieving old man—loyalty like that is rare."

The air between them tightened. Fear, resentment, a reluctant thread of duty tugged through Harold at once. This was a door into Fort Bradley's true heart; it was also a room he had no business in. He tasted both.

"Sir," he said at last, voice steadier, "I'm no hero, but I enlisted to fight, not—" he gestured at glassware, charts, the white coat — "not this. But I've never run from something hard. I won't start now."

A quick flash crossed Victor's face—surprise, maybe respect. "Good," he said briskly. "We'll begin. Orientation. Protocols. Faces you need to know."

The day blurred and sharpened by turns. Victor set a pace that made Harold's calves burn, threading him through cold corridors where lights hummed and floors shone with fresh wax. Doors opened on rooms he'd marched past for months without ever entering: vault-high chambers where banks of capacitors sat like squat, sleeping trolls; racks of vacuum tubes warming the air with a faint baked-dust smell; oscilloscopes breathing green lines that jittered, then steadied at Victor's touch. He passed drafting tables crowded with slide rules and inked arcs. He saw steel pillars banded with copper and a cage where static lifted the hair on his wrist when he passed too close.

Soldiers posted at the choke points tracked him with flat eyes and patches he didn't recognize. White coats moved like a second species, heads bent over paper, voices low. A relay clicked; a wall of equipment answered with a rising hum that rode up Harold's spine.

Names and ciphers came fast. "Section Theta. Dr. Ames on fields, Dr. Crowley on phase analysis. If you're challenged: 'Faraday.' Response: 'Cage.' Clearance color amber for you— until I change it. Never touch a grounded bus with both hands." Victor spoke without slowing, wheeled him through checkpoints, made him sign and sign again. The Well of Souls —always the Well—showed up on every document and diagram like it was the center of gravity. He felt small as a tack in a span.

Curiosity pulled against fear until his skull ached. By the time Victor left him at a plain metal door, his head throbbed with code words and faces that would likely be gone by morning.

His new quarters looked like money had once passed this way: a real bed with a decent mattress, a narrow dresser, a sink, a reading lamp that clicked with authority, a radiator that knocked to itself when it warmed. He set the notebook on the blanket and sat beside it until his breathing slowed, then lay

back and dragged an arm over his eyes. Sleep didn't come.
Every time his mind emptied, figures from the notebook filled
it again—intersecting lines, latitudes, arrows that jumped
oceans in a pencil stroke. In the stillness he remembered his
father in Clearville, the even way he spoke when a job was to
be done; the day Harold had left with a stiff back and a head
full of heroics. That version of war had been dirty and loud.
This one ran underground and spoke in formulas, and for a
moment—God help him—it sounded like magic.

Magic isn't real. He told himself twice. The fact that it needed
repeating made his hands go cold.

When he slipped into dreams at last, it wasn't into beaches or
gunsmoke. Joseph rose up instead—the boy from Victor's
stories, all sun and river—and his face pulled tight in a scream
Harold couldn't hear. The world around him rippled into a vast
shaft that pulsed with a slow, living light, and the boy's
features thinned into that glow, down and down, as if the earth
itself had opened a throat to swallow—everything. Harold
reached—too late, too slow—and woke with his palm against
the notebook, heart hammering, the radiator knocking like a
distant signal he couldn't yet read.

Harold's world narrowed to halls and diagrams. Days smeared
into each other: up before reveille, boots whispering over
waxed tile, door latch thunking open into the same strip-lit
corridors. The light inside Fort Bradley had a personality—
harsh and unkind—and it left a film on his eyes by noon. He
walked past faces he used to know by name in the mess line—
privates, junior lieutenants, clerks with coffee breath—and saw
only moving parts, teeth on a gear turning some mechanism

Afternoons, the lab swallowed him whole. Victor had burned away the softness grief had left; what remained was all edge and purpose. He drilled Harold the way Collins drilled a platoon: acronyms until the tongue went numb, hand signals, color codes, what to do when an oscilloscope trace went from steady to sawtooth. The room smelled of hot glass; banks of vacuum tubes threw static fields that lifted the hair on Harold's forearms. He learned the sound of a relay clicking home, the thin mosquito whine of a coil under load, the taste of metal that came when a field woke up. "Telluric currents," Victor said so often the syllables wore grooves in Harold's head. Currents running like sap. Currents you could court, not command.

He shadowed Victor through secured spaces, a half step behind and slightly left, watching how doors opened when the right voice met the right lock. Scientists traded clipped sentences; guards with patches he couldn't place straightened when Victor's shadow crossed them. The chessboard still gathered dust on a high shelf. In its place came warnings in a voice that didn't quite allow argument. *Eyes open, Harold.* Sometimes Victor stopped mid-stride as if listening to a note Harold couldn't hear, then moved on.

Nights were torture. He lay on the new mattress and stared at the ceiling until the plaster swam, the notebook warm against his ribs where he tucked it under the shirt. Its pages were a maze—latitudes, dates, rings nested tight, margins full of numbers that meant something to someone, just not him. He traced the lines with a fingertip like a child sounding out letters, and the more he traced the less he understood. When sleep finally took him it didn't keep him: his father's face twisted with judgment; Joseph grinning with a fish on a stringer; Victor's blue gaze gone glassy and bright; and always the Well.

By morning the routine reset: hum of lights, disinfectant sting, the rifle's weight traded for a clipboard. He learned who nodded, who avoided meeting eyes, who flinched at the word "phase." He wrote codes on the inside of his wrist and scrubbed them off in the sink before lights-out. Fear ate at him in a careful, patient way; curiosity bit faster, and always seemed to be hungry for more.

\*\*\*

The summons crackled through the intercom. "Miller, report to surface receiving. Priority delivery."

The surface was for show; deliveries were usually made in the base's underground receive bay. But he signed the log at the checkpoint and took the stairs two at a time anyway.

Heat surrounded him. After weeks of strip-light and concrete cool, the West Virginia sun felt oppressive. The upper loading dock lay empty but for a single truck—olive paint faded to chalk, a refrigerator unit thudding a steady, mechanical pulse. Hot exhaust, diesel, the metallic sting of sun on steel—he squinted until the glare resolved into a driver standing stiff with a clipboard clamped in both hands.

"PFC Miller?" The man's voice was tight.

"Yes, sir." Harold's salute came on reflex.

"Sign." The board moved toward him. "Top priority for Project WOS. Lt. Col. Martin." The driver's eyes slid off Harold's face as the pen scratched.

Canvas snapped back. Cold fog breathed out of the bed, rolling over Harold. Inside: a man-sized transfer case packed in block ice, drains trickling, the hum of the unit filling the space between thoughts. His vision put a face to it—pale, waxed with chill, eyes fixed on the sky. Not just a frosty coffin—Joseph. His own mind did that to him; he couldn't stop it. He didn't lift the lid. He couldn't. His throat closed hard enough to hurt.

"This—this must be a mistake," he managed.

"Orders are orders, son." Pity creased the driver's mouth. "Body needs refrigeration. Scientific imperative."

Scientific Imperative. The phrasing rang wrong in his ears. Joseph wasn't a specimen. He was a boy who fixed radios, laughed loudly at riverbanks, and fought heroically on foreign shores.

Rage surged and broke with nowhere to go. He gripped the clipboard until the metal edge warped. Protocol caught him the way a drilled command. Verify the freight ID against the manifest. Read the seal numbers aloud. Initial here, here. Canvas closed. Locks checked. His hands moved; every motion felt like laying a stone on a grave.

The driver climbed back into the cab without meeting his eye. Harold took position by the passenger step and signaled the gate. As the truck rolled backward and was swallowed the shade of the ramp, cooler air rose off the slope and seeped through his uniform. He waited for the "cargo" to be unloaded.

Gears settled in his head as if they'd been waiting for this tooth to catch. Telluric currents. The Well. Victor's hands shaking around numbers. Whatever they were doing here, it reached past boundaries and borders and into places no order should touch. He began walking, eyes forward, and felt the truck's cold spill into him and settle.

\*\*\*

The lab had a different pitch when he entered—the hum no longer gentle, the ominous buzzing crawling up Harold's scalp. Heat bled off the racks of tubes; the air carried phenol and that scorched smell of warm coils. Victor hunched at a console with both hands moving, toggles and dials working under his fingers like obedient animals. He didn't turn when the door slammed its stop.

"What did you do?" Harold's voice came rough, scraping his throat on the way out.

Victor flinched, shoulders pinching, and looked over. Shock shuddered through the blue, then cooled to something unreadable. "Harold, this is not—"

"Not what?" Harold took two hard steps in, the worn notebook braced in his fist like a brick. "Was Joseph just—just a possession to you?"

Victor's jaw set. "Joseph died a hero's death. What happens to his body is a necessary—"

"Sacrifice? For what?" The words broke loose, loud in the tin room. "For a machine you don't fully understand? For power you can't control?"

"You understand nothing, boy." The evenness snapped. It came out like a spit. "There are forces at work here greater than fronts and flags."

Harold slapped the notebook down so hard a pencil jumped and rolled. Pages fell open—margin figures dark with pressure. "Is this the project's purpose? Numbers and lies? All of this—and him—boiled down to a diagram?"

Somewhere a relay clicked; the trace on a screen steadied like a held breath. Victor sagged onto a stool as if his joints had given. Age settled over him in a visible slump.

"There are moments," he said at last, barely over the machines, "when survival outranks virtue. When the measures left to you are the ones you swore you'd never take."

"You don't get to make that call," Harold shot back. The notebook crinkled under his fingers. "Not for him. Not for me. Not for anyone."

Victor lifted his head. Wretchedness made the blue in his eyes look washed, almost gray. "We're at a precipice, Harold. The axeis… and more than the axeis." His gaze skated past Harold to some far point, the way a man looks through a window in his mind. "Death—" he swallowed, a flinch of the throat "—death itself is the enemy only I can fight. The Well is the key."

"The key to what?" Harold said. He heard the steadiness in his own voice and only then noticed he'd found his spine. "Say it plain."

Victor's mouth worked once, twice, and shut. He looked down at the console. His hands—those capable, careful hands—hovered over the switches but did not move.

Harold stood his ground. He could feel the cold he'd carried up from the truck nested somewhere under his breastbone, a hard weight that wouldn't thaw. "If you're going to call this necessary," he said, quieter now, "you're going to call it by its name."

Victor didn't answer. The only sound was the lab's pulse—the fans, the tubes, the slow rise of a coil into tone—beating at the room's edges, banging on Harold's eardrums. He reached for the notebook, pulled it back to his side not looking away.

Harold heard his words as if from underwater. "Death?" It scraped his throat raw. "You're insane, Victor. Bringing back the dead—that's against nature, against God."

The lab's hum seemed to climb a note. Victor straightened from the console. The blue in his eyes went hard.

"Don't presume to grasp what you have no way of understanding," he said, voice low, tight. "You hold up faith like a shield and call it truth."

"Truth?" Harold shot back. "The truth is you've lost your mind."

Something in Victor's face loosened—no kindness, just age showing through the strain. He raked a hand through his unkempt hair and spoke softer. "The telluric currents aren't curiosities," he said. "They're rivers inside a greater ocean. Energy. Structure. We've mapped the edges of it."

Harold forced a laugh that didn't land. "Stop."

"No." Victor stepped closer, the machines' glow painting his cheeks. "Call it aether, the astral plane, or even Akasha—names change. The Sea of Souls does not. It surrounds us. Every mind that has ever been leaves a wake there." His voice dropped. "The currents are paths. With the right alignment, the right instruments, you can even connect to them."

A chill ran Harold's back and parked between his shoulders. He wanted to believe the words were no more than grieving madness—

"Joseph isn't gone," Victor said, urgent now. "Not entirely. He's entangled. I can pull him free. Not as he was—but stronger."

Harold shook his head until the room blurred. "Death is final. You don't get to lay hands on souls."

Victor's eyes gleamed, grief shining through the fever. "Can't I? What if this is the only door left? Imagine a soldier who cannot fall. An answer to invasion before it reaches our shores." His mouth wavered. "A living god, Harold. And my boy—alive again."

Nausea rose fast. The picture Victor painted—grand and glittering—gnawed at the one soft place Harold couldn't armor: the story of laughter on a riverbank.

"And him?" Harold asked, voice gone hoarse. "Would Joseph be Joseph?"

A pause—actual doubt—creased Victor's brow. "His...essence should persist," he said, choosing each word. "A memory, maybe. But it would still be Joseph."

He swallowed; the uncertainty showed for a breath. Then the steel slid back into place.

"Resurrection is rough work," he said, clinically now. "He would be a weapon first. The rest—would have to come later." His gaze glided to the oscilloscopes, to the steady green lines. "The potential changes the war. Changes the world."

Harold had the sense of a board set he'd never agreed to play— pieces already moving, the king he'd been told to guard no longer a man at all.

Victor's ruminations were the final nail. Harold saw the shape of it at last—the grief was real, but it had been harnessed, yoked to something colder. This wasn't saving Joseph. It was turning him into a thing.

"No," Harold said. The word came rough and small but true. "You've lost yourself. You'd pull his soul through a machine and call it mercy."

Victor's eyes sparked. "It's the only way," he snapped. "We are fighting for survival. Sentiment is a luxury we cannot afford."

Harold held the line. He thought of Clearville—his father's steady hands, work done plain. He thought of the posters that had filled his head with clean battles and banners. Then he saw Joseph as he had been summoned in stories: quick hands, loud laugh, wide grin for the world. Not a specimen. Not a weapon.

"I won't be part of this," he said, steadier now. Something in him had set hard. "Not your Well. Not those currents. Not your grandson."

Victor stared as if weighing a bolt in his palm and finding it light. "You dare defy me?" Fury worked into his visage. "A nobody. A gullible pawn."

"I'm no pawn." Harold straightened until his spine found its place. "I'm a soldier. I won't fight for this."

"You don't know what's at stake."

"Maybe not," Harold said. "But I can smell shit when I'm standing in it."

"Then you are dismissed, Private First Class Miller," Victor said. The cold in his voice didn't quite cover the crack beneath it. Pain showed and then was gone.

Harold's throat worked. There was nowhere to carry outrage here; Fort Bradley had no outside to shout toward. He swallowed what rose, put his hand to his brow with a salute that trembled, and made his mouth say, "Yes, sir."

He didn't look into the blue of Victor's eyes—didn't want to find pity there, or the unbending certainty that had replaced it. He grabbed the leather-bound lifeline out of reflex and turned out of the lab. The door's seal kissed shut behind him; the hum dulled to a body-felt throb in the hall.

The corridors he knew by heart had shifted. Strip-lights buzzed a half note too high. Shadows pooled where the floor dipped; vents breathed like sleepers. Faces passed—men he'd drilled beside—blank as masks, eyes sliding off him. He matched his breathing to his bootfall and kept moving, dwelling a single clear fact in a maze that had stopped pretending it was anything else.

***

His room had the dimensions of a cell and the kindness of one. He sat on the edge of the bed with Victor's notebook heavy across his thighs, the leather warm where his hands had held it

40

too long. He'd stood up to a madman and won nothing for it. He was a cog that had stopped turning, still trapped inside the machine.

The scream tore him out of a shallow doze. Not bugle—an electric wail, knife-thin and rising, set his heart to banging. He fumbled for the electric torch on the nightstand; the weak cone cut a slice through the room's stale dark. The air had that brittle charge it got before a storm.

He pulled on his shirt with clumsy hands, forgot the top button, dragged his belt through with the holster half twisted. The door latch stuck under his palm, then gave. The corridor beyond had been remade by red: strobes pulsed and paused, turning corners into yawning mouths, banisters into exposed veins. The klaxon owned the space between pulses. No boots. No shouted orders. Just the siren and the thud of his own blood.

"Hello?" he called, foolishly. Nothing answered but the next rise of the wail.

The floor was cold through his socks until the leather found his feet; then the soles slapped too loud. He drew the pistol because that was what you did when fear pooled, and moved. The red light made shadows crawl in the doorway gaps. His neck prickled; it felt like the corridor watched him pass.

At the next junction the light found the blast door. By day it stood open, a dead weight slid back on tracks to let men and carts through to the lab wings. Now it stood shut, steel face bare of handles, edges sealed. Along the jamb, symbols he'd only ever seen chalked on Victor's diagrams glowed a low, sour blue—circles inside circles, strokes like compass marks. They looked eerie in electric light, as if they preferred the dark.

41

He pressed close enough to feel the door's cold through his shirt. A hum came off it—not the thin whine of a coil but a deeper note that lived in the earth, a pulse more felt than heard. It stepped up his spine and nested behind his eyes. Somewhere beyond the steel, something cycled: a rise, a hold, a slow fall. Again and again. The rhythm of a heart that wasn't human.

Harold's mouth dried. This wasn't an evacuation. It wasn't a drill. The base wasn't afraid; it was announcing a birth.

The warning Victor had thrown at him—eyes open—slid back through his head as if it had been waiting for this door. Telluric currents. Alignment. Coupling. The Well. He pictured the truck's refrigeration unit thudding in the sun, cold rolling over his wrists. He pictured the notebook's rings and lines.

"Dammit, Victor," he breathed. The siren swallowed the words.

He put his palm to the steel. The plate trembled under his skin, not the shake of machinery but a live shiver like an animal's flank. His stomach turned over. Every instinct he owned—farm sense, drill sense, plain human sense—said step back.

Instead he stood there, the red light strobing his sight to pieces, the hum working on his nerves, and understood with a sick, clean clarity: Victor had gone ahead without him. The Well of Souls was awakening.

The doors parted with a sigh that didn't belong to any hinge he knew—a wet-lung sound that crawled over his skin. Every part of him wanted to back into the red-lit corridor, to take the lie of safety the night air could offer. He stepped forward instead, breath held against the taste of ozone.

His torch swept through the dark and found the room's heart: a ring of coils, their crowns spitting lace-fine arcs that braided toward a single, suspended sphere. Green, gold, and hard white ran its surface in restless veins; the light needled his eyes and made his fillings hum. These weren't the dead coils from Victor's diagrams. They pulsed as if something under the floor was breathing for them.

Within that light, held taut by nothing Harold could see, hung Joseph. Uniform torn. Limbs pulled long. The face was all wrong—the slack of sleep without breath. This was a stage. Victor's stage.

A sound ripped out of Harold and died in the noise. The notebook's pages in his head shuffled into place and made a picture he didn't want.

Victor was at the console, hands sure, eyes fixed. The panel belonged to a fever dream—bakelite dials, knife switches, lamps winking amber-to-green. Numbers rolled behind glass like odometers. The air had the hot-dust stench of overworked tubes.

"Victor!" Harold's voice hit the metal and came back even more desperate. He had to push the word through his teeth. "Stop."

Victor turned. The coils' light carved his face into sharp planes; grief and triumph both rode there, and something colder underneath. He had crossed a line and burned the bridge behind him.

"You have to stop this," Harold said, throat raw. "Let him go. Let him rest."

"Fool," Victor murmured, not unkind. Contempt, pity; both fit. "You've no notion what you're looking at. What I've brought to heel."

"Brought to heel?" Harold's stomach turned. "You've desecrated your own grandson. You're wrenching at his soul." The word felt childish in his mouth until the sphere answered with a low pulse he felt in his gut rather than ears.

He moved because standing still made him shake. Each step through the heat was a small fight. The pistol rose without thought, the metal biting his palm, arm straightening until the front sight found the space between Victor's eyes. He didn't want to fire, but he needed Victor to see that he could.

"Turn it off," Harold said, the echo making him sound like more than one man. "Now."

For the first time, the demand cut through. Victor's gaze slid from muzzle to man to Joseph in the odd light. The coils chattered and sang; the sphere's surface crawled with new patterning, veins tightening, then loosening, as if trying on a rhythm.

"Please, just turn it off." Harold held the sight steady, breath in, then out, the way Collins had taught him when the target was paper and the worst you could do was tear it. Fear sat in his gut like cold iron, but it had edges now. It felt like purpose.

Behind Victor, a gauge climbed. The needle trembled past a red hash. The room's pitch shifted—one more note layered on, too low for hearing, high enough to burn the throat.

"Victor," Harold said, quieter. "Don't make this worse."

A guttural roar rolled out of the core. The coils answered with wild arcs. "Too late," Victor said, fear finally edging his voice. "It can't be reversed."

The world cracked.

A report like artillery fired in a vault, a white flare that burned through shut lids—and then nothing. The hum died. The air pressed inward until Harold heard his own blood as a drum. He could taste copper.

A low thrum returned—too deep for hearing until it was everywhere. A cold filament along the ceiling bullied a thread of light out of the long bulbs—one, then another—flicker by flicker until the chamber blinked back into view.

It was worse in full light. Machines shuddered and spit, hissing at ruptured seams. Ozone skinned the tongue. A gauge twitched in a circle. Sparks crawled like ants along a bus bar.

Joseph stood in the center.

He didn't rise so much as resolve there—light collapsing toward him with the sound of cloth torn underwater, stiff as a man braced against a gale. His first movements were wrong— jerks, resets, the body relearning how to be a body. Around him, light shed thin silhouettes that lagged and skated, figures out of phase with him—faces that weren't faces lashed out of his silhouette in a wash of pale luminescence. They didn't speak, but Harold felt the shape of noise in his mind: grief, fury, something like wind in a mine. Joseph's mouth worked. Words came as a mutter, a chew of sound with no structure. His features ran through a dozen masks—glee, rage, terror—and settled into a ruin that held those three at once. He wept openly. He barked a laugh that wasn't human. In his eyes there was only confusion and fear.

Hope left Harold like stepping onto a rung that wasn't there. Horror landed right after. This wasn't return. It was a twisting-back.

He shifted his grip on the pistol. The bite of the checkering steadied him. Victor took a step toward the boy he'd raised.

"Don't," Harold warned, but the word had no weight.

Joseph moved.

The jerky learning vanished. He crossed the space between breaths without crossing it—an arm out, fingers crooked—and something invisible hit Victor full in the chest. The man lifted, slammed, and went through the two-foot thick wall as if the concrete had been pressed wood. The sound of it—meat, stone, rebar—rattled the lab. Dust drifted in a slow sheet.

Joseph turned. His eyes—lit from within or possibly catching the room's light in some way Harold's mind didn't like—found the only other living thing in the room.

Harold's heart punched at his ribs. The pistol felt like a child's toy in his hand. He understood then, cleanly as a drilled command: Victor hadn't made a weapon he could point. He'd opened a door and let something walk through.

He set his feet—heels under hips, elbows loose—and kept the sight high on center mass because it was all he had to keep. The hum climbed a note. And Harold knew—with perfect clarity—that whatever Fort Bradley had been before this moment, it had just become something else.

Harold fired.

Muzzle flash punched the dark; the report slapped back off concrete and steel. Brass rang on the deck. He pulled the trigger again and again, hands locked, elbows loose the way Collins drilled into him. Powder smoke bit his nose. The slide hammered his palm. He walked the sights up the chest he'd been told was Joseph's and kept firing until the weapon told him he was done.

The rounds died on the body without a mark. No flinch. No blood. The face—ruined by too many expressions at once—held him as if watching an ant under glass.

Cold moved through Harold in paralytic waves. He'd brought a peashooter to bear against an act of God. The simple fact of it emptied his lungs.

Joseph lifted a hand.

The air bent—not wind, pressure. The room pinched around a point just in front of Harold's sternum, and his insides lurched as if an elevator had been cut free beneath his feet. Floor and ceiling traded places between heartbeats; the walls bowed inward, glossy panels taking his reflection and stretching it into a long, open-mouthed stranger. The coils' hum deepened until it lived in his skull. Metal screamed somewhere.

Heat bloomed behind his breast, small at first, then flooding outward. It wasn't a surface burn; it was a furnace door opening inside him. His vision narrowed to a white pinprick, then feathered into black. The world pulled on him in six directions at once—joints tugged, ligaments lit to wire—and his hands forgot the shape of the pistol. It sailed off, slow as a dream, and struck down with a sound he didn't hear.

Surfaces folded. The chamber became a trick of mirrors and bent glass. Gauges smeared into arcs. His limbs no longer agreed on where to be; elbows found wrong angles; fingers tried and failed to recall their count. The pressure climbed, climbed, until the scream he made stayed in his throat as if the air had congealed.

For a heartbeat he had only the eyes—Joseph's, holding the room's glow, steady with a child's confusion and something vile crouched behind it.

Then it took him.

Darkness came on like a dropped curtain—total, absolute—consuming the last of Harold's soundless shout.

**CHAPTER ONE**

Captain Theodore Bradley pressed a thumb into the knot under his ribs and waited for the spasm to ease. The "ergonomic" chair offered a hard plastic edge and little else. Healing had offered solace; the ache kept the bill unpaid. Three months of bed rest and four at this post on light duty had been almost more than he could stand after that landslide caught him on his assignment in the Rockies.

"Thursday already?" he muttered. A lift of his hand pulled the timestamp into his augmented vision: June 19, 2668. The implant he'd had installed in medical school—practical then—now layered both military OS and medical interface across his vision. He grimaced. *I never could get the hang of Thursdays.*

Time crept on his HUD, boredom growing with each passing moment. So, he idly swiped through classified files, headers blinking past on his AR. The motion held a familiar, forbidden pull. As a boy, he'd slipped into his father's study and read top-secret documents off a liquid-crystal screen while the house settled around him. Reprimands were occasional, consequences light—his distant father ignored most of it, and everyone else tolerated it out of quiet fear. He'd been the son of General Thomas Bradley—four-star giant, head of the Bradley family, a leading figure in the Telluric Foundation.

Now he had his own access code, and the privilege drew frowns. But their world ran on nepotism. Even a court-martial for unauthorized access would likely end the way most of his childhood had: a dismissive wave from his father.

A clanging thump—Lieutenant Mustang's utility bag hitting the floor—jarred him off the feed. The chair frame chattered; the knot seized beneath his ribs. Bradley let the headers scroll, letting another page populate while he reined in the flare of irritation, then looked up.

"Little warning next time, Mustang?" he said, annoyance plain in his tone and sharpened by the ache.

"Good morning, Sunshine," the lieutenant said, sarcasm flat and practiced. "Blessing everyone with your brilliance on this delightful Thursday, are we?"

"Still waking up deciding to be everyone's problem, I see?" Bradley shot back. The bite bled out as he settled too fast. Pain answered; he regretted the movement immediately.

"Not everyone's problem, sir—just yours." Mustang's gaze was cool, almost satisfied. "Seems an animal of some sort was prowling the alley near the dispensary where I get my morning tea."

Bradley's scoff died before it formed. The pain returned—part flinch, part dull throb. He pushed to his feet; a grimace pulled at his face and dizziness slid the room a fraction to the left.

"Not funny," he said, riding it out.

"The only thing funny here is you, 'sir,'" Mustang managed, the sound that followed more exhale than laugh. "But seriously, I did see something. Looked like a wolf. Or a dog—I don't know the difference."

His mind raced; panic welled up, and he tried to swallow it back. The Animal Ban of 2102 filled his thoughts—lecture after lecture, exercise after exercise. How could an animal breach the city's protocols? And if it carried the virus—another outbreak waiting at the door. The room seemed to drop a degree against the flush of his skin.

Mustang's mouth twitched as if the whole thing was a joke he was still deciding whether to tell. "Relax. It was an animal. Not exactly common inside the walls, sure, but… it's not some mutated monster."

Bradley stared at him. The knot under his ribs tightened like it had its own hands.

"Just an animal," Mustang continued, breezy, tossing the word around casually. "Back in the day people kept them. Took care of them. Whole species of emotional support—"

"Stop." Bradley's voice came out flat, not loud, but it stopped the lieutenant mid sentence. He felt the heat rise in his face anyway. "Don't do that."

Mustang blinked, caught off guard by the tone. "Do what?"

"Turn it into a story you can laugh at." Bradley swallowed. His throat had gone dry. His undergrad medical history course was already roaring through his mind—training vids, casualty maps, quarantine failure simulations. He could see the numbers spreading like time-lapsed bruises. "The reason the ban exists is because of those same animals."

Mustang lifted a shoulder. "You're saying the government outlawed pets because—"

"Because a spillover turned into an epidemic." Bradley heard the edge in his own voice and didn't bother sanding it down. "2101. Avian influenza jumped to… everything else. It rode anything that moved—pets, pests, strays."

Mustang's sarcasm thinned. "Chicago mustn't have gotten hit that bad," he said, and there was something defensive in it.

"I don't know if it hit everywhere the same. The outbreak that happened here was enough. Morgues overflowed. Warehouses became holding sites. And—then mass graves." He pressed his thumb harder into his ribs, willing the pain to anchor him. "They locked down. They culled everything. And then in 2102 they made it law—no companion animals, no exceptions."

Mustang held up both hands in mock surrender, but his gaze stayed skeptical. "Okay. So what's the plan, Captain Calm?"

Bradley felt the jab and let it pass. "Five-block quarantine around the sighting." The words came out procedural—because as long as he said them like a physician instead of a man picturing fever wards, he could breathe. "No unauthorized movement in or out."

Mustang's eyebrows rose. "For one dog."

"For a vector," Bradley snapped, then caught himself—wiped his hand over his face, forcing the next words to land like orders, not suggestions. "Standard protocol is elimination on sight. But since it's been moving freely, we need it alive long enough to test it. If it's carrying anything—virus, bacteria, something engineered—capture gets us a path. No capture means we guess. And guessing is how you end up stacking bodies."

Mustang didn't smile, didn't laugh. Simply nodded.

He exhaled. "Fine." The sarcasm tried to come back but words failed him.

***

Mustang grabbed his utility bag and was already moving. The strap hardware clicked; the door slammed hard against the frame as he rushed out. "Open channel, Sergeant Knight," he said, breath leveled—the subdermal carry turning low speech into command. A soft trill confirmed connection.

"Knight here."

"Deploy four squads to Sector Two, full riot gear," Mustang said. "Establish a five-block cordon around the food and drink dispensary. Get local constabulary support. No movement in or out."

"Yes, sir. Consider it sealed tighter than Captain Bradley on parade duty," Knight replied, humor leaking through the line.

"And Sergeant—minimize casualties. Civilians and ours."

A beat. Then Knight, flatter: "Understood, sir."

Mustang arrived as the last barricades locked into place. These weren't battle-hardened Corps veterans, but the line moved with drilled efficiency—hands on clamps, boots setting braces, polymer clacking against steel. A low murmur rode the cordon; the air smelled of baked metal and hot plastic.

He spotted Sergeant Knight and jogged over.

Knight snapped to attention with a sharp "Sir!" His squad followed a beat late, shoulders stiff. Mustang logged it: some of them would feel this in the morning.

"At ease, Sergeant," Mustang said. "Situation."

"Nominal, sir. Barriers are finishing up now. Civvies are cooperating, but… do we really need the constabulary? Bunch of useless half-wits—can't hold a thought. Like sleepwalkers. And the civilians, sir—they're… docile. Following orders, sure, but I've never seen people so listless."

"Maybe humanity's turning over a new leaf," Mustang said with a shrug. "Be glad it's not another Columbia. I still get nightmares from those riots. Nasty business." He pointed with two fingers. "Deploy Level-Three hazmat teams to scan the area. I want reports every fifteen minutes. Have the constables set up swabbing stations for infection checks."

Knight hesitated. "Sir… what exactly are we looking for?"

Mustang's answer came a shade too flippant. "Apparently, a dog. Captain thinks it might be carrying a world-ending virus." He let the dryness stand. "Lucky us—we get to be saviors of humanity."

# A LIGHT FOR THE LOST

*** 

Bradley plunged into the archive, flooding his augmented vision with hits on the 2101 influenza outbreak. Articles stacked and scrolled in regimented columns; timelines, abstracts, citations—years of data sluicing past even with the filters tightened. The clock ribbon in his HUD crept forward, each minute a small insult.

He kept refining. Narrowed dates. Adjusted keywords. The counter still spat back four million results. He drove his fists into the desk—dull thud, no echo—then scrubbed a hand through his hair.

At some point the fluorescents dimmed; didn't register when. Pressure built behind his eyes—steady throb at the temples. The more he read, the less there seemed to be. Paragraphs repeated word for word, errors and all. "New analysis" meant the same sentences in a different order. Even the journals were echo chambers: no treatment protocols, no vaccine workups— nothing but restated caution.

"This is absurd," he said, hands flaring uselessly at the empty room. "Even the medical journals are regurgitations. No treatment plans, no vaccine research—nothing."

*Enough with the public layer.* He blinked out of the open search and into the classified interface, keyed in his authorization, and ran the query again—same terms, new door—hoping the answers weren't drowned in noise.

***

Reports stacked; nothing changed. Scattered trash, smudged paw marks, the occasional dropping—echoes of a presence that refused to be caught. Mustang, despite himself, had to admit Bradley kept the brass pacified even as their search turned up only dead ends.

"Damn dog," he muttered. "Probably slipped the quarantine and ran off to be someone else's problem." He glanced at the empty street before entering his apartment building. "Not a single civilian has even sneezed. Maybe the virus died out. Or maybe it decided to be a head cold—like most of these bugs do, if you believe Bradley." He shook his head. "Half the time, I can't even understand what the guy's saying. He's been muttering about 'epidemiology' and 'antigen-antibody complexes' so much his head must be spinning." A dry huff escaped him. "Guess that's what happens when you cram too many fancy words into your brain, huh, Captain?"

He let the question die and stripped out of his uniform, eager for heat and noise to scour the last few weeks off his skin. The shower came on scalding; steam climbed the tile. He worked shampoo through his dark hair and let the water drum his shoulders until his thoughts receded to a tolerable hum.

Static ripped the calm apart. The priority channel crackled; Bradley's voice cut through. "Mustang, get to the office. Now."

Mustang flinched, a crawl running through his skin. "It's the middle of the night, Captain," he said, weariness snapping at the edges. "This damn dog can wait till morning. I need sleep."

"No, it can't. And we're not talking about the fucking dog. I can't say more on an open channel. Just get here." Bradley's composure frayed on the last words.

Heat couldn't wash that tone away. Mustang killed the water, toweled off fast, and hauled on a clean uniform. The apartment door slammed hard enough to rattle the walls. He took the stairs two at a time toward the office blocks, cursing under his breath.

Mustang pounded down the empty streets, sweat already beading his brow. "Just what I need in the middle of the night," he muttered, swinging wide around a corner to keep his pace. "This had better be earth-shatteringly important, Bradley. Or be so out of your mind I call a shrink instead of shooting you."

He slipped into the darkened office building on the balls of his feet. The silence was heavy, stitched together by the distant hum of ventilation. Curfew had been in place for hours; the corridors that buzzed by day felt alien now—hollow, stripped of voices and motion. Unease worked under his skin. In recent months he'd watched Bradley cycle through indecision, frustration, even flashes of fear. But the panic in that call had been something else.

His palm hovered near his sidearm as he scanned the shadows. He cleared each entryway by habit—edge, sweep, advance— senses dialed up. He hadn't realized how unsettling a familiar space could be when the lights were down and the noise gone.

Annoyance at being dragged out warred with a prickle of anticipation. Adrenaline sharpened the edges of everything, a welcome jolt after weeks of slog—even if the reason for it set his teeth on edge.

A muffled banging echoed up as he started down the stairs to their shared office. Mustang drew his pistol; the faint hum of its charge cycling up braided with the ventilation's drone. He slid along the wall, eased down the last steps, and leaned into the corner. The tactical light sliced the dark. A strip of brightness seeped from the office door.

He nudged the door with his boot, opening a narrow wedge. The light walked the room in clean sections. Silence had settled over what looked like the aftermath of a small storm—flex-pads scattered, a chair on its side, drawers yawning open, as if a violent gust had rolled through.

A low, incoherent murmur leaked from the connected restroom. Mustang shifted his weight, tightened his grip, and moved toward the sound.

The door blew open with a crash. Bradley stumbled out—shirt askew, eyes wild—spitting curses and flinging his arms. Mustang's heart hit hard; training kept his index high on the frame. Oblivious, Bradley seized the overturned metal chair and hurled it, the screech and clang ricocheting around the room.

"Captain, it's all right," Mustang said, voice even, muzzle steady on target. "Calm down."

Bradley spun, blue eyes blown wide and unfocused. "What?! No, it's most certainly not all right!" His mouth outran his thoughts. "Did you even know? Of course you didn't!"

"Let's assume it's fine for the next sixty seconds," Mustang cut in. "Calm down enough to tell me what's going on. Then—and only then—I put this away."

The weapon finally registered. Bradley's chest hitched; he took a long, shuddering breath. A thin line of control returned to his gaze. Mustang watched it settle, then eased the pistol down and holstered, the charge whine fading as the room's tension bled off by degrees.

Bradley gave a short verbal command; his AR chimed and pushed the transfer through. He stared past the room as if the wall could answer for him. Mustang braced.

Bradley slumped into the chair like gravity had decided he was done evading it. His eyes didn't quite track Mustang—like his brain was still somewhere inside the digital archive.

"These files…" Bradley said. The words scraped out of him. "The public record is a complete fabrication."

Mustang focused on the overlay, fingers swiping through layers of redaction. The classified blue washed his vision and made the room feel colder than it was. "You can't be serious?"

Bradley didn't respond immediately. He swallowed, then forced it out. "The epidemic. The Animal Ban. The whole public narrative—" he made a small, exhausted gesture, like sweeping dust off a table, "—it's a cover."

Mustang's mouth tightened. "Cover for what."

Bradley's gaze lifted to him, and something in it warned Mustang that whatever came next would ruin sleep for a long time.

"A citywide experiment," Bradley said. "It's labeled Serenity-adjacent."

Mustang's brows jumped before he could stop them. "Serenity?" He barked a short laugh that wasn't amused. "The government's little 'happy pill'?"

Bradley nodded. "Not the formulation they tell the public about." His voice flattened the way it did when he was trying not to panic. "Stronger. More addictive. The notes talk about compliance metrics. Habit loops. Behavioral suppression. Control over comfort."

Mustang stared at the scrolling lines, then realized his left hand had curled into a fist. He forced it open. In Columbia, they'd dosed whole blocks in the weeks before the riots—officially "to stabilize." Mustang had watched the streets go soft-eyed... then insane. One in twenty, the document said, had an "adverse" reaction described as behavioral dysregulation and acute agitated psychosis.

He swiped to another header. "Project Ouroboros." He said the word out loud and didn't like the taste of it. "What the hell is *that*?"

Bradley shook his head, barely. "It's buried under procurement language." He tapped a line with two fingers on his own overlay, highlighting it for both of them. "Resource allocation. Infrastructure development. Expansion of 'processing capacity.'"

Mustang leaned forward and scrolled. "This reads like a public works budget."

"It does," Bradley said. "Until you look at the auxiliary contracts." His eyes slid to Mustang again—quiet, intent. "Waste disposal."

The room went still in that way that's worse than noise. Mustang felt the phrase move through him like a draft under a door.

"Waste disposal," Mustang repeated, slower. "Like garbage."

Bradley's lips pressed together. "Like people." He didn't dress it up. Didn't soften it. "Missing persons reports. Population adjustments. 'Relocation.' And then disposal volumes that spike in the same districts."

Mustang's throat tightened. "You're telling me the rumors are real." His voice came out harder than he meant. "People vanishing. The… processing plants."

Bradley's jaw flexed. "I'm telling you the paperwork supports the conspiracies."

Mustang straightened, trying to find the angle that made this make sense without collapsing the world. "Bradley—this stuff is stamped five centuries old. More." He did the math without wanting to. "Five and a half centuries. Why are we digging up something practically archaeological?"

Bradley didn't look away from the overlay. The light from it made the hollows under his eyes look deeper. "Because it isn't archaeological." He tapped the corner of the display where the status flags lived—little clean tags that should have said CLOSED, ARCHIVED, DECOMMISSIONED.

They didn't.

"The experiment," Bradley said, voice tight, "is still active."

Mustang stared at the word *ACTIVE* until it stopped being a label and became a declaration.

He let out a breath that sounded like surrender. "So you're saying… the epidemic story—"

"Smoke," Bradley said.

"And the Ban—"

"A lie," he responded, and his eyes finally met Mustang's. "They took a city's living things away, told everyone it was for safety, and created a dependency on a corporate government that has been using everyone and disposing of the evidence."

## CHAPTER TWO

New New York rose out of the flats like poured slate—glass, steel, and gray walls too clean for honest work. Jorgen tasted dust at the back of his throat and told himself the kid was still vertical. But the sentiment didn't buy time.

"Should've stayed put," he muttered, toeing a pebble down the broken verge. Bradley had run home to a place that never wanted him. If he'd reached the boy an hour sooner —hell, five minutes—maybe. Would the kid have believed the rockslide wasn't an accident? That the same hands that hauled him back into this gleaming anthill had set the trap in the first place?

The official route had been a comedy. Gate guards in mirror-polished boots looked his Rocky Mountain papers over like they were a joke and gave him the company line in smooth voices: no affiliation, no visa, no entry. Wouldn't even take a message. Stupid bastards. He'd threaded worse nets for the syndicates with one eye closed and the other half-shut.

He leaned into the wind and studied the wall. City folk hated dust and sweat; they also forgot where they put their tools. Ten minutes of quiet wandering found him a maintenance depot slouched in the lee of the rampart. Door on the fritz, maglock tired. Inside: spools of rope, sacks of concrete, coils of cable, bundles of rebar. No inventory clerk and no cameras he couldn't lie to.

He worked quick. Swapped the barrel on his compressed-air rifle to a higher gauge so the rebar would ride true. Twisted a crude grappling head out of bent steel and cussed it into shape until the points would catch. Hefted rope for dry rot, picked the least sorry length, tied his knots by feel. Then he slit the concrete bag and palmed the dust up his sleeves, into his collar, across his face and hair until he matched the wall's cold gray. Dirty, sure—but nothing beats concrete camouflage in a city.

Twilight turned the city bruise-purple. Heat from the day still bled out of the stone; baked glass and hot metal hovered in the air. Jorgen braced, breathed, and fired. The rifle gave a flat cough. The rebar soared over the lip of the outer wall and clattered on the floor of the run. He reined in the slack and then leaned hard on the rope. No give. Good.

"Too old for this shit," he said to nobody, set his boots, and climbed.

The rope rasped his palms through the gloves; grit worked into his cuffs and eyes. Halfway up, a gust pushed city noise over him—the layered hum of turbines, a freight-rattle, the insect buzz of thousands of watts feeding the city. He kept his eyes on his hands and his hands on the work.

He topped out with a knee over the coping and lay still, heart working like a small hammer. The city unfurled on the far side:

a cityscape of boxes that reminded him more of coffins than buildings. Steam ghosting from vents, towers shouldering one another for space.

Jorgen rolled to a crouch and let the ache settle where it belonged. He didn't typically like people. But he liked the kid. Innocent wasn't the word—too clean for the world. Always trying to fix things. In a place like this, that kind of hope got stamped out.

"All right, boy," he said under his breath, "I'm coming."

He scanned for a descent that wouldn't end with a broken leg and a polite arrest: service ladders. Cable trays. A vent stack with handholds. There—maintenance rungs set into a shadowed return. He tested the first rung, then the second. Stone-sound.

The wall radiated cool against his cheek as he swung down. Below, the city's glow pulsed like a heartbeat, promising danger, noise, and a whole lot of assholes. He set his jaw and continued his descent, quiet as a rumor, every move spent like money he could not afford to waste.

He wasn't up against the cunning ridge wolves and syndicates he knew; if he kicked this anthill, sheer numbers would bury him. Good thing the keepers were lazy. He'd have tripped alarms ten times by now if they weren't. The ease of it bothered him. Too easy meant a different kind of trap.

The maintenance rungs ended on a blank drop. Wind worried the wall and brought the city's perfumed reek up to him. He scanned left: a fire escape clung to the next building, all rust and loose bolts, groaning like an old hinge. No glass-breaking, no sirens—that made it his best bad option.

"Right, then," he breathed, and leaped.

Air knifed past his ears. He hit the ladder hard enough to rattle teeth; iron bit through his gloves and the whole rig shuddered under his weight. Red flaked into his palms like salt. He rode the sway, counted two breaths, and moved. Mountain habits did the rest—keep three points, keep your hips close, test before you trust. He took it down fast and quiet, boots finding the outside rails instead of the resonant plates, hands skimming past burrs and oil-slicked joints that stank of rain and rust.

Street level rose out of steam and shadow. He dropped the last six feet, knees protesting, and flattened into the seam between receptacles and wall. The concrete dust he'd smeared on earlier did its work; under LED light he turned the same soft gray as the bricks. He listened. Distant turbines. A service drone whining somewhere overhead. No footsteps.

Annapolis, he reminded himself. Find Annapolis without catching a net.

He slid the rifle strap back into the groove his shoulder knew and checked his satchel by touch: city map folded to a soft square; the compact energy blade in its sheath; the flask that smelled like pine smoke and mean winters.

He wasn't naive. Cities had their own predators. You didn't track prints here; you read reflections, blind corners, the rhythm of cameras, where the trash didn't settle because boots came through too often.

He adjusted—rolled on the outside edges of his soles, let the sound get swallowed by the hum of the grid. The city tried to turn him around with its angles: towers throwing wind like fists, alleys that dead-ended at service doors and keypads, signage that meant nothing unless you'd been born to it. He let the confusion wash past. One block. Then the next. He matched himself to the dark edges of things, moved when the cameras looked away, froze when their little red eyes winked back.

Daylight was for hiding. He learned the seams quickly: storm drains that breathed cool algae stink; sewer grates where the air rose wet and sweet with rot; an abandoned row where the floorboards whispered and pigeons should have owned the rafters. Grim hotels. Nights gave him a longer leash, once the curfew hit and the streets went clean of civilians. Not free—never that—but close enough. A complete blackout was impossible, but he could limit his exposure, making himself a ghost in the digital rain. Keep to the blind cones behind lamp poles. Use the overhang where signage broke the sightline. Let the dust on his clothes cloak him from big brother.

The sprawl mocked him with its size—fifteen-minute cells chained from the ocean to the mountains, from the old Virginia line up into Massachusetts, each one whole unto itself and none of them offering a ride. Transit existed, but not for him, not for most; the roads sluiced traffic past neighborhoods without touching them, veins that didn't feed the flesh. So he walked, and he watched, and he kept a line in his head that bent toward Annapolis.

Days collapsed into a loop: map the cameras, move the body, vanish, drink, move again. Steps counted out on damp concrete, breath measured so it didn't fog in cold light. Supplies thinned to lint. The gray paste the locals queued for was not an option. Not even food. He could smell it from half a block: vitamins and plastic, a wet mineral tang that clung to the tongue just thinking about it. Water was easier to come by—condensers weeping into public taps, runoff caught in clean gutters—sometimes metallic, occasionally breath-taking odor of chlorine, but it kept his joints working.

What set his teeth on edge wasn't hunger at first. It was the quiet. No stray dogs nosing bins. No moths stuttering in the bright lights. Not even a gnat. The air swirled, the lights hummed, turbines sang under everything, but life gave this place a wide berth. As if the wild had looked at New New York and said, Keep it. And Jorgen agreed.

Hunger came on steady after that—an ache under the ribs that soured his temper and dulled his senses if he let it. The feeding stations were bait. Drones drifted in lazy figure-eights overhead, lenses warm, patient; scanners washed faces in pale halos and remembered who blinked. One wrong angle, one red-light chirp, and he'd wake to a white room with the corners rounded off. He watched the lines anyway, learned the rhythm: pouch in, head down, and go. The slurry looked like gear grease in a sterile bag.

Smoke and fat rose in his mind when he didn't want it: goat steak on a flat rock, hiss of snowmelt over coals, the clean snap when you cut across the grain. His mouth watered; his belly cramped in reply. He told it to shut up and kept walking.

He stayed to the seams. Back alleys where rain pooled and the cameras blinked on a two-count. Service corridors that smelled of abandonment and cold metal. He moved when the grid looked away, paused when it didn't, let the concrete dust on his clothes buy him another minute of anonymity.

A sound caught him mid-step—small, out of place. Not the servo-whine of a drone. Not the distant keen of a siren riding the air. A dry rustle, quick and cautious, tucked under the hum like a secret.

He froze. Let his breath go narrow. Listened.

There. Again. Organic. Alive.

Hope wasn't a word he trusted; it still lifted his spirit, a warm prickle behind his sternum. Maybe the city hadn't murdered every scrap of honest life. Maybe there something tucked into its underbelly.

He shifted his weight, soft on the edges of his boots, and ghosted toward the sound. Every sense opened—eyes tuned to shadow within shadow, ears sorting the city's thrum from that small noise, nose catching the faintest trace of musk under wet concrete. He followed the rustle as if it were a trail in snow: careful, hungry, and very much alive.

A brown shape skittered, too large for a rat and too fluid, slipping into a seam between buildings. Jorgen's head came up. Curiosity—starved as anything else—woke.

He dropped to a crouch, heart knocking hard against his ribs. The gap was barely a man wide, a slit where the wind died and the dark thickened. Hunger pinched, but that ember of wildness burned hotter. This was proof the city hadn't killed everything in it.

He snugged his bag and slid in sideways. Brick rasped his shoulders. The air tasted of exhaust with an earthy thread beneath it. He followed that thread like a lifeline. Far in, a weak glow bled around a corner, not daylight but the steady sick warmth of a failing bulb.

The seam opened without warning into a long chamber—vaulted, ribbed with conduit, a forgotten maintenance tunnel. Incandescents hung in cages, half of them dead, the rest buzzing on their last leg. Dust lay on the machines in soft drifts; belts sagged on frozen pulleys. Somewhere a compressor wheezed and caught like a life-time smoker, and the whole space trembled to the rhythm of tired gears driving an ungrateful city.

He tightened his grip on the rifle. Worked the lever; the action hissed and settled. The gauge read 175 PSI. Three shots, and each weaker than the last.

Leaky bastard. He should have had it charged to full, but couldn't have afforded the noise topside.

The smell shifted. Oil gave way to something sour and hot— rot, piss, fur left wet. The machine noise turned into a blanket of sound that tried to smother finer details.

Grease-brown fur flashed at the edge of his sightline. Then it came—out of the pipework in a blur. His first thought was a squat dog. Then it stood.

Not a dog. A rat, big as a medium hound, planted on its haunches and hissing. Black bead eyes, teeth the color of old corn, patchy coat clotted with filth. Ears torn to scallops. Tail thick as a wrist and scabbed.

"Shit," Jorgen said, just loud enough to feel it in his throat. He kept it in his periphery and looked for the rest. Nests didn't come solo.

"Don't suppose y'all are offering tea and biscuits," he added, dry as dust.

Adrenaline cut through the ache in his gut, cleaned the edges of the world. He'd heard travelers mutter about scavengers that got big in the places people forgot. Well, here they were. He measured distance and backdrop, counted his three shots, and began to move the way a man moves when failure means getting eaten.

He brought the rifle up, sighted the centerline of the skull, and held. The gauge in his periphery might as well have been a death-clock, three good breaths of air left. Waste one and he might not buy a way out.

They stared at each other across the hum and wheeze. The thing's whiskers trembled. His shoulders did not. Hunger on both sides, different coats.

The rat screamed. The sound tore down the tunnel and came back layered—answers from the dark racks and pipe nests beyond.

"Fuck me," Jorgen said, bandana up to cut the stink. He shifted two steps to put his back near a rib of conduit—no blind side, smaller front. Running wouldn't pay; the swarm had the legs too and his had years on 'em. Fold or play the bad hand. He set his boots. "Come on, then."

They came like a thrown net—brown and black, tails whipping. He let the lead one fill the sight. The first shot coughed out of the rifle, a clean hiss against the industrial groan. The big rat folded as if a string had been cut, grease-matted fur blooming red.

The pack paused, a ripple of doubt, then poured forward over their own dead.

He worked the lever; the action hissed and bit home. The rest he met with wood. He choked up on the stock and used the butt like a hammer, short, ugly arcs. *Thwack*—jaw. *Crack*—temple. He felt the jolt in his elbows, smelled the hot-copper note of fresh blood under ammonia and rot. The narrow aisle paid him back; only two could hit at once. He kept them in that choke and made them earn the inches they got.

Claws skittered on metal. A smaller one slipped past at shin level, faster than regret. He booted it into a spinning belt. Another launched high from the pipes—he took it out of the air with the second shot, the hiss lost under the compressor's dying wheeze. The body hit and slid, smearing.

One shot left.

Pressure mounted anyway. Weight against his thighs, scrabble at his calves, the kind of persistence that ate mountains. Sweat slicked his back; his hands found worse purchase with each swing. Breathe steady, he told himself.

Pain found him—just above the boot. Teeth sank into his calf muscle and tore sideways. Heat flooded down his sock. He roared, more air than word, and stamped back, trying to pin the biter. Another body slammed his hip. The rifle skittered from his grip and clattered on the grated floor, ringing like a bad joke.

"Shit."

He went low by choice, shoulders tight, blade out with a snap. Cold hilt, sure weight. He drove the point under the jaw of the one on his leg and levered hard. It let go in a gout of stink and steam. He kicked it free and put his boot on its neck until the twitch quit.

The tunnel was alive. Machine noise washed everything to a flat roar; only close sounds survived—his grunt, their hisses, the wet scrape of fur on metal. He edged sideways until the conduit rib kissed his shoulder again, fenced his front with the long knife, and found the rifle's position with a glance.

"Not your snack," he told them, voice rough through the cloth. "Not today."

They tested him in waves, and he answered—steel in, steel out, heel down, elbow through. The bandana filtered dust and not much else; the stink lived in his head. Blood warmed the inside of his boot and made each step loud. He felt the old fatigue reach for him the way cold reaches into joints—and he shoved it off with the same stubbornness that had gotten him over a hundred bad passes.

One shot left somewhere on the floor. A blade that hadn't failed him yet. And the simple math he'd always trusted: keep the window small, keep the hands moving, keep your feet.

Blood hit the air and the stink drove the horde mad—tails lashing, teeth snapping—as they tore into one another for a heartbeat. It bought Jorgen a breath. Nothing more.

He braced through the fire in his calf and got steel back in his hands. The knife's worn leather fit his palm like an old truth. He cut short and ugly—thrust, rip, heel down—space too tight for pretty work, fury doing what reach could not. Claws raked his sleeves. Teeth worried at his pants. He gave ground only to take it back.

"This ain't over, you filthy shiteaters!" he barked, and threw himself for the rifle.

He hit on a roll, felt jaws snap inches off his heel, and came up with the stock in hand. Pain receded under the white heat of adrenaline. He shouldered the rifle and found a target that wasn't fur.

The compressor.

Its shell bulged and sweated; paint blistered around a rusty seam. He had one shot left and no clean way out.

Make it count.

He squeezed. The round hit with a dull, ugly thunk, left a ragged mouth in the steel—the pressure went feral. The tank screamed and tore itself apart.

A wall of air hit first—then the sound, a slab that swallowed all others. Shards scythed the tunnel. A white wave of compressed air and shrapnel turned meat and fur into spray. Jorgen slammed shoulder-first into brick; grit filled his teeth; his ears went to a high, electric whine. Pressure burned his lungs. Copper touched his tongue. He coughed and red flecked the back of his bandana.

When the shockwave peeled off, the machine's wheeze was gone. What moved did so in jerks and twitches.

He blinked through the spin at the edges of his vision. Rats lay in heaped shadows, some still, some not. A length of shrapnel warbled to a stop somewhere in the dark.

Whether he'd outsmarted the rats or merely traded one death sentence for another, remained to be seen.

# CHAPTER THREE

Alysha stood at the glass, dusk burning the city down to embers. From this height, New New York crawled like a glittering fungus over a table of what the humans called concrete. Months of careful pulls on quiet strings had led to this—Lucas, tonight. He'd even sent the dress: a weaponized whisper that hugged her curves and threatened to reveal even more. Pity twitched and died; purpose burned hotter.

Lucas built nightmares—in clean rooms with white coats and black budgets—war made elegant and exportable. Her part was simpler: let him taste what he'd sold before he earned the only mercy he'd ever get. She touched the pendant between her breasts, cool weight steadying her pulse. Quent's handiwork—gnome craft braided with human tech—turned corporate scanners into liars. Agents had slipped into these cities before and vanished into footnotes—precious few survived, and none of them had gotten this far. She was the only one left. Every family broken by the human machine stood in the room with her like ghosts.

She moved and the silk sent a soft hiss through the penthouse hush. The apartment smelled of glass cleaner and decadence. Her perfume rode over it—sweet on the first inhale, edged with a pheromonal hook meant to catch "dear" Lucas by the balls. "Them's the breaks," Dandrag, her mentor, would've said, chuckling, when the work got messy.

The door chimed. She set her mouth into the smile Lucas liked and walked, hips teaching the light how to behave. The plan was simple enough: the perfect date, one laugh too close, one hand too trusting, a trip to the R&D facility with no one but him to hear her lullaby.

The smile melted when the door slid open on Lawrence instead. Not Lucas. The bodyguard filled the frame like a load-bearing wall. Disappointment flashed, hardened to cool disdain. He gave her a long, workman's appraisal—professional, but intentionally slow.

"Where's Lucas?" she asked, tone wrapped in silk.

"Waiting in the car." Lawrence's voice rumbled, something close to amusement shining in his eyes. "Standard procedure. Body search before you step into the Telluric Foundation's ride." His gesture to the hall was brisk enough to bruise.

Alysha's chin tipped a fraction. "Keep your hands to yourself, Lawrence. One wrong touch, and you'll regret it."

No flinch, no leer—just the job, the implacable patience of a man who'd put bigger problems on the floor. The white dress clung, daring him to be human. He stayed stone.

Fine. Procedure today. Lucas tonight.

She let the smile return, softer at the corners, as if fondness could be worn like fabric. Fingers brushed the pendant once more, a private reassurance. The city howled mutely through the thick walls. Revenge, she reminded herself, has a cadence. She would keep time.

Once Lawrence cleared her—no weapons, nothing to argue about—Alysha checked the mirror, teased a little air into her flaxen hair, and followed him out. Two birds with one stone, she thought, and let herself enjoy the proverb.

Lucas's car waited—the machine had better manners than most men: doors that sighed shut, leather that exhaled a cold, expensive smell, an opaque partition raised like a drawbridge. Scenic route, then. He wanted the city to perform for her—lit rivers, curated ruin, the polish Lucas mistook for power.

In the dark box of the back seat, he reached for her with clumsy confidence. Heat, cologne, the wet sweetness of a man who believed position was foreplay. Alysha let him crowd her, then gave him a smile and a hand to hold and nothing else. The part required patience. A flinch or a slap would waste months.

The difficult work was already done—in the pale hours before dawn, Lucas heavy and slow beside her, brain lax with pleasure and pride. He'd talked. Of course he had. He'd walked her through his toys the way a boy shows off contraband, and he'd sung the codes he'd carved into himself by repetition. Access like a tattoo you couldn't laser off. The research servers opened to her, and one file waited with a name that made all of this worth it.

Project Godspear.

The project name sounded ridiculous. The contents did not. Not a weapon so much as a caged event: chaos wired to flesh, kept under by a steady drip of tetrodotoxin. A simple interruption and the thing would awaken. There was no "safe." There was only on or off, and "on" meant the city learned what Lucas had dealt abroad.

She watched their reflections skim the black glass, perfume a steady thread in the recycled air. The pendant at her throat sat warm against skin, Quent's work quietly lying to every scanner they passed. Other agents had vanished into these cities and left no names behind. She was still here. She would make this count.

The partition hummed; the driver turned without asking. Lucas squeezed her knee as if that closed a sale. Alysha turned her head as if to listen better, chin tipping, lashes low. Inside, the arithmetic stayed static: keys in hand, path to R&D, only thing left was to starve the drip. Survival odds for her—slim. Cost to New New York—crippling. If the thing reached farther? So be it.

A smile touched her mouth, the kind that never reached her eyes. Tonight was for oblivion.

***

"Mustang, what the hell is going on?" Bradley snapped into the comm, ears still ringing. The blasts had punched the air and left a hush filled with high-pitched ringing.

"Dog's dead," Mustang came back, amused in a way that made Bradley's forehead bead with sweat. "Might want to get your ass over here, *Captain*. Knight'll guide you in."

He swept his squad. Wide eyes. "Perimeter," he ordered. "No one near the blast zone until I say." Boots scattered on grit; rifles came up. He ran.

Knight waited at a tight alley, riot shield slung over his shoulder, blaster at low ready as if this bored him. Goose flesh crawled up Bradley's spine. Knight tipped his chin in a go on motion, and Bradley slid into the dark.

A dead end stood where the alley should have opened, city-issue concrete. Knight didn't blink. He stepped up and palmed the wall. Light bent—just a hair—like heat over stone.

Bradley reached out. His fingers met not stone but pressure, a static nip that pushed back. He pressed harder. Tingling washed his skin as if he walked through cold rain. His hand passed through.

On the far side, the world turned into a vivid nightmare. Gear whine. Action rattle. The breathy pulse of a compressor.

The stink hit first—burned propellant, hot oil, meat. Then he saw it: the dog torn into wet abstracts.

Every nerve in him lit. His jaw locked so hard his molars squealed; his skin went cold and hot in a single shudder. Hand went for his sidearm on instinct—too slow. He was already dead. Visions of the rounds walking up his chest and chewing through the meat filled his mind.

Time resumed and nothing. No flash. No impact. Just that terrifying whine.

Mustang's laugh detonated in the chamber—delighted, and probably the first genuine laugh Bradley had heard from the man.

"Hilarious, Mustang," Bradley said, heat seeping into the words. Knight slipped through behind him with a grin he at least tried to hide. "How sure were you that friendly fire wasn't on the menu?"

Mustang shrugged, a hint of a smirk lingering on his lips. "Confident enough. Looks like it ran through its last rounds on that unfortunate canine. This place has clearly seen its share of scavengers, probably drawn in by the scent of the first victim." He gestured around the room, his eyes settling on the mangled remains of the dog.

"Makes sense," Knight offered, stepping closer to examine the scene. "But why the fancy light show? Why not just a regular wall?"

Bradley raked a hand through his hair, pulse easing back from the cliff. "Access," he said, already mapping angles. "Whoever built this wanted to slip in and out without a demo team." The turret, the shimmer-wall, the dead mutt—everything pointed to an entrance, not a dead end. Under normal circumstances he'd have kicked it up the chain of command. But after what he'd learned about the Telluric Foundation, silence was probably safer.

A low rumble rolled through the two stacked sets of doors ahead. Cool air pulled across his skin.

"Did you hear that?" he murmured, palm finding the familiar weight of his sidearm.

Knight cocked his head. Mustang, too.

"Ventilation," Mustang said. "Big system. Place is massive if it needs that much air."

"And probably heavily secured," Bradley answered, eyes cutting back to the shredded carcass. "Let's see where this access point leads. There's a good chance we'll find something interesting."

Knight held up a hand. "Before spelunking into a mystery bunker, maybe we call friends. This could be beyond the scope of our current resources, and walking in blind could get people killed."

Bradley chewed his lip. Trust was a ration these days. "Backup's a gamble," he said. Knight frowned. Bradley sighed. "Knight—"

The comms snapped to life. "Sir," Corporal Rodriguez cut in, "inbound backup just reported. Did you request it?"

Both officers looked at Knight. He lifted both hands, palms out.

Mustang took the channel. "ETA, Rodriguez?"

"Ten minutes, sir."

"Ten," Bradley echoed, feeling the ground tilt. He keyed to the outer team. "You've got five to get clear. Break contact and rendezvous at the barracks. Move."

A look flashed between Mustang and Knight—worry, calculation, too many questions for the moment. Mustang didn't wait.

"Knight, you're on need-to-know. Here's what you need: The Foundation's rotten. Centuries of human experiments—rotten.

This hole?" He jerked a thumb at the doors. "Most likely theirs. That 'backup' isn't rescue. It's a mop."

The comm sputtered again, Rodriguez's voice climbing. "Sir, vessels incoming fast! No room to run. They're ordering us to disarm and surrender for questioning."

"Run!" Bradley barked, instinct hitting first.

"Belay that," Mustang snapped over him, voice gone iron. "Comply, Corporal."

He touched his right ear. A small blade flashed; he winced, dug behind the cartilage, and tugged free a rice-sized device glistening with blood. It ticked in his palm like a guilty tooth.

Bradley's jaw set. "We don't abandon our people."

Bradley tasted rust at the back of his throat. Mustang's voice came low, hard-edged. "They're already walking corpses, Bradley. The Foundation'll make an example if we fight. If we ghost out, maybe they don't get all of us."

Knight didn't dress it any better. "Unseen," he agreed with Mustang. "If you're right, They'll silence the perimeter either way. If we vanish, they have to search. That buys us minutes, maybe more."

"That time buys us a chance for what?" Bradley snapped, heat under the words. "To live another day while our men—"

"Like the sergeant said," Mustang cut in, his expression offering no comfort. "Dead either way. Better to try to make it mean something."

The truth sank like a stone into his guts. Bradley's jaw worked; he stared past them at the breathing doors and heard the distant thrum of inbound rotors through the concrete. If there was a way to save his men, he didn't know what it was. There was no way to balance that equation, and math never lies.

He swallowed it, all of it. "Fine. What now?"

\*\*\*

Jorgen cracked an eye. The world answered with a low groan and a needle of ringing in his right ear. Pain had mapped him from ankle to shoulder. He lay half on, half off a mound of ruined fur and pipe shrapnel—the remains of the things that had tried to eat him.

He rolled to an elbow. The move stole his breath. A wet gleam waited under a leaking valve; condensation pattered into a shallow dip in the concrete. He dragged himself there and dipped a hand. Cold. He peeled out of his leathers one inch at a time—buckles tacky with blood, fabric glued to torn skin—and found the scrap of soap he'd lifted three lifetimes ago. The first pass set every cut on fire. He grunted, washed anyway. Grit came off in gray ribbons; chalky dust turned the puddle the color of milked stone.

He checked the damage like a mechanic: calf punctures from the bite, a slice along the ribs where a shard had kissed him, a dozen lesser tracks. He tore a clean shirt into strips, twisted a pad for the calf, and cinched it down until the throb dulled to a manageable thud.

The flask came next. Mountain liquor—pine smoke and bad decisions. He took a pull; it hit like a thrown match, set a line of heat from tongue to gut. He poured the rest over the worst of it. The sting buckled his knees; he rode it out with his jaw locked and breath short.

Hunger spoke up, it always wanted its say. He ignored it long enough to work, and crawled the shaft searching for anything dry—insulation paper, a heap of cable wrap, a strip of pallet wood hiding behind a compressor housing. He rolled tight tinder balls, shaved a curl of rubber to catch spark, and worked his old striker until the heap took. The first lick of flame put real warmth on his hands. Smoke hung low before tucking itself into the ceiling maze, lost in the machine-stink.

The fire would dry the leathers.

He dragged two of the bigger rats from the pile and set his knife to them. Skinning was ugly business—fur singed at the edges, a sour note of ammonia under everything—but his hands knew what to do. He cleaned them, skewered meat on stripped wire, and fastened it over the flames. Fat hissed. Grease popped onto his knuckles. The smell wasn't goat on a ridge, but it was meat.

The first bite fought him—stringy, stubborn as boot leather. He chewed until it gave. The second went easier. He ate because not eating was worse; tomorrow had a price and he'd need the strength to pay it.

Vents began to pull the smoke up and away, a steady draw he could feel on his cheeks. Small mercy. With food in him—grumbling but in—bandages tight and the fire settled to coals, Jorgen turned to the bad news.

Weapons.

He swept the floor with his boot, felt under pipes, checked where he'd bled. No knife. The absence landed harder than he liked. He found the rifle and wished he hadn't. A spiderweb crack split the junction where the micro-compressor met the charge reservoir; the housing flexed with a faint, hopeless tick when he thumbed it. Fatal. No pressure.

"Dammit," he said to the shaft, to the rats, to the city. "That stupid boy better be damn grateful when I find him."

Hours slid past on the backs of small chores—feeding the coals, rotating the leathers, tightening the wrap on his calf until the throb dulled to a knock. When the hides finally gave up their damp, he pulled them on. Familiar weight. Familiar squeak at the shoulder seam. He slung the broken rifle anyway. Something to hold on to.

Paint stencils marked the wall: **K-94 MAINT. TUNNEL**. Not city utilities. *Odd.* He eyed the tunnels and the oversized carcasses cooling in the dark. Experiments gone feral, or sewer stock overgrown on what leaked down here? "Answer's probably as ugly as it is useless," he muttered, voice coming back in broken cracks.

No sense wasting more time.

The climb back out of the tunnel was agony. Lacerations burned where the soap had stripped them clean. His calf screamed, then settled to a steady complaint. He moved like he always had when climbing out of the shit: three points, test before you trust, don't look down. Not that there was a drop here; it was just hard to stay vertical when the world was spinning.

Night lay over the city when he eased the grate and slid out. Cool air hit his face; LEDs washed the alley a sick blue. He took a knee and let the ring in his ear fade to a tolerable whine.

Map out. The line he'd walked the last few days hooked toward the fringe of Annapolis.

Close.

He found a tight nook behind a dead chiller unit—dry, out of the camera cones, with a line of sight on the alley mouth—and made it his refuge for the day to come. Curfew would give him the road again; he'd move under the cover of night, ghost into the building where Bradley had supposedly been stationed, and sit on his hands until morning.

He checked his wraps. Checked his water. Checked, again, for the knife he knew he didn't have.

"All right," he told the dark. "You stubborn bastard, I'll tell it to you straight. After that, you'll have to choose."

Dragging the kid out would be harder than walking alone. Company might still be worth the trouble. He shut his eyes, counted his breaths to ten, and let the city's hum settle into something he could sleep to.

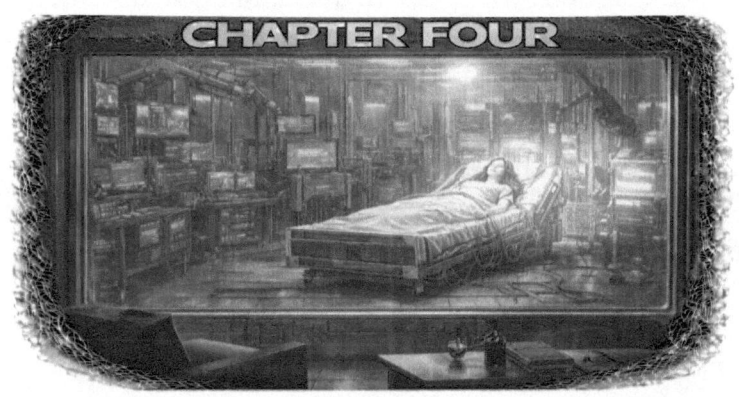

# CHAPTER FOUR

Lawrence, the hulking brute, stayed on the ground floor. Lucas's gaze kept straying to the white silk that suggested more than it revealed. He rode the elevator with her for the spectacle and wouldn't scuff a shoe giving a tour. Let him look. His clock was ticking in hours and minutes, not years.

The tour started on twenty-seven. A junior designer—Justin —bounced into patter about cosmetic modifications: dermal weaves, pigment shifts, bone micro-scaffolding. He talked function, process, black-market routes, and even bragged that the citizenry of New New York couldn't legally buy them; the California archipelago was their field. The more he spoke, the brighter he got. Waste, Alysha thought, not unkindly. A tragic waste of talent.

"Cosmetic enhancements?" Lucas cut in, annoyed at the mundane pageantry. "Who cares how you look when the city's about to be a herd of mindless drones?" His eyes slid from Justin to her, claim written in his gaze, punctuated by the extra beat he let his stare linger at her hip.

Justin missed it, or chose to. He kept going, eagerly answering her pointed questions with grateful detail. She fed him prompts, nodded in all the right places, and felt Lucas's posture go iron—shoulders tightening by degrees. Again with "the breaks." None of this was a choice. Trust wasn't on offer. If Justin guessed what she was, he'd hand her over or try to be a hero. Loneliness pressed in—wrapped in voices and unwanted affections.

They reached Weapons R&D. Arrays of locked cases glowed under glass.

She leaned closer to Justin, letting silk whisper. "Tell me about the energy blade," she murmured, voice soft enough to invite confidences that shouldn't be voiced.

A sound came out of Lucas—half growl, half sigh. Her mouth twitched, almost a smile.

His jaw set so hard the hinge popped. He shouldered past Justin with enough force to stagger him. "Enough," he said, the pitch climbing. "This is our date. He's only here to entertain."

Alysha widened her eyes just so—startled, contrite, but never weak. "Oh dear," she breathed. "Did I upset you, Lucas? I was only curious about the blade." A fleck of challenge flared in her blue eyes and went out again before he could reason out its meaning.

She let a fingertip brush the pendant at her throat, a private reassurance, then turned back to the display with careful patience. Let him seethe. Jealousy was a door. Tonight, she intended to walk through it.

Lucas's glare tightened to a slit, possession warring with presentation. He scoffed and pivoted to a glass case, palm leaving a fogged crescent on the pristine lid.

"This," he said, gesturing at a prototype energy rifle with a hand that wasn't quite steady, "is what matters. Not some glorified pocketknife." He tried to voice authority and missed.

Alysha tilted her head, the silk at her shoulder whispering as she looked from Lucas to the rifle. "A rifle?" Soft, almost indulgent. "A bit bulky for me, don't you think?" Her gaze slid to Justin. "And the blades are still in development, yes?"

Justin, trying to blend into the white walls, cleared his throat. "Y-yes, miss. Highly experimental—unstable, even. The Atlanta Alliance is… ahead of us in a few parameters."

She stepped closer to Lucas, lowering her voice until the hum of the lab almost swallowed it. "Fascinating," she breathed, the word skimming his ear. "But a little… unwieldy for me." Her fingers ghosted his sleeve—no more than a suggestion—and he visibly shivered; Alysha was positive it had nothing to do with the cold, filtered air.

"There must be something more… selective," she went on, sweetness threaded with challenge. "Something that doesn't rely on brute strength so much as"—her eyes traced his suit seam down, then came back up and held—"finesse."

Color climbed his neck. Annoyance sparked and guttered under something needier. "There's nothing more effective than these prototypes," he blustered, squaring his shoulders. "They're the future of warfare."

She let a small laugh ring like a glass chime—pretty, empty, and calculated. Justin flinched at the sound and then pretended he hadn't. "Oh, I'm sure," she said. "But surely there are projects they don't parade past 'just anyone.'"

Her breath brushed his ear again. "Perhaps later," she murmured, "you could show me something off the books. Something that might hold a girl's attention longer than glowy sticks and overheating swords."

Lucas's breath caught. His eyes shifted from her mouth to the reflective glass, to Justin's nervous profile, back to her. In the clean, humming heart of the lab, doubt took root—not about her, but about whether he was doing enough to impress her. He straightened, again trying to project authority.

"Finish up, Justin," he said, voice roughening to something he hoped sounded more masculine. "I'll handle the rest of the tour."

"Off the books, you say?" he echoed, voice gone husky. Possession slipped; something raw and eager showed through. Alysha met it, quick to set the hook.

"Just a peek," she purred, honey-soft. "What really makes New New York tick. And it would be a shame," lashes low, smile precise, "for a pretty face to leave without a proper souvenir."

Playful on the surface. The look behind it said something else entirely. She wasn't hunting trinkets. She wanted an audience —with the worst thing humans had ever dreamt into being. Lucas's bravado wobbled under the heat she fed him.

"A souvenir, huh?" A smirk tugged. He cut a glance at Justin, who seemed to fold smaller under the weight of Lucas's scrutiny. "Maybe there's an arrangement that could be reached," Lucas murmured. "Discretion is key, doll. One wrong move and—"

He left the threat hanging. Alysha didn't blink. Danger sweetened the air.

"Discretion is my middle name," she whispered, fingertips tracing the line of his sleeve. "Why don't we discuss the details somewhere... quieter?"

His eyes darkened—desire elbowing suspicion—ego trying to keep its footing.

Justin gathered himself and slipped away, shoulders hunched, swagger abandoned. For a heartbeat he glanced back—defiance blazing in his eyes, sharp and human in a city of glazed obedience. Waste, she thought again, and the feeling stung.

The elevator swallowed them, doors sighing shut in the lab's antiseptic light. Stainless steel walls offered three versions of them in pale reflections. Lucas leaned close, breath warmed by expensive cologne as he palmed the biometric plate.

"Top-secret labs aren't known for scenic views," he said with a smirk.

The scanner blinked green and the car lurched upward, a metal box sealing them in with their reflections. Alysha steadied her breath, met Lucas's gaze, and let a playful spark ride her eyes.

"Maybe," she whispered, close enough for her perfume to do its quiet work. "But I'm interested in a different kind of view. Something more...electrifying."

He chuckled—too loud in the small space—then watched her mouth until the doors hissed apart.

The corridor beyond wasn't sterile white; it breathed color. Holograms rolled down the walls in layered streams—data spirals and bioluminescent patterns pulsing like a foreign heartbeat. The air ran cool across her shoulders. Every footfall came back twice, once from the floor, once from the glass. Months of careful work brought her to this artery; the pulse under her skin kept time.

Lucas, a symphony of self-importance in a lab coat, droned beside her—specs and acronyms, all noise she let slide off. Her eyes worked the doors, numbers and placards clicking past like rungs on a ladder.

Materials Testing—000451. No.

Genetic Enhancement—101352. No.

Another run of meaningless sequences; the mask tugged at the edges as panic tried to lift its head—then—000002: GODSPEAR.

Heat snapped along her nerves, followed by a clean, steady focus. Real. It exists.

Lucas stopped short at Advanced Robotics—003964—and palmed the plate. Wrong lab. Close enough for him. Not for her.

She let him usher her in. The smile went away between one breath and the next; what replaced it was all hard line. Lucas faltered mid-sentence, the word "dexterity" dying in his throat.

"Enough talk, Dr. Thorne," she said, voice clipped to an edge. "Take me to Godspear."

A blink. Confusion, then reflexive bluster. "Godspear? Dollface, you don't—"

"Further commentary on your part is unnecessary," she cut in, stepping so he had to tilt his chin up to keep her eyes. "That's what I'm here for. I'm done listening to you play tour guide."

"I can't just—"

She struck—short, economical. A heel-of-hand strike popped his nose; cartilage crunched; blood sheeted over his lip and onto his teeth. The room's filtered air turned copper.

He stumbled into a bank of glass. She was on him before the cameras could decide what they'd seen, a hand on his coat to steer him into the blind wedge under the corner sensor. The pendant at her throat sat warm, lying to every reader in reach.

"Listen," she said, low and malicious. "You can walk me there like a genius with a very exclusive date, or I can drag you there by the collar while you leak on the tiles. Either way, I'm getting in that lab."

His breath sawed; his eyes shone wet with pain and something like clarity. He nodded, eager to comply.

"Good," she murmured, easing him just enough to let him breathe. "Clean yourself up enough to swipe without bleeding on the plate."

He fumbled a cloth from a drawer, pressed it to his nose, and swiped at the bloody mess, hands shaking. "You have no idea what you're asking," he mumbled through red.

She watched the door cycle open in her mind, felt the old fear try one more time and fail. "On the contrary," she said, guiding him back toward the hall. "I know exactly what I'm asking."

Outside, the pulse-light of the corridor folded around them again. Alysha set their pace—unhurried, intimate, the picture of a privileged tour. Lucas kept up because he had no choice. And ahead, behind 000002, the song she'd come to unleash waited in the dark.

Lucas walked up to the biometric scanner, but hesitated to open the lab.

She slammed his palm to the bio-plate and angled his face over the scanner—calculated risk. The device whirred. Red blinked once, twice. A green bar swept across his swolling features. Lock disengaged. The door sighed.

Relief hit like a wave—and then purpose returned. She yanked him in with her and, before the sensor cycle could complete, drove him into the blind wedge beneath the corner camera. Two quick elbows to the cheekbones. A heel-of-hand across the bridge of his broken nose. A chop to the larynx to rasp his voiceprint. A stamp that shattered the first knuckle of his right thumb. Targeted, efficient, cruel because it needed to be. When she stepped back, he could breathe, but nothing about his face or hand would read clean on a scan again.

This was why she'd come.

Alysha crossed to the observation pane. The chamber beyond hummed with sterilized air and soft machine breath. On the bed lay a child—twelve, thirteen at most—pink hair spilling across white sheets in a blush-bright river. Even sleeping, she was vivid in a way the room could not dull.

Rage rose so fast it sparked the air around her. Not a weapon. A girl.

Sapphire eyes would catch light and throw it back in colors that weren't human. Flame feathered along Alysha's forearms; her hair lifted in a heat halo and brightened, threads of gold bleaching toward white. She turned her hands to the inner door. Fire erupted, searing and hungry. Polymer blistered. Metal glowed and sagged. Alarms drilled the air; plastic fittings evaporated; safety glass laced itself with fractures. Lucas's blazer smoldered, acrid smoke slicking the back of her throat. Through it all, the girl lay quiet, as if napping in the evening sun.

The door wouldn't melt through—not fast enough, not without throwing shrapnel into the room.

Alysha dismissed the flame.

"Fine," she said, voice steady again.

She lunged for Lucas, the power in her grip surprising him. He squirmed in her grasp, his eyes wide with terror, but she hoisted him effortlessly, using his body as a battering ram. With a sickening crunch and a spray of sparks, the white-hot door buckled inward, its warped hinges groaning in protest.

She left him there on the floor beside the bed—burned and broken—a poor offering and a worse apology, but the only one she had. The pressure in the room built against her—subtle at first, then gathering, a field like the calm before a storm. It prickled her skin the way old magic did, power pooling and drawing strength.

The girl shifted. Fingers twitched. Lids fluttered.

*** 

Dust hung thick as gauze in the shaft of light knifing through a cracked pane. Bradley's whistle bounced around the cavernous space, swallowed and returned by rows of steel shelving, bowed under the weight of old industry—what would now be considered hulking consoles with dead LCDs, crates stamped with ghosts of logos, coils of cable as thick as his wrist. The place smelled like cold iron, old oil, and cardboard gone soft with age.

"Welcome to my little nest egg," Mustang said, grinning as he muscled a crate onto a scarred workbench. The impact sang metal-on-metal. "Officially: scrapped. Unofficially: corporate trash turned hobby that got out of hand."

"Why do you have all this?" Bradley asked, eyes tracking aisles, corners, even as he took it in.

"I like to tinker," Mustang said, popping the latches with his thumb. "Regs say no 'major alterations' to issued kit. Regs don't say I can't play with decommissioned gear everybody thinks got melted." His grin widened.

Knight's mouth tugged, sour. "So, you've always had some dissension in you."

Mustang pried the lid back. Inside: nested boxes, each labeled in a neat, obsessive hand. He flipped one to Bradley, one to Knight. They hesitated a beat—curiosity, caution—then opened.

Mustang pulled his own free. It looked like sleek glasses that had kept growing—braided leads draped from the temples to a slim battery the size of a deck of cards. "Since we ditched our AR implants," he said, voice dropping, "we go dark. No microtech they can ping. These are the next best thing—local-only overlays, hardline link, encrypted broadcast capability."

"Next best thing or a beacon?" Knight countered. "Half this junk should have military tags. You sure you didn't just put a lead line on us?"

The grin faltered, then came back. "Fair," Mustang said. "Except, I stripped the firmware, burned the old RFIDs, and installed chimeric signal converters. No handshake, no ping. If I'm wrong, you get to say 'I told you so' while we run."

"Quite the collection you've amassed under everyone's noses," Bradley said. He swept the benches with a tighter eye now, cataloging. Dusty relics, and between them, the bones of a fight: compact energy rifles, humming faintly; power cells stacked like bricks; tools laid out the way a man lays out a life's work.

He reached for a blade. The hilt fit his hand like an old habit; the vibro-emitter's low thrum settled his nerves in a way he didn't admit out loud. He tossed its twin to Knight, who caught it and tested the balance with a small, approving tilt.

Mustang tapped the "glasses." "Heads-up will give us multi-spectrum imaging and IFF."

Bradley nodded. "Useful."

Knight moved to the nearest shelf, hands already sorting: batteries that still held charge, a roll of carbon tape, a pouch of optical fuses. "You calling these 'plasma rifles' to sound cool," he said, "or are they the deconstruction emitters R&D field-tested sixty years ago?"

Mustang's mouth twitched. "So-called 'plasma.' Don't call them by their government name in case anyone's listening."

He had another crate open and was emptying its guts. He slung a heavy vest at Bradley; it hit with a dull thud, pouches bristling with purpose. Bradley shrugged in, cinched it tight, and started loading—sealant, gauze, coagulant injectors, a roll of sutures, tourniquets—each piece finding a home out of habit. Soft clicks and muted snaps built a quiet rhythm under the warehouse's low electrical hum.

On the workbench, Mustang pulled up a holo-map. Light climbed off the table in pale planes: streets, then the superstructure beneath—sewers, maintenance runs, access nodes—the city's undercarriage glowing in wireframe. Data points pulsed where his fingers tapped, paths knitting and unknitting as he tested routes.

"We won't have long here," he said, voice gone flat. "Either we punch out of the city and find someone willing to hit Telluric with us… or vanish into the lost lands and make quiet lives that last." He looked up. The bravado was gone; resolve stayed. "We're fugitives. But I'm not finished. I won't die like that dog, nor do I plan on letting those bastards get away with what they've done."

Silence held a beat—heavy with the things none of them needed to say: fear, anger, something hardening in the gut.

Bradley passed Knight an extra cell and an injector kit; Knight checked seals with methodical fingers, then snapped the kit onto his belt. Mustang marked two exits in quick succession and ghosted a third route for when the first two soured.

# CHAPTER FIVE

Alarms ripped the night open. Yellow strobes pulsed off wet concrete, painting Jorgen in a blinking bullseye. So much for ghost work. He'd planned to slip a seam; now every lens in the district felt like a sniper scope.

Panic scraped at his ribs—old instinct, useful if you owned it, dumb if you didn't. Curfew meant no crowds to vanish into, no noise to drown him out. Street level was a stage under a floodlight. He needed a hole to hide in.

He checked doorways: obvious. Alleys: short or boxed with cameras. The sirens dipped, slid, came back at a pitch that crawled along the spine. He felt his pulse stumble, breath wanting to quicken for no reason but the sound. Sonic crowd control—panic on a dial, compliance on the next. He tugged his bandana up anyway, more habit than help, and worked his jaw until his teeth set to his rhythm instead of theirs.

A deeper rumble rose over the keening. He looked up. Transports—sleek shadows—skimmed rooftops, their wash rolling grit down the facades. Not for him. They cut a line toward a far tower that stood out of the grid like a knuckle. Jackboots moving heavy somewhere else.

"Fine by me," he muttered, though the city's answer—apathy—itched. Back in the Rockies, porch lights would bloom; people would call porch to porch. Here, nothing. Empty streets, eyes closed by law. "Whatever, sheeple."

He pushed off the wall, leg complaining inside the wrap, and hunted low. Sewer access took too long to find—stamped steel hiding under a skin of runoff. The sirens' pitch shifted again; an edge of needle-whine crept in from somewhere close. Drones queuing up, he thought. More trouble.

Jorgen spun, bolted for the alley mouth—and stopped dead. A girl—pink hair wild, hospital gown flapping—ran the centerline, hands clamped over her ears. Terror had wiped every other thought off her face.

"Shit, shit, shit—double shit," he breathed. Part of him, the pragmatic part, screamed that this wasn't his problem. He already had a mission, a tangled web of his own making. But the other part, the one forged in the heart of the Rockies, the one that couldn't ignore a damsel in distress, especially a child, roared in protest.

He stepped into the open and threw his arms wide. "Hey! Kid! Here!"

She staggered, locked on him, confusion slipping over the terror like thin ice. She wobbled toward him, still pressing her ears, shoulders hunching at every siren pulse.

"Why are there so many suns, and why are they all yelling at me?" she cried, voice muffled by the volume of the sirens.

"Suns?" he echoed, blinking. The strobes hit the wet street and threw light up like knives. He forced a smile that felt like a cracked mask. "Not suns. Alarms. They're loud and stupid, that's all. Eyes on me."

The manhole yawned at his feet, breath of cold iron rising. He angled her that way and she flinched hard, panic freshening in her eyes. "I don't want to go where it's dark," she whimpered.

"Hey, hey—it's all right," Jorgen said, keeping his voice low and even while his pulse ran hot. "We can't stay topside. It's too exposed. Down there's the only safe bet. But…" He crouched to her height, pitched it to a conspirator's whisper. "If you promise not to tell, I'll show you a magic trick."

She nodded—tiny, shaky. He shrugged out of his jacket and wrapped it around her shoulders, turning hospital white into anonymous leather.

It wasn't his strongest suit, this "sweetness" business, but the situation demanded some creativity. Her bright, wary eyes searched his face. After a long beat, she gave a tiny nod.

"Good," he said, relief loosening his shoulders. He closed his eyes, and a faint, shimmering light began to emanate from his body. A low hum filled the air, growing steadily louder. Then, a miracle. The light coalesced around his head, forming a brilliant halo that banished the immediate darkness.

The girl's mouth fell open. Terror blinked out, wonder rushing in to fill the space. She clapped, a quick, delighted patter, bouncing on her toes despite the sirens.

"See?" Jorgen said, tilting his head so the light washed her face. "A little sun that likes you. Doesn't yell."

She smiled—sudden as sunrise.

"Now," he went on, keeping the cadence calm, "I'll go first. Maintain three points of contact as you climb down."

Another nod. He set his long coat tighter around her shoulders, then eased onto the slick iron rungs. LED whitewash leaked around the skewed cover, his halo casting a soft circle on the ladder shaft. She followed at a slow, steady pace.

"Attagirl," he murmured. The sirens dulled with each rung.

***

Karl prodded the sorry excuse for a rodent turning on his makeshift spit. Fur singed and curled, adding a bitter top note to the undercity's usual bouquet—rust, piss, and the sweet rot of something that had died and been forgotten. Smoke licked his eyes. He blinked grit out and rotated the spit another half-turn. The fat hissed. A bead ran down, flared, and went to ash.

He had, as his sister would say, royally screwed the grotto bat.

She'd warned him—sharp tongue, sharper sense. *Stay in the high country where the air is clean and the coin is honest. Traders and plainsfolk from Sateria will keep your stall busy enough, Karl.* But no; he'd chased a different shine. He wanted more than steady custom—he wanted stories, handshakes with strangers, a name shouted across crowded markets. He believed down to the bone that commerce bridged anything if you let it:

102

species, old grudge, bad history. Coin and fairness. Weigh true, cut straight.

The humans he'd found up here had a different ledger.

In a crowd, with his hood up, his height passed for human, if on the short side. Unfortunately under daylight, dwarven features read true: the set of his bones, the cut of his clothes, the color in his beard. Pride warmed him when he thought of Arnasta—the forge-city's stamp on his soul—but pride had little to do with running for one's life from a rush of scared lost-landers and their makeshift weapons. "Unforeseen," they'd called him. Creature. Evil. The word had been laughable right up until the chase made it life-threatening. One bad leap across a broken catwalk, stone crumbled like stale bread under his boot, and the world opened its throat and swallowed him.

He'd landed in the sump under the gleam. A labyrinth that stank and breathed, built to carry away all the city didn't want to see. Months had sloughed past, one into the next, like grease down a pipe. He'd mapped a few corridors by hand—chalk ticks at corners, a private miner's chart for earthworks that didn't love him back. Every ladder he climbed delivered him to more of the same: blind doors and locked grates. Human ingenuity impressed him even as it set his nerves on edge; they'd built a whole second city just to forget the first.

He poked the rat again. The skin split; stringy meat showed. He tried not to taste it yet. He was a son of Arnasta and had a palate—coal-roasted trout on a ridge, bitter greens in vinegar— but hunger made a man grateful for what didn't kill him. "Stone and slag," he muttered, more habit than oath. "Cook, you little beast."

Smoke twined into his beard. He scrubbed at it with knuckles scarred by honest work. He was no master smith—his sister got those hands, fine as a jeweler's—but tools had always loved him. He knew a good edge, a true level, the sound a hammer makes when the strike is right. He'd brought the best of their works down the mountain: chisels that would bite granite and thank you for the meal, hinges that wouldn't squeal even if you begged. He'd offered them with respect. Finest in existence, he'd said, and meant it. Blank stares had turned to snarls as they tossed away his wares and grabbed for him. Law had become cudgel.

He stared into the little flame and let himself imagine—for a heartbeat—the machines he'd seen up above when he still thought he could walk the surface like any other man. A conveyor that moved without ox or man to push it. A lift that climbed in its own iron throat. Lights that burned cold and never ate a wick. He didn't like how much these people trusted such things, but he'd be lying to say his mind didn't tick at the possibilities. Bring even one back to Arnasta and you could change opinions. Bring two and you could change lives.

The rat hissed and dripped. He tore off a mouthful and chewed until it relented. It tasted of smoke and stubbornness. He swallowed, grimaced, and went again. "Karl, you fool," he told himself around the heat. "Dreamed of markets and fell in a sewer."

Water plinked somewhere far down the tunnel, regular as a clock. Warm air breathed from a vent and then cooled again as some hidden fan—he thought, the word new and useful—cycled off. Far above, something heavy passed—a rumble that trembled the grime on his little spit and sent dust motes dancing in the one thin blade of light that found this forgotten chamber through a broken pane.

He pictured his sister when he told her this story and had to laugh, a dry bark that startled a pair of pale roaches. She'd roll her eyes, curse him at all the right places, then put tea in his hand and bread on a plate and make room for his machines if he was able to bring any home.

He wouldn't give despair the courtesy of a seat. Not here, not ever. He was Karl of Arnasta, stubborn as bedrock. He'd trade his way out if he could. He'd steal his way out if trade failed. He'd find a ladder that led to sky and the bruise-blue of proper mountains. And if, along the path, a machine or two happened to fall off the back of the humans' steamless wagon? Well. He'd find them a loving home.

Karl worked a strip of meat off the spit with his teeth. Texture beat aroma by a nose, but it was still several valleys shy of a proper meal. The undercity, at least, spared him rain. Tonight's nook had walls but no roof—good walls, too, high enough to break the rat-lines and let the smoke billow straight up. Fewer bites. Fewer headaches. Call it a win in a place that didn't hand out many.

Voices shattered the hush—closer than he liked. He froze, rat halfway to his mouth.

"Ugh. Smells like something died."

"And someone's roasting it," another voice added, deeper, amused in a way that suggested size.

Old fear pricked the back of his neck. The feral crowd he'd met topside had taught him what human mouths could shape when they were full of zeal and prejudice. Still… these sounded more like men off duty than wolves on a scent.

A third voice drifted in, edged with a grin. "Doesn't smell half as bad as Jorgen burning deer steaks when I was stationed out west."

A startled snort from the first. "Wait—you have friends who cook deer?"

"Apparently friendship can't discriminate against culinary… creativity."

"What's a deer?" the deep one asked, genuinely lost.

Karl's grip eased. Banter, not baying. Potential customers—maybe they were in the market for a new friend.

"Actually," he called, voice rough from disuse, cutting in before they could answer, "it's roast sewer rat. Not the most delectable dish, but it fills the belly."

Silence held a heartbeat, then the deep voice rumbled a laugh. "Found our chef." Volume without threat. "Come on out, friend. No need to hide from a little conversation. Especially if you're offering food."

He stood, joints popping, and stepped into the guttering light. Three shapes resolved out of shadow: one tall and narrow at the shoulders; one compact, near Karl in height, coiled tight in a way that read dangerous; and a third built like a gatehouse—dark skin, shaved head, weapon easy in his hands.

Their posture was loose. Curious eyes, not hungry ones. Karl let a wry smile tug his mouth and lifted a calloused hand.

"Looks like the company might be better than the menu," he said. "Karl's my name, friends."

The tall, slender one approached with deliberate slowness, palms up—universal peace. Seeing Karl's open grin, the others eased a fraction. Their guns dipped from high-alert to the kind of watch a man could hold while he talked business.

"Evening, Karl," the tall one said, stopping just outside arm's reach. "Is it your supper we smell?"

Karl glanced at the spit and snorted. "Supper's a generous word. But I'll share what there is." He tipped his chin at the makeshift fire, at the circle of light that made strangers into faces. "Sit with me, if you like."

"Name's Bradley," the slender one said, stepping in with a hand and a surprisingly warm smile. Dark hair, blue eyes that missed little, a cheerfulness that didn't belong down here and somehow worked anyway. He tipped his chin at the others. "Mustang. Knight."

Mustang inclined his head. Mixed blood in the slant of his eyes, compact build—short but likely fast. "Pleasure," he said, smooth on the surface while his gaze inventoried corners, exits, the height of the walls.

Knight only grunted. Bigger than the door, dark skin sheened by the fire, a white scar scoring one cheek. His eyes looked like they'd been narrowed so long they forgot how to soften.

"Don't mind him," Mustang added, offering the closest thing he had to friendly. "Knight forgets how to smile. Too many years watching the wrong side of things."

"The honest side," Knight rumbled, not quite disagreeing. His glance slid to the spit. "Besides your culinary... experiments, you've made a cozy den."

Karl puffed a laugh. "'Cozy' isn't the word, friend. But desperate times." He lifted the spit, let fat hiss and pop. "Rat roast and decent company? Closest I've had to a feast in months. Trade you a bite for a story. I promise it eats better than it smells."

Something eased in the air. Even Knight's jaw unclenched a notch.

"A fair trade," Bradley said, settling on a broken crate, eyes bright with mischief that didn't quite hide the watchfulness. "Though this rat of yours better live up to the sales pitch. I've heard things about undercity cuisine…"

"Cityfolk and their stomachs," Karl scoffed, mostly for show. He nicked off a sliver, blew on it, handed it over on the knife's flat. "You haven't lived until you've tried the local delicacy." He slid the blade through and skewered another taste. "As for stories, I've got plenty. Want the one about how I became king of this sewer palace, or the two-headed dog I wrestled last week?"

Mustang huffed. "Start with the palace. Dogs—with or without extra heads—can wait."

Knight accepted his slice, sniffed it once, then ate like a man who understood hunger. "Try not to oversell the throne," he said, deadpan. "We're short on crowns."

Karl's grin tugged wider. A small fire crackled in counterpoint to the rat's sizzle; warm grease and iron scented the little room. Three strangers, guns easy at their shoulders instead of hungry in their hands. Maybe not a rescue. But at least they were friendly.

He hooked the spit back on its wire and sat. "All right," he said, the old market-voice slipping on like a glove. "It began with a cart of world-class goods, a bad decision, and a city that didn't know what to do with a trader who talks too much. Eat while I tell it. Stories always go down better with something hot."

# CHAPTER SIX

Jorgen kept his voice low, a steady murmur against the tunnel's sweat and sour air. "So, what's a fella call you?" The tunnel breathed around them—and somewhere far off a pressure regulator cycled—*click, hush, click*. They'd put real distance between themselves and the uniforms, but adrenaline wasn't done with him yet.

The girl didn't answer. She just walked, small hand welded to his. Silence since he'd shushed her at the drop, but that grip spoke plenty. He gave it a squeeze back—still here, kid.

"Mouse?" he tried. "Too quiet, even for you." A corner of his mouth twitched. "Spark, then. Got a bit of fire—"

She shook her head hard enough to set pink hair dancing.

"All right, fine. Pinky, on account of—well." He looked down. She was already smiling up at him. "Pinky it is."

They needed a hole to breathe in, somewhere to let the shakes bleed out. For the first time in a long time, he wasn't alone. He felt needed. Bradley was still a job waiting to be finished, but with Pinky's hand in his, her need was more immediate. He'd handle this, then the other.

The refuse of Annapolis's underbelly spread ahead—arrows of corridors and sumps, slick stone, maintenance stencils ghosting past in chipped paint. His steps were soft and tired. Pinky's were small and tireless, eyes wide inside the gold-white ring of light he kept low and tight over his brow.

"Hey," he said, squeezing her hand. "You're doing great, Pinky. Really." The smile he found was brief but honest. "Proud of you."

Her grin flashed quick and bright, a little sun in the grime. Warmth cut through his fatigue—and then the sound came.

Footsteps. Faint, but clear. Not the wash of runoff. Human rhythm. One-two, one-two, with a hard heel that slapped the wet. Soldiers, or someone who liked boots.

"Come on," he whispered, the softness gone. The light around his head dipped to a sliver.

They ran the dark at a controlled clip—no splashes big enough to sing out, no panic to burn air. The tunnel changed its shape under their pace—corners turning dicey, echoes stacking until they felt like they were being followed by their own noise. Pinky trembled but held his hand like a lifeline.

This was not his turf. Thousands of miles from the mountains he knew like his own scars. Every bend here could be a trap or a gift. He let his senses work: a colder draft on the left, warm air to the right, a trickle underfoot that sloped by a hair. Then— thank you—dim green showed ahead: a junction, smeared with maintenance lights and stenciled numbers flayed by time.

"Hold on," he rasped, angling Pinky toward the smear of light. A maintenance hatch crouched in the wall—half-buried under slime and flaking paint—four ancient bolts fuzzed to lumps by rust.

He killed the halo to a thumbprint of glow. The broken rifle came off his shoulder and became a pry bar. He set the butt against the corroded cam-latch and leaned in. Metal cried. Threads grated like sand in teeth. The seconds stretched and the boots came louder—hard rhythm on wet concrete, echoes stacking until it felt like they were in his chest.

The hatch gave an inch, then another, groaning like a waking animal. No time for finesse. He shoved it wide enough, pushed Pinky through, and slid in after her. He let the door settle instead of slam, caught it with his boot so the latch didn't ring, then eased it home. Dark took them.

For a beat it was just their breathing—hot and ragged, loud as sirens in the box of his skull. He eased the halo up to a whisper. Gold-white leaked from an inner light he had always had but never reasoned out why. It was enough to draw lines out of the black: a vertical shaft dropping into deeper shadow; iron rungs slick with condensation; numbered stencils eaten by mildew. The boots outside went past, the sound going soft, then softer, then gone.

Pinky pressed against him, small and shaking, eyes huge in the dim. "What now?" she whispered, first words in hours. Fear there, same as his, but smaller, more fragile.

"We go down," he said, and made it sound certain. "Only way that isn't back."

He tightened the coat around her shoulders, checked the knot on the bandana at her ears, then put her hand on the rung and his palm over hers. "Slow steps, kidThree points," he murmured. "Short steps. Don't rush it."

"Easy now," he said, and started down into the undercity he didn't know, toward air that stank but didn't reek of uniforms and alarms. "You're doing great, Pinky."

\*\*\*

"Following those drainage lines is a long shot," Bradley said, his voice low, strain bleeding through. "They could dump us into the Atlantic. New New York didn't wall the coast for the view."

Mustang snorted. "You think I don't know that? But, it's still our best shot at breaking the grid. We can't live in the drains."

"We can't vanish either," Knight said, a growl that didn't carry. "The Foundation's corruption won't stop if we run. We need proof—records. Crack that open and maybe the other megacities stop pretending they don't smell the corpse."

Karl shifted in the shadow behind them. "My sister always said running won't solve anything," he offered, voice quiet but steady.

"And how—exactly—do we get 'proof'?" Mustang's edge sharpened. "Short of kicking in their front door?"

Bradley exhaled, a thin thread of calm knitting. "He's right. We won't find answers in the drains. K-94 looks like a starting point, maybe they left something we can use.."

Karl frowned, beard catching the strip light. "What is this K-94? And why say "The Foundation" like it's a curse? Who are they?"

Bradley scrubbed a hand through his hair. "It's complicated. Short version? Everything wrong up top tracks back to them and their experiments. K-94's a sealed complex. We think it's theirs." He didn't elaborate further.

"Doesn't matter what they did," Mustang muttered. The memory of dead men lived where sleep should be. "Breaking in's still impossible. They sealed it and murdered our people."

"We can't wait for leverage to fall in our laps," Bradley said, meeting Mustang's stare. "We have to take the initiative."

"With what?" Mustang let a dry laugh scrape out. "Harsh language? This isn't a street gang, 'Captain.' It's a megacorp with soldiers, armor, and a basement full of nightmares they haven't brought into the light of day. We try to stroll in, we end up as scorch marks."

"So what's your plan?" Bradley shot back, clipped. "Walk out empty-handed and hope the lost lands take pity?"

Knight cut through, steady as a wedge. "We need a way in that isn't a charge. A weakness—service duct, blind shaft, an access point they forgot to close. Something that doesn't announce we're coming."

Mustang rolled his eyes. "This isn't a sim," he said, even as he threw a wireframe into the stale air. The AR glasses conjured pale lines across darkness: storm mains, power runs, service shafts.

He swept a thumb to the redacted patch where K-94 should be. Thin arteries radiated from the dead zone.

"—tunnels," he finished, softer. "Unless you count the ones they pay minimum wage to forget."

Bradley didn't smile, but one corner eased. "Talk to me."

"City's bones run under the new walls," Mustang said, voice back to business. He marked three nodes south and east. "K-94 was fed by these grids before the last flood retrofit. Officially decommissioned. Practically? They left the roots and killed the juice. If we stay off the live trunk, we avoid active sensors."

"Choke points?" Knight asked, leaning into the ghostly map.

"Two," Mustang circled them. "We take them quiet—foam charges, not flash. Trip a mic and we walk, don't run."

Karl squinted at nothing—no AR, no context—then cleared his throat. "And if it all goes wrong?"

"Then we withdraw," Knight said. No drama, just fact. "Drainage to the coast stays Plan Z."

Bradley nodded; the decision clicked into place. "All right. We skip the ocean. We hit K-94 for a way into the lab. Mustang— find a route that never touches the live grid and mark every camera cone. Knight—inventory charges and sealant; prep foam, not flame. Karl…" He weighed the shorter man, the grit, the newness. "You stay with me. Anything that looks out of place or odd, you say it. Fresh eyes might catch something we miss."

Karl's brow smoothed. "Aye."

Mustang killed the overlay. Dark fell thicker after the brief light. Somewhere above, a pump kicked, and the pipes answered with a dull shudder. Far above, the city hummed.

"We move on the change of the watch," Bradley said, voice steady enough to slow hearts. "No heroics. We take the proof we can carry and leave."

"And if there's no proof to be had?" Mustang asked—not to snipe. Someone had to say it.

"There has to be something there," Bradley said. "But we aren't going to drown in a drain praying the ocean's kinder than The Foundation."

Knight's mouth twitched—approval, small but real. "Copy."

They stood. Packs whispered. Gear settled. The undercity took their heat and gave nothing back. Mustang reached out, two quick squeezes on Bradley's sleeve—ready. Knight checked one last buckle, eyes in their permanent squint. Karl shouldered stubborn hope like a pack.

Grasping at straws, Mustang thought. Maybe. But they were his straws, and he knew how to braid. He rolled his shoulders, mapped the route again behind his eyes, and started forward into the wet dark.

"There have to be others—people who'd fight if they had a chance," Karl murmured.

*Maybe*, Mustang thought. *Or maybe they were already embalmed in Serenity.*

"Maybe," Bradley echoed aloud. The undercity's cold had crawled into him, but his eyes still burned hot. "Getting to them, waking them—that's its own war. And Telluric's been dosing the city with Serenity. We need an antidote before we can even ask people to care."

"So we die with our eyes open—great consolation," Mustang shot back.

"Dying isn't the plan," Bradley snapped, then ratcheted his tone down. "But waiting for them to finish us off isn't either."

"I see something," Knight hissed.

They dropped in unison, lights dead. Up-tunnel, thin flashes needled the gloom—quick, off-angle, more reflection than beam. Karl stayed upright a heartbeat too long, peering; his white eyes caught the last of the spill.

"Karl, down," Bradley hissed. "And for the love of—quiet."

Bradley hooked his belt and yanked him down beside a broken conduit. Cold soaked Mustang's knees. Then a sound floated back—soft, bright, an impossible note down here.

A child's laugh.

Again. Light as glass bells. Mustang felt the hair rise on his forearms. "Well, that's creepy," he breathed.

Knight grunted; his jaw went tight. The glow ahead stuttered and died. The laugh didn't come again—for a moment it was just the drip, the damp.

The short, stocky Karl finally folded into a crouch, confusion in the tilt of his head but blessedly silent. Mustang cut a look across the line—Bradley, Knight, faces washed by the light from their AR units—and palmed his sidearm. The echo of that laugh threaded the dark, bell-clear and unnerving, like a dare.

Forward, Mustang signed. They slid from shadow, boots whispering on slime-slick concrete. The air tasted of mildew and salt. The air pressure shifted in slow waves—faint vibration you felt more than heard. Karl stayed at Bradley's heel, sure-footed in the dark; Mustang filed that away for later.

Light swelled with each step. He kept his breath even, heartbeat up but silent. They rounded the bend as one, weapons shouldered, lungs held.

Silence and a serviceable glow spilled from the structure.

Mustang's gaze sliced the room: ceiling, corners, floor. A small chamber sagging under neglect—walls flaking, waterlines ringed like a tub. A child's room by arrangement, not truth: a cot frame on its side, a one-eyed bear gone gray, wooden blocks scabbed with grime. The light came from a naked work lamp hung too high, too bright. No child. "What the hell," Mustang whispered. This smelled like theater. Someone had dressed the scene and waited for applause.

Bradley's focus ratcheted tight. "Eyes up," he said without moving his lips. "No tunnel vision."

Karl's hand touched damp stone and flinched. Mustang logged the twitch, kept moving.

Knight took point, weight forward, muzzle low.

His boot kissed not-floor.

A whisper of line.

The snare cinched and ripped Knight off his feet. His breath left in a bark as he flipped into stale air, blaster clattering off stone. Cable sang. A counterweight thudded somewhere in the dark.

"Contact—" Bradley pivoted—

A second loop bit. He went up fast. Pistol skittered, a black leaf into shadow.

Mustang was already moving—drop flat, roll clear of the web strung just above the grime line. "Don't thrash," he snapped, voice going razor-steady. "You'll tighten it." He swept for anchors, for the telltales, for the logic under the spectacle.

Bradley fought the buck. The cable chewed his ankle; the brake ratcheted another notch and lit his thigh. Upside down, Knight hung beside him—stone-still, eyes tracking, waiting.

No footsteps. No laugh. Only old pulleys complaining and water ticking time, counting how fast this could go bad.

Mustang took in the mess in one sweep: curses bouncing off the low ceiling, gear scraping, Bradley and Knight swinging like bait.

Karl stayed upright. Brave or lucky. In the blown-out light Mustang read the stagecraft—the cot frame angled to funnel feet, blocks scattered to pull the eye, lamp hung high to flatten depth. Worn boards weren't random; they were lanes. He shifted a half-step, weight soft, rifle easing to his shoulder.

Karl froze. Mustang saw the prickle ripple up Karl's neck a heartbeat before something jagged touched skin under his jaw.

"Think about your next move very carefully," a voice hissed, close and cold at Karl's ear so that only he could hear. "Don't do anything foolish."

Mustang slid his cheek to the stock, sighted through heat waves off the lamp. Above him, Bradley and Knight hung inverted, faces flushing, breath coming short. Mustang kept his own breath quiet and counted angles.

"Who are you?" Karl managed. "What do you want?"

A chuckle with no humor skittered around the room. "Answers come in time, outsider. For now, call it a test. What are three soldiers and one of the mountain folk doing in this shithole?"

"I fell," Karl said, truth rushing out. "Months ago—I don't know how many. The soldiers are my friends. They're helping me reach the surface. We mean no harm."

"I don't want to," the figure said. Pressure at Karl's throat eased a hair. "But your boys brought heavy steel. And those uniforms…" A pause with judgment. "They belong to people who don't like either of us."

*Unforeseen*, Mustang thought. He felt the word settle like grit under a lid.

"They're not like the ones up top," Karl blurted, too fast. "They're good men."

"That'll be enough of that," Mustang said, stepping out of shadow like he'd grown there. Rifle leveled, cheek to stock, sights steady. "Let him go. Hands where I can see them."

The hooded silhouette behind Karl shifted—tattered cloth breaking the outline. Real hesitation. Good. Mustang didn't blink.

"Lower the weapon," the figure hissed back, tension pulled tight. "We have more in common than you think."

"I highly doubt that, bottom-feeder," Mustang said, letting the contempt ride. The muzzle never wavered. "Only thing we share is wanting out of here. Odds are our reasons don't rhyme. Step back from his throat and we'll talk like neighbors."

Upside down, Knight saved air. "Bradley. Breathe. Don't thrash. You'll ratchet it tighter."

Bradley forced his lungs to slow. *Good. His head was back on.*

The shard bumped away and clattered to the floor. Karl slid sideways quick and came up at Mustang's flank, hands open, eyes wide. Mustang nudged him behind the muzzle line with a knee.

"Words won't buy it," the figure said. "But we share a bond. A friend of mine. Was hoping to find him before he made trouble." A beat. "Goes by Bradley."

The hood turned toward the dangling men. "Wouldn't you agree?"

A hand tore the old tarp from the form. Jorgen's grin hit the light—too wide, too pleased with himself.

Bradley's eyes went wide, then hot. "Jorgen?" Half disbelief, half fury. "Jorgen, you asshole—what kind of game is this?"

"I came with news, kid," Jorgen said, unbothered. "But first things first." He chin-pointed at the snares. "If your friend with the oversized cannon will kindly cut you loose."

Mustang's mouth twitched despite himself. He shouldered the rifle with deliberate care and stepped into the lamp's hard white. "You set a good stage," he told Jorgen, dry. "A little overbuilt. A little dramatic. Very… effective."

"Had an audience," Jorgen drawled.

*Fair.* Mustang crouched at Knight's cable, thumbed his multi-tool to a hungry hum, found the brake. Two quick cuts— Knight dropped, hit in a controlled fold, came up already retrieving his blaster.

Mustang cut the cable and took only a small amount of delight in the sound of pain the "captain" made when he hit the ground. Bradley bent, hands on knees, riding the skull-throb down.

"Better?" Jorgen asked, far too cheerful for a man who'd just shaved years off their lives.

"Ask me again when I can see straight," Bradley said, holstering with a snap. He leveled a look. "News. And why the trapeze."

"Wasn't sure who you were at first, and I'm too tired to keep running," Jorgen said, the grin settling toward business. He angled his head toward the dark. "Picked up a stray on the way. She's jumpy, and I promised I wouldn't take long."

"She?" Knight's eyes scanned the thresholds again, only with more intensity.

Jorgen's gaze ticked past them to the doorway. "You'll want to be decent," he said. "Kid's been through enough."

Hum and drip took the room back. He flicked Karl a nod. "Good head, mountain man."

"Karl," he puffed, finding a grin. "But I'll accept the compliment."

Bradley straightened, blood settling, anger banked to coals. "Next time—" he jabbed a finger at the pulley, "not so rough."

Mustang slid the rifle to ready, re-mapped the area out of habit, then fell in behind, thoughts already moving to contingencies.

# CHAPTER SEVEN

Mustang fought the grin trying to climb up his face. Bradley had praised and complained about Jorgen for months, but up close the man crackled—annoying, sure, yet magnetic in a way Mustang hated admitting. Karl looked like a stunned pup. Bradley and Knight dusted themselves off with the ritual focus of men erasing embarrassment one swipe at a time.

Jorgen vanished down the corridor and came back with his palm braced on the shoulder of a small figure half-hidden in a tan coat a few sizes too big. Hair the color of neon candy spilled into the light. Not dyed—too even, too loud under bad light. The girl's eyes were a deep violet, wary and stubborn all at once. Even Karl's easy smile hiccuped.

"This is Pinky." Jorgen's tone gentled. "We'll be looking out for each other a while—'til I can find a nice place for her to stay."

"Jorgen—" Bradley's words came sharper than he meant, concern tangled with leftover fury. "We're heading into danger. You can't bring her."

The playfulness drained from Jorgen's face; a harsh Rocky Mountain storm settled in its place. "Danger's the only constant, kid." His hand tightened a fraction on Pinky's shoulder. "Besides, she listens better than you ever did."

That one landed. Bradley flinched. Knight said nothing. Mustang kept his mouth shut and let the silence stretch.

"You wanted a why," Jorgen said at last, his voice roughing at the edges. "I came to warn you. That 'accident' in the pass? Not an accident." He looked to Bradley, then past him, like checking for witnesses. "I walked the site after they airlifted you. Found mining charges—clean placements under the bend. Not locals' garbage, not IEDs. And New New York crews doing cleanup in RMC territory. Somebody with pull wants you erased."

Bradley's gaze dropped to his leg like it had its own gravity. Mustang clocked the micro wince, the way his breath shortened —the man was replaying the fall whether he wanted to or not. Field medic, vertical lift, months of rehab and stubborn luck; Mustang had read the report and heard the gaps.

"Planned to tell you in your office," Jorgen added, shrugging it off with brittle humor. "Got distracted. Lucky for you I did, considerin' you boys were down here playing in the muck." His eyes glided over their gear, their grit. "What the hell are you doing down here, anyway—besides finding more trouble?"

Bradley sank onto a flipped crate and laid it out: the K-94 breach, the sentry gun and the retreat, Foundation dogs on their heels, the decision to cut implants and go to ground. He knifed a glance toward Karl and added the undercity detour that came with an unexpected friend who'd fallen out of the world. Mustang listened for soft spots and didn't hear any new ones.

While they talked, Karl drifted to the edge of the room and made himself useful. He coaxed a small fire in a sheltered corner with damp cardboard and splinters, then set a dented pot on a makeshift grate. Water hissed. He parceled out dried odds and ends from a waxed cloth with the ceremony of a chef and the resignation of a prisoner. The place filled with a thin, savory smell that fought the undercity's rot and almost won.

Pinky edged nearer the heat, shoulders still under Jorgen's hand. Mustang caught her watching the flame the way kids watch dogs—hopeful, but ready to bolt. He drifted his rifle to a low ready that said I see you, I'm not a threat, and pretended not to notice when her eyes slid to the weapon and then to his face, gauging which was more dangerous.

"All right," Bradley said finally, voice steadier, anger banked to coals. "We're not changing course. We still need to get into K-94. But if Telluric lit the fuse up there," he nodded toward the world above, "we treat every corridor like a kill box."

"Music to my ears," Mustang called, because it had to be said. He cut a look at Jorgen. "You bringing the kid means we move smarter, slower, and quieter—or we don't move at all."

Jorgen's mouth twitched. "Figure I can manage quiet when it counts."

"Prove it," Mustang said, dry as dust. He tipped his head at Pinky. "And teach her the same."

Pinky lifted her chin a notch, as if she'd understood the dare without the words. The pot began to steam; Karl stirred with a bent spoon, the metal clicking on thin iron, the sound small and domestic in a room that still smelled of mold and abandonment.

"Eat while you talk," Karl said, practical as a hammer. "Soup's better when it's hot, and it's easier to think on a full stomach."

For once, Mustang didn't argue. He took the heat, the thin broth, and the chance to watch. Jorgen kept himself between the kid and the door without thinking about it. Bradley kept looking at his men, counting them like a habit. Knight kept the perimeter in his eyes. Pinky kept one hand on the coat's hem like a talisman.

And Mustang kept the next moves building in his head— routes, contingencies, the math of adding two new variables to an already lethal problem. He let himself grin this time.

Fine. New plan. Same target.

Mustang couldn't turn his head off, so he put his hands on something that made sense. Jorgen's lines were right there— competent, effective, and old-school. He traced the path with his eyes: poly-wire invisible at a step's height, a snare loop tucked in shadow, counterweight hidden behind a lath panel, brake rigged from a scavenged pulley and a rusted pawl. No power. No heat signature. No EM chatter to trip a Telluric sweep. Strengths: silent and cheap. Weaknesses: anchor points not hardened, the brake squealed if you yanked too fast, lamp placement telegraphed the funnel. He filed it all without thinking, the way anyone else might breathe.

Knight ghosted off with a grunted apology and a fist pressed to his gut. City paste went down fine until you're fed real fat, that's when the troubles start. Mustang angled his body so the big man had a corridor to vanish down and the dignity to do it.

"Damn, kid. Looks like you stepped in deeper than just the sewers." Jorgen's voice carried over the quiet—none of the usual grin in it. "Sucks when home ain't what it used to be. News I brought... ah, skip the sappy. Let's give those bastards something to remember."

Mustang watched Bradley take that in. Chin tipped. Eyes narrowed, then distant. The man kept his face, but the gears behind it spun. Jorgen saw it too; the corner of his mouth twitched like he'd scored and hated the point.

"Maybe semi-retirement's gotten boring," Jorgen said, lids heavy, tone light. "Maybe I owe you a favor." Something lived under the joke. Mustang clocked it and let it ride.

Karl's stew started to win the air back from mold and rust—a thin, honest smell of salt and marrow. They ate. Jorgen told syndicate stories and took free shots at Bradley, and Bradley threw a few back, roughing the edges off the night. Pinky giggled at the right parts, small shoulders lifting under the tan coat like a bird shaking rain. Knight returned lighter around the eyes and sat with his back to the wall, listening like a man who didn't trust himself to relax but almost did. Mustang kept one ear on Jorgen's cadence and the other on the drip, the hum, the distant, never-asleep undercity.

When the bowls were dry and the cold came creeping in again, Jorgen stretched with theater he mostly meant. "Time to hit the hay. Or concrete—as it were. Split the watch?" He cut Mustang a look that said we're going to talk whether you want to or not. Then he peeled off toward a shadowed corner, Pinky in tow, the kid faking a yawn big enough to hide in. It worked; even Karl grinned.

Two hours later, Mustang put a knuckle to Jorgen's shoulder—firm, not hard. The man woke like an old fighter: one breath, one blink, one wince as the miles in his joints announced themselves. He took the seat Karl and Knight had cobbled from a busted crate and rebar, touched it in acknowledgment, then settled, rolling a stiff wrist as if pain were just something to be weathered.

"So," Jorgen rasped, voice sanded by sleep. "Let's cut to it." He eyed Mustang like a gunsmith appraising a jam. "Bradley dragged you into this, sure, but you don't read as accidental trouble. What's your angle?"

Mustang could feel Jorgen taking his measure—the old man-hunter's eyes had that steady, weighing look he'd seen on instructors and sergeants who'd lived long enough to be careful. He didn't bristle. He let the man have the read.

"I tried the model citizen thing," Mustang said, hearing the dry edge in his own voice. "Chicago-born, New New York–raised. Two flavors of authority telling me it was noble to serve, so I did. No questions." He let his gaze drift into the tunnel's dark, where the firelight couldn't reach. "Then Bradley dropped proof of a conspiracy—dates, names, procurement chains. The Telluric Foundation's in everything rotten. I could've turned him in." His mouth twitched. "Might've. Except he made a twisted kind of sense."

Jorgen's laugh was small and honest. "That's Bradley. Infectious idealism." The mirth thinned. "And he ain't wrong. You stand up sooner or later, with or without a city writin' your name on a wall. Took me longer than I'll admit to figure that out." He scrubbed a hand over his jaw, then tipped his chin, voice dropping. "Now keep your cool. Don't go for that rifle unless the world goes sideways. Understood?"

Mustang nodded, confusion creeping across his expression.

Jorgen raised his voice just enough to carry. "Hope you enjoyed the show, friend. We ain't meanin' you any harm, and I'm bettin' you ain't huntin' trouble. Let's skip the skulking and talk straight."

A seam in the dark unstitched. Mustang's hand found the rifle's grip and stopped there—because he'd said he would. A woman stepped into the heat, bright against the undercity's grime: forest-green clothes without a speck on them, blonde hair, pleasant form, posture like she'd never been cold or hungry a day in her life.

"How did you know?" she asked. Her voice was smooth, surprise riding under it.

"Lots of folks—and things—have hunted me," Jorgen said, all charm with a steel thread. "You're good. But there's a scent to you. Hard to hide, even down here."

She gave a neat little curtsy that belonged anywhere but this room of forgotten memories. "You may call me Alysha. A delight making your acquaintance. And you are correct, I don't mean you harm."

"Figured," Jorgen said, loose-shouldered now, though Mustang could see the way his weight stayed set. "So why the cloak and dagger?"

Alysha's shrug was light. "Saw you with the girl. Wanted to make sure you weren't some sewer-dwelling creep."

Mustang snorted before he could help it. The sound put a hairline crack in the tension. Across the low fire, the others slept like stones; only Pinky had her eyes open, the coat

131

bunched in her fists, pretending to breathe slow while she watched everything.

"Fair enough," Jorgen said, letting it go. He jerked his chin toward the pot on the warm bricks. "There's stew left. When everyone's vertical, we'll sort where we stand. If we're walking the same way, we can mind each other's backs."

Something unreadable moved behind Alysha's eyes—surprise, then caution settling back in place. She nodded.

Mustang didn't ease off the rifle, but he let his shoulders drop an inch, enough to say he could live with this for now. The undercity breathed around them—the damp stone, the quiet hiss of the fire, Karl's spoon ticking the pot as if supper with strangers was ordinary. Pinky shifted closer to the heat. Jorgen's hand hovered near her shoulder without quite touching.

"All right," Mustang said, more to the room than to anyone in particular. "We'll talk in the morning."

# CHAPTER EIGHT

Karl took to the newcomer like a tavern-keeper—easy smile, open hands—and Pinky shadowed Jorgen without a sound. Mustang and Knight wore their unease in the way they checked details that didn't need checking. Bradley didn't blame them. *You expand a unit without warning, you buy friction.* But Jorgen was an old variable in Bradley's math, and Mustang and Knight would back his call. The pact settled without words: sink or swim, they were tied to the same rope.

They packed light, redistributed weight, and set out—back to the spot where Jorgen's tale had him almost bleeding out. The K-94 maintenance access. The paint was ghostly, the numbers half-eaten by time, but they were there. Possibility, stamped in faded yellow.

"We need a win," Bradley said, keeping his tone even, not soft. "And I'm not sure you stumbling into exactly what we needed qualifies."

A breath of dry humor flickered across Jorgen's face as he pointed at the faded stenciling. "Lucky thing, too," he said. "If I hadn't been lookin' to die down here, I might've missed it."

Mustang cut the banter. "So what's the plan? Foundation goons aren't gonna let us waltz in for story time."

"No fancy plan," Bradley admitted. He felt the familiar weight of the sidearm, polymer cool through his glove. "We take what the place gives us—intel, schematics, anything that cracks this isolation. If they left heavy guns to guard an "abandoned" lab, it's not dead. It's buried. And the lengths they went through to bury it must be worth dying for, because they're definitely willing to kill to keep it secret."

"If it comes to it, I'm certain dying will be the easy part," Knight rumbled.

Pinky slipped her hand into Jorgen's. He blinked, then gave her that crooked smile of his. "Well, kiddo," he whispered, "looks like we're in for another adventure."

Bradley put them on the ladder in order: Jorgen first, light and sure despite the years; Pinky next, small feet careful on slick rungs; then Mustang, Knight, Karl; and Bradley last to watch the tail. The shaft swallowed sound. Metal groaned under old bolts. Dust shook loose, went to powder in his mouth. Mustang's beam knifed the dark and threw long, ugly shapes that seemed to move even when no one else did. Every ring of a rung came back at them twice as loud.

Air thickened the deeper they went—stale, warm, with that tang of neglected machines. Bradley set his breathing to the climb: in on the reach, out on the step. Pinky's coat brushed the ladder, a steady whisper below. Jorgen's boots kept a calm rhythm, and Knight's weight made the metal sing.

The ladder ended on a grated platform no bigger than a truck bed. Bradley swung off last and felt it flex under the stack of bodies. The space beyond was a throat of dull steel. A reinforced door sat embedded in the wall, surface scabbed with age, hinges overbuilt, seal intact. K-94 stenciled faintly under a smear of grime. He thumbed sweat off his eyebrow, leaned in, listened.

No fan whine. No footfall. Just the slow tick of metal and their own breath echoing the dark.

"This is it," he said, voice low. "K-94."

The lock was old-world ugly—bolted steel, swollen with rust, daring them to try. Bradley ran his fingers over the pitted faceplate, feeling for seams, listening for the lie. "Can we breach here?"

Knight was already unzipping the kit. "Built to last, but it shouldn't take too long," he said, setting the mag-cutter wedges along the faceplate, hands steady.

Crouched at the lip, Mustang watched the black drop below. "Question is what kind of persuasion we'll need after we get inside."

Bradley didn't answer. He was counting problems: no draft leaking around the jamb, dust sitting thick on the hinges—no recent traffic. Good for surprise.

The cutters buzzed to life—no bang, just pressure. The steel moaned and held. Second set, same result.

"Different approach," Jorgen said, the corner of his mouth tilting toward Alysha. "Your turn to shine, firefly."

Alysha stepped up without theatrics. She set her hands, concentrated, and the air took on a low, bright hum. No flame —just heat that bent the sightline and filled the air with a sweet-bitter stink of heated metal. The faceplate softened at the belly and groaned.

"What the hell," Mustang breathed. Knight's stance shifted— annoyance giving way to respect.

Metal whined high, then slumped. Knight moved fast, tools in, lever twist, pressure off the tongues. The door yielded a grudging inch, then another, swinging into a corridor that drank their light.

No one rushed it. Alysha's eyes found Jorgen. "How?" she asked quietly. "Calling me 'firefly'…you already knew."

Jorgen's smirk thinned. "Seen a few people with—talents in my day. I took a chance."

"Always the smooth talker," Mustang said, but Bradley heard the new caution in it.

He put a hand on Alysha's shoulder, steady pressure. "We all have secrets," he said. "Right now we have a mission."

He swept the threshold low with his beam. No tripwire. No pressure mat he could pick out under the dust. The air beyond was dead—no circulation, no fresh ion smell, only cold iron and dark. If there were sensors, they were sleeping or long blind.

Knight took point through the breach—shield up, muzzle low. Bradley tucked in behind him, eyes on Knight's off-side and the high lines, counting steps, angles, and places to die. Mustang's beam thinned the dark; Bradley kept his own light down, letting the walls come to them. Alysha and Pinky rode the middle with Karl, Jorgen ghosting the rear and checking their back trail.

The passage corkscrewed down, rough-cut and sweating machine oil. Single file, toe-quiet. Every scrape came back bigger. Knight slowed at each bend just enough for Bradley to clear the corner with him, then rolled on.

The tunnel shouldered open into a squat room with rusted hulks throwing broken shadows. A slump of ducting and shelves had collapsed into a waist-high barricade; Knight cleared left, Bradley cleared right, and the stack flowed in behind.

"Old maintenance office," Jorgen said from the barricade, voice low. "Nobody's loved it in a long while."

Bradley brought them through. Light found benches lined with tools gone orange, crates cannibalized into smaller work areas, paper schematics clinging to concrete in a skin of dust. Someone had worked here with care once.

A soft, out of place color tugged Bradley's eye—a cool blue on the far side, pulsing faint as a heartbeat. He felt Mustang aim for it without looking.

The thing humming there was a slab the size of a coffin lid. Wires had been spliced into its gut in little bundles; a liquid crystal panel threw the blue light in a steady wash.

Mustang whistled under his breath. "First-gen LCD," he said— reverence and hunger both. "Didn't think any of these survived."

"Air-gap it," Bradley said. "If it tries to talk to anything, I want it screaming in your sandbox not to whoever else might be listening."

"I like living too," Mustang muttered, already shouldering his pack open. He slipped a Faraday sleeve over the interface cabling, threw a tight local overlay off his AR, and started coaxing the relic into a conversation. The panel answered in fits—flickering lines, then a crawl of characters that meant nothing at arm's length and everything to someone who'd spent years prying at old systems. Dusty lights and mechanical whirs came alive, if muted from their original glory.

Pinky drifted toward the glow until Bradley's hand found her elbow and parked her behind Karl. She watched anyway, eyes huge, head tilted, like the code might blink and turn into a story.

Karl made himself useful, as always—quiet hands and keen eyes. He sorted through a toppled bin, rejected junk by touch, and came up with a spool of fiber that still had its sheen. "Good thread," he said, pleased without being loud about it.

Knight prowled the edges. He stripped a stack of plates off a wall grate and found a ventilation port black with dust. He reached in, felt collapse and dead air, and shook his head. "No flow. This box has been shut a while."

Alysha stayed near the choke point they'd come through, back to the wall, listening. Bradley examined the room again in slices: doorways, underbenches, ceiling lines, cable runs. No fresh footprints in the powder. No new smells. The hum was the only live thing in here.

"How long?" he asked without looking at Mustang.

"Depends whether this museum piece wants to play nice," Mustang said, fingers tapping a ghosted keyboard. "If it's just local logs, minutes. If it calls for a handshake upstream, we cut it before it squeals."

"Cut it either way if you see a transmit," Bradley said. He crouched by the side of the slab, following the cables back with his light. Not on city power. No glow in the indicator rails.

The panel spit a block of text and then a menu in a font that belonged to another century.

"Node K-94," Mustang read. "Maintenance archive. Subsystems: 'Utilities,' 'Access Control,' 'Incident Reports,' 'Personnel.'" A beat. "No network link. She's talking to herself."

"Start with Incident," Bradley said.

"On it." *Tap-tap*; the page rolled. Mustang grunted. "Dates are a mess. Time drift on the local clock. But... here." He expanded a line.

The panel ticked. Mustang swore softly. "Scrubbed records," he said. "But whoever scrubbed it didn't salt the ground. There's residue. I can reconstruct some headers."

The hum deepened by a hair—nothing most would hear. Bradley did. He cut a glance at the power bank. The charge LED climbed one bar as if on cue.

"Mustang," he said, quiet. "Pull the transmit pins. It's broadcasting somehow."

Mustang's fingers were already under the housing. "Already pulling teeth."

Pinky leaned around Karl's arm. "Is it... talking?" she whispered.

"Just to us," Bradley said, keeping his voice steady for her sake and everyone else's. He watched the blue light paint Mustang's cheekbones and thought about how fast a room like this could go from gold mine to grave.

"Two minutes," Mustang said.

"Two minutes," Bradley echoed. He reset his breath, let the silence come back, and kept counting doors.

Bradley noticed Jorgen's absence a heartbeat before the clatter —tools somewhere in the dark, the old man fussing with that air rifle. Fine. Let him have his ritual. After pulling the transmission pins, Mustang's fingers went back to ticking at the ghostly keys.

Pinky's gasp cut the quiet in half.

Bradley's head snapped to the screen. Lines of text bled to red, then the whole display strobed—error glyphs, a rising needle of a whine that raised his hair. The cool blue wash shifted crimson, painting the room like an operating theater.

"Mustang, we've got a—"

"I see it," Mustang bit off, eyes not leaving the interface. "Go find someone else's ass to crawl into and let me work."

Something moved at the double doors. A spider the size of a housecat skittered over the frame and onto the wall—sleek, metallic, with too few legs. The sound came with it: a spread of tiny metal feet ticking on grate.

"Contact," Bradley said, pistol up.

The room broke open. Pinky, bless her heart, launched into motion—darting, spinning, and dancing—peals of sound tearing out of her as if she were an alarm given legs. The pitch clawed at Bradley's ears but the drones hated it worse; the first unit stuttered in its arc, legs splaying.

Jorgen's rifle hissed and the bot blew apart in a spray of wire and black oil. "Eyes front," he growled, already walking shots across the doorway, keeping the threshold a storm of steel that forced more spider drones to misstep and tumble.

Knight went loud—shield up, blaster thumping in controlled bursts that turned clusters into wreckage. One drone latched Pinky's ankle before anyone could stop it; she cried out, skidding, and Bradley snapped a single shot that took the thing off her with a crack of ceramic. Welts already blooming. He shoved her behind Karl with a hand he didn't remember moving.

"Corner workstation!" he barked. Knight had a line of blood down his forearm. Bradley was on him, cinching a pressure bandage while his own thigh stung where shrapnel had kissed him. "Karl, pressure here." He grabbed the shorter man's wrist, planted it on the wrap across his leg, and let go. "Don't lift."

"Right," Karl said, jaw tight. A drone clipped his shoulder in passing; cloth sizzled. He didn't flinch off the task.

Mustang swore under his breath, hands a blur. "It isn't phoning home—it's a local connection," he said, half to himself. "Tripwire routine. Sit tight."

"Define 'tight,'" Bradley shot back, then bit it off. No time.

The doorway kept birthing hate. Jorgen bled from a line along his cheek and only stopped shooting long enough to reload. Knight, his wound now bandaged pushed forward, his shield edge came down on a crawler, crushing it flat; his blaster cored another three. The air turned to ozone and hot metal. Every bot that fell seemed to make room for two more, the tick of their legs building to something that felt like a hive living in the floor.

Pinky's wail faltered. She was still moving, but less spring. The siren in her throat losing to the volume of the drones crowding into the room. Bradley saw the tremor in her knees and the smear of oil on her bare calf and did the math: seconds to work with, not minutes.

"Mustang," he said, not looking away from the door as he thumbed a fresh energy cell home, "I need good news."

Mustang didn't look up. "I need more time!" His voice rasped through the haze, fingers rattling the holo-keys. "I'm close—damn security's stacked like an onion. Just a few more—"

A new sound rose and swallowed him: mechanical whirs layered into a single hive-breath. Down the passage, red pinpricks winked to life and multiplied. Not a handful—a damned army. The swarm's heart had found them.

Bradley's pistol tracked the mouth of the corridor. "On me," he said, more to hold himself steady than to move anyone; everyone was already engaged.

A blur cut past his sightline. Alysha. Quiet shadow no longer—she slid in with a long, curved blade that caught the room's bad light and gleamed with destructive potential. Too big to have been hidden anywhere on her frame. Bradley clocked the impossibility and shelved it—collapsible, conjured. Her sword didn't matter right now.

Knight never saw the spider dropping toward his spine. The clang of edge on chassis saved him. Alysha's arc took the bot apart in a shower of wire and sparks. She didn't stop. Dancer's hips, killer's wrists—clean cuts, no waste.

It still wasn't enough.

The corridor kept vomiting metal. Red eyes stacked in ranks. Legs ticked on grating, the sound burrowing into Bradley's head. The line bulged. Knight's shield met the first wave, blaster bursts turned groups into scrap, but gaps in their defenses opened anyway.

"One more layer—just one—dammit!" Mustang's voice frayed to wire.

"Karl, hold pressure," Bradley snapped. Knight was leaking from the thigh now—new puncture—and the earlier gash along his forearm hadn't had time to clot. Bradley slammed a clot-pad into the arm wound, taped, yanked the thigh tourniquet a quarter turn tighter even as the big man fought on. "Breathe, Knight."

"Breathing," Knight ground out, eyes never leaving the door.

Jorgen fought like a man who'd already died once and wasn't keen on a repeat. The patched air rifle hissed and spat steel bearings; drones pitched, fell, twitched. One latched his forearm anyway, pincers biting deep. Jorgen tore against it and barked something obscene that blurred in the noise.

Pinky moved because standing still meant dying. The siren in her chest tore loose again—high, bright, weaponized fear. Bots nearest her seemed to falter, legs splaying, gyros whining. She stumbled, the sound stuttering, ankle swelling angry where one of the crawlers had found meat before.

"Hold—" Mustang's fingers blurred, words sawed off by concentration. "Just a few more seconds!"

Alysha spun between two heavies, blade flashing, limbs hitting floor in metal clatter. For half a breath Bradley thought they had it contained.

The new unit changed the math. Bigger body, armored skirts, heavier servo whine. It hit Knight like a door and pinned him flat. The claw assembly ratcheted down, lined for the throat.

Pinky screamed.

Time went thin. Bradley's brain already stepping through an answer: fire the pistol and risk a ricochet into Knight's face, or close the distance and try to lever the claw. Jorgen, trapped under his own synthetic parasite, could only bellow. Mustang was inches from killing the room or saving it.

"Now, Mustang," Bradley yelled—not a shout so much as a trigger.

The room died all at once—light, sound, everything. The swarm's hum cut mid-breath. Black rushed in, thick as Tuesday's gray goo. Bradley held his breath, counted to three, listening. Ragged draws. Metal settling. Knight's choked grunt and the scrape of his shield. Alysha's blade whispered.

"We're…alive," Bradley said, and heard the relief in it.

"For now," Jorgen answered from the floor, prying steel from his forearm by feel. Wet sound. A swallowed curse.

Static licked his ears. The dead LCD hiccuped, pulsed, then woke on a whisper of power. A single prompt blinked, multiplied, then poured code. Blue washed the room; eyes squinted against it.

"Partial access," Mustang rasped, already back at the keys. "Security's still a dogpile, but I can pull basics."

Lines resolved. A low-res holo of their world rose out of the air —offices, workshops, a handful of adjoining rooms. Gray fogged the rest. Unknown. Bradley felt Pinky's shoulders dip beside him when she saw that fog; his own gut mirrored it.

He shoved the feeling aside. Work. Knight first. He pulled the patch and pushed gauze into the ragged bite on the forearm, tape tight, tourniquet one notch looser on the thigh to bring the pulse back without letting it gush. Knight's jaw flexed but he breathed on cue. Karl moved when Bradley tapped the kit—no questions, good hands—fresh pads, antiseptic, a strip of coagulant for the worst of Jorgen's forearm grooves.

"Could be worse," Mustang muttered, squinting through the low-detail wireframe. "At least we know the local rooms."

"'Local rooms' won't get you what you need," Jorgen said, voice gone gravel. He jerked his chin at the gray. "Half a map is one step from useless."

The adrenaline bleed left a cold steadiness in Bradley. "We don't have exits, but we have options," he said, eyes on the projection. "We start with what feeds us or moves us. Storage here, and… here." He pinched to zoom—one block stenciled SUPPLY, another unlabeled but laid out like a cache room. "If there are rations, charges, batteries—it's worth checking out. After that, we scout for a primary interface or server room off this branch." He slid the map to a faint ladder icon choked in gray.

"Right, let's get the lay of the land. Figure out what the hell this place was, what's still lurking out there in the dark." His gaze fell on Alysha, who, until now, had remained a silent. "And you, little firefly," he continued, a hint of curiosity in his gruff tone, "what else can that fancy blade of yours do?"

145

Alysha's eyes stayed on Knight's bandage for a beat. When she answered, her voice was even. "It cuts what needs cutting." She shot a glance at Bradley, then back to the dark beyond the projection.

"Good," Bradley said before Jorgen could wind it up. He checked his spare cells by touch. "Mustang, leave the console on a loop, pulling anything it can scrape—logs, access, labels. If the power cycles, we won't lose the crumbs."

"On it," Mustang said. He set a crawl, wrote a dumb little watchdog to yank anything with a filename, and squirreled it to a local buffer. "If it goes down, we'll have what we have."

"All right," Bradley said, letting the room hear the decision in his voice. "We need to split up. Mustang and I will stay on the system—dig for anything we can use. Jorgen, I need you to take the rest of the group ahead. Knight'll be your shield. Be careful."

"There's a ventilation shaft…" Mustang mused, highlighting a thin green line. "Doesn't look promising, but it connects to other areas—might be worth checking out on your way. I'll send the details to Knight's AR unit."

## CHAPTER NINE

Jorgen took point, Pinky tight to his hip. Karl hauled the gunna without a word; Knight brought the shield and those steady, watchful eyes. Alysha slipped behind them, blade asleep at her side. The holo-map died as they left the office. Dark folded in. Only Karl's rescued flashlight cut a narrow lane through dust and gloom.

"Hold," Jorgen rasped, hand up.

There it was—a faint skitter of metal, crosswise above. Pinky pressed harder into Jorgen. He tipped his chin toward a side run.

Stairs.

They moved that way, their footfalls soft. The treads complained in long, tired notes. Jorgen set each boot flat to kill the ring and kept two fingers on the rail so he'd feel a break before he saw it. The others matched his cadence, hearts pounding, asses puckered.

At the bottom, a wide room opened—damp, sour, and stale with mildew. The light cut across rust-furred benches and the ribs of dead crates. Their path was clear enough.

"Elevator shaft," Jorgen said. A mouth of black split the far wall, thick hoist cables hanging pitted and quiet.

"Looks inviting," Knight muttered.

"Might be our only way down." Jorgen nodded at the lines. "Karl."

The dwarf went to the cables like a smith to stock—thumbed the jacket, rapped a knuckle, listened. He tugged and watched for the slow, even twist that meant the cores were still true. Again, from a different height. He gave a short nod.

"They'll hold—if we don't bounce too much."

Jorgen worked a harness from rope: waist wrap, quick chest hitch, tail cut. He ran the line through a figure-eight on an eye bolt sunk low in the wall, tested the knot, added a prusik he could thumb if the world got stupid. Check the anchor once more—out of habit, not doubt.

"I go first," he said. "If the line jerks twice, haul my old ass up. If it sings, cut it. Don't argue."

Knight answered with a single nod. Alysha had already angled to watch their backs. Pinky's fingers found Jorgen's sleeve; he squeezed once and passed her hand to Alysha.

"Don't worry, darlin'. I won't be long," he said in answer to the pitiful look on her face.

Karl raised the flashlight. Light fell into the throat and died fast. Jorgen swung his boots over the lip, let his weight settle into the rope, and started down slow, soles skimming the wall.

Above, the old cables creaked like winter trees. Pinky watched, eyes wide. Sweat silvered Knight's brow, but his stance didn't waver.

Moments stretched. Every scuff was a shout, every shadow a waiting drone. At last Jorgen's voice drifted up the shaft— gruff, winded, relieved. "Got a set of doors I can work. Ledge feels solid... another one a dozen feet below. I'll check it next."

Karl set to rigging harnesses they could use with the cables. Knight shouldered past his own pain and took the next descent. Alysha moved like a whisper, sure and balanced even in the cramped dark. One by one they slipped off the lip and vanished. Karl, last up top, squeezed Pinky's shoulder and sent her onto the cable with a steady, "You're all right, kid," before tying himself on.

Jorgen clung to the shaft wall on the lower ledge, the glow from above barely silvering his fingers. Even with the flashlight, the space felt tight, rusted plates pressing in at the edges of his mind.

"Another workshop," he rasped, testing a door's play with his boot. "Let's see if—"

Metal screamed. The ledge under them lurched. Rust pebbled down like rain, choking the shaft mouth in grit. Then the kind of silence that packs your chest with ice.

Relief tried to surface—no one had fallen—when a sharp SNAP knifed the dark above. Karl's flashlight jittered into a strobe and died. Blackness took everything.

A scream tore loose. Karl...

Jorgen swore under his breath, forcing the panic down where it belonged.

"Pinky!" he bellowed up the chimney, voice raw. "Talk to me!"

Breaths first, small and ragged. Then her answer, thin with fear. "One of the things holding the vines broke. I'm okay—I think. I don't know about Karl. He's just hanging there!"

If that line went, the dwarf would drop a long way. Jorgen tasted copper and made the choice.

"Hold on, Karl!" He forced steel into his voice. "I'm coming up."

He fumbled with the makeshift harness he'd used going down, palms slick now, and swung for leverage. A rusted ladder hugged the wall—rungs of antique mercy. It looked older than his worst memories and twice as offensive, but it was what they had. "Knight! Alysha!" he shouted. "Get ready to take him!"

Jorgen tested the first rung with half his weight. It moaned. He climbed anyway. Every rung sang a complaint into the black. He kept three points at all times, his breath low and even, his eyes on the dim smear where the upper ledge should be.

Above, Knight and Alysha worked by feel, bodies braced against the floor, hands searching for a swinging boot. Jorgen reached the right height, leaned out, hooked Karl's line with his forearm, and pushed it toward waiting hands.

"Got him," Knight grunted.

"Easy," Jorgen warned. "Don't jerk him—"

They hauled in—*damn, Alysha was strong.* The primary cable sang, then softened. Karl's boots thumped the edge. Fingers found harness, belt, beard.

Karl collapsed on the ledge, shaking and breathless, the laugh that burst out of him half sob, half victory. Jorgen stayed on the ladder long enough to be sure of their success, then climbed the last rungs and rolled onto the ledge beside them, chest a furnace, hands burning with rust.

"No one else having a heart attack?" he managed.

From above: a small, wavering "What's that?" From beside him, Knight's low, steady, "No." Alysha's hand squeezed his forearm—answer enough.

Jorgen let his head thump the wall once, hard. "Just me then," he said, voice back to grit. "Outstanding. No more heroics."

Jorgen tried to calm himself despite his chest sawing, pulse rabbiting in his throat. The ladder sang once more and went still. Dust hung in the beam of Karl's now-cracked flashlight—and beyond it, a faint wash of glow.

Boxes. Old, square-jawed machines with resin faces and soft, inviting LEDs.

Pinky's breath caught. "More magic lights! And they're pretty!"

Karl edged closer, brow knitting. "What in the… what are those?"

Even Knight's granite softened a shade. "Relics."

Alysha drifted to the nearest unit, palm brushing the cool panel. "They hum," she murmured. "Faint, but… alive. To what end?"

Jorgen couldn't help the grin. It tugged at his face even as his ribs complained. "History class, kids," he rasped. "These are vending machines. They used to sell things."

"Sell?" Pinky echoed, baffled and delighted all at once.

"Snacks. Drinks," Jorgen said, nostalgia creeping in despite himself. "You fed them credits—money—and they spit out what you picked."

"Like magic?" Pinky asked.

"Like laziness with good branding." He shrugged. "Some days a cold soda beats conquering the galaxy."

Knight snorted. "Colossal waste of time and technology."

"Depends on your priorities," Jorgen said, pushing off the wall. The backlit menu flickered like an old eyelid. Maybe, just maybe. He rapped the casing, listening for a fan, a relay, any whisper of life. Something hummed back. He traced a hairline seam and levered it with a knuckle and a curse.

A service panel scraped open, complaining all the way. Dusty cubbies stared back—most empty.

Pinky's face fell. "Nothing…"

"Always one last, forgotten morsel," Jorgen muttered. He reached deep, fingers combing past grit and dead air until plastic crackled under his nails. He pinched and tugged.

A crinkled mylar pouch slid free—colors time-bleached to ghosts, letters aged to nonsense.

Knight's composure slipped. "What in the abyss…"

Alysha tipped her head, studying the faded print. "The inks are… ancient."

Jorgen turned the bag in the light, mouth quirking despite everything. "Ladies and gents," he said, "behold: the height of civilization." He didn't open it. Not yet. Just let the weight of the absurd little triumph settle the room, steady their breath, and remind them the past hadn't quite let go.

Jorgen held the bag up, the grinning cartoon mascot oddly familiar in this buried world. "Behold, Cheese Toes," he announced with mock pomp. "A delicacy from a bygone era." He gave it a shake. Something actually rustled.

"Can you... can you eat it?" Pinky asked, wonder and worry braided in her whisper.

Jorgen tucked the bag under Knight's nose, sniffing with theatrical care. "If the preservatives they pumped into food back then did anything right..." He shrugged and ripped it open.

A soft gasp circled the room. He bit a single neon-orange curl and let the fake cheese bloom across his tongue. "Stale," he judged, "but not half bad." He offered the bag to Knight with a little bow. "Your reward for valor, brave warrior."

Knight stared, unreadable, then the corner of his mouth twitched. "Well..." He tried one, then another, a slow smile ghosting across his face. "I'll be damned. Not the feast I expected, but not the worst I've had."

Hesitant chomps and surprised noises followed as Knight parceled out the loot. Alysha inspected a puff like evidence, tasted, and gave a small, clinical nod. Pinky made a face, spit the crumb into her hand, and shuddered. "It tastes like... feet."

Chuckles rippled. Jorgen let his gaze roam the other machines, the old backlit panels winking. An idea tugged. "If this relic lasted," he mused, tapping a rusty faceplate, "then maybe…"

Karl caught on at once. "Other foodstuffs?" His eyes brightened. "Aged delicacies…exotic, forgotten cuisines…" He trailed off, already bartering in his head.

Knight finished his share and grunted—agreement, skepticism, maybe both. "Could be a fool's errand," he rasped, "or the only way to resupply. Worth checking."

Pinky pitched her rejected curl into a corner, lips set. "It tastes icky. I don't like it." The dim light sparked in her eyes. "Can we go do something fun now?"

Alysha, silent until then, lifted a finger toward a faint opening at the far end. "There," she said, voice soft but sure. "Something feels…different." A beat, then—almost self-conscious—"Warmer, somehow."

Curiosity drew them as one. The vending relics and their stale treasure fell behind as they crossed the threshold. A whisper of warmth touched their skin, comforting against the underground chill, but growing with each step—an invisible thread pulling them deeper. Pinky tugged Jorgen's coat tight and shivered. "Creepy," she murmured. "It's like walking into light… but prickly."

Jorgen narrowed his eyes and took the room in like a threat assessment. The tight corridor spilled into a cavern big enough to swallow a rail yard. Dim emergency strips threw long, shaky shadows; everything else sat in the half-dark.

Pipes webbed the ceiling, vanishing into poured concrete. Along one wall, hulking machines slept under a skin of frost, white rime veining their housings. Across from them, a run of metal doors bled a soft, sinister warmth. Alysha's step hitched; her hand drifted to the curve of her blade without thinking.

"This place…" Knight breathed, the gravel in his voice edged with awe. "It's—"

Karl moved closer, eyes tracking the pipework like a smith reading heat lines. "Ingenious," he muttered, his accent thick in the echo. "Cooling circuits… but for what?" He laid a calloused palm to a frozen run, listening with his fingers. "Different workings, same principles. There's a heart beating here." He shifted, feeling the faint thrum beneath the frost. "And heat," he added, almost reverent. "Not the kind from a forge, but power all the same."

His gaze slid to the glowing doors. He lifted his hand, chin angling toward them. "And there—that's where it all flows. The source. The true heart of this inverted, metal mountain."

*** 

The stale air of the tunnel whipped past Mustang's face, his footfalls drumming a hard rhythm on cold concrete. Behind them, the whir deepened—the ugly purr of a spider drone hunting.

"Faster, damn it!" he snapped, glancing back. In the dim, the drone's single red eye burned like a coal.

Beside him, Bradley grunted. "I'm givin' 'er all she's got, Lieutenant. Any bright ideas to lose this thing?"

Mustang's AR flickered overlays across the dark—routes, angles, dead space. "There." A slit of a side passage. "Dead end, but we might shake it."

Bradley didn't hesitate. He braked hard, skidding into the slot and pressing flat to the wall. The drone overshot, screeching as it hunted the corner.

Mustang wedged in beside him, jaw tight.

Bradley hissed, drawing his pistol. "What is the deal with those things?"

"More annoying than you," Mustang said, breath clipped. "Triggered when we got close to something." His irritation flared. "This wasn't part of the plan."

Bradley lowered his head, resolve hardening. "Tells us we're close. We were headed for servers and records, right?"

"Yeah," Mustang said, replaying the holo-map in his mind.

"Then maybe that drone activated because we were on the right track," Bradley said. "Security protocols. If it's meant to protect, it's not exactly going to let us pass."

"So you're saying the bot just verified our target."

"Exactly. Let's hope there aren't more between us and those records."

Mustang's fingers flew through a ghosted interface, trying to bite into the drone's systems. "Damn it," he breathed. The old code was stubborn as bedrock.

"Anything?" Bradley whispered, listening for the whir to return.

"Security's ancient but effective," Mustang said. "Whoever built this place built it to last." His eyes cut to the mouth of the blind. "Looks like it's going to be up to old-fashioned firepower."

Bradley nodded, the energy pistol heavy in his grip. A small blast wouldn't put the thing down for good. "Need bait," he said, voice gone flat. "Give you a clean line—long enough to hit something vital."

"I don't like this, Bradley..." Mustang's brow tightened.

"Yeah, well, neither do I," Bradley shot back. "Dying's worse. Don't miss." He drew a breath, slid a shoulder out of the crevice, and showed the drone a slice of motion.

The whir spiked. The spider rounded the corner, red eye locking. Limbs rose, arcs crackling between its nodes.

"Now!" Bradley barked, breaking cover.

Mustang's rifle snapped, the report savage in the tight space. A lance of superheated plasma cored the drone; it spasmed, shrieked—metallic tines on ceramic—and twitched like it might spit one last reflexive shot. Then the red went out. The steely carcass hit laminated cement, smoking.

Bradley let the breath go. "Hell of a shot, Mustang."

Mustang dipped a nod, already crouched over the wreck. "Might strip something useful—"

"No time," Bradley cut in, holstering the pistol. "That shot just rang the dinner bell."

Mustang glanced at the ruined chassis, then back to the tunnel. "You're right. It bought us a window—let's use it." He shouldered the rifle; his AR flashed as he reoriented. "Server room's a few passages down."

They ran. The tunnels threw back their footfalls, light skidding across damp concrete. Every corner felt rigged for an ambush.

Mustang scanned his surroundings, mind already corridors ahead—if the records were intact, if there was any power keeping the servers active—

A cold draft met them at the threshold. Dust hung in narrow beams cutting through cracked panels. Somewhere deep, a faint electrical hum lingered—the ghost of a pulse in the facility's forgotten mind.

Racks of ancient servers lined the walls, their blink patterns throwing green and amber freckles into the gloom. Bradley let out a low whistle. "Guess someone forgot to kill the lights."

Mustang didn't take the bait. The glow from his AR washed his cheeks as he scanned the immediate area. "Power's still on," he breathed. "Let's hope the brains aren't fried." He palmed a dust-caked panel. "Fun part starts now."

Behind them, the door thudded shut—heavy, final. Bradley spun, hand finding his sidearm. "Hey—what did you—"

"Insurance," Mustang said, fingers already moving through a floating lattice of icons and code. "If drones—or anything else —come knocking, this buys time."

Bradley let it ride. He paced the rows, reading scuffs and dust like a medic reads a chart. Old, intact, humming. No scorch, no pry marks. Positive signs for their current situation.

Mustang's whisper hissed through the fan noise. "Ancient OS. Layer cake." Awe and irritation bled together in his tone. Lines of symbols cascaded across his projection as he tunneled, tested, backed off, tunneled again.

Bradley's anxiety rose with every passing second as his boots clicked a slow rhythm. Lights blinked like patient monitors. "You sure you've got it?" he muttered.

"Few more firewalls," Mustang said without looking. "Code's degraded in places. Need a backdoor that still leads somewhere. Active defense keeps slamming every—"

A dull thud hit the sealed door. Metal rang; dust drifted. Bradley pivoted, pistol up. "Mustang…"

"Not me." Mustang's tone flattened. Another hit—harder. The panel shivered in its frame.

They traded a look. Whatever was out there had weight.

Mustang accelerated, hands strobing across the projection. "Almost—almost…"

The door jumped under a third blow. Fine grit sifted from the lintel.

"Focus," Bradley said, sliding to the hinge side, safety off, stance set. The pistol felt small.

"Got it," Mustang hissed. Data dumped into his view—file names, log stubs, the promise of order. "Now to—"

The scream of tearing metal shredded the room. The door bowed, locks shrieked, sparks hiccuped where bolts tore loose. Angry red spilled through the widening seam. Bradley fired, a white-hot bolt lancing into the gap.

A mechanical roar answered.

CHAPTER
TEN

The doorway looked like something had bitten a hole in the wall—metal bent inward, edges warped and blackened. From that torn frame, a bulk of shadow detached and stepped through. For a heartbeat it was only mass and movement, blocking what little light there was. Then it shifted into the light spilling from the ceiling strips.

Segmented armor plates caught the glow, dull and scarred. Joints flexed with a hydraulic grind. In the center of its head unit, a single red sensor swelled from ember to coal, washing the room in a thin, bloody sheen.

Bradley's stomach tightened. The grip of his energy pistol was tacky under his palm as he snapped it up on muscle memory. *"That is not a spider drone,"* he said, with more than a little panic.

The machine answered with an infrasound shriek—an electronic scream that set his teeth on edge and made the old server racks vibrate. It stepped closer, heavy feet punching dents into the metal decking.

Mustang was already moving. "Hang on," he yelled over his shoulder. Holographic panes bloomed into the air around him in a cascade of pale blue—strings of archaic code, schematic overlays, warning sigils combating the crimson glow of the drone's eye. His fingers cut through them in quick, controlled arcs, tapping, dragging, stitching invisible pathways together. "The drone—I saw an override hook in the suite. Give me a minute."

The words shouldn't have helped, but they did. A small, stubborn thread of hope pulled at Bradley's chest. He held his shot, tracking the sensor as it locked onto him. The red point narrowed, focusing. A faint targeting tone started to pulse in his earbud, in time with his pulse.

"Mustang," he said, throat gone dry. "Clock's running."

"Got it." Mustang's tone flattened—banter gone, all work. "Initiating shutdown. Now."

The room lurched as if someone had yanked on the rug beneath their feet. A deep hum rolled through the floor. Static crawled up Bradley's forearm where it pressed against the pistol. Across the towers of antiquated hardware, rows of indicator lights winked out, one after another, plunging the server banks into dead, matte black.

The drone spasmed. Its shriek cut off mid-cry, leaving a ringing emptiness. Armor plates quivered. The red sensor flared wide, then collapsed down to a pinprick and went dark.

Bradley let out half a breath, shoulders loosening. "Nice work —"

The sensor flared back to life before he could finish, much brighter this time, a harsh, angry red that painted his hands and the pistol in blood-color. The drone steadied, planted a foot, and straightened to its full height.

"Didn't take," Bradley said through his teeth. "Need a new plan."

Panels in its torso and shoulders irised open with mechanical clicks, revealing nested weapon systems and stubby launch tubes. Metal limbs shifted, locked, reformed. The machine's outline went from bulky to predatory.

"Here we go," Mustang muttered.

The first volley hit the room like a hailstorm. Bolts of energy and micro-missiles tore out of the drone on a roar of displaced air. Bradley dove sideways as the spot where he'd been standing erupted. Server housings exploded into jagged shrapnel. Razor-edged fragments keened past his ear, close enough that the wake stung his skin. Impact blooms left molten craters in the racks; hot metal spat across the floor and skittered under his boots.

Behind him Mustang swore. "Override tripped its defense tree. It adapted."

"Then put it back to sleep," Bradley snapped, rolling behind a dead terminal. He came up on one knee and fired. His pistol barked bright lances of white-blue energy that slammed into the drone's chest. The shots left scorched rosettes and smoking streaks on the armor but no penetration.

"Working on it," Mustang said. The holographic projections around him reconfigured in a frantic cascade. "Its code's a junkyard—legacy code grafted on top of garbage. This is a nest of protocols someone fed through a blender and let ferment."

The drone advanced with slow, confident steps, each one thudding through the decking. Bradley moved with it, keeping low, using the server towers as shifting cover. Every time he leaned out to fire, the sensor snapped toward him, that red eye jerking to meet his muzzle flash. The room had been cool when they came in. Now the air tasted baked—every discharge added another layer of heat and noise: the crack of his pistol, the drone's deeper report, the stuttering whine of servos changing torque.

Another blast from the drone's forward cannon slammed into the rack just above his head. Metal screamed and split. Shards rained down, pinging off his shoulders and catching in his hair. A wash of superheated air rolled over him, close enough to singe the hair along his neck.

"Hang in there, Bradley!" Mustang called, voice tight but controlled. His hands were a blur through the ghostly interfaces, palms leaving faint afterimages in the air. "Almost through its outer shell. Just need a clean hook."

Bradley could feel his pulse pounding all the way up into his jaw. He tasted metal, copper at the back of his tongue—fear, adrenaline, the tang of ionized air. The drone kept coming, sensor a steady crimson bead—always tracking him.

It spat another volley. Smaller projectiles this time, fast enough that he didn't really see them—only the stitched line of impact they carved across the room. Server towers disintegrated into clouds of shrapnel and plastic dust.

Bradley threw himself sideways, hitting the deck hard and sliding behind the next rack. The floor burned his palms through his gloves. The blasts chewed through the metal where he'd been, carving glowing trenches in the server housings. Superheated air punched past, bringing with it the sharp, acrid reek of burning insulation and fried circuits that clawed at his nose.

"Come on, Mustang. Come on." Bradley's voice barely cleared his teeth. His heart hammered against his ribs so hard it felt like it might burst. He pressed his shoulder into the torn edge of the server rack, felt rust bite through his jacket, and risked another glance.

The combat drone was closing the distance in steady, brutal steps. Its armor was streaked with soot and burn marks where his shots had landed, but it moved with the slow assurance of something that didn't know how to be afraid. Red sensor burning, plating flexing, it had the look of a metal predator that had finally scented blood.

Behind Bradley, Mustang's fingers kept flying. The holographic panes around him had collapsed into a tighter cluster—concentric circles of code and targeting glyphs rotating over his hands. His jaw was bunched, lips pressed around the wordless sounds of someone thinking too fast to talk.

"Come on," Bradley whispered again, more to himself this time.

He couldn't wait to see if it would change its mind. He exploded from cover, boots crunching through glass and scorched plastic. The world narrowed to the stagger in the drone's gait and the exposed joints at its knees.

He raised his pistol, sighted on the closer leg joint, and squeezed the trigger in disciplined bursts. White-blue lances tore across the space between them. The shots chewed into the spaces between the overlapping plates at its knee, burning through secondary armor and into the softer mechanics beneath. Sparks fountained out in a shower of bright, spitting starbursts.

The drone loosed an electronic screech, a grating distortion that fuzzed the edges of his hearing. It wasn't pain—these things didn't feel—but it sure as hell sounded like anger. Its stride faltered as that leg tried to lock and failed. The sensor jittered on its mount, no longer perfectly aligned with its gun barrels.

It fired anyway.

The volley went wide. Instead of carving a line through Bradley's chest, the projectiles tore into the server banks off to his left. Plastic exploded, steel housings shredded, and a row of still-powered indicator lights burst in a chain of tiny flares. Glass and molten fragments rained down in a stinging cascade that peppered his scalp.

"Legs are compromised!" Mustang shouted, excitement cutting through his strain. "You've got it limping—keep hitting the joints!"

Bradley didn't bother to answer. He shifted his weight, drew a quick breath that tasted like hot metal and burned insulation, and pressed the advantage. His world became a rhythm: step, sight, fire—step, sight, fire—each burst walking along the same line of weakness. Energy impacts hammered into the already-damaged knee assembly, then climbed to the opposite leg where servos whined in protest.

The corrupted machine stumbled, one step turning into a stagger that punched gouges into the decking. Its armor shrieked as plates ground out of alignment. Hydraulic fluid—dark and iridescent—spattered across the floor, smoking where it hit hot metal.

Bradley shifted his angle and drove a shot into the seam of the nearest weapon pod. The blast caught exposed wiring and something critical underneath. The pod detonated inward on itself with a hollow, metallic bang. Shards of housing clattered across the floor; a stream of scorched cabling swung free like severed tendons.

The drone reared back, sensor flaring white-hot for a heartbeat before snapping to yellow. An inhuman roar tore out of its speakers, all clipped distortion and static.

"It's not done yet," Mustang warned. His voice was closer now, threaded with urgency. "Power graph's spiking—capacitors overcharging. One bad feedback loop and this thing turns into a fragmentation grenade. We need it offline, now!"

Heat was bleeding off the machine in waves he could feel against his face, even at this distance. The air around it shimmered slightly, rippling with the excess.

He drew a breath through his teeth, tasted smoke and copper, and moved.

No scream, no blind rush—just a hard, driving push forward. He cut in toward the drone's weakened side, boots skidding on grit and puddles of coolant. The machine tried to track him, torso rotating with a tortured whine, but its ruined leg lagged behind, dragging a half-beat out of sync.

Bradley angled low, bringing his pistol up almost level with the deck, and fired into the last solid joint bearing the machine's weight. The blast punched through the overstressed coupling. Metal ruptured with a wet, crunching crack. The leg folded in on itself, and the drone's mass went sideways.

It crashed down like a dropped engine block.

The impact shook the floor under his boots. Server towers shivered; one toppled in slow motion, snapping cables as it went and slamming into the drone's torso with a hollow, echoing boom. A storm of sparks erupted where torn conduits kissed exposed metal. Wires writhed and spat light as raw current arced across the mangled frame.

For a heartbeat, the only sound was the labored whir of failing servos and the high, rising whine of something spinning past tolerance. The sensor cycled wildly through colors—yellow, red, white—before shrinking, dimming, and finally guttering out.

The whine cut off.

Silence rolled in, thick and unreal. No shriek, no gunfire, just the distant tick and ping of cooling metal and the soft hiss of burning insulation.

Bradley stood there, pistol still leveled, chest heaving. The ringing in his ears faded enough that he heard his own breathing—rough, ragged pulls that scraped his throat. His arms felt heavy, the muscles in his shoulders and back trembling from the sustained tension. A dull ache bloomed in his right wrist where the recoil had worked its way down into scar tissue.

He took two careful steps back from the wreck, not letting the muzzle dip until he was satisfied nothing on the chassis was trying to move. Only when the sensor stayed dead and the last of the flickering arcs winked out did he finally lower the pistol.

The room smelled like a burned-out transformer. Dust motes and ash drifted through the slanting light from the ceiling strips, turning the air into a slow, gray swirl.

Bradley let himself sag against the nearest upright server rack that was still standing. The metal was warm under his shoulder. His legs shook, a full-body tremor he couldn't quite suppress.

Across the debris field, Mustang picked his way over fallen panels and shattered housings. He emerged from behind a half-collapsed bank of servers, blinking through the haze. His AR glasses sat crooked on his nose, one lens smeared with soot. Dust and sweat had carved pale tracks down his cheeks. Despite it all, his grin was wide and bright, adrenaline still burning in his eyes.

"Well," he said, taking in the wreckage with a low whistle, "that was…educational."

He planted his hands on his hips, boot nudging a twisted piece of drone casing. "And impressive. I have never seen a man work that hard to erase a room from existence. You know these racks were older than both of us, right?"

Bradley's laugh came out as more of a rasp. It scraped the back of his throat in a way that felt almost good. "Yeah, well," he said, swallowing against the dryness, "seemed like a bad time to get sentimental."

He jerked his chin toward the ruined drone, its legs twisted under it, armor peeled back in jagged petals. "Besides," he added, letting his head rest against the rack behind him, "you can't argue with results."

Mustang toed a chunk of twisted casing, then shrugged, dust flaking from his shoulders. There was still an edge of adrenaline in his eyes, but under it Bradley caught something else—reluctant, almost grudging respect.

"Can't argue with that," Mustang said. "But hey—" his voice shifted, the humor dropping out "—that thing wasn't running standard drone firmware."

Bradley followed his gaze to the wreck. The drone lay half-pinned under a toppled server bank, armor warped, sensor dark. Even dead, it looked coiled.

"No," Bradley said. His throat felt raw; the word came out low and rough. "It was corrupted. And possibly overclocked." He let the thought hang a moment, eyes tracking the blackened ceiling, the half-lit strips overhead. "Makes me wonder…"

Bradley dragged the back of his glove across his forehead, smearing sweat and grime into a new pattern. "Anything left to salvage in this graveyard?" he asked, voice coming out hoarse.

Mustang straightened, rolling his shoulders like he was shaking off the mood. A faint, satisfied curve tugged at his mouth. "Most of these antiques are toast," he said, nodding to the buckled servers. "You and your friend over there were… thorough."

He lifted his hands and called up a fresh cascade of holographic panes. They flared to life above his wrists, strings of text and data tags hovering in the smoky air. "But the override bought me a window," he went on. "Long enough to siphon off a few juicy streams before everything went kablooey."

A flick of his fingers expanded a list. File names marched down the projection in sterile white.

"Project Serenity," Mustang read. "Project Ouroboros." He shot Bradley a look over the tops of his skewed AR glasses. "Looks like we've got confirmation."

The names hit with a small, precise weight. Bradley felt his jaw tighten. Serenity. Ouroboros. The same ghosts he'd first tripped over in buried summaries and redacted memos—the crack in the story, the proof that the avian flu of 2101 hadn't even existed.

Mustang scrolled further, his brow furrowing as new labels slid into view. "Project Godspear. Project Spearhead." He snorted once, humorless. "Definitely not vaccine programs."

His finger paused on another line. "Project Redemption," he read more softly. "That one's not ominous at all."

"And then there's this cluster," Mustang added. He tapped again, bringing a new set of entries into focus. "Subject 00001. Subject 00002. Subject N3-1505."

Bradley's attention sharpened. "Subjects," he echoed. "Not test batches. People? Animals? What were they doing down here?"

"Don't know yet." Mustang shook his head, eyes never leaving the scrolling text. "Metadata's thin from this side. But the pull's still running. Everything I could hook before the systems cooked is on this drive, but I'll need time to defragment it."

He dropped his hands, letting the projections shrink to a neat, hovering column at his side. When he glanced over, the spark in his eyes had shifted—less exhilaration now, more hard focus. "Let's just hope the answers don't make us regret what we find."

Bradley met his gaze and held it. The fear from the fight was still in him, somewhere deep, but something steadier now sat on top of it.

They finally had more than suspicions, redacted files, and news articles that failed the CRAAP test. They had file names, subject tags—threads they could drag into the light and wrap around the Foundation's throat.

He gave a short, grim nod. "The Telluric Foundation wanted this buried," he said. "Too bad."

His eyes went back to the drone, to the shattered racks, to the faint glow of Mustang's data column hanging in the burned air. Whatever was waiting further down, they weren't walking into it blind anymore.

A glint cut through his fatigue. Bradley scrubbed a hand over the stubble along his jaw, already trying to think three moves ahead. "Time to regroup," he said. "We can't do this alone."

Bradley tapped the temple of his AR glasses. The lenses brightened, UI ghosting over the wrecked server room as the squad channel opened with a soft click.

"Knight, status." His voice came out rough. "You guys still breathing down there?"

Static flooded his ear, a rushing hiss that made him wince. For a moment it was all noise, like someone grinding sand through a speaker. Then Knight's voice punched through in broken chunks.

"…ey! Brad…copy…barely…found something…"

Mustang's head came up. "Knight, say again," he cut in, fingers already fluttering through a fresh spread of holo-controls. "We're pulling mainframe data now—"

Another wash of interference, sharper this time. The channel spat syllables and dead air.

"…generation…massive…feels like…heart of this…"

A cold line of adrenaline slid down Bradley's spine. Power generation. Heart of the complex. He traded a quick look with Mustang.

"Knight, we need a location," Bradley said. "Ping us a marker —anything. Put it on the grid."

More static. The reply came in shattered fragments, words buried under noise.

"…find…coordinates…system's…weak…"

"Damn it," Mustang muttered. His jaw tightened. "Hold on, I'm punching through." He tore open another layer of options, rerouting their feed through narrower bands, boosting output, hopping to quieter slices of spectrum. The holo-map appeared above his wrist through the lenses of the AR unit and fractured into nested wireframes as he forced the system to listen.

For a few seconds, nothing. Just that restless hiss.

Then a single tone chimed in Bradley's ear, clear as a bell. A blinking marker appeared on Mustang's floating map—a blue pulse deep in the tangled schematic of tunnels and chambers.

"Got him," Mustang breathed. Louder: "Signal's dirty as hell, but it's there."

He zoomed the projection with a twist of his fingers. Corridors unfolded like a holographic ant farm, levels stacking on top of one another. He traced a glowing path down through the maze. "He's several decks below us and farther in," Mustang said. "Close to the central shaft. That 'heart' he's talking about? I'm betting it's the main generator."

Bradley watched the pulsing marker, jaw flexing. "All right. Finish the pull." He swept his gaze over the ruined room one last time—the toppled racks, the dead drone, the haze of smoke hanging under the ceiling strips. "Grab what you can carry. We link up with the others and go meet Knight's 'something.'"

He could feel the weight of it settling on his shoulders: not just rogue hardware and corrupted drones, but whatever the Foundation had buried in the dark and then walked away from.

While Mustang hunched over his display, shepherding the last trickles of data into the portable drive, Bradley picked his way through the wreckage. The combat drone lay on its side, half-crushed under a fallen server bank, armor peeled and twisted. Thin curls of smoke still rose from torn conduits, smelling of hot plastic and burned oil.

"Don't get sentimental on me," Mustang called without looking up, the edge of his old tone creeping back in. "The spider-bots aren't going to hold a vigil for their buddy."

Bradley snorted once. "Not my type."

He stepped closer to the wreck, boots crunching over glass and scattered fragments. Something under the warped plating caught his eye—a dense block of housing wedged under a bent strut, still intact enough to hum faintly against the palm when he pressed his hand to it.

He set his pistol aside for a moment and got both hands on the broken panel. Metal groaned as he pried it loose, muscles in his forearms burning. With a final wrench, the section came free, revealing the primary weapon array nested inside. A faint, residual charge thrummed through the casing.

"Hello," Bradley murmured.

He hooked his fingers under the array and lifted. The weight dragged at his shoulders; he had to set his stance to keep from overbalancing. He turned back toward Mustang with it resting against his hip.

"We might want this," he said.

Mustang finally tore his focus from the holo-feed. His gaze climbed from the array to Bradley's face, one eyebrow ticking up. "You sure you can handle that thing? Looks kinda heavy."

"Guess we'll find out," Bradley said.

Mustang huffed a quiet laugh, the corner of his mouth twitching. "Given what this place is, might be some useful tech in there. But, you're on your own lugging that thing around."

He thumbed the download closed with a decisive tap. The holographic panes folded down into a single, floating status bar: TRANSFER COMPLETE. He snapped the drive from its port and slid it into a hard case at his belt.

"Data's secure," Mustang said. "Whatever the Foundation was doing with Serenity, Ouroboros, Godspear—all of it that survived—we've got their ghosts on a leash now. At least on a drive."

Bradley shifted the weapon array higher against his shoulder. The joint in his shoulder creaked softly, compensating for the added mass. The glowing path on Mustang's map stretched out ahead of them in a thin blue line, diving into deeper levels.

He fell in beside Mustang as they headed for the ruined doorway, boots leaving prints in the dust and soot. Each step toward the corridor felt heavier, as if the air itself thickened the farther they went from the surface.

"Ready as I'll ever be," Bradley said under his breath.

He wasn't. Not really. No one was ever ready to walk into the kind of secrets The Foundation had welded shut and left to rot. But the route was lit, they had names and subjects and a teammate calling from the dark.

Turning back had never been part of the plan.

*** 

Jorgen was the first to spot them. He turned from the machine at the center of the chamber, weathered face splitting into a grin that crinkled the creases around his eyes.

"Well, if it isn't the data-wrangling duo," he called, his voice echoing off concrete and steel. He swept an arm toward the machine like a game-show host presenting a prize. "Look what we found. Beats vending machines any day, wouldn't you say?"

Bradley's boots crunched over grit as he stepped into the light. The "prize" was a generator the size of a small house, a mass of turbines and armored casings sunk into the floor. Thick power conduits clawed up from its shell and vanished into the ceiling. The whole thing throbbed with a low, continuous hum he could feel through his soles and running up his legs, like standing next to a caged storm.

Knight stood off to one side, rifle slung but ready. His face stayed flat, but the relief was there in the looseness of his shoulders when he saw them. "Generator's live," he said, voice gravelly. "Place is swimming in power. Enough juice to light the whole megacity and then some."

Bradley's gaze snagged on Alysha.

She hovered at the fringe of their loose circle, just inside the spill of the overhead lamps. Her strange blade was sheathed, but her stance was coiled—weight forward, chin slightly down, eyes fixed on the generator's core as if waiting for it to move. The slow rise and fall of her chest looked controlled, deliberate, like she was forcing herself not to flinch.

Pinky stayed half behind her, one small hand hooked in the back of Alysha's short cloak. The girl's purple eyes slid between the generator and those rejoining the group, wide and alert.

"What is this place?" Bradley asked, voice dropping without him meaning to. It felt wrong to speak loud with that much power humming underfoot. "And what in hell did they need this kind of output for?"

He glanced toward Mustang. If anyone in the room was already building answers, it would be him.

The space itself was a cavern carved out of old infrastructure— high ceiling lost in shadows, walls bristling with conduits, breaker arrays, and ancient warning placards half-obscured by dust. The air was warmer here, carrying the stinging, unnatural odor of sulfur and the faint stink of lubricant. The generator's low thrum sat under everything, steady as a heartbeat.

Mustang wasn't looking at the hardware.

He stood a few meters back from the generator, shoulders tight, gaze fixed just past the edge of reality—on an AR overlay only he could see. The color had drained from his face, leaving his freckles stark against his skin. His fingers hovered in the air, not moving.

"Mustang?" Bradley said. That knot of unease in his gut cinched tighter. "Talk to me."

Mustang blinked, as if dragged up from underwater, and snapped his head toward Bradley. The urgency in his eyes was cold and clear. "Problem," he said. "Big problem."

He swallowed, then words started to catch up with his thoughts. "Finishing that download gave us a cleaner handshake with the mainframe. Enough bandwidth to stop scraping and actually listen. And—" he jabbed a thumb at the empty space beside his head "—something just tripped a perimeter alert. Ground level."

Jorgen's grin vanished like someone had thrown a switch. "Perimeter?" he said. "That means—"

"The Foundation," Mustang cut in. His tone had gone hard. "Troops. Heavy armor, full tactical. They're inside the facility."

He flared his fingers, ripping away the generator's schematics and calling up a different layer of data. Map lines and camera icons bloomed in the air. He dragged a feed to the external projector node on the corner of his AR glasses; a grainy black-and-white image flickered into existence on the wall—security cam footage from a stairwell.

Figures in armored rigs moved through the frame in disciplined formation, weapons up, visors blank and reflective. They swept corners with the unhurried confidence of people who knew they owned the ground.

Pinky made a small, sharp sound. Her fingers tightened on Alysha's cloak. "The bad men," she whispered, the words trembling.

Knight muttered a curse under his breath. "How the hell did they track us here?" he growled, hand tightening on the grip of his blaster.

"Pick your poison," Mustang said, eyes skimming the feeds while his fingers danced through translucent menus. "We left footprints the second we woke this place up. But I've got a strong candidate."

He pulled the facility map up alongside the camera feed and tapped a blinking node representing the server room above them. "That little shutdown stunt we pulled on the combat drone? I didn't just slam a door. I slipped a worm into their back end while everything was screaming."

Bradley's mind moved with his words, slotting pieces together. "They lost contact with the drones," he said slowly, "so they sent in a team to see why."

"Cleanup crew," Mustang agreed. "With a side of 'trace the breach and hit it with a hammer.'"

He zoomed in on the feed. The image jumped closer, flattening into washed-out gray. The Telluric soldiers advanced down a corridor, helmets turning in short, efficient arcs. Closer to the edge of the frame, the picture fuzzed and warped in places, as if patches of the hallway were smudged out. Distortions crawled a half-step ahead of the lead elements—warped outlines where the image refused to resolve cleanly.

"Also," Mustang added, voice dropping, "that worm? It's chewing on their systems right now. I'm piggybacking on their network—pulling their comms, their helmet cams, anything I can suck down before they notice the extra mouth."

He pointed at the shifting smears in the feed. "Those glitches moving before the squad? That's not bad reception. That's active camouflage phasing in and out of the overlay."

Bradley felt his jaw clench. The words came out a growl. "Ghost Cloaks."

Alysha stepped in closer, leaving the generator's glow behind. The black-and-white footage washed her face in a sickly pallor as she watched the armored shapes advance through the upper corridors.

"You have access to their systems?" she asked, eyes narrowing. Her voice had a sharp, hungry edge.

"Some," Mustang said. He didn't look away from his overlays. "Not enough to shut them down."

A dangerous light stirred in Alysha's gaze. "Then this changes things." She turned to Bradley, studying him as if weighing a blade in her hand. "You wanted answers, soldier? It seems the answers are walking straight to you."

For a heartbeat, something rose in Bradley's chest—hope, or the rough outline of it—before Knight cut it down.

"That won't work," Knight said, the growl in his voice flat and certain. He shook his head. "These aren't architects. They're grunts. Even if we grab one, you'll get ranks, serial number, and a rehearsed blank stare. They don't know what the Foundation's actually doing."

Alysha's attention slid to Knight, frustration tightening the line of her mouth, then back to Bradley. "Then you are willing to die without answers?" she asked quietly.

Bradley felt the question land like a weight. His pulse ticked in his throat. The idea of dying here, in some forgotten power vault, tasted like bad meat. But so did the thought of walking away while The Foundation wiped their tracks clean and rewrote the story topside.

"We need to know what they're hiding," he said. His voice was low, clipped, more statement than plea. "That's why we pulled the files. Those names, those subjects—that's leverage. We use what we've got, stay alive, and live long enough to pull the rest into the light."

Mustang sliced through the tightening silence. "We can argue ethics when we're not about to get ventilated," he said. "Right now, we need an exit that doesn't run straight into a firing squad."

He dragged the facility map to the front of his projections, brow furrowed as he scrolled deeper. Corridors and shafts unfolded in blue wireframe, spiraling down beneath their feet. "This place is a rat's nest. There's got to be a less…welcoming way out."

"Down," Pinky said.

Her small voice trembled but carried in the humming space. Every head turned.

"What?" Jorgen asked, softening his tone. He shifted slightly so he was half between her and the generator, half between her and the projected soldiers on the wall.

Pinky pointed at the ceiling, then at the floor between her boots. "They came from up there," she said, nodding toward the stairwell on the video feed. "So...we go the other way."

Alysha dropped into a crouch beside her, bringing her eyes level with the girl's. "Perhaps she is right," she murmured. "The soldiers hunt near the surface. Deeper...there may be paths they are not yet watching."

Knight's gaze narrowed as he watched the feeds—one showing the kill squad sweeping methodically downward, another the labyrinth of lower levels sketched in incomplete lines. "Risky," he said. "But holding here is suicide. They stack charges on that door, we're done. I say we move."

Bradley looked to Mustang.

Mustang lifted one shoulder in a half-shrug, eyes shifting between his projections and Pinky. "Schematics get less reliable the farther down we go," he said. "Lots of blank space and 'no data.' But she's not wrong. Up is occupied. Everything else is a question mark. And this whole place is already a gamble."

The generator's hum pressed at Bradley's ears, steady and indifferent. He took in the scene: the hulking machine throbbing with stolen power, the team's faces lit by ghostly AR light and the dancing static of distant cameras, the Foundation soldiers on the wall drawing closer with every second.

He felt the decision settle into place.

"Then we gamble," he said. The words came out steady. "We take our proof and get out of their kill box."

Knight took point, rifle up, every line of his body tuned toward the dim stairwell at the edge of the chamber. The concrete steps beyond dropped into flickering light, edges softened by dust and neglect. Jorgen fell to the rear, one broad hand resting lightly on Pinky's shoulder, crowding his bulk between her and any open angle.

Alysha slipped into the middle of the column, her blade now sheathed at her hip. She walked with a quiet grace, gaze combing the shadows as if she expected the walls themselves to reach out and grab them.

Bradley slotted in just ahead of Jorgen, the scavenged weapon array cradled awkwardly against his chest. The thing was heavy, its dead weight dragging at his arms, but he was convinced it would be necessary to have it with them. The glow from Mustang's map traced a pale line in front of his boots, pointing them toward the stairwell like a runway.

He glanced back. Mustang was still anchored where he'd been standing, eyes lost in layers of scrolling data.

"Mustang," Bradley hissed. Their footsteps were already echoing off the vaulted ceiling. "We need to go."

Mustang jerked, as if shocked. "I know, I know," he said, fingers still darting across his projections. "Just trying to find us a little edge—a blind spot, a bypass, anything to cover our collective asses on the way down…"

"Those soldiers have better tech than you do," Bradley snapped, not breaking stride. "You want an exit? You follow us."

Mustang hissed a curse under his breath but his fingers still flew, throwing a last flurry of commands into the air. Status bars closed, windows collapsed. With a tight flick of his wrist he killed the AR spread, the light around his hands guttering out. He slapped his pocket to make sure the hard drive was still secure, palm flattening over it, and jogged to catch up, boots ringing on the metal.

Their path sloped down into the dark.

The stairwell railings were orange with rust and flaked under their grips. Each step sent dust boiling up in dry, choking clouds. The hum of the generator faded behind them, replaced by the hollow, bone-deep quiet of old concrete and rusted steel.

The only sounds were their own—ragged breathing, the scuff of boots, the occasional long, complaining groan as the structure shifted somewhere out in the unseen.

They pushed through crumbling stair flights and into narrow access halls where condensation dripped from broken pipes onto their heads and shoulders, cold against hot skin. In one passage, water pooled ankle-deep across buckled tiles, reeking of mildew. They filed past rooms full of dead machines—rows of consoles and cabinets furred with dust, cables dangling like vines. Whatever this place had been built for, time hadn't just forgotten it; it had started to eat it.

Up ahead, Knight's low curse snapped through the silence. "Damn."

Bradley pushed closer. The corridor had simply stopped. Ten meters ahead, the ceiling had come down in a jagged crush of concrete and twisted rebar, turning the passage into a solid wall of rubble.

Jorgen blew out a breath through his nose. "Figures," he muttered. "Soldiers ain't our only problem. Hit the wrong support down here and the whole place'll come down on our heads."

"We keep moving," Bradley rasped. His voice felt as worn as the walls. He slid his gaze from the real corridor to the ghostly overlay on his AR. Mustang had thrown him a limited feed— just enough to see the upper-level cams and a blinking icon for the Foundation team.

On the inset window above his left eye, grainy footage showed armored figures working their way deeper with patient, methodical precision. The Ghost Cloaks were harder to see— patches of dirty static sliding just ahead of the formation, where the image refused to settle. At their current pace, the regular troops were hours out from this depth. The Cloaks? Best-case, tens of minutes.

The knowledge pressed against the back of his skull like the barrel of a gun.

He was starting to feel the first thin threads of panic when Knight gave a surprised grunt. The big man's head tipped, eyes tightening as he studied his own overlay.

"Hold up," Knight rumbled. "There might be another way."

He lifted a hand and traced a line through the air. On Bradley's HUD, a faint second route lit up—an irregular web threading around the collapse, diving into a mess of ancillary lines beneath the main corridor. Knight zoomed in, filtering out the noise.

"Collapsed piping," he said. "Old maintenance runs. Tight as hell, but they snake around the block." He stabbed a thumb toward the rubble. "Should spit us out on the other side."

Bradley's heart kicked, hard. Not a clean escape, but better than waiting here for the bad guys.

Before he could answer, something new blinked to life at the edge of his vision—a red numerical cascade ticking steadily downward. For a second he thought it was a glitch on the Foundation feed. Then he realized it was anchored to his system UI, not theirs.

"What the hell is this?" he demanded, stabbing a finger at the air where the timer hung over his AR field.

The accusation hit Mustang first. Bradley turned on him, anger already building, but it faltered when he met Mustang's eyes. There was no flinch there, no guilt—just a flat, cold intent.

"That timer?" Mustang said. His voice had gone very calm. "That's not a complication. That's our exit strategy."

Bradley felt the bottom of his stomach tilt. "You set the reactor to overload," he said. It wasn't really a question.

Mustang's answer was a thin, crooked smile that didn't reach his eyes.

Jorgen barked out a harsh, disbelieving laugh. "Exit strategy?" he echoed. "Sounds more like suicide to me, boy."

Mustang's smile didn't change. "Those troops upstairs aren't here for crackers and tea," he said. "They're here to sterilize the site. Make sure no witnesses walk out to tell anyone what The Foundation buried under their feet."

He jabbed two fingers at the ticking red numbers only he and Bradley could see. "This place is a liability now. With an overload in play, they've got a choice—keep chasing us into a collapsing furnace, or cut their losses, seal the exits, and let the meltdown and the secrets cook together where no one can see."

A shiver of unease moved down the line of them like a physical thing. Pinky edged closer to Jorgen. Alysha's hand drifted toward her sheathed blade. The air felt tighter, the walls closer.

Knight's weathered hand tightened around the stock of his blaster. His gaze locked on Mustang, dark and measuring.

"You're suggesting we…"

"That we bring this whole damn place down on their heads," Mustang finished for him, voice flat but eyes hot. "We give them a choice: walk away from this hole and whatever's left of their precious projects…or stay and get buried with them."

The words hung in the stale air.

Bradley felt the idea slide over his skin. It was insane. It was exactly the kind of scorched-earth solution he'd spent a career trying not to need. But he couldn't deny the cold, brutal logic of it—it was the kind of thing Mustang would think of. Hell, Mustang probably knew it was something *they* would think of and got a tight twist of satisfaction at the thought of the Foundation watching their salted earth strategy sink their own monster into the ground with them in it.

Images flashed up unbidden: city blocks, homes, people who had no idea what slept under their feet. The generator's hum became a low, threatening note. If the overload climbed too far, if the containment failed—

He clenched his jaw. There were a thousand ways this could go wrong. But standing here waiting for Ghost Cloaks to cut them down was the one outcome he could guarantee.

Get the data out. Live. Drag the Foundation into the light. That was the mission. Everything else was already broken. He could feel bad about the civilian casualties later.

He met Knight's eyes.

The older soldier's face was all hard lines and shadow. No enthusiasm there, no shock—just the grim acceptance of a man who'd seen too many bad options and knew this counted as one of the better ones. Knight gave a short, guttural sound that might have been a snarl and turned toward the narrow gap his overlay had marked in the rubble.

"On me," he said, and squeezed sideways into the dark slit of the maintenance tunnel. Concrete scraped his dura-glass shield as he went.

Jorgen followed, shoulders turning to fit. He let out a low, dark chuckle as he ducked under a sagging length of pipe. "Well, boys," he rumbled, voice echoing off metal, "guess we're goin' out with a bang, not a whimper."

Pinky's eyes were wide in the dim light, pupils blown. She reached for Jorgen's hand without looking away from the ruined corridor. His rough fingers closed around her smaller ones, steady and warm. He gave her a quick squeeze and, over her head, shot Alysha a last, measuring glance.

Alysha stood at the mouth of the tunnel, half-turned toward the way they'd come. Her hand rested on the hilt of her sheathed blade, every line of her body coiled but still. There was no fear in her face, only a focus—as if she were listening for the exact moment the hunters would step into her reach.

"Go," she said quietly. It wasn't a suggestion.

Mustang checked the red numerals ticking at the edge of his vision, then the map, then Bradley. "No do-overs on this one," he said. His attempt at levity didn't quite land. He ducked into the tunnel after Jorgen and Pinky, one hand brushing the wall to steady himself, the other hovering near the drive under his jacket.

Bradley shifted the scavenged array higher onto his shoulder. The metal bit into his skin; joints protested as he redistributed the load. The weight felt right and wrong at the same time— both a promise and a sentence.

The world narrowed to rough walls inches from his face, and the scrape of his jacket against the sides of the tunnel. Behind him, Alysha's footfalls fell in, light and precise.

The countdown timer rode the top of his vision, its red numbers pulsing against the dark. Each tick shaved away another second of borrowed time, carving out a future measured not in miles or hours, but in how far they could get before the fire reached them.

# CHAPTER ELEVEN

Knight took point into the facility's lower service runs, his AR display throwing a ghostly lattice over the walls—stress fractures and warning glyphs riding the cracked concrete ahead. The tunnel had the claustrophobic feel of bad infrastructure: rebar exposed in long cages, insulation hanging in strips, old conduit split and curling. Every heavy step sent a faint tremor through the shell around them, as if the whole section was carrying a load it could not afford.

Water dripped from unseen cracks overhead in slow, irregular beats, pattering into stagnant puddles that filmed the floor in greasy reflections. Their weapon lights cut thin cones through the gloom, catching motes of dust and mold spores hanging in the air. The smell was a dense mix of rust, wet stone, and something old and sour that clung to the tongue. With every downward step, the weight of the whole complex seemed to settle a little heavier on their shoulders.

"These tunnels weren't built for comfort," Jorgen grumbled, shoulders scraping both sides as he forced his bulk through a pinch-point. Flakes of concrete dust snowed off the wall onto his roughspun shirt. "And they sure as hell weren't built to last this long without maintenance."

Ahead, the floor had buckled, slabs shifted into uneven ridges. Alysha took Pinky's hand and guided her over, tiny bare feet finding purchase on the tilted concrete. Pinky's fingers were white-knuckled around Alysha's; her breathing came in quick, shallow pulls, fear radiating off her like heat. It mirrored the tight edge coiled in everyone's gut.

Knight raised a fist, bringing them to a halt. "Hold," he rasped, voice barely a scrape in the confined space.

He swept his gaze along the length of the tunnel, then back to the AR overlay. Red markers pulsed over the ceiling and upper walls, clustering in ugly constellations. Hairline cracks the lights barely picked up were etched bright in his view.

"This section's bad," he murmured. "Load points are spiking. It's already failing in three places I can see."

Mustang's curse came out low and bitter. "The timer's not slowing down," he muttered. The numbers in his own vision kept falling, a relentless red march. He pulled up a quick flood of data—material fatigue estimates, load curves, radiation from the reactor starting to climb. "Maybe if we spread out, keep the pressure even, go one at a time—"

"Or," Jorgen said, snorting, "we could just blow a hole through the damn wall and save the tiptoeing."

"And bring the ceiling down now rather than waiting?" Bradley shot back. "We're trying to escape, not become permanent fixtures."

A sharp crack snapped through the quiet. Knight's head whipped up. The tunnel answered with a deep, warped groan—metal and concrete arguing under load. Dust sifted down in a thin curtain, stinging eyes and tongues. Above them, one of the fissures Knight's AR had flagged split wider, running fast across the ceiling.

"Damn it," Knight growled. "Decision time. We push and risk getting buried, or we sit here and die when the reactor goes."

The ceiling sagged another fraction, visible now—it was caving in.

"Go! Now!" Knight roared, driving back through the line and shoving at shoulders, packs—anything that got the line moving.

Behind them, the ceiling finally lost the argument with gravity. A slab of concrete the size of a single-seat grav-lift tore free and smashed down where they'd been standing seconds before, throwing up a suffocating cloud of dust and chips. The noise punched through Bradley's chest like a physical blow.

Under it came a second, uglier sound—the tortured scream of metal shearing. A support beam somewhere behind them buckled, the wrenching groan rolling down the tunnel like thunder.

Jorgen, closest to the collapse, twisted mid-stride, eyes going wide as he saw where the next failure line was headed.

"Knight!" he bellowed, voice raw. "Look out—!"

Knight moved before anyone else.

\*\*\*

Bradley saw his head snap toward the warped I-beam, saw his face set—not surprise, not fear, just the hard, flat realization of a man reading the end of a story. Then Knight was moving, boots hammering toward the failing section.

"Knight—" Bradley started.

Too late. The beam shrieked as it tore free, concrete crumbling around it in jagged chunks. Knight lunged underneath, shouldering into the sagging metal with a guttural sound that was half curse, half battle cry. The impact drove him down to one knee. Rust and grit exploded across his back. The whole tunnel shuddered, then the collapse slowed—just enough.

Another slab hit somewhere behind them with a concussive thud that punched the air from Bradley's lungs. The floor lurched sideways. Dust turned the beam of his weapon light into a solid, choking column. He skidded, boots sliding on loose debris, and slammed a hand against the wall to keep from going down.

Through the haze he caught a glimpse of Knight.

The older soldier was braced under the I-beam, shoulders jammed against cold steel, arms locked, every muscle drawn up like a coiled cable. Veins stood out in his neck. His teeth were bared, breath coming in harsh, ragged bursts. The beam groaned across his back, the sound of tons of concrete trying to finish what they'd started.

"Knight!" Bradley's shout came out raw, scraped by dust and panic.

The others had stumbled to a stop, instinct dragging them back toward the collapse even as survival screamed at them to run. Jorgen's face was a grim mask under the dust; Pinky's eyes were huge, wet lines cutting through the grime on her cheeks. Alysha stood taut, hand on her blade, gaze fixed on the sagging ceiling above Knight as if she could cut it down to size.

"Get…out of here," Knight rasped. The words buzzed through the AR channel and the ruined air together. "Leave me. You won't…make it otherwise…"

The ultimatum hung there, heavy as the beam itself. Overhead, the tunnel complained in long, drawn-out groans, cracks creeping like black lightning across the ceiling. Every sound carried the same message: you are out of time.

Bradley felt panic claw up his chest, hot and wild. Under it, something else dug in—the simple refusal to walk away. Not now. Not here.

"Not happening," he muttered.

Mustang appeared at his shoulder, materializing out of the dust with his AR lenses still glowing faintly around his eyes. The usual dark humor in him was gone; what was left was pure focus.

"We can take some of the load," Mustang said, voice tight but steady. "There's a support strut back along the wall. If we can lever it under the beam, give him a wedge…"

He didn't have to finish. Bradley was already moving.

They scrambled back, boots slipping on rubble. The support Knight had flagged earlier lay half-buried in debris—a rusted length of heavy steel half as wide as either of them, welded once into the tunnel's skeleton and snapped loose by earlier impacts. Bradley and Mustang dropped to it together, fingers scrabbling for purchase.

The metal was slick with dust and corrosion, resisting his grip. It didn't want to move. Bradley dug his boots in, felt the floor grit under his soles, and hauled. Mustang braced beside him, grunting with effort. The beam shifted a few centimeters, then caught on broken concrete.

"Come on," Mustang hissed through his teeth. "Come on—"

Their breaths sawed in and out, hot knives in dust-burned throats. The cramped tunnel gave them barely any room to work. There was no good angle, no clean swing, just brute force against an object that had no interest in going where they wanted it.

They needed leverage.

Bradley's gaze snagged on the wall—a length of rebar and pipe jutting from a cracked panel, bent but still fixed solidly in place. An idea snapped into place.

"There," he said, already reaching. He seized a loose length of pipe that had fallen in the earlier collapse, hands slipping over grit until he found the balance. He jammed one end of it over the protruding steel, forcing it down until it bit and held, forming a rough hinge.

"Get on it," he told Mustang, voice harsh. "We'll use it to lift the base."

They threw their weight onto the far end of the makeshift lever. The pipe flexed, complaining, but it held. The buried end of the support beam started to rise, inch by stubborn inch, grating against debris. Bradley's shoulders screamed. Something in his back twinged like a live wire.

Back at the collapse, the tunnel's complaints grew louder. A sharp crack ran down the line of the ceiling, followed by a fresh rain of grit and fist-sized rubble. Knight's muffled cry punched through the channel as a chunk of concrete glanced off his brow and tore a bloody line across his cheek.

His grip on the I-beam slipped a fraction. The metal dropped that same fraction. The sound it made was terrible.

"Now!" Bradley snarled, more at his own body than at Mustang.

They drove into the lever, every muscle burning. The pipe flexed almost to the point of failure. The support beam finally lurched free of its bed with a metallic shriek.

"Go, go—" Mustang gasped.

Together they man-handled the freed strut toward the choking cloud where Knight held the ceiling up. Every step was a fight against mass and cramped space. Dust stung their eyes, turned every breath into a cough. They slid the far end forward like a battering ram, the metal ringing as it smacked through rocks and debris.

"Down," Bradley barked.

They jammed the tip of the support under the sagging I-beam, angling it until it bit into a crack in the floor and caught. Bradley dropped his shoulder against the rear of the strut, Mustang alongside him, and shoved.

The beam groaned, shifting its weight onto the new support. Knight sucked in a ragged breath as some of the pressure lifted from his back. Not enough. The ceiling above them continued to sag in fits and starts, pressing down on the I-beam, which pressed down on their fulcrum.

Mustang let out a wordless yell and pushed harder, boots skidding on loose stone. Bradley followed, vision tunneling, muscles shrieking as if they were being peeled apart. The steel bit deeper into the floor, sparks spitting from fresh fractures.

The strain on Knight eased by degrees, but it was still there— enough that his arms trembled, boots grinding into the shifting rubble for purchase. The tunnel around them felt like it was exhaling in long, agonized groans.

In the corner of Bradley's vision, the countdown on his AR kept ticking, each red digit flipping with calm, mechanical precision: 16:12. 16:11. 16:10.

Every second they clawed back from the collapse bled out somewhere else, flowing downhill toward the reactor.

They heaved. They breathed dust. The steel sang under stress.

Hope felt like it was slipping through their fingers just as surely as the seconds on their displays—both of them grinding away under the same ruthless pressure.

With agonizing slowness, their stolen support beam began to earn its keep.

The metal against Bradley's shoulder bit into flesh; his arms shook so hard his hands felt like they might slip right off the steel. But the strut edged deeper under the sagging I-beam, and the weight pressing down through Knight's frame eased by fractions. The big man's back was still bowed under the load, but his stance widened, boots gaining a little more purchase on the rubble.

Sweat and blood poured down Knight's face in muddy rivulets, cutting dark lines through the pale dust. His jaw was clenched so tight Bradley could hear the faint grind of teeth through the comm. His eyes, narrowed against the falling grit, stayed fixed forward—no plea, no panic, just a stubborn, blazing refusal to fold.

Then a different sound pushed through the chorus of groans and metal shrieks—a low, deep rumble that came from beneath instead of above.

The floor in front of Knight bulged, like something exhaling under pressure, then gave way. Cracked slabs and rebar dropped out of existence with a sharp, tearing roar. A hole yawned open at their feet, swallowing concrete and twisted steel in a rush. Damp, cold air sighed up from the darkness, thick with the smell of earth.

The shift ran through the tunnel like a wave. The ceiling's weight, seeking a new path, followed the failure line. Chunks of concrete and shattered supports tore free and plunged into the new chasm in a grinding cascade. For one sick heartbeat Bradley saw Knight tilt toward the drop, the I-beam dragging him in like an anchor.

Then the world lurched again. The I-beam slipped, its crushed seating crumbling away. With a tortured screech it slid off the fulcrum and dropped into the void, taking most of the ceiling's anger with it.

Knight pitched backward as the load vanished from his shoulders. He hit the rubble ass first, sucking in great, ragged lungfuls of air. His face was a mask of sweat, dust, and smeared blood, but his eyes were bright and alive, the shock of still-breathing burning hot behind them.

"Get him clear!" Mustang shouted. His voice cracked on the last word, raw with adrenaline.

Jorgen moved like the floor wasn't still trying to kill them. He barreled through the thinning dust, hooked an arm under Knight's and hauled, dragging the bigger man backward just as their makeshift strut snapped out of its notch with a shower of sparks and dropped uselessly below.

They stumbled away from the edge, coughing, eyes streaming tears of dust. Behind them, the tunnel continued to tear itself apart. Sections of ceiling sagged and broke away, falling in a slow, relentless chain reaction that chased the collapse deeper into the new hole. Each impact sent another shudder through the walls, each shudder another reminder that they were seconds from joining the rubble.

Bradley hooked his hands under Knight's opposite arm, taking some of the weight. Knight's legs moved, but sluggishly, like he was wading through molasses. Together they lurched down what was left of the corridor.

He risked a look back over his shoulder. The passage behind them was gone—just a broken lip of flooring and, beyond it, a churning mess of dust, shattered concrete, and twisted metal dropping into the dark. Any path back through the old tunnel network had been neatly erased.

The red countdown in his AR pulsed at the top of his vision, indifferent to the chaos. Mustang's version would show the same numbers, marching on.

"Over here!" Mustang's shout cut through the ringing in Bradley's ears.

Bradley turned in time to see Mustang pointing past the jagged edge of the collapse, toward where the floor had not just collapsed but torn open. A ragged mouth in the stone yawned off to one side—wider, more deliberate than the random breakages around it.

"Another passage," Mustang said. "Hole's big enough to fit us if we squeeze."

Jorgen maneuvered Knight that way, Pinky glued to his side, one small hand wrapped tight in his torn sleeve. They edged through the gap single file, brushing past broken rock and twisted rebar. The air on the other side felt different—cooler, cleaner, carrying a hint of raw stone instead of rust and rot.

The dust settled enough for their lights to penetrate, and Bradley's first clear look stole what breath he'd gotten back.

They stood at the lip of a tunnel that dwarfed the cramped service runs they'd been crawling through—an enormous bore vanishing into darkness in both directions. The ceiling arched high overhead, lost in shadow; the floor stretched out in a smooth, gentle curve, maybe twenty feet across at its narrowest. Their weapon lights caught only slices of it at a time, revealing more emptiness beyond.

The rock under Bradley's boots wasn't carved. It was too uniform, too deliberate. The wall nearest him was smooth to the touch, worn in long, shallow arcs that caught and threw back the light in uneasy patterns. The space felt—strange. Not in the way of failing concrete and bad engineering, but in a deeper, quieter way, as if they'd stepped out of one story and into another without meaning to.

"What in the hell…" Mustang breathed. His AR stuttered as he tried to map the tunnel, projections pixelating wherever they met this new geometry. "This isn't on any of The Foundation's schematics. There's nothing this big, this deep."

Knight, still catching his breath, agreed. "Doesn't match anything in the facility layout. Looks like a mine bore, maybe, but…oversized. Twenty feet at least." He reached out and brushed his fingertips along the nearest wall. The stone was unnaturally smooth, almost polished. "And it doesn't feel like machine work."

Alysha moved past them without a word, drawn forward as if the tunnel were calling her by name. Her steps were silent on the stone. She scanned the walls, eyes tracing the rhythmic ridges that ran along the curve—marks too regular to be natural, too imperfect to be a drill.

She lifted a hand and laid her fingers against one of the grooves. The touch was light, almost reverent, as if she were reading a story written in stone.

"No machine," she said at last, voice carrying in the vast, hollow space. "This was not made by metal teeth."

A chill ran the length of Bradley's spine. His grip tightened on the weapon array he was still lugging around.

"Then what…" he started, the question dying as it left his mouth, swallowed by the dark and the hum of the ticking numbers in his sight.

Karl stepped up beside Alysha, eyes narrowed. In the harsh cut of their weapon lights, the smooth wall picked up a dull sheen.

He laid his broad, scarred fingers in the same grooves she'd traced and followed them, palm flattening here and there as if weighing the stone.

"She's right," he said after a beat. His voice came out low and certain. "Stonework doesn't lie. This wasn't poured or drilled. Compression striae." His thumb tapped along a faint line of stratified dust. "Something *passed through* here, sometime after this place was built."

Alysha turned, the strange sigils on her blade catching the light in a faint, oily shimmer. Her gaze tracked the tunnel's curve into darkness.

The reactor's countdown was one threat; the image of some unseen giant worming through tunnels under the facility was another, older kind of fear. Bradley felt it sink cold into his gut. It was easy to imagine the darkness ahead bulging, stone splitting around something they'd never see coming until it was on them.

Mustang stared at the walls as if they'd personally offended him. His usual swagger was gone. "Yeah," he muttered, the red numbers of the timer pulsing at the edge of his vision. "Guess we're not just running from fire anymore."

He dragged in a breath that rattled. "We're burning time we don't have," he said louder. "Reactor doesn't care what dug this hole. We need distance and stone between us and that blast. Or we're ghosts when it goes."

Bradley swept his light along the tunnel. Every hollow became an eye, every shadow a crouched shape. A moment ago the bore had looked like salvation—a way out from under collapsing concrete. Now, standing in it, he was unsure. The darkness ahead didn't feel empty; it felt unmeasured.

"Deeper, then," Jorgen grunted behind him. He rolled his shoulders, making his wiry frame look even more stubborn than usual. "Whatever carved this, it went down and away. We follow the path. Question is—" he nodded toward the fork ahead, where the bore split left and right into equal darkness "—which way keeps us alive?"

Karl had no visor, no AR wash across his eyes—just calloused hands and a lifetime of reading stone by touch. He crouched, set his palm flat on the floor in the center of the tunnel, then shifted, feeling along first one side, then the other. He closed his eyes, face turned slightly as if listening for a sound only he could hear.

"Fresh scuffing in both," he murmured. "Not from what carved it. Lighter loads. Feet, drag marks…something." His brows pulled down. "We're not the first though."

A shiver went down Bradley's spine that had nothing to do with the temperature.

"But which way gets us farther from the core?" Mustang pressed. The ticking in his ear felt louder now, like the timer had found a voice. "Which way is deeper?"

Karl opened his eyes. In the dim light, they looked almost black. For the first time since Bradley had met him, there was a hint of hesitation there.

"Can't swear it," he said. "Feels like more pull that way." He jerked his chin toward the left-hand tunnel. "Low hum in the rock."

It wasn't the clean certainty Bradley wanted—just a gut call, the kind of instinct that had kept Karl alive in the sewers and undercity for months, alone. Here, in this deep place, it was still more credibility than anyone else had.

Bradley's jaw ached from grinding his teeth. On one side: reactor fire. On the other: whatever had carved this monstrous vein, and whatever had come through after. There wasn't a good door to choose. Just one that would slam behind them— or on them.

"Left it is," he said. The words felt like they weighed more than they should. He caught the others' eyes in turn—Mustang, Jorgen, Knight, Alysha, Pinky—and saw his own fear reflected back, wrapped in the same fragile layer of resolve.

He took the lead with Knight, weapon lamp throwing a tight cone down the left-hand bore. The smooth walls slid past in their peripheral vision, their lamps carving crisp, skittering shadows that leaped and twisted like they were laughing at the attempt to pin them down. Boots slapped stone, breaths dragged in and out of dust-rough lungs.

The air shifted as they ran—cool, carrying the dense, mineral smell of deep places. Under it was a faint dampness, a hint of something wet far below, like a buried river or lake.

The timer burned at the edge of Bradley's vision, numbers ticking down in hard, red flips. Each change felt like a punch behind his eyes. It had stopped being information and become a rhythm—hammering in his ears, driving his legs, insisting that forward was the only direction left.

They had no idea what waited deeper in the earth. They didn't know what had made this tunnel, or if it was still here, somewhere ahead, waiting. But turning back meant the reactor, the surface teams, the kind of death you saw coming. Whatever was in front of them was, at least, still unknown.

Jorgen, all wiry tendon and age-scarred muscle, ran like a man half his years. Pinky rode on his hip, arms locked around his neck, face pressed into his shoulder. When she dared to look up, the light from Mustang's rig cut her features out in pale slices—too wide eyes, lips moving with small, choked sounds she probably thought no one could hear.

Alysha flowed along the flank, a smear of motion at the edge of Bradley's lamp. She moved with clipped, economical steps, head tilting at every faint echo. Her hand never strayed far from her blade. Every so often she would glance back, counting heads, then turn forward again, eyes narrowing as if she could force the dark to give up its secrets.

Bradley held his pace, the damn weapon array heavy against his shoulder. He still didn't understand why it felt so important, but he knew that it was. Fear ran under his skin like current, but it stayed in its lane, channeled into speed. He did not let himself picture the thing that had carved this passage. He didn't try to imagine jaws or claws big enough to leave gouges in bedrock. That way lay paralysis. All that mattered was the distance growing between them and the facility.

Time stopped behaving like time. It stretched and snapped, a rubber band at the edge of breaking. They ran until his lungs burned and his thighs felt full of broken glass, until every breath rasped, but the marching red numbers told him it had only been minutes.

The tunnel kinked sharply right, forcing him to cut his speed and pivot. As he rounded the bend a chill bled through him, the air suddenly colder. There was a taste to it now—metallic, faintly bloody, a tang that brushed the back of his tongue and sent a tight shiver along his spine.

His beam swept the walls and caught new damage. The stone was no longer just smoothly carved; long gouges ripped across the surface, deep scrapes that crossed the original flow of the tunnel. Something had happened here—

Movement flickered at the edge of his sight.

Bradley's heart lurched. He snapped his head toward it, weapon swinging to cover, breath held. The lamp showed only more stone, more curve, more black beyond its reach. No shapes, no eyes. Just his own pulse thudding in his ears.

Exhaustion's getting cute, he thought, jaw clenching. He pushed forward.

The earth chose that moment to roar.

The low rumble they'd been half-aware of—part reactor, part distant structural failure—spiked into a full-body assault. The floor heaved sideways, a violent ripple that knocked his feet out from under him. Bradley hit the stone hard, air punched out of his chest. Around him, the others went down in a tangle of limbs, gear slamming into rock. The blast of sound turned the tunnel into a drum, every surface amplifying the shock.

Dust exploded from the ceiling in a choking wave. Their lights jittered wildly, then went out entirely, swallowed by the sudden chaos. Pinky's scream cut through it all, high and piercing, a thread of pure terror in the noise.

Jorgen was up almost before he'd finished falling. He grabbed for Pinky, hauling her against his chest and curling his body around her as grit rained down. Even in the weakened glow from Knight's flickering lamp, Bradley imaged the look in the girl's eyes—naked, animal fear.

"What the hell was that?" Jorgen roared, voice bouncing down the tunnel, half fury, half refusal to roll over and die.

Mustang pushed himself up onto hands and knees, coughing. The holo-ghost of the timer that had been burning in his vision shuddered, dissolved into a whirl of static, then went flat. He blinked hard, eyes wide and hollow.

"The reactor," he rasped. "She went early. We lost the curve. It blew ahead of schedule."

Bradley's stomach dropped as if the floor had vanished again. All that running, all the seconds they'd stolen, and the detonation had moved the finish line wherever it wanted. The meltdown wasn't something behind them anymore, a wave to outrun. It was a fact carved into the world around them.

The shock faded by degrees, replaced by guilt, all the lives lost. In that pause, the tunnel's own voice crept back in—the slow trickle of dust, the rasp of rock sliding against rock, the low, continuous groan from somewhere below that vibrated up through his hands. The whole passage felt like it was thinking about whether to hold together.

The bore stopped feeling like a refuge and started feeling like a throat that might close without warning.

Their lights sputtered and died. HUDs glitched once, twice, then winked out under the reactor's electromagnetic slap. Karl's flashlight flared bright—then gave up with a soft pop.

Darkness fell fast and absolute. For a few blind heartbeats there was nothing but breath and the scrape of bodies shifting.

Then a thin line of cool light appeared.

Alysha had drawn her blade. In the black, it was a pale, steady sliver—marks along its length catching some inner glow. It hung there in the void like a single, narrow promise, the only thing that kept the tunnel from erasing them completely.

"Power surge," Mustang muttered, mostly to himself. "EMP… damn it…" His voice thinned out, then he forced something like cheer into it as he ducked under Knight's arm and took some of the bigger man's weight. "Hey, systems might come back up later," he added, breathless. "Y'know…assuming we don't get pancaked first."

The joke fell flat in the dark.

Bradley understood what he was trying to do. Throw a little light into the void, even if it was fake. But the reality sat heavy on all of them: buried under God-knew-how-much rock, blind, and more turned around than when they'd started running.

Jorgen's hand tightened around Pinky's shoulder, drawing her in against his side. It wasn't gentle, but it was steady. "We'll get through it," he rumbled. No promise, no talk of sunshine on the other side—just a statement, wrapped around a core of iron that none of them could miss.

Karl's voice came from the dark a moment later, blunt enough to cut through the thin veil Mustang had tried to throw over things. "Time's not our friend," he said. Even the short man's usual rock-solid tone had a crack in it. "If the lights don't come back…"

He didn't need to finish.

Without their rigs, without Karl's flashlight, this place stopped being a tunnel and turned into pure void. Every faint scrape sounded too close. Every breath echoed like it belonged to something else. The stone felt nearer inside Bradley's skull than it did at his shoulders, pressure building from all sides.

A pale blade eased closer, ghost-light playing along its edge.

Alysha stepped into the center of the group's ragged circle, her weapon held low. The faint glow that clung to its etchings brightened as she focused, her eyes half-lidded in concentration.

"We should go," she said. Her voice was little more than a whisper, but it carried.

The air around the blade thickened, then sparked. Flame bloomed along the metal in a sudden, hungry rush, wrapping the length of it in a tight, controlled sheath of fire. Heat licked at Bradley's face. Shadows that had been absolute now jumped back, revealing rough walls and tired faces in sharp relief. The tunnel shrank from infinite black to a space they could see, however small.

Her bearing was no kinder than Karl's words, but they were actionable. Movement meant choice. Choice meant they weren't corpses yet.

Bradley shifted the salvaged array in his grip, the now familiar heft grounding him. "Better than waiting for the ceiling to pick a winner," he rasped. "Lead on."

They fell in behind her.

The tunnel changed character again. What had once felt like an escape route now read as a system of veins inside the same buried beast—no less claustrophobic for being wider. Alysha's blade-fire painted the walls in bronze and shadow, bringing out every curve, every old scar in the stone. The light didn't reach far, but it was enough to keep their boots moving in the right direction.

Without  the HUD to map how far they had come or to even tell time, it was impossible to tell how long they had been moving. Pain settled into Bradley's legs and lived there. His shoulders ached from the weapon's weight. Knight's breaths grew louder and more ragged as he leaned on Mustang more and more. Pinky stopped making sounds at all, her face pressed into Jorgen's shoulder still wrapped in his longcoat, fingers locked tight in the fabric lining.

The air down here was thicker, sour with old stone and a faint, unsettling damp that clung to skin and hair. Condensation beaded on the walls and occasionally broke free to patter onto their shoulders, cold and startling in the warmth of their exertion.

The fire along it burned steady at first, a clean, bright line. As they pushed on, though, Bradley started to notice the way it fluttered at the edges, the way it dimmed before she pulled it back under control. Her steps, once effortless, took on a hitch. The hand not on the hilt brushed the wall more often, fingers scraping for balance.

By the time Bradley realized how much the fire was costing her, her movements had gone slow and deliberate. Sweat slicked her brow, catching the flicker of the flame.

Still, she kept it raised. Still, the fire burned.

And they kept walking after it, deeper into the earth, because the only thing more terrifying than what might be ahead was staying where they were and letting the dark finish what the blast had started.

They took only the briefest of rests—backs to the cold, sweating stone, shoulders touching more for comfort than necessity. Their voices stayed low, breathy scraps of sound as they passed around the last of their water and ration bars. The food tasted like dust and salt, but it put something in their stomachs besides fear.

Bradley kept one eye on Knight.

In the unsteady glow of Alysha's blade, the bigger man's injuries were harder to ignore. His face was gray under the grime; the muscles in his jaw jumped whenever he shifted his weight. Every movement pulled at ribs that had taken the full kiss of that I-beam. Knight wore it like an inconvenience, but Bradley had seen enough broken men to recognize how close that front was to giving way.

It was Karl who broke the quiet.

"Let the flame rest," he said. His voice wasn't loud, but it was certain. "I'll take over."

For a moment nobody moved. Mustang's head jerked up, eyes reflecting the blade-light like an animal's. Static still rippled at the edges of his dead AR lenses, a useless ghost of systems that weren't coming back online.

"How," Mustang said, "are you going to see anything without her light?"

Karl shrugged, as if the question barely needed a breath. "Miner's eyes," he said. "You spend enough years underground, the dark stops being a stranger."

Bradley almost snorted. He knew a cover story when he heard one. He'd seen Karl in lightless stretches before, moving too sure, reading his surroundings the way Mustang read tactical exercises. This was more than "eyes adjusting." But if Knight and Mustang wanted to take the explanation at face value, so much the better. They'd already had their belief system kicked a few times today.

No sense adding another weight to the pile.

Alysha gave a single small nod, then exhaled and let the power drain from her blade. The fire winked out in a breath, severing their world down to black. Pinky choked on a gasp. Jorgen's arm tightened across her shoulders, pulling her in against his chest until her forehead rested against his collarbone.

There was nothing—no light, no depth, just the sound of the slow creaking of stone settling. Then Karl spoke again.

"Follow close," he said. "Keep your hand on the person in front of you. Don't drift."

He produced a coil of pliable wire from one of his many hidden pockets; now Bradley heard it rasp through Karl's hands as he worked. One by one, they felt the line bump their fingers and then loop around their waist or belt, getting cinched off with quick, practiced tugs. A lifeline, crude but solid.

Bradley figured Karl was a dwarf, and dwarves had a long, ugly history with humans—enough that the old stories said they didn't show you all the tools they carried unless you'd bled together or they were watching you bleed out. Karl clearly wasn't ready to lay his cards on the table, but he also didn't seem to be any kind of threat.

Bradley couldn't blame him. Trust was expensive.

Karl set off along the right-hand wall, one palm skimming the stone, feet sure despite the dark. The wire tugged gently at Bradley's wrist as he fell in behind, then again as Knight, Alysha, Jorgen, Pinky, and Mustang lined out in his wake. Mustang took the drag position by choice, watching the darkness behind them with dead optics.

The tunnel changed again.

Under Karl's guidance, the path twisted harder, angles sharper, as if they were moving through knotted roots instead of a clean bore. The walls no longer felt uniformly smooth when Bradley's shoulder brushed them; here the stone was pocked and jagged.

Karl moved faster than Bradley would have thought possible for someone so stocky. The dwarf's boots found the right spots instinctively, stepping over unseen ridges, skirting drop-offs Bradley only sensed when cold air brushed his ankles. Bradley stumbled more than once, boot toe catching on a lip of stone.

Gratitude edged into his frustration. Down here, when HUDs and training and firepower had all been stripped away, it was Karl's unique skills that mattered.

The deeper they went, the more the tunnel felt like it was squeezing in on them. The walls closed just enough that Bradley's free arm brushed rock with nearly every step. Sometimes his fingertips slid over a plane as smooth as worked stone; sometimes they snagged on pitted surfaces, tiny holes and fractures that chewed skin.

Pinky's soft, shallow breaths drifted along the line, occasionally broken by a tiny, involuntary whimper she swallowed back. Jorgen answered those with low, half-heard curses—aimed at the stone, at The Foundation, at fate—

anything but her. Alysha's voice came rarely, just a quiet word when Knight's pace faltered, her shoulder taking more of his weight for a few strides. Behind them, Mustang's boots scuffed in a different cadence, pausing now and then so he could turn and listen, wire going taut between him and the others.

Until something changed in the dark.

At first Bradley thought it was his eyes playing tricks again—a suggestion of shape where there shouldn't be any. But when he blinked, the faint impression remained. A soft wash of color, not white, not the harsh blue of LEDs, but a muted, ghostly glow.

"What is that?" Mustang's voice drifted up the line, rough with fatigue and threaded with a strand of wonder.

Karl grunted. "Fungus," he said. "Deep stuff. Makes its own light." He ran his fingers along the wall; when Bradley's hand brushed the same area a second later he felt a slight give, a damp slickness on the stone. "Means we're close to natural caverns."

The faint luminance grew as they moved, resolving from a suggestion into visible patches along the walls. Smudges of blue-green radiance clung to the stone in irregular blankets, turning the rock into a surrealistic landscape. Tiny pinpoints of cold white dotted the darker stretches—spore clusters pulsing faintly with a rhythm Bradley couldn't feel.

The tunnel began to widen again, ceiling climbing away, lost in the soft glow. Karl led them through one last kink and then stopped short.

Alysha sucked in a breath. Even Knight let out a low, involuntary whistle.

The tight passage opened into a cavern so large its shape was hard to trust. The fungal light crawled over everything—wide sheets of blue-green on the walls, pale tendrils hanging from the ceiling, constellations of spores dusting ledges and outcroppings. Rock spines rose from the floor in uneven ranks, their edges rimmed in sickly color.

For the first time since the blast, Bradley could see more than a few meters in any direction.

It didn't make the place feel any less alien; if anything, it sharpened the strangeness. The ghostly illumination only made the depth of it more surreal. It was beautiful in a way that made him feel a little manic.

Light seeped from every surface, turning stalagmites into frozen waves and the ceiling into a low, mottled sky. Pinky's small gasp cut the silence; fear left her face, replaced by wide-eyed wonder. Beside her, Jorgen let out a low, honest whistle.

"Keep close," Karl said.

His voice rolled through the cavern, steady and low. He turned in a slow circle, eyes tracking ledges, shadows, the dips in the floor. "These caves aren't cut like the tunnels above. Natural pockets, bad footing. Could be anything around the next bend."

The darkness was gone, but the fungal light didn't banish the shadows so much as teach them new tricks, making them sway and ripple at the edges of vision.

Bradley adjusted his grip on the salvaged array. The cold of the metal grounded him. For all the wrongness, the glow meant life of some kind still clung down here. Life needed air, water, pathways. Maybe some of those paths led up.

For now, the cavern was space to breathe.

They followed Karl deeper into the luminous heart of the cave, boots whispering over stone. The glow thickened as they went. Fungus bloomed in wild clusters, smearing the walls in denser bands of light. The rock underfoot smoothed out, rounded by old water, and their shadows lengthened, black and sharp against the blue-green wash.

They slowed without meaning to, pulled up short by the sheer strangeness of it. Their ragged breathing eased. The cavern's silence settled around them—no hum of machinery, no distant thump of failing infrastructure—just the crisp drip of water somewhere ahead, each drop echoing like a pin struck on glass.

The air cooled further, turning damp against Bradley's skin. The smell changed too, trading for rich stone and something almost fresh, like wet earth after rain—muted but present in the back of his nose.

He felt curiosity stir under the fatigue. Karl hadn't just kept them alive—he'd led them into a pocket of the underworld that felt…less dead. A hidden fold humans hadn't yet poisoned.

Pinky saw it first.

She sucked in a sharp, delighted breath and wriggled free from Jorgen's hold. Before the old bounty hunter could get a proper grip on her, she shrugged out of his bulky coat, leaving herself in dirty white shorts and the compression wrap across her chest.

"Pinky, where are you—" Jorgen started, concern roughening his voice.

Too late.

The girl sprinted ahead, bare feet slapping stone, and launched herself in a fearless arc toward a shimmering hollow in the cavern floor.

The pool looked like someone had poured starlight into a stone bowl. Its surface caught the fungal glow and fractured it into a thousand shards, light jagging back and forth as Pinky's small body hit the water with a splash that rang off the chamber walls.

The water wasn't the murky, stagnant kind Bradley had expected to find underground. It was startlingly clear. In the shifting gleam he could see movement below the surface— sleek, silvery fish darting in quick bursts, twisting away from the disturbance, and fat, sucker-mouthed creatures clamped to submerged rock, their circular jaws working as they grazed on the same faintly luminous algae that freckled the cavern walls.

"Lets make camp," Bradley said, dropping his bag and removing the line from his waist.

# CHAPTER TWELVE

The others went down hard.

Within minutes of bedding against the rock, their breathing settled into the uneven rhythm of exhausted sleep. Knight slumped with his back to a smooth outcrop, head tipped forward, hands still near his rifle. Pinky was curled into the hollow of Jorgen's side beneath the old man's coat, her "snores" a little too regular to be real. Even Alysha and Karl slept like sprung traps at rest—still, but with that coiled readiness in them.

Bradley and Mustang kept first watch.

Their camp lay within sight of the pool. Its surface caught the cavern's blue-green glow and broke it into shifting patterns that climbed the rock above like reflections off a ceiling. It would've been easy to stare and let the rest fall away; instead, Bradley's gaze kept drifting back to the shadowed gap where they'd entered the cavern, half expecting fire or something worse to pour through.

He worked the salvaged weapon array in his lap, fingers moving by habit. The housing was scorched, plates warped from the fight and the collapse. Underneath, though, the guts were mostly intact—coils, capacitors, bundles of fiber cable. His thumbs brushed over scorched circuit traces, mapping possibilities. Could he rewire the charge, dump it into something shaped, something defensive? Probably not down here, not with this junk and no tools. But he could at least strip out anything Mustang might be able to use to repair their gear.

Across from him, Mustang crouched over a mess of ruined hardware—projection lenses, cracked housings, ragged lengths of optic fiber. He muttered to himself as he sorted through it, curses woven into a rhythm that sounded more tired than angry. The lenses still held a faint charge from the EMP blast; they sparked occasionally when he touched solder points together, little blue gnats of light dying before they were born.

A short distance away, Knight's breaths came slow and deep, the sound steady in the cavern's hush. For all his earlier insistence that he was fine, his color had gone bad and the set of his mouth said every inhale cost him. At least he was down long enough for his body to try to catch up.

"Any luck?" Bradley asked quietly.

Mustang snorted without looking up. "This is like trying to repair a symphony with a sledgehammer," he said. "I might get *something* to play again, but nobody's gonna recognize the tune."

Bradley huffed a faint laugh and went back to his own mess of parts.

Silence slid back in. Water in the pool lapped softly at the rock, disturbed now and then by a glimmer of silver below the surface. Pinky's pretend snores rasped in their corner. Somewhere above, a drop fell from the ceiling and hit stone with a sharp, solitary tick.

Mustang's hands slowed. His gaze drifted over to where Karl lay with one arm behind his head, face turned toward the cavern roof, then to Alysha, curled with her back to a fungus-lit wall, blade across her knees even in sleep.

"You think we can trust them?" he murmured. The bravado was gone; this was the quiet voice he used when the noise in his head got turned down. "Her, with the sword that catches fire. Him, walking around down here like it's midday."

He stopped there, the rest of it implied. *Unforeseen.* Things that fed on chaos. Things the Foundation trained them to spot and burn.

Bradley took his time answering. Alysha was still an unknown —half feral, half priestess of something he didn't have a name for. Karl was easier to read: blunt, loyal, turning sideways only when talk brushed too close to what he really was. Both of them had carried their share of the weight down here. Both had taken hits for the group.

"I trust what they've done," Bradley said finally. "That's what we've got." He kept his eyes on the weapon array, voice low. "Karl held the line when the tunnel tried to kill us. Alysha kept us moving when the lights died. Whatever else they're keeping in their pockets doesn't erase that."

Mustang chewed on that for a moment, jaw working. "Sure," he said at last. "And, hey, they haven't tried to eat us. Or melt us. So that's a win on the Unforeseen front."

The attempt at humor was there, but it had a flat edge. He went back to his tools, shoulders hunched.

They sat like that for a while—two silhouettes in the cavern's ghost-light, sharing the same tight band of responsibility. Bradley turned a capacitor over between thumb and forefinger, mind running through diagrams that only existed in memory. Mustang stripped wire with his teeth and a multi-tool, piecing together the skeleton of something that might, if they were very lucky, talk to the outside world someday.

The first watch was always the longest. The body hadn't surrendered yet, the mind still busy playing every ugly what-if it could conjure. Out there in the half-dark, past the edge of the fungal glow, the earth rumbled occasionally as the blast's aftershocks worked their way through the stone. Each one sent a faint tremor through the floor and a ripple of unease up Bradley's spine.

Later, when the shadows felt heavier, he'd put a hand on Jorgen's shoulder and drag the old man up into the waking world. Knight's discipline would do the rest, pulling him from sleep to share the watch whether Bradley asked or not. For now it was just the two of them, their pile of tech, and the slow, steady pulse of light across the cavern walls.

Bradley shifted his grip on the weapon array and kept his eyes on the dark mouth of the tunnel, counting each breath until it was someone else's turn.

For now, Bradley let his gaze drift over the sleeping line of them and tried to make sense of it.

Knight, his walking vanguard, slumped but unbroken. Mustang, his tactical right hand, curled around a mess of dead tech like it might still answer him. Alysha, a blade out of some half-remembered myth, coiled even in sleep. Jorgen, grizzled bounty hunter. Karl, wandering merchant with hands that knew stone. And Pinky—an innocent, or something close enough—pulled into the crossfire of a war she couldn't possibly understand.

None of it should have fit together. Yet here they were, breathing the same cold air, sharing the same patch of stolen safety.

His eyes returned to Pinky. She lay in a tight curl beside Jorgen, the coat pulled up over her ears, one eye slitted just enough to watch the world. The fungal glow turned her hair into a pale halo against the rock. Something hot and stubborn sparked in Bradley's chest at the sight. Against every sane prediction, they'd clawed their way this far. He glanced at Mustang, gaunt face washed in blue-green. The same tired resolve looked back at him.

Time dragged.

When the first watch finally felt like it had earned its name, they nudged Jorgen and Knight awake. Jorgen came up with a grunt and a crack of stiff joints, settling beside the pool with his rifle across his knees, expression carved from old stone. Knight blinked himself upright more slowly, eyes narrowing against the ache in his ribs as he shifted to join him. He didn't say much; he didn't need to.

Mustang arched his back, wincing as muscles protested. "Go rack out," he told Bradley, voice rough but edged with a gruff kindness. "You're not doing anyone favors staggering around like a concussed mule tomorrow."

Bradley didn't argue. He found a strip of rock near the others and lowered himself onto it, easing the salvaged weapon within reach. Heat radiated off the sleeping bodies around him; it bled some of the cavern's clammy chill from his hide. Alysha and Karl lay as they had before, still as statues yet somehow ready. Pinky cracked one eye as he settled, watching him sidelong, then squeezed it shut again in an exaggerated imitation of sleep.

Sleep didn't cooperate.

Every time he let his eyelids fall, his mind spat up spider-drones dropping from ceilings, the tunnel choking closed, the bright red tick of the timer as the core climbed toward meltdown. His chest tightened, breath hitching in echoes of earlier panic.

"Can't sleep either?" Mustang's whisper drifted over from a few feet away.

"Nope," Bradley sighed. He shifted, making a sliver of space on the rock as Mustang eased down beside him. "Head won't shut up."

"Same." Mustang huffed a quiet, humorless laugh. "Five years ago, if you'd told me I'd be camping in a glow-worm cave under a blown reactor, on the run from New New York alongside my CO and  a sword-witch, I'd've called for a psych eval."

Despite everything, Bradley's mouth twitched. "Not exactly the inspirational poster they promise in recruitment."

Shared misery had its own gravity. Side by side, they stared up at the cavern ceiling, where bioluminescent patches stippled the rock like distant, warped stars. The drip of water echoed somewhere out in the dark, weirdly reminiscent of the nights he'd spent in the mountains with Jorgen, watching real constellations while frost crept over their sleeping rolls.

Gradually, the hard edge of wakefulness softened. Exhaustion seeped in around the fear. Bradley's thoughts slid from the immediate—camp, weapon, blast—to the people threaded around him. Pinky's too-bright eyes. Jorgen's haunted tone when he thought no one heard it. Knight's quiet steadiness, the way he had thrown himself under an I-beam without hesitating. Mustang's brittle jokes over hard truths. Karl and Alysha, strange and necessary.

If this patchwork alliance could survive drones, collapsing tunnels, and a reactor going critical, maybe there was a line somewhere ahead that didn't end with all of them dead, lost in these tunnels. Maybe.

He held onto that *maybe* as his breathing finally began to deepen.

\*\*\*

Jorgen and Knight sat their watch by the glowing pool.

The soft, shifting light painted long shadows across their faces, carving age and fatigue into sharper relief. Reflections from the water climbed the cavern walls in slow, wavering bands, like ghosts pacing just out of reach.

Jorgen's big hand slipped under his shirt and found the familiar weight of the locket he kept on a thin chain against his chest. He thumbed it open with a practiced motion. In the dim, alien glow, the image inside was barely more than shapes—the ghost of a woman's smile, the blurred outline of a boy at her side. His calloused thumb traced their faces anyway, mapping details his eyes no longer needed to see.

For a moment, the bioluminescent cavern fell away, and all he felt was that tiny circle of metal warming under his touch.

"Tell me about him," Knight rasped.

The question was soft, but in the cavern's hush it sounded loud. It cut through the drip of water and the faint lap of the pool.

Jorgen's fingers tightened around the locket. He drew a slow breath that sounded like it scraped his chest on the way in. "Danny," he said. The name came out rough, worn from use. "Wanted to be a doctor. Said he was gonna make enough to buy me and his momma a house with a pool." His mouth twitched. "Sun, grass, idiots splashing, all that. Wanted me to retire. Get out of running down dogs for the syndicates."

A bitter chuckle slipped loose and died quickly. "Damn fool kid. Never stood a chance."

Knight's eyes stayed on the glowing water, but his focus had gone far past it. "How old?" he asked. The two clipped words carried more weight than a speech.

"Twelve." Jorgen swallowed. "Twelve damn years old."

Grief ran between them like a river under stone, unspoken but there all the same. The cavern's soft light made the pool shimmer, a quiet, living thing in a world that kept grinding lives apart. It only made the memory of what had been taken feel sharper.

After a long time, Knight cleared his throat. "We fight for what's left," he said. It wasn't a question.

Jorgen grunted, low and steady. "For the girl. For Bradley." His gaze slid from Pinky's sleeping shape to the tangle of bodies where the others lay. "Maybe for a shot at something that looks like peace. If that's still a thing."

Their words lingered and settled, another layer on top of all the others they carried. Two men—one grizzled, one still in his prime—sat shoulder to shoulder, both carved up by different wars, both choosing to keep standing anyway. Whatever else they were, they shared that.

They kept watch at the edge of the shimmering pool, rifles across their knees, eyes tracking the slow play of light and shadow on the far walls. For a few hours under the fungal glow, the horrors above and below felt distant. Not gone, but held at bay. Jorgan didn't expect peace for himself, but maybe the young'uns could see something close to it.

*** 

When the next shift came, Alysha and Karl took their turn.

The cavern hummed around them in its own quiet way. The blue-green light painted the stone in soft gradients, casting faint halos around each patch of fungus and turning every drip of water into a tiny flash. That slow, steady life made Karl's skin prickle. This was stone, but not the kind he knew—too alive, too old.

227

Alysha stood a little apart, slim frame outlined in the glow. Stillness seemed to cling to her; she didn't fidget, didn't pace. She watched the tunnels with the same calm she'd shown under the collapsing ceiling, as if the dark was something she understood better than the light.

"You don't sleep much," Karl said. His voice rumbled out, cutting across the drip and distant echo.

She looked at him, those unsettling blue eyes catching the dim light. "Sleep is for the untroubled," she said. Her tone was soft, almost absent. "There are echoes here. Old ones. This world beneath the world remembers."

A shiver walked up Karl's spine—the old dwarven respect for deep places tangling with a miner's suspicion of anything he couldn't measure with tools and calluses. "Reminds you of home, then?" he asked, a hint of challenge under the grit.

For the first time, something eased in her gaze.

"Not the Arnasta you would know," Alysha said. "Not halls of hammered steel and the ring of forge-fire." A ghost of a smile touched her mouth. "My home was greener. Pyrefly Marsh, at the edge of Sateria. The hum of wings at dusk, the smell of damp earth, and the glow of moon tulips…"

Karl grunted, trying to reconcile the image in his head—fog-wrapped marshes in northeastern Sateria—with the blade-slim warrior at his side. It didn't fit, not at first glance. But he'd seen the way she moved under falling stone. There was steel under that reed-straight frame.

"Suli, then," he said, matter-of-fact. His thumb brushed along the intricate carvings on her blade, feeling the shallow grooves. "Not like us. Not born with a mountain sitting on your skull."

Alysha's fingers came to rest on the weapon beside his, touch light, almost protective. "The echoes are different under your cities," she murmured. "All that forged iron. The heartbeat of stone. Creation humming in the bones of the world." She tipped her chin toward the dark beyond the fungal glow. "Here, older things breathe. Stranger ones. The marsh had its whispers too, if you knew how to stand still long enough."

Karl found himself listening harder than he'd meant to. There was more to her than the blade and the haunted eyes— something that rhymed with his own sense of the deep, even if the notes were different.

"Why'd you leave?" he asked.

Her gaze slid back to the pool. The light caught in her eyes and didn't quite reach the shadows behind them. "They came," she said quietly. "Humans. Machines. Fire." She swallowed once. "There was a lot of noise. A lot of blood. I ran. Hid in the reeds until the smoke stopped. When I went back…" Her jaw tightened. "There was nothing left to go back to."

For the first time, the shape of the pain behind her calm made sense to him. She wasn't just some hedge-warrior with a trick blade—she'd been put through the same kind of forge his people used on steel.

"The surface," Karl grunted, "isn't short on monsters."

"Different faces," Alysha agreed, bitterness threading her voice. "Same hunger. They burn, they take, they leave scars and call it progress."

The cavern settled around them again. Dripping water. The soft pulse of fungal light. The weight of too many dead places neither of them would see again. Karl's eyes drifted to the sleeping shapes nearby—humans who had put their lives in the hands of a dwarf and a Suli with every reason in the world to hate their kind. He wondered, briefly, how far that trust could stretch before something inside one of them finally tore.

For the moment, the lines between them blurred. Dwarf and Suli, iron and sorcery—none of it mattered as much as the fact they were still breathing and still facing the same dark.

Karl drew in a breath that tasted of damp stone and distant water. "The forge-city of Arnasta isn't much to look at from the outside," he said, voice softening despite himself. "But when you're in it…you've got the clang of hammers all day, the heat of the forges, veins of ore singing under your feet. Rock above, rock below. Feels like being held. Until it decides it's had enough of you."

He spoke of the mines without boast, just a steady respect—for the narrow shafts, the sudden shifts in the stone, the way a misread echo could drop a ceiling on your head. He admitted, almost sheepishly, to the itch that had finally driven him topside: the urge to see skies that weren't carved, to trade good dwarven work for strange things made by stranger hands.

Alysha listened, eyes on the glowing fungus clinging to the walls. In her stillness he felt a recognition, an understanding of living in a world that was beautiful and merciless in the same breath. Different soil, different ghosts—but the same hard bargain with the places that had made them.

\*\*\*

By the time the others started to stir, the cavern smelled more like a real camp than an alien oasis.

Alysha and Karl had already been and come back, their boots damp, hands slick with eel-mucus. Now they worked side by side over a small, carefully banked fire, movements practiced and efficient as they split the long, pale bodies, stripped guts into a neat pile, and skewered the meat on improvised spits. Fat hissed as it dripped onto hot stone. The scent of roasting fish—oily, rich, edged with smoke—curled through the cold air and wrapped itself around the sleepers, dragging them up from whatever bad dreams had claimed them.

Pinky woke laughing.

She slid free from under Jorgen's coat and made straight for the pool, splashing her bare feet in the shallows. Her hands chased the darting silver shapes just under the surface, fingers splaying as the fish skipped away in sudden bursts of light. Jorgen trailed after her to the edge and dropped into a squat, the cavern's glow softening the hard planes of his face. In its wash, the lines around his eyes looked less like scars and more like something gentler, worn by time instead of violence.

Knight eased himself upright against a smooth slab of rock with a sharp exhale he tried to hide. Every shift pulled at bruised ribs and muscle, but even hurting he refused to stay flat and not doing something. His gaze kept swinging between Pinky's chaos at the pool and Mustang's chaos a few meters away.

Mustang sat cross-legged in a halo of scavenged tech, hunched over like a penitent at a shrine. Dead circuits, cracked lenses, warped housings—the wreckage of three different systems piled in front of him. Sparks spat occasionally as he bridged

231

contacts, each flare met with a muttered curse or, sometimes, a low, satisfied grunt when something gave him a hint of life.

Breakfast didn't last long. There wasn't much to go around, but hot protein and salt went a long way in quieting the worst of the shakes. They ate perched on rocks or crouched by the fire, fingers greasy, saying little. The pool's light shimmered up at them, making everything look oddly peaceful—if you pretended the tunnels behind them didn't exist.

Afterward, they drifted into a loose circle near the water's edge —a quiet council.

"We stay here," Knight said. His voice was rough, but the certainty under it was solid. "I need time to get back on my feet. Mustang needs time to make miracles out of trash. We've got clean water, protein that swims up to say hello. That's more than we've had anywhere else."

Karl nodded, bracing his hands on his knees as he leaned forward. "Old cuts branch out from this pocket," he said. "Natural ones. Seen three already." His beard twitched as he frowned toward the shadowed exits. "Could be a warren down here. Might find a way out. Might find something worse. Either way, no harm in catching our breath before we poke our noses in."

"Pinky needs it," Jorgen added, not taking his eyes off the girl as she tried to coax one of the braver fish into nibbling her fingers. Her laughter bounced around the cavern, bright and strangely clean. "Hell, we all do."

Bradley let his gaze move around the ring of them—Knight propped but present, Karl's steady bulk, Alysha with her blade across her knees, Mustang already half turned back toward his pile of parts, Jorgen and Pinky framed by that impossible pool.

A handful of broken people and one very strange kid, carved out of different worlds and shoved together beneath the earth. Somehow, they were still here.

"All right," he said. The word felt heavier than it should. "We rest. We regroup. But we don't plant roots. Mustang—whatever you can squeeze out of that mess…"

"I'm on it." Mustang cut in, a specter of old energy in his eyes. "Eye, ear, spark, I'll take whatever I can get. Anything's better than bare hands."

A thin thread of order stitched itself through the next stretch of time. He wouldn't call it normal, or safe, but it became a routine.

Karl vanished into the tunnels in measured bursts—never long enough to worry them, but long enough to come back dusted with damp grit, muttering about side pockets and deadfalls. He scratched marks into the rock with a shard of metal, crude maps that only he truly understood, glancing back at the fungus-lit chamber each time like he was making sure it was still there.

Knight started the slow war of healing. With Pinky as his self-appointed drill sergeant, there was nothing gentle about it. She would toss pebbles at him in lopsided arcs, demanding he catch them with either hand. Then she'd plant herself in front of him and insist he "walk proper," fingers hooked in his belt as if she could drag him upright by will alone. Every overreach sent a flash of pain across his features he tried to swallow. Bradley and Jorgen traded looks over her head—equal parts worry and reluctant approval. Knight needed the push. What was left of their med-kit was a sad joke; if his body didn't do most of the work, nothing would.

Pinky turned the cavern into a kingdom.

She named the bolder fish first—the one with the torn fin, the one that stayed close to the rocks. That one was Queen, that one Scout, that one Sir Bubbles for reasons she never explained. She built stories around them in a constant murmur, tales of underwater cities and glowing crowns, her voice threading through the drip of water and the occasional clank of metal from Mustang's work area. The sound was too bright for this place and exactly what it needed.

Mustang became the other constant.

He knelt in his circle of busted equipment until his legs went numb, shoulders hunched, fingers blackened with burned insulation. Curses came first, low and inventive as he pried fused parts apart or watched a promising circuit die under his hands. But every so often, his tone shifted: a sharp, startled bark of laughter when a patch job stuck, a pleased hum when a fragment of holo flickered to life over a lens. Nothing that resembled a full system yet, but each tiny success was a wedge hammered under the weight pressing down on them. Proof that the world outside this cave still existed in copper traces and half-charged capacitors.

Bradley watched it all from the edge of the pool or from a perch near the fire, the cavern breathing around them. For the first time since they'd gone underground, the future didn't feel entirely like a straight drop. There were forks now—risks, dangers—but also chances. That was enough to hang onto, for as long as the glow held and the stone stayed where it was.

Bradley peeled back bandages with careful fingers, nose wrinkling at the sharp tang of antiseptic over damp stone and fish smoke. The bruising along Knight's ribs had gone from ugly black to a mottled yellow-violet, but the swelling had eased. No angry heat, no bad smell. For down here, with what little they had, that counted as a win.

The salvaged weapons array was gone from his own kit now, passed over to Mustang piece by piece. In their current state, the squad's rifles were just dead-weight—brittle stocks and cracked housings. If anyone could coax a charge or a shot out of the mess, it was Mustang. Bradley stepped in only when asked, offering an extra pair of hands or another way to route a cable. The rest of the time he stayed out of the lieutenant's way and pretended the hollow feeling in his gut wasn't the instinctive dread of facing whatever came next with nothing but metal clubs.

When the walls felt too close and the weight of decisions started to grind him down, he found Jorgen.

The old bounty hunter didn't say much. Never had. But he'd tilt his head toward an empty spot by the pool, and Bradley would drop down beside him, letting the glow play over their boots while Pinky narrated the adventures of Sir Bubbles and Queen Fin. Jorgen's encouragement came in short, rough-edged pieces—a grunt that meant *you did right*, a flat "he'll pull through" when Bradley's eyes kept straying to Knight. It wasn't much by normal standards, but down here it landed like full speeches.

Alysha kept to the edges.

She'd put her hood up again, the greenish fabric of her forest cloak swallowing most of her outline. She moved along the cavern's perimeter, always within earshot—the soft scuff of her boots on rock, the faint jingle of metal at her belt—but rarely within arm's reach. When Bradley looked up to track her, he'd sometimes catch her standing very still, half turned away, eyes fixed on the pool.

More often than not, her gaze settled on Pinky.

There was nothing predatory in it, Just a quiet, raw sadness that didn't match the hard efficiency she'd shown under fire. The girl would be laughing at some private joke with the fish, water up to her knees, and Alysha would watch with an expression that looked too old for her face—like someone listening to a song they hadn't heard since before everything burned.

Bradley had been too busy counting threats and rations to put it together until then.

They were all spinning in their own storms. Knight hiding pain behind discipline. Mustang holding himself together with projects and profanity. Jorgen balancing one kid he'd lost against two he'd somehow picked up. Karl walking the stone to keep from thinking about what lay above it. Alysha carrying a marsh full of ghosts behind her eyes.

He wasn't any different. He just wore his whirlpool in checklists and patrol routes.

Watching Alysha watch Pinky, the realization settled over him like the cool air off the pool: this wasn't just about surviving the reactor, or The Foundation, or whatever had carved these tunnels. It was six broken edges and one strange, stubborn child trying not to cut each other while they figured out how to keep moving.

***

Each day settled heavier on Bradley's shoulders.

The danger, the decisions, the knowledge that if he broke, they all broke with him—none of that was covered in training sims or field manuals. He took what scraps of calm he could find, shallow breaths grabbed between waves.

One of those scraps was Jorgen.

Bradley found him perched on a smooth rock by the pool, boots planted wide, eyes fixed on the clear water. Pinky was curled at his side, head pillowed against his ribs, asleep or close enough to it.

"I need to borrow some of your coffee," Bradley said.

His voice came out rough with fatigue.

Jorgen blinked, dragged back from wherever his head had gone. "What makes you think I've got any?" he rumbled, suspicion automatic.

Bradley almost smiled. In a world that had come unhinged, Jorgen's reflexive grumpiness stayed nailed in place. "Because you," he said, "are exactly the kind of bastard who'd ride out the end of the world with a secret stash. If anyone here walked into hell with their vices intact, it's you."

A flash of surprise crossed the old man's eyes, quick as a spark. Then his mouth tugged into a broad, uneven grin that pulled one out of Bradley in return. With a grunt, Jorgen dug into the depths of his pack and came up with a battered tin that had seen more years than most recruits.

Gratitude hit Bradley harder than he expected.

He took the tin like it was something fragile, not dented metal, and set to work. The scrape of beans under the improvised grinder, the first sharp threads of scent twisting into the cold, damp air—it all felt like ritual. A tiny piece of the old world, stubbornly refusing to die down here.

By the time he poured the first cup, the cavern smelled faintly of home: bitter, burnt, familiar.

Jorgen accepted his mug with another grunt, fingers closing around it as if someone might change their mind. He didn't say thanks; he didn't have to. The way his shoulders eased as he took the first sip said enough.

Bradley poured two more, hands shaking just a little from exhaustion and the cramped work of grinding. He passed them off without fanfare, then found himself turning toward the edge of the camp where Alysha sat apart.

She was half-turned to the wall, hood up, one hand resting on stone as if listening to it. Her eyes were distant, shadows pooled deep around them.

"Coffee?" Bradley said.

The word sounded almost ridiculous in this place of glowing fungus and carved rock—as out of place as a sunrise.

Alysha looked over, surprise slipping clean through her usual guarded mask. For a moment she just studied the steaming cup, then took it with both hands, careful, as if it might vanish.

She lifted it to her mouth. As the bitter warmth touched her lips, something shifted in her expression—less hard, less distant. Not quite a smile, but there and gone, like she was tasting a memory as much as the drink.

Hope, Bradley realized, didn't always show up in grand speeches or clean victories. It hid in small, stupid things—a cup of coffee in a cave, a kid laughing at fish. His job wasn't just to keep them alive . It was to hunt those moments down and feed them, so they had something left to fight with tomorrow.

"Thank you," he said.

The words came out quieter than orders ever did. He took a small sip, letting the bitter heat burn a line down his tongue and throat. "For what you've done. Getting us this far."

Alysha watched him over the rim of her cup. In the bioluminescent wash, her green eyes looked almost backlit. "You're welcome," she said. No softening, no extra weight. "But it serves me too."

Honest, at least. A clean reminder of what they were—an alliance of overlapping interests, not some storybook warband. She moved by rules he barely understood, pulled by loyalties and losses he'd only glimpsed.

He held her gaze. The mug was warm between his hands, an anchor in the cold. "Still," he said, "we're tied together now. If one of us slips, we all pay. That's risky for everyone."

For a heartbeat, he saw something shift behind her eyes. Not agreement, exactly, but recognition. Respect, maybe.

Silence settled, but it wasn't knife-edged anymore. Water dripped somewhere beyond the pool; the faint bubbling of one of Pinky's "royal subjects" broke the surface and vanished again. Bradley found himself talking—lighter than mission reports, heavier than small talk.

He told her about Jorgen's tin. How the old man acted like generosity was a disease but had still handed it over without real hesitation. How the first curl of coffee scent had hit like a hand on his shoulder from another life.

Alysha listened, head tipped slightly, as if trying to fit this into some framework she knew.

"There was a rite," she said at last. She tasted the words as she chose them. "A shared drink. Bitter. Before the hunt. Before battle." Her gaze dropped briefly to the cup. "To bind the group to the same fate. To admit you might die together."

Bradley nodded. That he understood. "Warrior's brew," he said.

That drew the smallest ghost of a smile from her, there and gone in an instant.

He noticed her hair when she shifted, turning a little toward the pool.

It caught the glow strangely. What had been a clean, pale blonde now carried a faint copper at the roots, threads of darker color that hadn't been there before. At first he blamed the fungus—this place played hell with shadows—but the more he looked, the more he saw it: a seam of new color running out from her scalp, like something bleeding through from beneath.

"Your hair…" he started, then hesitated. The question felt weirdly intimate out here, a hand reaching toward something he couldn't define.

Alysha's eyes narrowed a fraction. "What about it?"

He shifted his grip on the cup, searching for the least intrusive way to say it and failing. "It's…changing," he said. "There's copper in it now. At the roots." He made a vague motion near his own temple, hoping it helped.

She reached up, fingers threading through the pale strands, brushing them forward into her line of sight. For a second her expression went blank.

"A trick of the light," she said. Too quickly. "This place bends color. The glow—" she gestured at the walls "—it lies."

But something unsettled had crept into her voice. The mask was still there, just thinner. Bradley's gut told him the light wasn't the problem.

"Does it hurt?" he asked. It came out softer than he'd meant, stripped of command.

She met his gaze squarely then. For a heartbeat the distance in her expression cracked, and he saw the edges of whatever storm was chewing at her from inside and the green starburst taking over her irises.

"Not like a wound," she said finally, barely above a whisper. "But...yes." Her fingers caught on a strand where the copper showed strongest, rolling it between thumb and forefinger as if it were foreign. "It feels like something is being pulled out, slowly." She exhaled. "Like being...bled from a place you can't bandage."

Alysha, for all her uncanny edges and blade-born poise, wasn't outside this place's reach. Whatever was crawling through her hair from the roots up could just as easily be working on the rest of them. The question sat between them, unspoken and cold: had they traded one kind of death for another by hiding here?

He could push. Ask what "bled" meant. Demand more than fragments. But the set of her shoulders, the way her hand stayed on that copper strand, told him exactly how far he'd get

—cryptic answers, deflection, and another wall. They didn't have the luxury of that argument right now.

"It's…striking," he said instead, forcing a thin edge of lightness into his tone. "Suits you."

The words tasted flimsy against what she'd just admitted.

Alysha's mouth twitched, almost into something sharper. "Perhaps," she said. The dryness was back in her voice, pulled over whatever she'd let slip. "It is a strange thing, though. Watching yourself change and not understanding why."

The bitter scent of coffee still hung in the air between them. The cavern seemed to draw in around it, the soft drip of water turning into a slow count they both ignored. Bradley stared into the bottom of his cup, watching the last dark trace slide along the metal as he tilted it. His mind ran in tight circles— radiation, fungus, something in the rock, in the water. All guesses. No answers.

He felt the responsibility like a hand on the back of his neck, pushing.

"You know," he said, breaking the silence, "you can sit with the rest of us. It's not healthy, being out here on your own all the time."

The words came from the same place as his orders, but without the bark. He'd seen too many people fold inward under strain, carving themselves off to keep the others "safe." It never worked. Isolation just made you easy to break.

Alysha's eyes widened a fraction, surprise cracking her calm. It was gone almost immediately, replaced by the familiar hardness.

"I am where I need to be," she said. The curtness couldn't quite hide the edge of something else—self-directed anger, maybe. "Birds fly with their own kind for a reason."

He heard the resignation under it. The way she clung to the idea of distance like armor. Different flock, different sky. Easier to accept being alone than risk losing another nest.

"We're safer together," Bradley said. He leaned forward slightly, elbows on his knees, not looking away. "We need you."

He felt the word *we* land between them. Not a tactic, not a scrap of diplomacy—just the truth as he saw it. Whatever this was, it lived or died as a group.

She held his gaze. Something uncertain flicked through those sharp green eyes. Under the cloak, under the blade, under the copper seeping through her hair, she was still human in the ways that mattered—tired, hurt, balancing on the same edge as the rest of them.

"Perhaps," she said at last.

It came out more as a sigh than agreement, but the resistance in it had thinned. She didn't move toward the others—not yet— but she didn't turn away either.

Down here, where victories were measured in inches and breaths, Bradley took it for what it was. A small shift. A hairline crack in the isolation.

Bradley rose, setting the empty cup aside. The unease didn't leave, but he shoved it down where all the other worries lived and focused on the one fight he could actually step into.

He held out his hand.

No speeches, no orders—just a palm offered between them. It wasn't about hauling her upright. It was an admission that he saw the weight she carried, and a quiet promise that she didn't have to drag it alone.

Alysha just stared at it. Distrust and surprise moved across her face, old reflexes trying to slam the door shut. Then, slowly, she lifted her own hand and set it in his. Her skin was cool; her grip, when it closed, had the compact strength of someone very familiar with blades and bad odds.

He pulled her up, careful not to make it look like help she could refuse later. Enough pressure to steady, not enough to trap.

Something loosened in her expression—almost relief, almost grief—gone before he could pin it down. The fortress was still standing, but he felt one stone shift in the wall.

"There's strength in numbers," he said. His voice came out rougher than he liked. "And right now…" He searched for the right phrase and settled for the honest one. "We need every scrap of strength we can get."

Alysha met his gaze. The sharp greening of her eyes had lost some of its edge, tempered by the simple fact that they both knew exactly how bad things were.

"You might be wrong," she said. The defensiveness was still there, but muted. "My strength could be as dangerous as anything we're running from."

"Then we deal with that too," Bradley answered, not backing off. "Together." He let the corner of his mouth twitch up. "Besides, if we don't get those comms working, Mustang's going to blow a gasket. And I'm not fighting that monster by myself."

That finally pulled a real reaction out of her. The smallest ghost of a smile curved her lips.

"No," she said. "I suppose you're not."

**CHAPTER THIRTEEN**

Bradley and Alysha were halfway back to the warm blur of light that marked their camp when the cavern jumped.

A sharp *crack* split the quiet, ricocheting off the stone like a gunshot in a bunker. It was followed at once by a high, hoarse chorus that could only be Pinky trying to yell a battle cry and an anthem at the same time.

Bradley and Alysha traded a look, then hurried the last stretch, boots scraping over damp rock.

They rounded the bend into chaos.

Mustang knelt in the middle of it, coated from hairline to boots in a fine dusting of tech grime. Bits of wire, scorched plating, and gutted housings littered the ground around him like the aftermath of a small, very specific explosion. In his hands he cradled Knight's blaster, holding it upright like a holy relic.

Knight leaned against a nearby rock, weight carefully off his bad side. His face was caught somewhere between stunned and amused, eyes a little too wide to be fully confident in what he was seeing.

Pinky bounced in place, bare feet skidding on the stone, fists pumping as she shrieked encouragements that made no sense at all.

"IT'S ALIVE!" Mustang bellowed, raising the weapon overhead with a theatrical flourish. "Behold the birth of Frankengun! Or—wait—Lazar-blaster? No, that's awful, give me a second—"

Alysha, all composure again, took in the mess with a single cool sweep of her gaze. One eyebrow arched. "And this… scientific achievement required no magic?" she asked, a faint edge of amusement tugging at her mouth.

Bradley couldn't hold it in. Laughter ripped out of him, raw and welcome. The knot in his chest loosened a notch.

"That involved fire," he said, stepping in to clap Mustang on the shoulder, "and an unholy amount of swearing. Don't lie."

Mustang preened, shoulders squaring as if he were on a stage instead of standing ankle-deep in broken parts. "Genius is a messy process," he informed them. "Sometimes it requires a little…thermal persuasion to convince fried circuits they want to live again."

Knight finally found his voice, rumbling a half-growl, half-laugh. "If that thing blows up in my hands, I'm decking you," he warned.

Pinky latched onto Bradley's leg like a limpet, staring up with wide, shining eyes. "Can we shoot targets now?" she burst out. "Rocks? Mushrooms? Or maybe a fish—just a little one—"

Bradley dropped into a crouch so they were eye to eye. "These are for keeping us safe," he said gently. "Only when things are really bad. That's what they're for."

Her face fell for a heartbeat, then bounced back the way it always did. "But we can still practice, right?" she insisted. "I wanna be the *best* safe-keeper."

"We'll see," he said, which in Pinky's world translated to *eventually* and kept her from arguing.

Mustang, riding the high, swung the newly resurrected blaster up into demonstration position, the weapon a patchwork of original parts and whatever he'd bullied into cooperating. The charge indicator stuttered but steadied. He grinned like a madman.

Alysha's dry commentary and Bradley's rough laughter moved through the camp like clean air, cutting into the stale fear that had been hanging there for days.

Then bootsteps hammered against stone.

Jorgen and Karl came barreling around the curve of the tunnel, weapons half-raised, eyes hard and searching. They took in the scene—the smoke, the weapon, Pinky's wild bouncing—with a single sweep.

"Trouble?" Jorgen barked.

Mustang, never one to waste an audience, flicked a glance at Jorgen and Karl, then lobbed Knight his blaster.

"Trouble?" he scoffed. "Please. You're looking at a *breakthrough*. Witness the glory of reverse-engineered genius."

He pivoted and, with a smaller flourish, tossed Bradley his sidearm.

"Yours too. Give it a spin. My rifle still needs sweet-talking, but the basics are live."

Bradley caught the weapon. The familiar weight settled into his palm. The tiny indicator on the side glowed a steady, reassuring line. A jolt of adrenaline cut through the fatigue, snapping his brain from hiding and hoping to armed and ready.

Across the way, Jorgen's weathered face creased into a wolfish grin. Approval flickered behind the old man's eyes.

Karl ran his hand along the cavern wall in an absent habit, eyes on the pistol. "That's good work," he admitted. The respect in his voice was reluctant but undeniable. "Didn't think you'd get them singing again."

They slid back into something like a training ground after that.

Pinky, quick to adapt, converted her earlier battle cries into target practice orders, pointing at rocks and broken stalactites with grand, sweeping gestures. "That one's a monster! No, *that* one. Pew it! *Pew it better!*"

Blaster fire answered her. Bradley and Knight took turns, spacing out their shots, reacquainting themselves with recoil and trigger break. The bolts slammed into stone with satisfying thuds, chips skittering across the cavern floor. Muscle memory came back fast—stances adjusting, breathing syncing to each squeeze. Out here, under rock and fungus-light, it felt almost like a live-fire exercise from another life, twisted but familiar.

Jorgen watched from a nearby ledge, arms folded, expression gruff. Pride still managed to leak through in the way his mouth twitched at a particularly tight grouping. Even favoring one side, Knight moved like the soldier he was. Bradley's shots grew smoother, more confident, each impact an unspoken refusal to roll over for whatever waited in the dark.

Time blurred—marked by Pinky's increasingly absurd scenario-building and Jorgen's occasional low-voiced critique —until Mustang finally rose from his rat's nest of parts, eyes shining.

"Finally," he announced, lifting his rifle reverently. "She's officially ready for her debut. Now all we need is a suitably dramatic target."

Bradley couldn't help grinning. "Pretty sure Pinky has a list. I just don't trust her aim yet."

"Nonsense," Mustang sniffed, mock-offended. "This lady is a precision work of art, not some brute-force cannon. And the best part—" he added, with a conspiratorial wink, "we're never running out of ammo again."

That pulled the attention of everyone within earshot.

Knight raised an eyebrow. "Yeah, that part. I was going to ask how you planned on charging the mags when we're under a couple hundred meters of rock."

Mustang, sensing his moment, shifted into lecture mode. "Simple," he said, tapping the modified butt of the rifle. "Molecular deconstruction module. Converts matter to pure energy on the fly. You feed it mass, it gives you a firing solution. Rocks, dirt, whatever…" He gestured toward the cavern around them. "Congratulations, the world is now your ammunition crate. Courtesy of the Foundation weapon array Bradley lugged down here with us."

Karl's eyes tracked the rifle, then the stone overhead, then back to Mustang. His jaw worked once.

"And this," he said slowly, "actually works?"

Mustang puffed out his chest. "Only one way to find out."

He plucked a pebble from Pinky's carefully sorted pile, thumbed open a narrow port in the rifle's stock, and dropped the stone inside. A faint hum rose in pitch, the modified butt of the gun pulsing with contained light.

Then he shouldered it, sighted lazily on a gnarled knot of rock across the cavern, and squeezed the trigger.

The shot cracked through the air like lightning from a bottle. The targeted stone, roughly fist-sized, didn't just chip—it *vanished*, exploding into a spray of grit and molten fragments. Sparks flared bright white and gold against the blue-green glow, briefly painting the cavern in stark shadows.

Pinky shrieked in delight and launched into a fresh barrage of improvised war cries, already lunging for another pebble.

Bradley looked surprised giving way to wary curiosity. They'd both learned long ago there was no point interrogating Mustang's process. Results were the only metric that mattered, and for better or worse, this one had just lit up the room.

Mustang spun, riding the high, and pressed modified magazines into their hands. "Here," he said, eyes dancing. "Field test time. You can shower me with praise later." He jerked his chin at Bradley. "And yeah, good call on that weapon array. Half this brilliance came out of its guts."

Warmth cut through Bradley's lingering tension. For all Mustang's showboating, there was genuine respect under the jab. It landed like confirmation of what Bradley already knew: none of them were getting out of this without every set of hands pulling weight.

Knight turned the magazine over, the faintly glowing core pulsing like a caged heartbeat. "Containment field?" he asked, thumb tracing the seam along its edge.

"Exactly," Mustang said, pleased. "Keeps the wild stuff corralled until you tell it to misbehave."

Jorgen let out a low whistle. "Damn clever," he remarked. "Didn't think I'd live to see the day you could shove random junk in your butt and come out with a loaded gun."

That earned an honest laugh from Mustang and a couple of sidelong winces from the more literal-minded.

Karl shuffled closer, the stone-dust crunching under his boots. He bent to inspect the rifle, his scarred fingers ghosting over the new housings and jury-rigged conduit. "Efficient," he grunted. "In theory. Question is how long it lasts."

Mustang's grin shifted from wild to intent. "Long enough," he said. "Those array components? Older design, but they were playing in a bigger league. We lose a bit to heat, sure, but the tradeoff is no more praying for a charging station." His dark eyes sparked. "Matter in, shot out. As long as we've got rocks and trash, we've got ammunition."

Pinky tugged hard on Bradley's sleeve, eyes wide and shining. "Can I shoot now?" she begged, bouncing in place. "Please? I wanna make something explode like Mustang did!"

Bradley dropped into a crouch. "Not today," he said, letting a smile soften the refusal. "These are still too touchy. But soon? We'll set up a real range, and you can practice for when it counts. Deal?"

"Okay! I'll be the *best* safe-keeper," she declared, already scanning the ground for more "ammo."

But over the next few days the cavern did become a range.

Shots thundered in measured bursts, bolts slamming into chosen targets with impacts that shook dust from the ceiling. Bradley and Knight fell into old patterns—stance, breath, squeeze, check—pushing themselves until their muscles burned and their shoulders ached. It was a familiar pain, the kind that came with purpose instead of pointless strain.

Mustang moved between them, tweaking field strengths, watching discharge patterns, scribbling frantic notes on a battered slate. Every so often he'd bark, "Hold fire!" and snatch a weapon to check a readout, nodding or swearing under his breath before handing it back.

Pinky took her new title seriously. She scurried along the edges of the cavern, collecting pebbles and bits of rubble, organizing them into neat rows by size and "explodiness," announcing each new category with great importance. "Big boom. Medium boom. Sparkly boom."

But as the session wore on, another reality crept into focus.

The guns got hot. Not just warm from use, but *hot*—the containment cores flaring a little too brightly, the metal around them radiating heat against gloved palms. More than once, Bradley felt an uncomfortable prickle along his fingers and called a halt, setting the weapon on the rock until the hum subsided and the glow dimmed.

Knight did the same without being told, jaw tight as he flexed stiff hands in the cooler air.

Between volleys, they found themselves forced to step back, weapons resting on stone while the new tech bled off excess heat. The cavern filled with the smell of ozone and scorched dust.

"Damn," Mustang muttered, dragging the back of his wrist across a sweat-streaked brow. "Thermodynamics. Always the one to ruin a good party."

The last shot still rang faintly in the stone. Heat shimmered off the rifle's stock; the air around the muzzle had that sharp, metallic tang that came after too many discharges in too little time.

Knight thumbed the release and eased the modified magazine out with care, like he was handling an unstable grenade. The core inside glowed a sullen, angry orange, light pulsing against his scarred knuckles. "Overheating's not a footnote," he said. "We lean on these too long, they'll cook themselves—or us."

Bradley nodded, feeling the same knot of worry tighten under his ribs. The rush of getting their guns back bled into something more sober as he watched thin tendrils of heat haze curl off the vents. "We'll need a workaround," he said. His gaze slid up to the cavern ceiling, tracking the drips and the slow swirl of dust, then back to Mustang. "Some way to bleed that off before it bites us."

"I'd need a real heat sink for that," Mustang replied, frustration edging his voice. He snapped the rifle's panels shut with a little more force than necessary. "We're swimming in rock and fungus, not radiators. Down here, this is the best we're getting unless the mountain's hiding a fully stocked lab behind Door Number Three."

Jorgen, who'd been leaning on a boulder watching the whole display with his arms folded, gave a low whistle. "Never a dull moment," he said. He pushed himself upright, joints popping, and reached for Knight's crutch where it rested against the wall. "Come on, soldier. Show time's over."

Knight slid the hot mag back into the rig with care, then took the crutch. With Jorgen braced at his side, he started the slow walk back toward the fire and the pool, each step a stiff, deliberate refusal to stay down.

Bradley watched them go, the chemical light from the bioluminescent fungi painting their retreat in muted blues and greens. The weapons in their hands ran hot, their escape routes were guesswork, and the world above them wanted them dead —or worse. But every problem they tripped over, they'd carved into something they could use. Imperfect guns, limping strides, jury-rigged tech;

It wasn't much. It was still forward.

\*\*\*

The fire threw restless shadows across the cavern walls, making the stone seem to breathe. Smoke from the cookfire curled up into the dark, threading with the damp, mineral smell of the underground and the oily tang of roasting fish. It was a strange mix.

Mustang hummed tunelessly as he worked, sitting cross-legged in his usual nest of parts. The glow of his multi-tool flickered across his lenses, turning them into shifting squares of light. Each brief spark was a promise: connection, signal, some thin cord back to the world above instead of this buried, forgotten place.

Jorgen sat a little apart, cradling his cup as if it held something rarer than coffee. The steam rising from it mingled with the smoke, softening the lines in his weathered face.

Pinky had finally burned through her last reserves. She lay curled beside him, cheek pillowed on his leg, one small fist still full of pebbles—the "ammo" she'd spent the afternoon sorting for their monster-rock war.

Near the fire, Knight tended the skewered fish. He turned each spit with the focus of a man who refused to be useless, even with half his body protesting. To anyone else it was just cooking; Bradley saw the same stubbornness Knight put into holding a firing line now aimed at something as simple as not burning dinner.

Bradley leaned back until the rough stone took his weight. It dug between his shoulder blades, a far cry from the upholstered chairs and polished floors his past life had held, but that world felt like someone else's history now. He let his gaze move around the circle: Mustang's restless energy; Jorgen's quiet, almost grudging ease; Knight's squared jaw and careful movements; Pinky, small and limp and utterly trusting; Karl with his steady presence and scuffed hands; Alysha—

Alysha was the one who caught him.

She seemed to relax, and moved closer. Cloak still on, blade within reach, but her shoulders were lower, her posture less coiled. She sat near enough to feel the heat of the fire, not hovering in the dark at the edge. For the first time since they'd met her, she looked less like a blade waiting to cut someone's throat and more like another tired fighter grabbing warmth while she could.

Karl felt it too. He leaned back beside her, the ghost of a smile easing his normally hard-set features. Exhaustion still dragged at him, but for the moment it sat behind his eyes instead of pulling him down. He'd walked the tunnels, gathered dried fungal stalks that passed as wood, brought back eels from some hidden side pool. They had food, a fire, and enough people awake to listen for trouble.

It wasn't victory. It wasn't the sky. But it was four stone walls, warmth, and breathing bodies in the same circle. Down here, that was its own kind of treasure.

The fire cracked, sending up a shower of sparks. For a while there was only the pop of fat in the flames, the occasional murmur, the soft drip of water somewhere in the dark.

Then the cavern exploded with sound.

A triumphant yell ripped across the chamber, followed by the clatter of metal on stone and what sounded suspiciously like Mustang attempting a victory dance in boots not meant for it.

Bradley jerked upright as Mustang sprang to his feet, both hands held high. In one of them, a pair of AR glasses gleamed faintly, their tiny status lights blinking steady green.

"They work! THEY WORK!" Mustang's voice reverberated off the stone, ragged with relief and sheer glee. "Two fully functional!" He waved one pair overhead, then shoved the other toward Bradley. "And look—"

He thrust a third set straight into Knight's hands.

"Targeting restored," Mustang crowed. "We have our eyes back."

For a second, Bradley just stared at the glasses, feeling their weight in his palms. The tiny hum of active circuits brushed his fingertips. Hope hit him like a physical thing—tight, sharp, electric. He let out a whoop that echoed nearly as loud as Mustang's.

Jorgen, startled out of his quiet by the outburst, barked a laugh and lifted his coffee in an unspoken toast, grin splitting his beard. The firelight caught on his teeth and the metal rim of the mug, turning the gesture into something bright in the dim cavern—one more small, stubborn flare against the dark.

Knight, still braced on his crutch, pushed away from the rock and limped toward the noise. "Let me see," he rasped, that old command edge flickering back into his eyes.

Mustang handed over a pair of glasses with an exaggerated bow. Knight slipped them on with slow, practiced care, thumb and forefinger making the tiny adjustments by muscle memory. A few grunts, a low string of numbers under his breath as he tested range and resolution followed. Then he gave a short, decisive nod.

"Not bad, Lieutenant," he rumbled at last. The respect was grudging, but real. "Not bad at all."

Even Alysha drifted closer from the edge of the firelight, drawn in despite herself. The bioluminescent glow turned her features sharper, her hood a dark halo. "What is it?" she asked, curiosity briefly softening her usual reserve.

Pinky shot upright like she'd been spring-loaded, pebbles scattering from her hands. "Are we playing a game?" she blurted. "Can I play too?"

Mustang, beaming, swept into a fast, sprawling explanation, hands carving shapes in the air. "Comms, sensor feeds, tactical overlays," he said. "And that's before I start bolting on upgrades. This is just baseline connectivity—wait until I get the rest of the suite running."

Bradley's mind snapped to the one question that had been gnawing at him since the glasses first blinked to life. "Can we access the hard drive from K-94?" he asked. The words came out harsher than he liked.

The bubble of celebration thinned.

Mustang's grin faltered as the implication landed. "Yeah," he said after a beat, voice dipping. "Should be able to jury-rig an interface. Drive's in here somewhere." He dropped to a crouch by his pack, shoving aside wires and casings with sudden focus.

Around the fire, glances passed like quiet signals. Hope and unease, both riding high. The drive had become easy to forget in the scramble to stay alive—a dead weight at the bottom of a bag. But it was still there.

Jorgen tipped the last of his coffee back and set the mug down with a small, decisive clink on stone. "No better time than now," he said. "Let's see what kind of nasties they buried with it."

Knight shifted, the leather of his brace creaking as he adjusted his stance. Even this deep, with fish crackling over the fire, a shiver ran through him. "Secrets," he said quietly. "Or a signed death warrant."

"We already cashed that," Mustang said without looking up. "This is just the fine print."

Pinky, picking up on the change in tone without understanding why, edged closer to Jorgen and wrapped both arms around his elbow. Alysha's posture tightened again, shoulders drawing in, eyes going sharp and watchful.

Mustang finally found the hard drive, a scarred block of metal and plastic, and set it by the fire. Cables snaked from it to a scratched interface plate, then up into the AR rig perched on his brow. He slipped one pair of glasses onto his face, the lenses flaring with faint overlays only he could see.

The cavern quieted. Fire popped, water dripped, and the soft hum of booting tech filled the spaces between.

Mustang's fingers moved through invisible menus, tapping and swiping at phantoms. Light played across his lenses, reflections of windows that weren't there. His usual smirk drained away by degrees, replaced by a hard, intent focus.

"All right," he said finally, voice low. "We've got directories. Where do we start?" He highlighted a column only he could see, shoulders tensing as he scrolled. "Project names. Codenames."

Bradley didn't have to think long. "Start with Ouroboros," he said. The name tasted like metal on his tongue.

Alysha's gaze flicked to him, then to Mustang. Her voice dropped to a murmur. "Ouroboros," she echoed. "The serpent that devours its own tail. A symbol of cycles. Of creation…and of destruction."

Mustang's voice thinned in the cavern as he read, each sentence landing like a blow.

"Project Ouroboros. Established 2101…" He swallowed, lip curling. "Primary objective: destabilize biological matter to… maximize caloric yield."

The fire popped. No one moved.

Jorgen's scowl deepened. "Fancy talk for grinding people into rations," he muttered. "Meat is meat to them."

Pinky shivered where she sat pressed to his side, fingers worrying at a pebble. Knight gave a short, contemptuous, humorless laugh.

"Dead bodies. Bio-waste. That's their solution?" he said. "Disgusting, but efficient. That's The Foundation all over."

Alysha said nothing. Her eyes drifted from the fire to the black throat of the tunnel and back again, as if she were listening for something else layered over Mustang's words.

Mustang flicked to the next entry. His tone flattened, going clinical to keep from shaking. "Companion Animal Ban of 2102…correlated as phase one. 'Initial biomass acquisition.'"

He stopped reading there. The implication didn't need help.

Bradley's fist cracked against the stone at his side, pain spiking up his arm. "So they started with pets," he said tightly. "Worked their way up to anything that couldn't fight back. Anything that could be tagged as 'waste.'"

Silence pressed in, thick and sour.

The fire's smoke seemed to turn rancid with it. Project Ouroboros stopped being a name and became a picture: vats, hooks, quiet rooms where the dead never left the system. Survival, profit, control—whatever excuse they'd told themselves didn't matter. All Bradley heard in it was *acceptable losses*.

"If this is what made it into the project logs..." Mustang shook his head. "We have no idea how deep the rot goes."

Alysha's voice cut through the crackle of the fire. Soft, but sharp enough to draw blood. "It is an abomination," she said. "That kind of hunger does not belong in the world. To do this to those outside their walls is evil enough. To feed upon their own..." She trailed off, jaw clenched.

The knowledge hung over them like a toxic fogbank. Stomachs churned; no one reached for the fish. Bradley looked at Pinky's small, trusting profile and felt something cold and steady ignite in his chest, fighting off the first wash of despair. At least Karl, snoring softly a little way off, had missed this. One less back to load it onto.

Guilt followed on the heels of that thought. It should've been *her* they'd spared. Not the dwarf. The child.

Jorgen tipped his mug back and gulped the last bitter dregs, face twisting. "Fuel for nightmares," he said. "But we still gotta sleep."

Even Mustang's usual spark had dulled. The glasses sat askew on his nose, the wash of scrolling data reflected in his eyes like distant fires. Whatever loyalty or numb resignation had kept him working for The Foundation before, it was gone; what remained was raw disgust and a self-directed fury that made his hands shake.

He knew he wouldn't sleep—didn't know if he would ever sleep again.

They parceled out the dark the way soldiers always did when there wasn't anything else to control. Knight, leaning heavier than he'd admit on his crutch, agreed to share first watch with Mustang and his new "eyes." Alysha took the second without hesitation, her blade already within reach. Bradley volunteered for third—those dead hours when the fire burned low and the mind did its worst work.

Jorgen and Pinky settled on a patch of moss, his leather satchel shoved under her head for a makeshift pillow. She curled against his chest, small hand fisted in his coat. His eyes stayed open longer than hers, staring into the shifting light, knowing exactly what waited for him when they finally shut.

The fire cracked, sending up a thin ribbon of sparks toward the unseen ceiling. Around it, they lay down one by one—not because the knowledge had grown lighter, but because this was what there was: a circle of heat, a handful of guns, a hard drive full of nightmares, and the simple, stubborn choice to be alive when the next watch began.

## CHAPTER FOURTEEN

The faint wash of AR light painted Mustang's face the color of cadaver, hollowing his eyes as he scrolled through the K-94 drive. Around him, the cavern had settled into its false night—low fire, soft snores, the drip of unseen water—but for Mustang there was only the sickly glow of menus and the steady flick of his fingers.

Project Serenity stopped its banality two lines in.

He skimmed, then slowed, then forced himself to read every word.

"…mass distribution vector…ration-based delivery… primary agent: Serenity, with variant formulations S-2 through S-9…"

The jargon was clinical, the intent anything but. Civilians. Issued food. Compliance baked into daily calories. The "subjugation of the populace" translated down into dosage charts and supply chains, cross-referenced with the ration program like it was just another logistics problem.

His stomach turned. He could almost taste the chalky tang of the gray goo they'd all grown up on.

He flipped past Serenity's appendices before he put his fist through the stone.

Project Spearhead scrolled up next, a handful of references snagging his attention in spite of himself—"localized temporal shear," "island anomaly," "civilian compartmentalization." An island stuck in its own stuttering time.

He bookmarked the directory with a twitch of his fingers and forced himself on. Curiosity could wait. This couldn't.

Project Godspear sat deeper in the tree, locked behind a higher clearance. The folder opened on a forest of dense notation, math and terminology that made even his well-trained brain feel half a step behind.

"Ascended entities…Well of Souls cross-reference… extradimensional resonance," he read under his breath, voice dry. "Sure. Why not."

He opened the first video file.

A man sat strapped to a chair in a sterile room, wires and leads running from his skin to a wall of equipment. Mustang recognized the old hardware, mid twentieth century stuff, all sharp edges and bulky housings. The prisoner's face was already wrong before he spoke—eyes unfocused, expression sliding like the muscles couldn't agree on who was driving.

The questions were mundane at first. Name. Origin. Symptom lists.

The answers weren't.

Voices collided in the man's throat—different cadences, different word choices, fragments that didn't fit together. He saw the moment one of the researchers realized it, saw the tilt of the head, the greedy spark behind the glass.

As the interview continued, the room seemed to tighten. The audio picked up soft, irregular taps Mustang first took for bad compression—until one of the scientists turned, frowning at the wall.

Knocks. Behind the camera. In the ceiling. Places nothing should be moving.

Lights dimmed by fractions, then snapped back. Equipment readings spiked without inputs. The prisoner laughed in three different voices. A mug slid two centimeters across a table with no hand near it.

By the time the screaming started, Mustang already knew what direction this was heading. Knowing didn't help.

One monitor imploded like it had been hit from the inside. A researcher jerked sideways, blood blossoming in the air as something invisible caught him. Another went up and over, spine bending at an angle no body should. The chair shook, restraints biting deep into the prisoner's skin as he thrashed.

The feed caught only flashes—wet impacts, bodies flung against glass, the echo of desperate orders drowned in noise. At the end, the room was a red smear of motion, gear and people and pieces of both pulled apart by nothing Mustang's eyes could track.

The video cut to static mid-scream.

Mustang realized his hand hurt. He'd driven his fist into the stone beside him, skin split across the knuckles. The dull throb was nothing compared to the cold that had settled into him.

This wasn't a rogue program or a lab accident. They'd reached into something they didn't understand and yanked—and the thing on the other end of the rope had yanked back.

He dragged in a breath that tasted like fish smoke and stone dust and hit the next file before he could think better of it.

The world on screen shifted.

Same era, different environment—what looked like the remains of a military installation, all collapsed corridors and scorched concrete. The recon team's gear was outdated, heavy armor plates and stubby rifles that looked clumsy compared to what Bradley and Knight carried now.

They moved through the wreckage in silence. The only sounds were the crunch of debris under boots and the distant hiss of cooling metal. The camera passed over bodies—or what was left of them. Limbs severed clean, torsos opened like someone had taken them apart to see how they worked, and then forgotten to put anything back.

Whoever had done this hadn't bothered with bullets.

The team's formation tightened as they pressed on, weapons up, beams cutting thin corridors of light through the dust. Mustang's shoulders crept up as if he were the one clearing corners.

Then they saw her.

She lay at the center of what might once have been a command hub, framed by collapsed beams and shattered screens.

Unconscious. Breathing. Completely untouched by the carnage around her.

Mustang zoomed the feed in without thinking.

Olive skin, unmarked. Hair an impossible pink that spilled around her like a stain of color on the gray floor. The white shift she wore was simple, sheer—but it caught and held light in a way the camera couldn't quite read, edges fuzzed by a faint luminous haze.

The recon team, hard men by voice and posture, went quiet in a way no order had prompted. Rifles dipped a fraction. One of them swore softly, not in fear, but something close to reverence.

When they reached her, their movements lost the usual jerkiness of combat footage. One checked her pulse with careful fingers; another draped a field blanket over her shoulders as if afraid she'd break. They secured her to a stretcher with the kind of gentleness Mustang had never seen in any Foundation op vid.

The screen stuttered as the stretcher lifted.

Then the feed cut.

Mustang stared past the floating menus, past the blink of icons, into the rough curve of the cavern wall. His eyes weren't really seeing the rock. They were still trapped in the clash between two images: a room painted in blood, and a woman lying untouched in ruins like something fallen out of another sky.

Victim? Weapon? Or something the word *subject* didn't even begin to cover?

He forced himself back into the directories under *Project Godspear*. File after file opened into chaos—scanned notebook pages, jittery video logs, screenshots of equations dragged half off the page in haste. Digitized photos of ragged handwriting filled his vision. The research team's confusion bled through in every line: circled phrases, underlines gouged into the paper, arrows pointing to the same words over and over.

"Dimensional anomaly."

"Unnatural energy signature."

The same terms, repeated until they lost meaning and became a mantra of not understanding.

One image froze him.

A block of text, shaky but clear, underlined so hard the strokes had nearly torn the paper:
*Subject maintains she is the harbinger of the new dawn, Anaku'tawa.*

A chill slid down his spine. *Harbinger.* Not subject, not weapon. Not even "patient." A herald of something new, something big enough they had to wrap it in myth to get their heads around it.

Was she their masterpiece—a goddess built in a lab? Or had Telluric just…found her? Pried open some crack in reality and dragged out the first thing that answered?

The answers weren't in the top-level summaries. They were buried deeper, nested inside subfolders and cross-references, a whole labyrinth of bad ideas that made the rest of the K-94 drive look almost sane.

He dug.

The woman's face followed him from file to file. Olive skin, luminous gown, that shock of impossible hair—and suddenly, uninvited, another face slid over hers.

Pinky.

Smaller, rounder, streaked in dirt and fish-water and wild joy. Same bright, impossible color family. Same kind of *wrong* beauty, like somebody had taken the world's palette and shifted it half a tone.

His stomach lurched. He scrolled back, pulled up a tagged still image, then another. Cross-referenced with a subject list. *Subject 000002.*

"Come on," he whispered. "Tell me I'm seeing patterns where there aren't any."

The text didn't care what he wanted.

Subject 000002: female. Unknown chronological age. Phenotype inconsistent with recorded family lines.

A line of cold sweat slid between his shoulder blades. For a second he heard Pinky's laugh in the back of his head, echoing against the cavern stone. He swallowed hard, bile burning his throat.

Daughter? Avatar? Echo? Whatever she was, whatever *this* was —it wasn't coincidence.

He braced his back against the stone and pushed on, opening the subject files one by one. Every clip, every log, drove the nails deeper.

Experiments dressed up as "trials." Reality bending where it wasn't supposed to. Rooms that went wrong without warning. *Termination attempts* listed like maintenance schedules.

Again and again they tried to break her—poisons, blades, bullets, containment fields that could shear steel in half. Again and again, the reports ended the same way: *failure to terminate*. Anomalous feedback. Unknown interference. Systems fried. Personnel lost.

Mustang gagged more than once, choking on half-digested fish and bitter coffee. He had to pause, knuckles pressed to his lips, eyes squeezed shut until the wave passed.

No morality. No brakes. Just another problem to solve, no matter how many people they fed into it.

As the hours blurred, a pattern began to pry itself out of the horror.

He scrubbed back and forth between time stamps, watching the woman's face change frame by frame, decade by decade. In early footage, she was ageless—self-possessed, gaze steady, words sharp despite the restraints. In later clips, after weapon trials and "incidents," she looked...younger. Softer. Confused.

The more they tried to kill her, the less she seemed to understand what any of it was.

He double-checked the dates, the metadata, the time stamps burned into the bottom of the screen. They didn't lie. The same subject number, the same impossible energy readings, the same pink hair—and every attempt to end her had peeled years away instead of adding them. Their "ascended being" wasn't aging.

She was *un*-aging.

Not the mother, then.

The realization built up, a pool of acid in his gut as the files laid out who this was.

This wasn't a descendent, or even some clone.

The same girl.

"Holy shit," Mustang breathed, the words ripped out of him more than spoken.

His hands shook as he scrubbed back through the key points and committed the stamps to memory—dates, sequences, file IDs. Decades of footage, different cameras, different teams, the same monstrous ritual of study and slaughter repeating under new faces and new budgets.

He sat there in the dim, AR glow ghosting his features, and knew three things with painful clarity: he had to tell the others; he could *not* tell Pinky; and whatever they thought they were fighting topside, it was only the shadow of something much, much worse than they could have imagined.

\*\*\*

Activity buzzed through the fungal grotto, but the mood stayed heavy, grim. Knight moved among them without the crutch now, gait still stiff but no longer halting. Every unaided step was both a relief and an alarm bell—bones knitting too fast, bruises fading too clean. Healing like that never came without a bill.

Fish bones piled at the edge of the pool, pale against slick stone. The schools that had once flashed beneath the surface were thinner now, streaks of silver instead of clouds. Their sanctuary had limits, and it was starting to show.

Alysha waited until the bustle swelled—Mustang muttering over hardware, Karl packing gear, Jorgen arguing with Knight about how much weight he should carry—then crooked a finger at Pinky.

"Come," she said quietly.

She led the girl a little way from the others, where the bioluminescent fungus painted the cavern wall in soft blues and greens. There, in that gentler light, Alysha unfolded something from beneath her cloak.

It was a dress. Brilliant white, with puffed sleeves, the hem and bodice banded by a bright rainbow that glowed faintly in the grotto light—a scrap of festival color in a world of stone and shadow.

"This was my sister's," Alysha said. Her voice had gone distant, edges softened by memory. "I want you to have it."

Pinky's eyes went huge. She reached out, fingers hovering a breath above the fabric before she finally touched it. The cloth was smooth beneath her grimy hands, the stitched rainbow catching the fungus-glow and scattering it in tiny reflections. She dragged her fingertips along the colored bands, slow at first, then faster as the reality of it sank in.

A giggle burst out of her. Then another. She hugged the dress to her chest, wriggling with a joy so bright it seemed to shove the cavern's chill back a pace. A moment later she was twirling, bare feet slapping softly on damp stone, the dress flaring out around her like a captured cloud.

When she flung herself at Alysha, the impact almost staggered the Suli. Pinky's arms locked around her waist, small fingers digging in with surprising strength. Alysha hesitated only a

274

fraction of a heartbeat before folding her arms around the girl and hugging back, tight.

The promise was wordless but unmistakable: *mine to guard.*

The sharp sting behind Alysha's eyes took her by surprise. Smoke, damp, ghosts—everything tangled together. She blinked hard, but one tear escaped anyway, tracking a clean line through the grime on her cheek.

Across the grotto, Jorgen watched them with his hands wrapped around a half-packed kit bag. The faint, crooked smile that tugged at his mouth made him look years younger, softening the lines carved there by too many bad jobs and too many empty bottles. For a moment, with Pinky spinning in that ridiculous rainbow dress and Alysha letting someone hold on to her, it almost looked like a normal camp after a hard day's work.

The moment didn't last.

Bootsteps slapped stone in a hurried rhythm, too sharp to be casual. Jorgen's smile faded even before he turned.

Mustang was threading through the stalagmites at a near-run, AR glasses shoved up on his forehead. The usual cocky tilt to his mouth was gone; what remained was tight, grim focus. He headed straight for Bradley like a homing beacon, one hand already reaching for the other man's shoulder.

Knight, propped near the fire just before, pushed himself upright. He left his makeshift crutch leaning against the stone without seeming to notice and crossed toward Jorgen with a steadier stride than he'd had any right to this soon.

"What's got Mustang spooked?" he asked, voice low, gravel roughened both by healing ribs and something older.

Jorgen flicked a glance toward the two men now huddled at the far edge of the camp, half hidden by a curtain of stone. Mustang was talking fast, shoulders tight; Bradley's head was tipped down, brow furrowed, listening hard.

"The drive," Jorgen said, mouth flattening, "it's worse than we thought."

Knight followed the line of his gesture, eyes narrowing as he watched Mustang practically pull Bradley a few steps farther from the others, out of Pinky's earshot. Bradley went willingly enough, but there was a stiffness to him—a man bracing for impact he couldn't yet see.

The two soldiers exchanged a look, the kind that didn't need words. They'd both been around long enough to recognize the posture of bad news.

A heavy quiet settled over their side of the grotto, muting the clatter of gear and Pinky's distant laughter. Jorgen nudged a loose stone with the toe of his boot, sending it skittering across the slick floor. The faint clack-clack echoed off the cavern walls and came back thin.

The glow of the fungus, the dress swirling around a child's legs, the smell of cooking fish—none of it felt real. Just a fleeting mirage the world had thrown up to mock them before the next wave hit.

Pinky came skipping across the grotto in the rainbow dress Alysha had given her, white fabric flashing in the fungus-glow, hem flaring with every hop. She looked like a shard of daylight dropped into the cave—too bright, too clean—against the low murmur of packing and the tight faces of grown men pretending not to stare.

Jorgen dropped into a crouch to meet her, knees popping. He dragged a hand through her hair, mussing the carefully combed strands until they stuck up around her shoulder.

"There you are, little terror," he said, forcing his mouth into a grin. "Ready for another adventure?"

The word *adventure* still worked on her, but not like it had. Doubt crossed her face, quick and small. Her gaze slipped past him, toward the bend of stone where Bradley and Mustang had disappeared. The rainbow skirt swished once, then stilled.

"Are we going to see more monsters?" she asked.

The tremor in her voice hollowed him out. He didn't feel like spider drones or dark tunnels were all they had to worry about. Jorgen felt the answer rise and shoved it down.

He cupped her cheek with his calloused palm instead, thumb smudging a line of dried algae from her skin. "We'll face whatever comes after us," he said, keeping his tone steady. "That's what family does."

She leaned into his hand like it was the most obvious thing in the world, some of the tension easing from her shoulders. The dress flared again as she shifted closer, small fingers bunching in his coat.

Knight watched them from a few paces off, weight braced subtly on his bad leg. The sight hit him harder than he liked to admit: Pinky in that ridiculous dress, clinging to a man who smelled of coffee grounds and gun oil; Alysha standing a little ways back, hand resting on the hilt of her blade, eyes soft in a way they never were in a fight.

*Family,* Jorgen had said.

Ragtag, misfit, broken—but down here, under tons of stone and somebody else's sins, they were all they had. Keeping the kid safe, keeping any of them safe, felt less like a duty and more like the last line between them and becoming the thing they were running from.

Knight's gaze slid back to the mouth of the side tunnel where Bradley and Mustang had vanished. No voices drifted out, no flicker of AR light. Just stone and shadow and the knowledge that whatever was on that drive had already started to change the way Mustang moved, the way Bradley set his jaw.

He didn't know what they were about to bring back to the fire. Only that it wouldn't be small, and it wouldn't be something they could put down again.

In his gut, he felt it settle like a lead weight: whatever secrets they'd unearthed were going to shove this whole strange little family deeper into the dark—a nightmare with no clear edge, and no guarantee there was a waking world left at the end of it.

\*\*\*

The cavern seemed to narrow around them as they stepped away from the firelight and the others' voices, slipping into a pocket of shadow between two curtains of stone. Fungal glow didn't quite reach here; the air felt cooler, damp against Bradley's neck.

Mustang's words, low and tight, sat between them.

"Bigger problems," he said.

He didn't raise his voice, but the way he said it—flat, stripped of all his usual swagger—made the phrase land heavier than any shout.

Bradley clung to the last scrap of optimism like a reflex. "Ouroboros. Serenity." He kept his tone even, like he was working through a tactical brief. "They can't reach beyond the city, right? Supply lines, jurisdiction…they're still contained."

Even as he said it, he heard how stupid it sounded. He'd already seen what *contained* meant, in Foundation terms.

Mustang shook his head. The gesture was small, but decisive. "It's not Ouroboros," he said. "Not Serenity. Godspear." He flicked his fingers, and a chain of icons spooled into Bradley's AR field. "Look for yourself."

Bradley accepted the feed. A white room filled his vision— hard lights, a drain in the floor, steel restraints bolted into a chair.

A woman sat strapped at the center of it, bare feet hanging above the grate.

Olive skin. Hair the color of spun candy, bright even through the compression artifacts. Her eyes—wide, bewildered, furious.

The scientists moved like they were doing inventory. Calm faces. Clipboards. Questions delivered in flat, practiced tones. The woman answered at first, voice distorted through the ancient mic, threaded with an accent he couldn't place.

Then the "testing" started.

Needles. Arcs of light across her skin. A field humming up until the camera jittered and the walls bled static. Instruments spiking with no reason. The image stuttering.

She screamed—until the sound broke into something hoarse and animal, and Bradley's stomach clenched like a fist.

The feed jumped.

Different room. Different lab coats. Same subject number burned into the corner of the frame.

Same hair—shorter now.

Same face—younger.

Her eyes were worse. Less defiance. More confusion, as if she'd forgotten the rules of being a person and kept having to relearn them between shocks.

Another jump—faster this time, like Mustang was unwilling to linger.

A smaller body on the table. A too-big restraint cinched down. Someone—some idiot with a fake conscience—had left a stuffed toy within reach like it might anchor her.

She clutched it with both hands.

Her hair was still that impossible pink.

And her eyes—

Bradley made a sound he didn't recognize, something raw that scraped up his throat. The lab flickered, and for a heartbeat it wasn't the chair he saw—it was the grotto behind Mustang. Pinky in that ridiculous rainbow dress, laughing as she splashed at the pool. Pinky tilting her head like she understood more than she did.

Those eyes.

"Oh, shit," he breathed.

Mustang killed the feed with a twitch of his fingers. The AR peeled away, leaving rock and fungus and the low murmur of packing.

"We were wrong," Bradley said, barely audible. "About what she is."

Mustang's jaw clenched. "Jorgen finds out she's their favorite test subject?" he said quietly. "He'll go back up there with his rifle and a death wish. We'd never get him turned around."

He didn't have to say *and I wouldn't blame him.* It was in his eyes.

Bradley scrubbed a hand over his face, grit rasping against his palm. Off to his right, over Mustang's shoulder, he could see Knight by the fire, methodically breaking down and reassembling his rifle. Jorgen hummed under his breath as he counted ration packs, the tune low and aimless. Normal motions. Normal habits. They looked small against what he'd just seen.

Pinky darted through the edge of his vision, chasing something only she could see, Alysha shadowing her like a pale ghost. The new dress flared and spun, a bright ring of color in the blue-green light. Pinky laughed, high and clear.

It felt like being stabbed, slowly.

"We can't go back," Bradley said. He heard the decision harden in his own voice. "Not to them. Not to that city. They turn people into rations and lab notes. Ouroboros, Serenity…those are bad enough. But this…" He shook his head. "Godspear is something else. I don't even know what that fight would look like."

"Suicide," Mustang said bluntly. "On their turf? With what we've got? Yeah." He huffed out something that wasn't quite a laugh. "They poked a hole in reality, Bradley. And when something looked back, they strapped it to a table."

Bradley swallowed, metallic bile at the back of his throat. The urge to storm back into the wider world and drag Telluric into the light burned hot and useless inside his chest.

"We still need the others to understand what we're up against," he said. "They need to know The Foundation isn't just corrupt. They're…anti-human. We show them enough of the projects to make that clear." His gaze flicked again toward the little cluster around the fire. "But we don't tell them everything. Not about her."

He met Mustang's eyes, voice dropping. "Pinky doesn't hear a word of this. Not if we can help it. She gets to be a kid for as long as we can steal that for her."

Mustang looked past him, toward the dress, the spinning, the laugh. His usual sarcasm was gone when he nodded.

"Yeah," he said quietly. "Yeah. She's been carved up enough already."

Bradley exhaled slowly, forcing his thoughts into an order that resembled a plan.

"We frame it as anomalies," he said. "Time distortion, psychological fallout, whatever you can make sound plausible. You talk about interference scrambling memories, experiments leaving gaps. Enough truth to be useful, not enough to crush her."

Mustang's mouth twisted into something that wasn't quite a smile. "Half-truths with a science garnish," he muttered. "I can work with that."

Bradley glanced back toward the others one last time. Jorgen's rough hand ruffling Pinky's hair. Knight's steady motions over the blaster. Alysha's watchful stillness at the edge of the firelight.

They were already neck-deep in a nightmare they didn't understand. If there was even a sliver of light left to hold on to —even if it was built on careful omissions—then it was his job to keep it burning.

"For now," he said, "we keep her safe. From them. From what they did. From knowing."

He straightened, shoulders squaring, the decision settling over him like armor.

"Let's go tell the others what we *can* afford to."

It was a flimsy shield and Bradley knew it. One hard question, one wrong scrap of truth, and the whole thing would come apart. But it was all they had—thin cover between a little girl in a rainbow dress and the fact that her life had been an experiment.

For now, her laughter had to be louder than anything on that drive.

"Bradley! Mustang!" Jorgen's voice rolled through the grotto, rough and echoing off wet stone. "You two done whisperin' sweet nothings back there?"

The sound snapped the moment in half. Bradley's jaw tightened, the frustration there and gone in a blink, replaced by

283

the flat, controlled calm he wore for the rest of them. Mustang blew out a breath through his nose.

"Looks like break time's over," Mustang muttered, trying for a smirk and almost getting there. His eyes, still blown wide from what he'd seen, gave him away.

They stepped back into the light of the fungal glow and fire embers, sliding into motion without discussion. Packs were cinched, bedrolls slung over shoulders, weapons checked by touch and habit. Karl appeared from one of the side passages, beard dusted in fine grit. He moved like a man whose hope had worn thin.

"Well," he grunted, shifting his pack higher on one shoulder, "looks like we're playing a guessing game for a while. Tunnels split every which way. No sense to them I can trust."

Jorgen snorted, the sound halfway to a cough. "Always comfortin' knowin' we're lost as a tick in a sheepdog's ear," he said, tipping back his canteen for a quick swig. The cool water smell mingled with damp rock and old smoke.

Knight, leaning on his scavenged crutch, eyed the shadowed mouths of the tunnels with a soldier's impatience. "Any direction's as good as another," he said tersely. "Unless you've got something better than vibes and guesswork, Karl."

Karl's brow furrowed as he ran thick fingers over a nearby wall, feeling the cuts in the stone rather than looking at them. "Not exactly," he said. "These tunnels—" he jerked his chin at the rough passageways around them "—aren't all natural. Some've been widened. Pick marks. Chisel scars. Different ages layered over each other."

"The marks on the stone," Alysha added, stepping closer, her hood shadowing copper-touched hair. Her fingers ghosted along a scored groove. "Crude. Hand tools. Old, but not ancient. Definitely not human."

Mustang let out a low whistle, the sound bouncing down the tunnel ahead. "So the Foundation built their toy box over somebody else's den," he said. "Great. Nothing creepy about that."

Karl nodded. "One main tunnel shows more wear. More dust kicked up, more scuffing. Something's been using it. Recently." He pointed down a broader passage where the floor was smoother, the faint track of many feet worn into the stone.

"Traffic?" Jorgen echoed, brows climbing. "Down here?"

"Footprints, bits of broken stone, a few tool chips." Karl shrugged. "Could be people. Could be…something that likes tools. Either way, it's a trail."

Pinky, who'd been hovering at Alysha's side, bounced on her toes. "Are they friends?" she asked, eyes bright. "Can we play with them?"

The adults shared a look—full of things they'd never say out loud.

"Let's hope so, little one," Jorgen rumbled at last, forcing the corners of his mouth up. "For now, we'll follow Karl. Might not be the way out, but it's better than standin' still."

They formed up without needing orders—Knight near the front despite the lingering stiffness in his leg, Karl leading by touch and instinct, Jorgen and Pinky together, Alysha gliding just off their flank like a pale shadow. Mustang fell in behind Bradley, adjusting his glasses, already assembling half-truths and cover stories in his head.

Bradley took one last look back. Pinky skipped beside Alysha, skirt flaring, chattering about the colors on her new dress. Alysha listened, expression softer than he'd ever seen it. The sight twisted something in his chest.

*We'll tell them,* he promised himself, turning toward the darker throat of the tunnel. *Knight, Jorgen, Karl—they deserve to know what we're really up against. We'll do it careful. We'll do it together. And we'll keep the worst of it off her shoulders for as long as we can.*

Then he faced forward and moved out with the rest, deeper into stone and uncertainty, carrying secrets that felt heavier than his pack.

But Pinky... she deserved to stay in the dark a little longer, at least about this. Let the nightmares belong to the adults for now. If this buried world could buy her even a narrow pocket of peace—a few more days of splashing in luminous water and naming fish and pretending monsters were just stories—that was a kind of victory he wasn't willing to surrender.

So Bradley took the only mercy left to him. He let her laughter set the pace, that bright, ridiculous sound bouncing off fungus-lit walls, a thin thread of defiance in the oppressive weight of the earth. The rest—the files on K-94, the butchered science of Ouroboros and Serenity, the things Telluric had done to the girl —could wait until they stopped again, until he and Mustang had found the words.

Until then, he gripped his weapon and held that sound in his chest like a talisman. That small, stubborn joy was the measure now As long as Pinky could laugh like that, there was still something human left to salvage from the ruin of ambition and cosmic horror.

# CHAPTER FIFTEEN

The deeper they pushed, the more the fungus claimed the rock around them. Pale strands webbed the tunnel walls, thickening into ropes and curtains of glow. Light seeped from every tendril—soft green at first, then sharper, almost sour on the eyes, until the darkness thinned but never quite left. The air turned cool and wet, carrying a faint, organic tang that clung to the back of Bradley's throat.

Alysha moved through that light like she belonged to it. Her hair, once a pale blonde, now burned with copper— bright, metallic, her once blue eyes now a brilliant emerald. She'd stopped tugging her hood forward, stopped flinching when anyone looked too long. If the change bothered her, she hid it behind that distant stare and the short, quiet answers she gave Bradley whenever he pressed her about headaches or weakness. Each time, he caught himself checking the roots, watching the color creep.

Karl kept them on track. His silhouette, solid and compact, anchored the front of the line. Even with the fungal glow painting the tunnel in ghost-light, he swept every shadow with a miner's suspicion, boots feeling for faults in the floor, free hand trailing the rock as if reading it like braille.

Knight's change was harder to ignore. The crude crutch was gone, abandoned somewhere back in the stone. He walked now —no swagger, but with a steady, controlled stride that should've taken weeks to earn back. Every so often his jaw clenched and a muscle jumped in his cheek, but he never asked to slow down. The speed of it set Bradley's nerves on edge, some part of him convinced the bill for that kind of recovery hadn't arrived yet.

Between them all, Pinky darted like a spark thrown from a fire. The rainbow dress Alysha had given her flashed in the green gloom, a riot of color against mold-slick stone. She skipped from hand to hand—Jorgen's, then Alysha's—peppering them with questions about glowing mushrooms and underground monsters, whispering secrets into ears and demanding new ones in return. Her high, breathless chatter washed over Bradley and Mustang like a pressure release valve, thinning out the ache in his chest for a few heartbeats at a time.

The relief never lasted. The weight of what he and Mustang knew rode just behind his ribs. K-94's file tree lurked behind every AR menu, a rotten tooth they kept worrying with their tongues. The truth needed to be shared eventually; they both knew it.

When they finally stumbled into an older chamber—a bubble of space where the tunnel widened and the ceiling vanished into shadow—they fell into the familiar pattern without thinking. Packs came off, gear was sorted, filters checked, rations divided. Someone claimed a corner for waste, someone else cleared a patch of floor for sleeping bags. In minutes, the ruin of some long-forgotten hall—carvings worn soft on the walls, broken plinths half-swallowed by fungus—had become a camp.

The light here pooled and shifted, clusters of fungus clinging to carved reliefs like strange moss, outlining half-erased figures and symbols in blue-green halos. Under that steady glow, Alysha's copper hair seemed brighter still. She moved more slowly now, shoulders dipped, one hand braced on the wall more often than before. Sweat beaded along her hairline despite the chill. Twice, as she and Pinky gathered dried moss from the margins of the chamber, she paused just a second too long, swaying as if the stone had rolled under her feet.

"I'm gonna rest my old bones," Jorgen murmured, cutting through the low whisper of movement. The usual bite in his voice was dulled. He unrolled his sleeping bag in the far corner with none of his typical grousing about drafts or rocks, didn't even glance at the food they were portioning out. He just lowered himself onto the bedroll, turned his back to the fire, and was snoring within minutes—a deep, ragged sound edged with pure exhaustion.

Knight watched him with a frown, arms folded, weight settled carefully on his good leg. "Something's off," he said under his breath, eyes tracking from Jorgen to Alysha and back again. "She's running on fumes, and he never skips a meal. Not out of greed," he added when Bradley looked over, "out of discipline. You keep your strength up, or you die tired."

Mustang, crouched with his toolkit spread around him, didn't bother with a joke. He just gave a tight nod and bent over the gutted rifle core in his lap, tools ticking and scraping in quick, restless bursts. The jitter in his hands wasn't only from caffeine.

Bradley took it all in—the carved stone and crawling light, the hunched shoulders, the too-deep sleep. The chamber should have felt impressive, almost sacred, with its old marks and vast, resonant hush. Instead it was a snapshot halfway through a slow collapse. The glowing fungus could paint the walls as pretty as it wanted; it couldn't hide how hard this place was grinding them down.

"We need to talk," Bradley said.

His voice was low, but it cut through the soft drip of water and the faint crackle of Mustang's tools. He stayed seated, elbows on his knees, gaze fixed on the green-lit stone between his boots, then lifted his eyes to the others.

"Not about escape. Not about whatever's waiting in the dark." He swallowed, feeling the dryness in his throat. "We need a plan—for if things go sideways."

Silence pressed in around them. Alysha's copper hair gleamed where she sat with Pinky nestled against her in a mound of moss. Knight leaned against the carved wall, arms crossed, weight subtly favoring his once-broken leg. Mustang's multi-tool whined down and died in his hand.

What's happening to them isn't normal.

The thought slid through Bradley's mind. Alysha's hair tarnishing day by day, her stamina bleeding away. Knight's bones knitting too fast, strength flooding back in ways that felt wrong. If the caverns were changing them this quickly...how long before that change spread? How long before it became something worse?

His eyes snagged on Pinky.

She lay half-curled against Alysha bare feet tucked under herself, thumb absently tracing a groove in the stone. Her lashes fluttered; he couldn't tell if she was fully asleep or listening the way kids did—soaking up more than any of them wanted.

What if she's not just a victim? What if they made her into—

He shut that door hard.

"The questions aren't going away," he said, forcing himself to keep talking. "We can't just keep running and pretending nothing's changing. Not with Alysha…not with Knight. We need to think ahead. Decide what we do if someone starts to slip. If they can't keep going. If they—"

The word died in his mouth. Can't say it. Don't make it real.

Mustang looked smaller than Bradley had ever seen him. The AR haze over his eyes couldn't find him a road out of this one.

"Yeah," Mustang muttered. "Feels like it's not just the tunnels trying to kill us anymore." He gestured with one hand at Knight, at Alysha. "Feels like we brought something down here with us."

Knight met Bradley's gaze across the faintly glowing chamber. No bravado there, no shrug-it-off soldier act. Just a grim acknowledgment.

"Bones shouldn't heal this fast," he said quietly. "Not at my age." His jaw flexed. "Not sure how long I can pretend it's just good luck."

On the moss bed, Pinky shifted, murmuring something unintelligible. Alysha's arm tightened around her for a heartbeat, then loosened. She blinked herself fully awake, pupils wide in the fungal light. Sweat shone along her hairline despite the chill.

Her eyes moved from Bradley to Mustang, then to Knight, reading the room without a word. She looked older in that moment, not in her face but in the way her shoulders slumped, like the stone itself had settled on them.

Nobody rushed in to fill the silence.

Mustang did, eventually.

"We have to talk about Pinky," he said.

Mustang's dark eyes were steady now, all the chatter burned away. "She's in more danger than any of us," he said quietly. "If the Foundation finds her? If anyone finds out what she is —"

"Is it because she's the Godspear?" Alysha murmured.

The words slid out of her on a breath, half-asleep, half-something else. Her eyes were fixed on the ceiling, but the name dropped into the chamber like a stone into still water.

"No."

It echoed off the carved walls, a little too loud. Pinky flinched against Alysha's side. Knight's hand tightened reflexively on his rifle grip, knuckles whitening. The fungal glow seemed to dim for a heartbeat.

Mustang lifted a hand toward Bradley, palm down. Sit. Breathe.

"She's not the Godspear," Mustang said, slow and deliberate. "She wasn't made by that project. She was a test subject." His jaw clenched around the word. "They weren't trying to create a weapon. They were trying to find a way to kill her."

He looked from Bradley to Alysha, then back. "That doesn't make her safer. It makes her...valuable. To them. To anyone who hears the word 'ascended' and smells a payday." His mouth twisted. "If word gets out she's special, there's going to be a line of people trying to drag her back into a lab—or worse."

Alysha's head turned at last. The copper in her hair caught the ambient light in molten streaks. Her eyes were clearer now, but no less tired.

"How did you know that name?" Bradley asked her, softer, though suspicion still leaked through.

Alysha blinked, slow. "You two aren't the only ones carrying secrets," she said. She looked down at Pinky, fingers tightening on the girl's shoulder.

The response did nothing to ease the knot in his gut. Godspear was classified well above top secret. What else did she know?

Knight shifted, the faint rasp of his boot on stone loud in the hush. His blaster stayed pointed at the floor, but his forearm corded with tension.

Bradley felt anger surge up through the nausea and clamp around his ribs.

"No," he said again, quieter this time but no less fierce. "She's a kid. She's a victim. Not a weapon, not a project, not—"

The rest jammed in his throat, images from the K-94 files rising behind his eyes—lab lights, restraints, pink hair slick with blood. He bit down hard enough to taste iron.

He forced himself to look at Pinky instead. At bare feet, at the hem of Alysha's sister's dress, at the little fist curled in the moss.

"Whatever the Foundation called her," he said, voice frayed, "they don't get to define her. Not anymore."

Mustang stepped in before Bradley could spin out any further.

He dropped down beside him, close enough that their shoulders almost touched, AR glow washing his face in sickly green. The usual smirk was gone. What sat there instead was worse— resignation.

"We've got to stop dodging this," he said quietly. "Pinky's not just another survivor. The files…what they did to her…" His eyes tracked to where she lay tucked against Alysha. "It goes deeper than we know."

Bradley's jaw clenched. "She's a kid."

"She was a test subject," Mustang said, not softening it. "They strapped her down and tried to break her. Over and over. We both know they are still out there—and they will want her back?" He shook his head. "There won't be negotiations. There'll be a hunt."

The words landed like a series of punches. Hunt. Not for them. For her. Their little pocket of light had teeth marks in her.

Alysha shifted, pushing herself up further. Exhaustion dragged at her, copper hair damp with sweat, but when she spoke her voice was clear, almost detached.

"I saw the Godspear file," she admitted. "Because of Lucas." Her eyes locked on Bradley's. "Righ before I killed him."

Cold slid down Bradley's spine.

Lucas.

The name carried weight for him that no one else quite understood. The face behind too many reports. The signature at the bottom of too many clearances. Not the genius he claimed to be, but he held the keys to the kingdom.

Mustang let out a low, humorless breath. "So the steward of the freak show finally took a long walk off a short pier," he said. There was satisfaction there, Mustang hadn't like the pompous little weasel either. "Simplifies one problem. Sort of."

Jorgen's absence from the conversation was strangely loud. He slept in the far corner, or pretended to. No snoring now. Just stillness. For a man who groused through everything until it mattered, the silence was out of place.

"'Architect' is generous," Bradley said, voice rough. "He had a few breakthroughs early on. Spent the rest of his career cashing them in." He scrubbed a hand over his face. "He was a steward. A gatekeeper. And if he's gone, that chair's already warm again. Someone else will be wearing his badge."

The truth of it settled over them like more stone.

Mustang's brief relief guttered. "One less bastard," he said. "Same machine." His fingers found their way back to his tools, moving faster now, like if he worked hard enough he could outpace the implications.

Bradley felt the mission reframe itself in his head whether he wanted it to or not. This wasn't just getting out of a maze. It wasn't about one lab, or one man, or even one island. It was the Foundation. Best case they got written off as dead, but given the lengths they had gone to try to kill her—unsuccessfully— they would never stop looking for her.

Across the chamber, Jorgen didn't move. No half-asleep grumble, no demand to be brought up to speed. Knight was right—something was off there, too. Was it the caverns, the stress, or one more slow-burning consequence waiting to surface?

Knight broke the silence with a voice that sounded more like the sergeant Bradley knew.

"Doesn't change what we do next," he said. "We teach Pinky to fight. To hide, to run, to shoot if it comes to it." His gaze slid to Karl. "And you find us a way out of this tomb before it becomes our coffin."

Karl gave a short, weary nod, hand resting on the carved wall as if feeling for an answer in the stone. No promises. Just that.

Bradley drew in a breath and pushed himself to his feet. He could feel their eyes on him—waiting for an order, even if none of them were technically his to command.

"For now," he said, "we sleep. Mustang takes first watch. Then Knight." He met the older man's gaze, weighing the too-fast healing and trusting it anyway. "I'll take third."

No one argued. They were past the point of pretending they were fine.

They broke apart in ones and twos. Mustang drifted toward the edge of the camp, rifle across his lap, AR lenses dimming to a low glow as he pulled up sensor feeds. Knight checked his weapon by touch, then settled in where he could see both the carved entrance and Pinky's makeshift bed. Karl eased down with his back to the wall, head tipped back, listening to the stone.

Bradley lay down last, close enough to reach Pinky if he had to. The moss was cold through his clothes, the air colder still, but heat churned in his gut—rage, fear, a grim resolve that refused to die no matter how much weight he stacked on top of it.

Sleep didn't come.

Behind his closed eyes he saw lab lights, restraints, pink hair slick with blood that wasn't there on the girl breathing softly a few feet away. He saw Lucas falling. He saw hands he didn't recognize rifling through the files Mustang had just read, picking up where the last monster left off.

He rolled onto his side, watching Alysha's copper hair catch and break the fungal glow. Pinky shifted in her sleep, a small hand resting on the older woman's arm. For a moment, the chamber was just that—a room with people resting in it, not the staging ground for a war they hadn't planned on fighting.

We protect her, he told himself. From the Foundation. From whatever's in those files. From the truth, if we have to.

Down here in the dark, that promise was the only thing that still stayed solid.

Eventually, his eyes slid closed, not from peace but from exhaustion. Mustang kept his lonely vigil at the edge of the light, and the ancient stone listened without judgment as their borrowed sanctuary drifted toward uneasy dreams.

Mustang glanced over once at Knight, whose gaze stayed pinned on Jorgen's sleeping form. They didn't speak, but the worry passed between them anyway.

Knight moved with that same quiet efficiency when his watch came up. He checked his blaster, adjusted straps, tested his rapidly healing leg with a few careful steps. On the surface he was all routine—angles, lines of fire, shadowed corners—but Bradley had seen the way Knight touched his own ribs earlier, as if feeling for a fracture that should still hurt and didn't. The speed of his recovery sat in Knight's eyes like a bad omen.

Sleep, when it finally dragged Bradley under, was shallow and sharp-edged. He dreamed in fragments: Pinky standing stock-still with a rifle too big for her hands; a woman with the same bone structure, older and broken, strapped to a lab chair while invisible things pulled her apart; the tunnels closing in, walls slick with a darkness that wasn't just the absence of light. Every time he jerked awake, the cavern was still there, humming softly around them, and the sense of something pressing in from beyond stayed lodged in his chest.

When his turn came to relieve Mustang, the handoff said more than either man did. Mustang's eyes were wide-awake tired, that wired look of someone who'd seen too much and was hanging on out of spite. Whatever jokes he might have cracked died behind his teeth. He passed Bradley the watch with a short nod and went to ground without argument.

Bradley took his post and found no comfort in the soft glow of the fungus or the steady crackle of the fire. The carvings on the chamber walls caught the light in ways that made them look like wounds. In the darkness beyond their camp, he saw more than threats: he saw Lucas, reduced to a detail in a classified report; Pinky, not a lucky stray but a stolen asset; and the possibility that whatever was changing Alysha's hair and knitting Knight's bones might already be inside the rest of them, waiting for its moment.

The idea of simple escape felt childish now. Getting out of the tunnels alive wouldn't be enough—not with what they knew, not with what Pinky represented. If anyone was going to drag this into the light and break it, it would have to start with people like them—tired, outgunned, but still breathing. It was ridiculous, almost laughable. But as he watched the others sleep, that impossible task was the only thing that made sense. It was the thin thread he wrapped around his own fear to keep it from unraveling him.

By the time they started calling it "morning," the cavern felt colder. Breaking camp should have been automatic—roll bedrolls, douse the fire, check weapons, move. Instead, everything dragged. Jorgen didn't sit up swearing at his joints. Alysha didn't wordlessly stretch, eyes already sweeping for threats. They stayed where they were, breathing shallow and even, as if sleep had sunk hooks in them.

They gave it time. Ten minutes. Thirty. Long enough that, on any other day, Jorgen would've already been complaining about ration choices and Pinky would've climbed onto him demanding a story. The longer the silence held, the worse the knot in Bradley's stomach got.

"Enough," he said finally.

Knight helped roll Jorgen onto his back while Bradley dropped to his knees beside the old man. He worked by habit: two fingers to the carotid, count it out; watch the rise and fall of his chest; check skin temperature with the back of his hand. Pulse steady. Breathing slow, but not labored. No clammy sweat, no glassy stare. He eased an eyelid open—pupil tightened to the light, then drifted back. Reflexes all there.

"He's not in shock," Bradley murmured. "Vitals are clean. It's not a head injury, not anything obvious." That was the worst part—there was nothing to treat.

Mustang hovered just outside arm's reach, AR lenses ghosting faint lines over Jorgen's body. "No radiation spike. No airborne toxins on my sweep." He glanced at Bradley. "On the system side he reads like he's napping, but biology says something different, I'm guessing."

"Yeah," Bradley said. "This is too deep for sleep."

They moved to Alysha. Bradley repeated the checks—pulse, breathing, skin, pupils. The same unsettling normalcy. Strong heart, good oxygenation, no fever, no signs of stroke. He pressed gently along her neck and limbs, feeling for swelling or hidden trauma. Nothing.

"She's the same," he said quietly. "They're both stable. They're just not…waking."

Knight's jaw flexed. "So not poisoned, not bleeding out, not dying." He looked from one still form to the other. "Can they be moved?"

"Yes," Bradley answered. "Carefully. There's no physical reason we can't. But I don't know what did this or what happens if it gets worse."

Mustang scrubbed a hand over his face. "So the rock isn't killing them, the air isn't killing them, and nothing's screaming on my sensors," he said. "But they're out cold and staying that way. That about sum it up?"

Bradley sat back on his heels, the stone biting through his pants. "More or less," he repeated, more for the others than himself. "But this isn't normal sleep. Something's got hold of them, and I have no name for it."

The uncertainty settled over the chamber like another layer of stone. The tunnels ahead were still waiting. Now they just had to decide whether they were carrying their people into whatever came next—or leaving parts of themselves behind.

Bradley felt the questions cutting tighter with every second. "We can't stay here," he said, eyes tracing the carved walls as if they might open into daylight. "But we can't just leave them either."

The options lined up in his head and all of them were bad— drag two unresponsive bodies through hostile tunnels, split the group and bleed strength, or sit in this stone throat and wait for something worse to find them.

Knight broke the silence. "We may have to consider that this is as far as they go." His jaw clenched on the words, the hardness in his voice at odds with the thin thread of hope still hanging there.

Mustang didn't even try for humor this time. He snapped his case shut, stowing the last of his gear with careful, deliberate movements. "We put some distance between us and this room," he said. "Find a spot we can actually hold. If they wake, we come back for them."

They all heard the rest: and if they don't, we say goodbye on our feet instead of lying down beside them.

Pinky moved through the chamber on a different orbit than the rest of them, her bare feet whispering over stone. She'd found a small fungal bloom that had managed something like a flower —pale, luminous petals cupping a core of faint blue. She carried it to Alysha with both hands, set it gently in Alysha's slack fingers, then looked up, waiting for the familiar flicker of awareness that never came.

"When is Alysha going to wake up?" she asked. Her voice wasn't sing-song; it was flat with a quiet, gathering worry. "And Jorgen. He's supposed to tell a story before we leave."

Bradley dropped to a knee to meet her eyes. The right answer and the kind answer weren't the same, and the lie caught halfway up his throat. "They're worn down," he said finally. "Bodies can only take so much. They just need more time."

Pinky frowned, a small line digging between her brows. She glanced from Alysha to Jorgen, then back. "They've had time," she said. "We've all slept. Why aren't they getting up?"

The question was simple logic, and it hit harder than any accusation. Bradley had nothing he could hand her that wouldn't fracture something important.

Mustang stepped in, his usual edge sanded down to something quieter. "Sometimes people go under deep," he said. "Deeper than us. It's still sleep, but it doesn't care how long the rest of the world waits."

"That's not good enough," Pinky said. Her face tightened, and for a second Bradley saw past the dress and the small frame— saw the subject that had been pushed past every breaking point and forced to adapt. "They're supposed to wake up. They said they would."

Her control snapped all at once. "No," she said, sharper now, the word cracking in the air. She stepped into Bradley's chest, fingers knotting in his shirt. "Wake them up. Do something."

He wrapped his arms around her because it was the only thing left he knew how to do. She shook against him, breath hitching, not the wail of a child throwing a fit but the ragged surge of someone who'd run out of ways to bend without breaking.

Knight looked away, jaw working. Mustang busied himself with a strap that didn't need adjusting. The cavern shrank to the small circle of Bradley's arms and Pinky's shuddering breaths.

He murmured assurances he didn't believe, feeling each one land like a fresh crack in something fragile. They were losing ground on every front—but this felt like the worst failure: that he could not promise her the simple, solid thing she wanted. That her world, already carved up and repurposed by other people's ambition, was shrinking again, one sleeping figure at a time.

Around them, the bioluminescent glow kept pulsing on the stone, indifferent. It threw soft light over two unmoving forms, over the weapons and packs and bedrolls, over the girl in his arms. Bradley held her tighter and made himself a quiet, brutal promise: whatever came next, whatever choices they had to make, he would not let the Foundation—or this place—take the last of her away without a fight.

Pinky's sobs bled down into raw little breaths, the sound scraping at Bradley's nerves. She stayed pressed against his chest, fingers knotted in his shirt, but the storm had passed— for now.

Karl stepped in close, boots crunching on gravel and brittle fungus. His lined face was all stone and worry. "Look," he said, voice low, the usual growl smoothed at the edges. "We're not leavin' them. Not like this."

Bradley's head came up. For a heartbeat something hot and stubborn flared in his chest—then the math slammed into it. Weight, distance, air, food. Knight barely back on his feet. Mustang running on fumes. Pinky. "Karl, we can't carry them," he said. "Not both. Not through that." He jerked his chin toward the black throat of the tunnel. "We slow down, we bleed out. All of us."

He hated how reasonable it sounded.

Karl didn't back off. He turned a slow circle instead, eyes tracking the chamber walls, the fields of pale stalks clustered under the bioluminescent wash. "Those," he said, stabbing a finger toward a stand of thick, dried growth. Each stalk was as tall as his shoulder, hollow and fibrous, their outer skin papery and stiff. "They're light, they're strong, and they're dead dry." He glanced back at Bradley. "We don't carry. We drag. Couple of travois, like we used in the collapse tunnels back home. It'll ride rough, but it's better than walking away."

Mustang let out a low whistle. For once, there was no joke sitting behind it. "Well, damn, Karl," he said. "Didn't have 'emergency field engineer' on your résumé."

Karl snorted. "My sister always said my head's full of more rock than sense," he muttered. "But I know what holds and what doesn't."

Bradley looked from the stalks to Alysha's still form, to Jorgen's steady, unreachable breathing. The idea was terrible. It was also the first thing that hadn't felt like surrender in hours. He exhaled through his teeth. "If I see signs they're crashing— airway, pulse, anything—I call it," he said. "No arguments. We don't drag corpses."

Karl met his eyes and nodded.

The room shifted around that decision. A resting place became a workshop in a heartbeat. Knight levered himself up with a grunt and went to work beside Karl, his movements careful but sure. The dwarf hacked through the thicker stalks with practiced blows, each cut sending a dry, papery crack echoing off stone. Knight stripped webbing from spare packs, the synthetic straps rasping over his palms.

Mustang dug into his gear with renewed purpose, coming up with buckles, clips, anything that might bite into fungus and hold. "Square frame, cross-brace at the hips," he said, falling into problem-solving cadence. "We don't want them flexing too much or they'll snap."

"Cross-brace, I know," Karl grumbled, but he took the suggestion, lashing the first frame tight. The stalks creaked, then settled. "See? She'll ride."

The air filled with small, concrete sounds: the squeak of cinched straps, the scratch of knife on dried stalk, the wet slap of repacked rations dropped into a lighter kit. Someone's hands smelled of sap and fungal dust; Bradley caught it every time he bent to check Jorgen's vitals—still strong, still maddeningly unchanged.

Pinky watched without speaking at first. Her face was puffy from crying, but her eyes were clear. When Karl waved her over, she came, palms skimming along the rough stalks, testing their give.

"Here," Knight said, holding out a length of cord. "You can help tie the ends. Tight as you can. No slack."

She wrapped the cord with precise, economical movements, fingers steady. "If this breaks, he'll hit his head," she said, nodding toward Jorgen.

"Then we don't let it break," Knight replied. The line of his mouth eased, just a fraction.

When they finally slid Jorgen onto the first drag and Alysha onto the second, the chamber seemed to exhale. The travois were ugly things—roots, straps, and scavenged gear twisted into shape—but the sight of their people lying on something that moved with them, instead of staying behind, did something solid to the group's posture. Shoulders squared. Chins lifted.

Bradley took one last pass: fingers to throats, counting beats; listening at mouths for the soft rush of breath; checking eyes under lids for anything that screamed terminal. Nothing new. No better, no worse. For now, that would have to be enough.

"Travel light," he said. "Anything we don't eat, wear, or shoot in the next two days stays here."

They stripped their kit to bare function. Extra clothing, redundant tools, a few battered luxuries—gone. Jorgen's battered tin of coffee made the cut by silent consensus. Pinky tucked it deep into Bradley's pack herself.

When they stepped back into the tunnel, the world felt heavier.

The walls closed in, slick with condensation and veined with glowing fungus. The air was thicker here, tasting of wet stone and the faint metallic tang of old water. Every sound seemed louder—the drag of fungus runners over rock, the scrape of boots, the low grunt each time the travois caught on a ridge.

Karl took the first harness, thick stalk runners hissing over the uneven floor. Jorgen's weight settled into the straps, pulling at his shoulders and hips. Knight moved ahead, clearing loose stone, marking low overhangs with a tap of his knuckles.

After a while Knight swapped in without a word, jaw set as the strain woke every not-quite-healed muscle in his body. Karl walked beside the load then, one hand on a cross-brace, keeping it level.

Mustang carried more than his usual share of gear, pack straps biting into his shoulders. He stumbled once when a runner snagged on a hidden lip of stone, catching himself with a muttered curse. "This was more elegant in my head," he said under his breath.

"Welcome to the real world," Bradley answered, shifting Alysha's travois around a jagged outcrop. The stalks rasped over rock, sending a fine spray of dust into the air. He tasted grit on his tongue, coughed it out, kept moving.

Pinky stayed close to the rear drag, one hand on the side rail as if sheer will could keep Alysha anchored to them. She didn't chatter. She just watched, eyes tracking every jolt, every sway.

Step by step, the tunnel took them. The work was ugly and slow and it hurt—but no one turned back. The litters groaned and slid behind them, four stubborn lines carved through the dust, proof they had chosen to carry their own.

The absence of sound from their fallen became its own kind of noise. Jorgen should have been snoring—short, ugly blasts that everyone complained about and secretly relied on. Now his chest rose and fell without a sound. Alysha, who normally breathed like she fought—controlled, measured, present—lay as quiet as carved stone. Every time Bradley checked them, fingers at throat, ear hovering near their mouths, he heard nothing but the tunnel: distant drips, the whisper of air moving through unseen cracks, the faint rasp of fungal fronds brushing stone.

Pinky moved ahead of the litters with a brightness that outshown the bioluminescence. She didn't skip so much as glide from patch to patch of stronger glow, fingers skimming the carved walls as if tracing old scars. Under her breath, she ran a low, steady patter—not quite humming, not quite words —murmured commentary to the beasts and figures etched in the rock. It sounded less like play and more like someone deliberately filling silence. Watching her, Bradley felt the double edge of it: the fragile semblance of normalcy she clung to, and the knowledge that the truths they were hiding from her could shatter it in a heartbeat.

The world narrowed to breath and drag. Their own inhalations came harsh and loud in the confined space, ghosts of mist catching the green-blue light as they exhaled. Behind that, the litters spoke in a steady grind: dried fungal runners scraping over ridges, bumping across runnels in the floor, hissing when they skidded through fine gravel. Words, when they came, were short and quiet—a warning about a low ceiling, a muttered count on a pulse check, a hoarse request for a swap on the harness.

Karl's scouting runs shrank. Where he'd once vanished for minutes at a stretch, now he rarely slipped more than one bend ahead before easing back into view, brows drawn tight. The fungus didn't help. Its glow smeared the edges of everything; growths on the walls became hunched shapes until you got close enough to see the texture, and every projecting root looked like a waiting hand. More than once, Bradley saw Karl pause, shoulders tense, before a slow breath and a visible shake of the head loosened him again.

Rest came when Bradley said it had to—when hands weren't closing properly on straps, when Knight's gait turned ragged, when Mustang started missing obvious footing. They would wedge the litters against a wall, lay out thin mats on wet stone, and collapse. Sleep, when it came, was shallow and hard: Knight jerking awake at sounds that weren't there, Mustang swearing in his sleep, Bradley jolted out of dreams with his hands already reaching for his pistol. More than once he woke to hear Pinky talking in the dark—soft, urgent sentences aimed at someone who wouldn't answer.

Still, something in them refused to fold.

When Bradley felt his knees threatening to give, Knight would wordlessly shoulder into the harness, jaw clenched, limp all but gone as he dragged Jorgen's weight forward a few more meters. When Knight's eyes went far-off and his hand drifted toward a phantom crutch, Mustang would walk beside him until his focus returned. Karl's doubt showed in the way he touched the walls, palm lingering on the stone as if asking it questions; but if Pinky's low, tuneless murmur picked up behind him, he would square his shoulders and push on, as if that fragile sound was reason enough to keep moving.

As the march stretched and blurred, the tunnels began to work their way under Bradley's skin. Every creak from the travois jolted his nerves. A shift of gravel behind him had his hand half on his pistol before he identified it as his own footfall. Once, a distant rockfall somewhere above sent a spill of dust down through a crack in the ceiling; for a full minute after, he couldn't shake the conviction that something unseen was pacing them in the rock overhead, matching their steps.

Knight's calm started to fray at the edges. On breaks, he rubbed his thigh or shoulder with a frown that was more puzzled than pained, as if trying to reconcile what his training said about healing time with what his body was doing anyway. He spoke less. When he did, it was stripped-down and sharp—distance, water level, rotation plan. No commentary. No gallows humor.

Mustang's jokes turned brittle. The first time one of the fungal growths drooped low enough to brush his hair, he started to crack wise about "hostile salad" and then stopped halfway through, expression going flat as the thought of what the Foundation had already done with biomass caught up with him. After that, when he talked, it was usually logistics— ammunition yield per gram of matter, how long the containment fields could handle the ambient heat, what kind of range they'd have if they had to fight in a corridor this narrow.

And under all of it, Pinky kept moving.

She didn't ask again when Alysha and Jorgen would wake. She adjusted blankets when the litters snagged, tucked loose corners in so their arms wouldn't drag, and occasionally laid her palm against Alysha's cheek as they paused to rest, as if checking for some temperature only she understood. When Mustang's voice went too quiet or Knight stared too long at nothing, Bradley would catch them glancing forward—to the slim figure in the rainbow dress walking ahead of their burdens, talking softly to the shapes in the stone.

Whatever was left of hope had chosen her as its avatar.

Pinky's cheer had edges now, but it still pulled them forward. When they stopped, she would pass around whatever she'd scavenged—a rock with a seam of quartz that caught the fungus light, a thumb-sized knot of violet growth that stained her fingers, a shard of smoothed metal she insisted was "lucky." She offered each with the same unembarrassed seriousness, waiting for them to look, to nod, to acknowledge that there was still something in this place worth noticing that wasn't teeth or concrete.

On one short, grudging halt, she peeled away from the others and curled up beside Jorgen's litter. The old flower Alysha had given her was a crumpled thing now, edges browned and curling, but she cupped it like something fragile and set it carefully in his broad palm, folding his fingers around it one by one. The cavern smelled of wet stone and stale sweat; under that, Bradley caught the faint, sour bite of dried coffee on Jorgen's breath as he knelt to check his pulse again.

"Wake up, Jorgen," Pinky murmured, not whining, not begging —just stating it, as if it were a step in a process. Her voice was low enough that Bradley almost had to lean in to hear. "I found a story stone. Princess. Very old dragon. You'll like this one better."

Jorgen didn't move. The only answer was the slow rise and fall of his chest and the distant tick of dripping water somewhere in the dark. Pinky waited a few heartbeats longer, searching his face for some tiny tell, then gave a small, tight nod—as if filing the attempt away—and shifted closer, shoulder touching his arm, eyes half-closed but not really sleeping.

Bradley's throat tightened. He pressed his fingers against Jorgen's wrist until he felt the steady thrum of life, then checked Alysha in the same practiced motions. Warm skin. Regular respirations. No change. Nothing he could treat. Nothing he could fix.

They moved again when he called it. Harness straps bit into shoulders already rubbed raw; breath rasped loud in the narrow space, pluming white in the cooler pockets of air. The litters scraped and bumped behind them in a constant undertone.

Ahead, Pinky walked just beyond arm's reach, dress dulled by dust, rainbow hem flicking with each step. Every so often she glanced back, checking that Jorgen and Alysha were still there.

Bradley locked his eyes on that small, stubborn silhouette and forced his legs to keep pace. Whatever waited at the end of these tunnels—it wasn't allowed to have her. As long as she kept walking, he would too.

CHAPTER SIXTEEN

The warning hiss ran down the line like a live wire. After so many days of nothing but their own footsteps and the drip of distant water, the new sound—shouts, metal on stone, a wet, ugly impact—felt surreal. Battle, here, now, somewhere ahead in the green-lit dark.

They bunched together without needing to be told, bodies closing in around the two lashed litters. The tunnel widened just enough for them to pull in tight. Fungal light washed the stone in sickly turquoise and green, every stray tendril throwing long, twitching shadows.

Bradley cut his hand through the air—down, still. His heart thudded in his throat, the ache in his shoulders and spine burning away under the clean, sharp rush of adrenaline. He strained to separate the echoes: a croakbark of command in a language he didn't know, a deeper roar that wasn't human, the crash of something heavy slamming into rock.

Knight slid forward half a step, blaster up. The pale glow on his face caught the tight set of his jaw, the way his eyes tracked the curve of the tunnel, searching for shapes beyond the curtain of green growth.

Mustang brought his rifle up and tucked tight into his shoulder, the muzzle steady even as his gaze scanned ahead. "Of course," he muttered under his breath, voice a rough scrape. "Perfect time for us to be down two bodies." He adjusted his grip, finger resting just outside the trigger guard, waiting.

Karl shifted his weight, boots grinding on stone. The noises from ahead—those guttural shouts, the heavy impacts—didn't fit the predictable dangers of bad rock and bad supports he knew. His hands tightened around his climbing picks, the closest things he had to weapons, the steel heads glowing in fungus-light as he angled himself between the litters and whatever might be coming.

Pinky pressed in against Bradley's side, slender fingers digging into his sleeve. He felt the tremor running through her. Her eyes were wide, not the blank, distant wide of shock, but sharp and focused, turned toward the sound as if she could see straight through the bends of stone.

Another crash. A scream cut off mid-breath.

Then Pinky snapped.

"We have to go help them," she blurted, voice too loud in the confined space. "They're losing. There's a thing down there— it's tearing them apart. A monster—-a real monster!"

Bradley's hand shot out on instinct, catching her by the upper arm before she could bolt. "Pinky, stop." He hauled her back against his chest. "You can't know that. You're guessing from the noise."

She twisted in his grip, not wild, not panicked—purposeful. "I'm not guessing." Her voice cracked, but there was no childish wobble to it. "I hear them. I understand them. They're calling for help. One of them is asking for his brother. He thinks he's dying."

Bradley stared at her, the foreign sounds still meaningless in his ears. The language echoing down the tunnel was a smear of whispers and swallowed hisses, meaningless to his ears. "How?" he demanded, disbelief and a cold dread knotting in his gut. "Pinky, how can you understand any of that?"

"I don't know." Tears tracked lines down the dirt on her cheeks, but she didn't look away from the shadowed haze ahead. "The words…they turn into pictures. Faces. Movements." Her fingers flexed against his sleeve as if she could pull him forward by force. "The thing ambushed them. It's too fast. If we don't go now, they'll all die."

The shouts ahead spiked again—someone barking orders, someone else screaming in a different register entirely. Something heavy crashed, stone shearing and skittering. Whatever was down there was still very busy.

Mustang's gaze jumped between the mouth of the tunnel and Pinky's face, running calculations that had nothing to do with ballistics. "You're not just catching tone," he said, more to himself than to her. "You're parsing it. Full semantic take." He drew in a breath, jaw working. "All right, Pinky—can you tell if the thing making that noise is talking too? Not just roaring. Talking. Can you tell what it wants?"

Pinky nodded, her focus tilting toward the distant clash. "No…" she whispered, a tremor running through the word. "It's different. Louder. Like…angry shouting. It's got too many voices."

The others stiffened; cold recognition slid through the group. Pinky—the one they'd done everything to shield—suddenly held an edge none of them had. She could hear and understand —the foreign tongue, the ragged cries, even the monstrous bellowing—they weren't just noise to her. In a heartbeat she shifted from protected stray to something far more dangerous: a key—a living translation node.

Knight voiced what they were all thinking. "This makes her more of a target," he said, the words flat, gravel-rough. "Whoever—or whatever—is down there might not let someone like her just walk away. Even if we do help them."

Protecting Pinky had been hard enough when she'd just been unlucky. Now she was an asset. People killed for less.

"Listen," Bradley said, his voice low, steady by force of will. "We need eyes on what's going on. Mustang, Knight—get forward, see what you can about the layout. Karl and I will hold here. Keep your distance."

Mustang cut a look at Knight, unease ghosting his dark eyes. "We're going in blind," he muttered. "Don't know the language, don't know the ground, don't know how many bodies in play."

Knight gave a short nod. He adjusted his grip on the blaster, fingers settling into familiar grooves. "If it's a fight," he said under his breath. "We go slow and dirty. Learn as we engage. Let the chaos cover us."

They slipped ahead, hugging the tunnel wall until the floor dropped away into a wider cavern. Fungal light bled across the stone below, sickly green and blue, just enough to sketch the scene in stuttering detail—reptilian figures in piecemeal armor, maybe a dozen of them, and opposite them the bulk of a scorpion-like thing that shouldn't exist: too much chitin, its barbed tail lashing through the glow.

The sound hit next. Steel on shell. Wet impacts. The layered hiss of reptilian speech tangled with the creature's chittering roar, all of it bouncing off the rock and shivering up through their boots.

"This ain't good," Mustang breathed, barely moving his lips. "They're getting torn apart down there."

Knight's gaze tracked the angles, the distances, the lack of anything resembling decent cover. "They're wide open," he said. "Shields, spears, rocks. Against that? They're not walking out."

Training and survival instinct screamed the same thing—fall back, watch, learn, don't step into someone else's slaughter. But the urge to move, to do something while living things screamed and died in the muted dark.

A muffled shout rolled down the tunnel behind them. They turned as Bradley, Karl, and Pinky came up at a crouch, firelight from the rear camp still clinging to their clothes. Shock and raw concern mirrored back at Mustang and Knight from their faces.

Pinky took one look at the chaos below and went rigid. "We have to help them," she said. The words scraped out of her cutting straight through the tension.

Bradley's hand settled on her shoulder, firm but careful. "We're working on it, Pinky," he said, eyes already back on the fight, measuring angles, timing, consequences.

Karl leaned out just far enough to see, then recoiled with a low curse. The glow caught every line in his face, carving years into the scowl. "Can't just stand here while they get peeled apart," he muttered. "But that thing…" He jerked his chin toward the monster below. "That's a nightmare with legs."

With the four of them pressed against the rock lip, the decision grew heavier by the second. Step in, and they painted targets on their own backs. Stay put, and watch outnumbered fighters get scythed down by something that should never have crawled out of any lab or cave.

How the hell were they supposed to walk away from that?

Mustang tried to split the difference between instinct and sanity. "Maybe…" he started. "Maybe there's a way to pull it off that mess. Drop some rock on it, make it look the other way for a few seconds…"

His gaze swept the chamber below and the stone arch around them. The place was too big, too open—more cathedral than tunnel. The walls were slick with fungus, soft and spongy where he needed crack and fracture. Anything strong enough to shift stone would light them up in the monster's sights before it even landed.

Knight crushed that thin thread of hope without ceremony. "Too exposed," he said, voice low. "Even if we turn its head, they're still dead on their feet. No cover, no fallback. They've got nowhere to go."

Silence dropped over them, except for the fight below. The sounds came up in jagged waves—stone ringing under heavy impacts, the wet crack of chitin meeting flesh, reptilian voices shredded into screams. The scorpion's layered hiss crawled up the rock like steam, sour and metallic in Bradley's mouth.

Pinky pressed herself against his side, fingers knotting in the fabric of his trousers. He could feel her shaking. She turned her face into his hip, as if the cloth could block out the noise.

Bradley tore his eyes from the carnage long enough to meet the others' looks—Knight's blunt assessment, Karl's tightening scowl, Mustang's pinched frustration. There wasn't a good call here, just different kinds of bad.

"We hit it hard," Bradley said. "We hit it fast." His voice came out rough, but steady. "Our priority is the wounded. We buy them a gap and we drag them out."

Karl gave a single, tight nod. "Reckon that's the only play worth making."

Mustang rapped his knuckles against the side of his rifle, a ghost of a grin tugging at one corner of his mouth. "Well, if we're doing something stupid, we might as well do it with style," he said. "I've still got charges left. We can make one hell of an introduction."

Behind Bradley, Pinky watched them from the shelter of his arm, eyes wide and too clear. She understood enough now to know there was no guarantee in what they were about to do. Fear pinched at her features, but there was something else under it—a stubborn, brittle hope.

They moved. Adrenaline cut through the mud of exhaustion, sharpening the world. Karl peeled off along the rim, boots whispering over the stone as he hugged the wall, looking for height and angle—somewhere he could reach the dried clumps of fungus without stepping into the open.

Bradley and Mustang slid closer to the lip overlooking the cavern, choosing what little broken stone there was to brace behind. The air down there felt thicker, hot with the stink of chitin, blood, and the rot-sweet tang of disturbed fungus.

Pinky latched onto Bradley's leg again as he took position. Her forehead pressed against his thigh, breath coming fast and shallow. He reached down, gave her hand a quick squeeze— one brief, wordless promise—and then loosened his grip so she could pull back if she needed to.

Below, the reptilian fighters regrouped and charged again, shields up, spears flashing in the fungal light. The scorpion met them like a closing trap. One heavy pincer snapped shut on a defender's torso, and the body folded with a sound Bradley felt in his teeth.

Time dragged. Each heartbeat slammed against his ribs, a countdown.

Karl's signal finally came—a low, sharp whistle that cut clean through the din.

Mustang settled his cheek to the stock, the rifle's containment core humming against his shoulder. He tracked the scorpion's head, waited for a gap in its wild thrashing, then squeezed the trigger.

The shot cracked the air, a white-hot bolt punching into the thick plating along the monster's skull. Chitin charred and cratered, fragments spinning off in glowing shards. The scorpion screamed—a layered, grinding shriek—and reared, tail lashing wildly as it tried to locate the new threat.

Bradley didn't wait. He ripped free of cover with a hoarse, wordless shout, boots skidding on the slope as he charged down toward the killing ground, every line of his body angled toward the creature. If it looked anywhere, it needed to look at him.

Up high, Karl thumbed one of Mustang's charges and slammed it into a clutch of brittle fungus stalks wedged in a crack. The blast punched heat and pressure across the ceiling. Desiccated growths went up at once, a curtain of fire and spores peeling away into the air.

Light flared—a sudden, searing wash that painted the cavern in violent orange and green. The scorpion recoiled again, pincers snapping at nothing as glowing dust rained over its shell.

Down on the floor, two of the reptilian warriors seized the opening. They broke from the line, sprinting for the crushed fighter still sprawled in the dust. Their hisses shifted tone— from panic to command—as they grabbed their comrade under the arms and began to drag, muscles straining against the stone.

Mustang rode the edge between panic and exhilaration. He braced, sighted low, and dumped another bolt into the thing's nearest leg joint. The shot sizzled across the cavern, punching into the pale seam between plates. Chitin blackened and blew apart in a spray of smoking shards. The scorpion lurched sideways with a tearing screech that rattled his teeth.

Chaos tore the battlefield into jagged pieces. They weren't trying to win—just to throw the monster off-balance long enough for the scaled fighters to drag their wounded clear. Heat rolled back at them in suffocating waves. The air stank of scorched fungus and cooked shell, a greasy, bitter reek that clung to the back of Bradley's throat. For a few heartbeats, they held—sheer stubborn will pressed back against the impossible.

For a heartbeat, it worked. The scorpion reeled, stunned, its front legs buckling as Mustang stitched more fire along the wounded limb. Cracks raced through its armor. Segments hung at wrong angles.

Bioluminescent threads boiled out of the wounds, knitting across splintered chitin with obscene speed. The green-white filaments thickened, braided, hardened, weaving themselves into a new shell over the exposed joints. What should have been mangled weakness became layered, glowing armor.

The creature's shrieks shifted—less pain now, more rage. It planted those freshly sheathed legs and drove its weight back into the stone, tail lashing, pincers snapping with renewed strength.

"Damn it," Karl spat, voice rough with disbelief. "The damn stuff's healing it."

Across the cavern, the surviving reptilian fighters had broken contact. They staggered toward the far wall, dragging a limp comrade between them. Their steps were uneven, some favoring wounded limbs, but they moved with purpose. The rhythm of their hissing changed—less despair, more harsh, driven intent.

Bradley stood too far out from cover, breath sawing in and out. The realization hit like a punch: their distraction hadn't crippled the monster. They'd just helped it molt into something worse. He found Mustang's gaze across the chaos—the brief flash of raw fear there matched the cold spike in his own gut.

They had no way to shout a plan to the reptilians, no shared words to warn them, no guarantee their fire wouldn't be turned on by grateful survivors the second the scorpion fell. They were fighting shoulder to shoulder with strangers and might as well have been ghosts for all the understanding between them.

The beast locked onto them, clustered eyes burning with a damp, glassy focus. It shook off the last clinging spores, turned its ruined-then-mended bulk upslope, and started forward. Stone shuddered beneath each step. Pincers rose, wide enough to crush a man in half.

Tactics thinned down to instinct: live now, think later.

While Bradley and Mustang fell back on angle and fire, Knight did what Knight had been bred and trained to do. He stopped thinking.

He hit the cavern floor like a riot line breaking—boots pounding, shoulders squared, every stride a promise of impact. His blaster came in close against his chest, less firearm than weighted baton, the butt and frame ready for bone and shell instead of clean, ranged shots. Dust and glowing spores burst around his legs as he drove straight at the thing, using its focus on Bradley as his opening.

The scorpion roared—a grinding, wet metal sound. Knight answered with a bellow of his own, raw and wordless, cutting through the layered hisses and the crack of energy fire. He wasn't aiming for a killing stroke. Every swing, every shoving impact, was meant to slam, stagger, and shove that massive bulk off rhythm—turning the cavern itself into a weapon as he forced the monster to react to him, not the other way around.

The scorpion's pincers scythed through the air, Knight met them head-on. Dura-glass kissed chitin with a teeth-rattling crack as his riot shield took the blow, shunting the massive claw aside in a shower of glowing spores. The impact numbed his arm to the elbow, but he reset his stance and stepped back in, forcing the creature to track him instead of the retreating reptilian fighters.

He moved with a speed that didn't match his bulk. Short, brutal pivots. Half steps. Shield snaps that turned killing arcs into glancing blows. Every dodge and parry came from drilled muscle memory and a hot, steady burn in his chestUnlike the others, Knight wasn't looking for an exit or a better angle. Bradley and Mustang thought in lanes of fire and fallback positions. Knight thought in lines that did not break. His bellowed curses hammered off the stone, a simple message hurled into the cavern with every collision of metal and shell: *no farther.*

Something got through, his forearm was bleeding but he couldn't stop to wrap it. The shield shook under another strike, edges biting into his forearm. His shoulders screamed, breath sawed harsh and hot in his throat, but his body absorbed the punishment and kept moving. He was exactly what he'd been trained to be in crowded streets and burning corridors—a wall that walked. He knew he couldn't bring the monster down alone. That wasn't the point. Standing in its way was.

His roars weren't battle speeches. They were the same wordless, grinding sound he'd made holding riot lines against stampeding crowds—the sound a human body made when it decided to endure until it fell over or the world died.

Their gamble had stalled. The scorpion's fungus-reinforced shell made a cruel joke of their earlier damage, proof that these depths were willing to repair their own nightmares. For a moment, all they'd bought was a few gasping breaths and a worse enemy.

Then something shifted at the edge of the fight.

The skinks—lean, scaled forms who'd been dragging their wounded toward the rear of the cavern—checked their retreat. One, taller and broader than the rest, straightened. A rough circlet of braided, bioluminescent fungus hugged its brow, casting pale halos across the ridges of its skull. It hissed, long and sharp, and jabbed its spear toward Knight, toward Mustang's flashes of energy fire, toward Karl scrambling along the wall.

The meaning wasn't in the words but in the posture. Recognition. Choice.

The crowned skink drew in a breath and loosed a piercing cry that answered Knight's roar note for note, a ragged, scaled echo of defiance. The others replied in kind. Their hisses rose, braid of sound over the thunder of the scorpion's rage, and then they turned as one.

Primitive blades and stone-tipped spears came up. Bare feet slapped wet rock. They charged back into the killing ground.

It wasn't the organized withdrawal Bradley had hoped to buy them. It was something narrower and fiercer—a shared refusal to die running. For a heartbeat, humans and skinks held the same line, shoulder to metaphorical shoulder, and threw themselves at the same monster.

The fight exploded outward. Karl, heart hammering, used their surge like cover. He scrambled higher along a ridgeline of stone, fingers digging into damp fissures, searching for another angle to throw heat and shrapnel down on the scorpion's flanks.

Mustang saw the shift and pushed his luck. He could feel the rifle's core running hot against his shoulder, vents fanning his cheek with scorched air, but he rode the edge anyway. "Come on, you bastard," he muttered, tracking for the gaps Knight forced open. Each time the NCO slammed his shield into a joint or drove the beast off balance, Mustang snapped a shot at exposed seams—charred plates, softer membranes, anything that might actually stay broken.

The scorpion went wild. Pincers snapped at Knight, at skinks darting under its reach, at the bright stutter of Mustang's fire. Its barbed tail carved glowing arcs through the spore-lit air. For all its power, it struggled to answer everything at once. Skinks darted in and out of range, stabbing at tendons and softer tissue, leaving thin lines of dark blood that didn't heal fast enough. Their smaller cuts didn't cripple, but they stole the monster's attention in ragged, vital pieces.

Behind the broken line of stone, Pinky pressed herself into Bradley's side and stayed there. Her fingers hooked into the torn fabric of his trousers, knuckles white against the dark material. She watched around the edge of his hip, eyes huge, throat working against the urge to sob or cheer. The sight of scaled fighters and humans moving in the same rough rhythm —Knight taking hits meant for others, skinks answering his roars with their own—hit her like something halfway between a nightmare and a story Jorgen might have told if he were awake.

The cavern shook with it all: the clang of shield on pincer, the crack of Mustang's rifle, the wet crunch of stone weapons biting into shell, the layered hisses of pain and rage. The monster's shrieks tangled with Knight's bellows and the skinks' answering cries until it was impossible to hear where one species ended and the other began.

The fight crested into a raw, deafening blur. Skinks darted under the sweep of chitin and fungus, their scaled feet slapping wet stone, crude blades flashing in the sour green glow. The scorpion met their courage with mechanical brutality.

One skink misjudged a step. A pincer snapped shut with a crack like splitting bone, and its hiss cut off mid-breath as the body folded, limp, into the claw. Another took the barbed tail full-on. The impact hurled it into the cavern wall; the dull, wet crunch that followed made even Knight flinch. For a heartbeat the charge faltered, their courage stuttering around those broken shapes on the stone.

Bradley felt each fall like a blow to his own ribs. From his position behind a fungal outcrop, he caught flashes of scaled limbs at wrong angles, the dark smear of fresh blood on stone, and felt doubt bite down hard. How many lives for a fight that wasn't even theirs? Knight, braced beside him, tracked the same carnage with a clenched jaw, the muscle in his cheek jumping with every impact.

The scorpion's tail came around again—wild, enraged, a whip of plated muscle and venom. Mustang was still fixed on a weakened joint, lining up another shot. He saw the blur too late. The tail hammered into his side and shoulder like a swinging battering ram. The sound—flesh and stone in the same brutal note—echoed through the cavern.

Mustang's scream tore loose as he went down. His rifle bounced away across the slick rock. He hit the ground on his back, breath blasted from his lungs, his right arm already hanging limp and swelling beneath torn fabric.

"Karl!" Bradley shouted, but the dwarf was already in motion. Karl scrambled across the uneven floor, boots skidding on slime, swearing under his breath as he lunged toward Mustang. The scorpion drove forward on him instead, pincers gouging furrows in the stone, forcing Karl to jerk back or be pinned.

The last two skinks hesitated. The fungal-crowned leader stood half-turned, caught between the wounded humans and the shattered remains of his own fighters. The crown sat crooked now, strands of glowing fungus dangling across one eye. Confusion and raw fear alive in his posture—charge again and lose everything, or cut their losses and leave these strangers to die.

Bradley felt the moment tipping toward collapse. "Fall back!" he bellowed, voice cracking over the clangor. "Regroup! Now!"

The order snapped through the chaos, but it didn't land on everyone.

Something in Knight broke along a different seam. The mounting casualties, Mustang's limp body, the backpedal he heard in Bradley's voice—it all slammed into him tearing at a wall he didn't even know was there. He planted his feet, shield up, refusing even the idea of turning his back.

"I am not running," he roared, the shout scraping up from somewhere lost to time and forced experimentation. "Never again!"

While skinks and humans peeled away in stuttering retreat, Knight continued to press the monster.

He drove forward with the full weight of his body behind the shield. The dura-glass rim caught the scorpion across the head, just above its clustered eyes. The impact rang through the cavern like a struck bell, sending a dull shock all the way into his spine. The monster reeled, its front legs skidding, tail jerking wild as it adjusted to the unexpected force.

Knight wrenched the shield off-line just enough to see past its edge. With his good hand he yanked his blaster up into the gap and squeezed. One, two, three shots—each one at full power, each one punching into the softer plates and fungal growth along the underbelly where it reared back. The bolts hit with sizzling pops, charring flesh and flaring spores into a brief, blinding spray.

The weapon protested in his grip. Warning tones shrilled; the casing grew hot enough to sting his palm. Knight felt the power core stutter. Smoke curled from the vents. Useless. He dropped it without a second thought, fingers tightening instead on the straps of his shield.

Then he went to work.

He slammed the shield into the scorpion again and again, hammering at joints, already-damaged plates, anything that gave even a little under impact. Each blow sent fresh fractures spidering through the dura-glass, hairline cracks that multiplied under the stress. Chips flew from the rim. The shield vibrated so hard his joints ached, but Knight barely registered it over the red haze roaring in his ears.

The scorpion's focus narrowed to him. Pincers snapped down, trying to crush the smaller figure that dared to stand alone in front of it. Knight slipped sideways on blistered feet, the movements ugly but efficient—half-learned dance from riot lines, not battlefield training. The claws slammed into the ground where he'd been a heartbeat before, spraying shards of stone.

He ducked under one strike, rolled his shoulder, and came up inside the arc of the next, shield catching and shoving the claw off-course. Each near miss grazed his armor, left new dents, ripped another strip of skin from his forearm where the straps dug in. But he kept moving, kept swinging, kept shouting his ragged refusal into the cavern air.

There would be no retreat, not for him. For this stretch of heartbeats, Knight's world had narrowed to one simple fact: if the monster wanted to push past him, it was going to have to go through him.

Tears gathered in Pinky's eyes as she watched, her small hands knotting into fists, knuckles pale in the green wash. Each crash of Knight's shield against chitin rang through the cavern, dura-glass on armor, a brutal, hollow report that rattled Bradley's ribs. Every near miss, every lunge of the pincers that missed Knight by less than inches, was a fresh reminder of how close the next second might come to killing him.

Knight's stand had nothing to do with good tactics. Bradley could see that in the set of his shoulders, in the way he drove forward when any sane soldier would have broken contact and fallen back. It wasn't strategy, or even survival—it was rage. It was a raw, guttural rejection of the thing bearing down on them and the black weight pressing in from all sides. Knight had

332

been injured; there had been nobody to fight; but now, he had a target.

Knight only relented his assault to brace for another heavy blow from the scorpion. The pincer made contact. The shield finally gave, dura-glass cracked with a sharp, splintering report and blew apart, shards spinning across the wet stone.

A pincer followed through—striking Knight across the chest and sent him flying. He struck the cavern wall hard enough that Bradley heard the air leave him in a single, ugly grunt. Knight slid down the rock, armor scraping, and crumpled at the base.

Through the blur he saw the creature rear, tail lifting high. Venom gleamed along the barb, fungal light catching in the wet sheen. It coiled to drive straight through him.

A shout tore out of Bradley, more instinct than language, as he threw himself forward. He knew even as he sprinted that he was too far.

The tail began to fall.

For a fraction of a second, time stretched thin. Bradley felt, with awful clarity, the helpless certainty: they were about to watch Knight die under that thing, smashed into paste on the cavern floor.

A blur of rainbow-lined white shot past his peripheral vision.

Pinky tore free of his reach before his hand could close around her sleeve. She was easily outpacing him, feet splashing through a shallow film of water, the rainbow hem of her dress snapping at her calves. Her face was a mask of terror and iron resolve, eyes locked on Knight and the falling barb.

The barb slammed into the rock above Knight with a crack that shook dust and spores from the ceiling. Chips skittered across the floor around her ankles.

When she stopped, Pinky turned and planted herself between Knight and the monster, feet apart, shoulders squared, arms flung out in a human barricade that would do nothing against that mass of chitin and muscle.

"No!" Her voice ripped through the cavern, high but not childish in its fury. "Leave him alone!"

The scorpion froze.

It loomed over her, all segmented bulk and clicking mandibles, beady eyes reflecting the fungal light in dead facets. For a breath, its entire frame went still, as if the sight of this tiny, unarmored thing standing in its path did not fit any pattern it understood. The barbed tail twitched, shifting a few inches instead of driving down.

Behind her, Knight clawed at the rock, trying to get his boots under him. Pain flared white-hot through his back and ribs, but he forced air into his lungs. "Pinky—" His voice came out as a ragged rasp. "Get back!"

She didn't move.

Heat from the scorpion's body washed over her; the air stank of venom, scorched chitin, and the metallic bite of spilled blood. Bradley's heart hammered in his throat as he watched that impossible standoff—an armored nightmare and a girl in a dress, squared off in the green gloom.

# CHAPTER SEVENTEEN

The cavern fell into a strangled hush at the center of the chaos. The scorpion's bulk loomed over everything—fungal light, skink bodies, shattered stone—until the whole world narrowed to a single point: Pinky, small and rigid, standing between Knight and the barb.

Then the thing's tail snapped in one fluid, predatory arc, venom beading along the tip like black glass. The air hissed as it cut through, and for a heartbeat the only sound was the rush of it falling toward her chest.

Bradley's roar tore loose before he knew he was breathing. It bounced off the stone in raw, broken echoes. Karl's fingers locked around a useless projectile, joints whitening. Knight, pinned under his own pain, tasted iron at the back of his throat—a hot, metallic failure he couldn't swallow.

The skink leader keened, crown of glowing fungus bobbing as its hiss broke into something closer to a wail.

The barb was a breath away from Pinky when the world snapped.

Light erupted from her—violent, sudden, nothing like the soft fungal glow that painted the cavern walls. It came in a single, searing pulse that punched outward from her skin, not white but a hard, prismatic glare that ate color and shadow at once. Bradley's vision went blank. Heat washed over his face, dry and electric, smelling of ozone and dust and sun-baked sand after a storm.

He threw an arm across his eyes, teeth gritted. For a second there was only the sound of excited air and the press of that light.

When the glare eased enough for shapes to return, Pinky wasn't there.

In her place stood a woman wearing the same rainbow dress, now hanging over a taller, impossibly composed frame. Bare feet on wet stone. Shoulders squared. The violet of her eyes was unchanged, but the look behind them was different—no confusion, no fear. Depth. Indignation. Something ancient and awake.

The scorpion recoiled as if struck. Its tail jerked back, barb dripping, mandibles ticking in a restless, uncertain chatter. The woman lifted her hands, fingers spreading as if she could feel the air around them like fabric.

When she spoke, the cavern carried her voice like a blow to stone.

"You dare to threaten me?"

The words rolled out of her, layered—Pinky's timbre buried under something older and colder, a resonance that made the hairs rise along Bradley's arms. Dust sifted from the ceiling with every syllable.

"Foolish creature," she said, and the contempt in it was absolute. "Behold the new dawn of Anaku'tawa."

Light gathered between her palms, not in a single beam but in a churning, condensed sphere. It spun on itself, threads of color braiding and unbraiding too fast for his eyes to track. The air around it warped, heat rippling outward, carrying the sharp tang of burned metal and ionized air. Sparks bled from its edges and fell upward instead of down.

She stepped forward, bare feet unflinching on the wet stone, and threw.

The sphere spun in her hand, growing with each rotation. It consumed the immediate area around the statuesque woman standing where Pinky should have been.

Everything vanished in light.

The blast chewed the darkness out of the cavern in a single instant. Pressure slammed into Bradley's chest, shoving the breath out of him. The sound of it ripped through his skull— too loud to process, leaving nothing but a high, shrill ringing. Heat crashed over them, a dry, baking wave that smelled of scorched chitin, cooked meat, and hot stone.

When the glare finally guttered out, afterimages floated in his vision—ghost-rings of color, burned into his sight. The front half of the scorpion was simply gone. What remained was a smoking ruin of blackened segments and fused armor, still twitching in reflex as viscous fluids hissed on the overheated rock.

At the center of the devastation, the woman stood alone.

Her outline shimmered, half-solid in the fading brilliance, dress whipping in a wind that wasn't there. For a heartbeat she looked unshakable—chin up, shoulders back, eyes bright with a fierce, terrible certainty.

Then something in her went wrong.

The triumph drained from her face, replaced by a flash of disorientation—fear, sharp and human, cutting through the goddess-like veneer. Her form wavered, edges blurring as if she stood behind water. The dress stuttered between sizes; her arms flickered thin, then small, then smaller again.

The light around her faltered.

With one last stuttering flare, the woman's shape collapsed inward, the brilliance folding tight and then snuffing out like a candle pinched between wet fingers.

Where she had stood, Pinky lay curled on the stone, knees tucked to her chest, bare feet streaked with dust. The rainbow dress bunched around her, far too large in places as if it hadn't had time to settle back to her size. She didn't stir. Her breathing came in small, shallow pulls, lashes damp against her cheeks.

Bradley stumbled to her, boots slipping in the slick mess left by the scorpion's remains. His heart hammered hard enough to hurt. He dropped to his knees beside her and reached out, hands hovering for a beat, afraid to touch. Her skin was warm —warmer than it should've been—but not burning. Pulse, when he found it at her throat, thudded steady against his fingertips.

Relief hit like a blow. It didn't erase the dread.

Up close, even in sleep, she looked…different. Not older. Not exactly. But there was a tension around her eyes that hadn't been there before, a faint shadowing in the skin beneath them, as if some part of her had stayed awake while the rest shut down. The echo of that other voice, that name—Anaku'tawa—still rang in Bradley's head, layered over her usual laugh, over every soft question she'd ever asked him.

Around them, no one moved.

The surviving skinks stood frozen, weapons slack in their hands, staring at the small, unconscious girl like she was more dangerous than the creature that had almost killed them. The leader's crown-glow painted its wide reptilian eyes, equal parts worship and fear.

Bradley swallowed hard, keeping his hand on Pinky's pulse as if that alone could anchor her to the version of reality he understood.

She was alive.

She was also something else entirely.

Knight forced himself upright, boots slipping a little in the slurry of chitin and cooked meat. His ribs protested, but he pushed through it, bracing a hand on the cracked stone. His eyes swept the cavern—not measuring firing lanes or cover this time, but trying and failing to wrap themselves around what he'd just seen. Half a scorpion the size of a truck lay smoking on the floor. The other half was gone. No blast marks he understood, no visible source—just absence and a girl curled where a goddess had been standing.

Karl stared at the same spot, jaw working under his beard. The damp stone still held a faint shimmer where Pinky had stood in that impossible light. He looked from that ghost of brightness to the small, sleeping figure in the oversized dress, and something in his usually steady expression fractured.

"What in the hells…" he began, voice rougher than usual, and then stopped. There wasn't language for that.

Silence pressed in, thick and wet. Even the fungus seemed to dim, its cold glow leached by whatever had just burned through the cavern.

Then a new sound cut through it—a slow, hollow tapping. Hard against wet stone, evenly spaced. Instinct snapped every head around toward the darkness.

The two surviving skinks emerged from the gloom at the edge of the fight. They moved differently now: no darting aggression, no flared crests. Their steps were measured, cautious, as if they approached something wounded and dangerous in equal measure. Between them, cupped in clawed hands, they bore a shallow stone bowl. Thick liquid sloshed inside—a viscous, faintly luminous slurry that clung to the sides, casting a pale, oily light across their scaled wrists.

They stopped a few paces from Pinky. Slowly, with the kind of care Knight had only ever seen around unexploded ordnance, the blue-tailed leader set the bowl on the stone in front of her sleeping form. Both skinks sank to their knees, heads bowed, tails low, hands spread in a posture that needed no translation.

Not just fear. Reverence.

Their hisses dropped to a whisper, the harsh edge gone. The blue-tail glanced up, crest twitching, then turned its narrow head toward Mustang. It jabbed the air, not at his rifle or his chest, but at his arm—swollen, darkening, hanging crooked against his side.

The smaller, brown-scaled skink eased forward. It extended a hand, palm up, as if asking permission from a man who could barely stand. Its fingers brushed Mustang's forearm. The touch was unexpectedly warm, the scales rough but careful, settling on the ruined limb with a pressure that was almost…reassuring.

A tight ripple of unease went through the group. In another fight, an injury like that would be an opening to exploit, a reason to finish a man where he stood. But there was no gloating in the skink's stare. Its pale eyes, slit-pupiled and unblinking, held something that read disturbingly close to pity.

It began to croon, a low, rhythmic chant that thrummed against the stone. The sounds were all throat and chest, guttural syllables rising and falling in a pattern that tugged at the nerves, not the ears—unfamiliar, yet oddly soothing.

With its free hand, the skink unknotted a crude pouch at its belt. It pinched out a mash of shredded leaves shot through with glistening spores that pulsed faintly in the dim light. When it tore them open, the air filled with a sharp, damp smell —earth after rain, crushed moss, something bitter and metallic beneath.

The skink tipped a measure of the luminous liquid from the stone bowl into the mess in its palm, working the mixture together with deft, stained fingers until it became a paste that clung like wet clay. Then, with the same strange gentleness it had shown touching Mustang's arm, it began to smear the salve along the swollen flesh and mangled joint.

Mustang drew a breath through his teeth. For a heartbeat his expression twisted, bracing for a spike of pain that didn't come. Instead, a coolness spread beneath the skink's hands, sinking through bruised tissue into bone. The raw, electric agony that had been chewing at his nerves since the blow ebbed, receding under the salve's slow-burning chill.

He flexed his fingers experimentally. The arm still hung useless, strength gone and joint shot to hell, but the pain had dulled to a distant ache, bearable where moments before it had been blinding.

The skink patted the last of the salve into place with a satisfied hiss and backed off, rejoining its leader. Both of them bowed again—first to Mustang, then deeper, to Pinky. Their hands spread toward the stone bowl and the clump of softly pulsing fungus beside it.

The message was painfully clear, even without Pinky's gift for tongues.

They thought she had done this. The blast. All of it. And now they wanted something back—blessing, favor, whatever passed for worship in these depths.

Bradley's stomach turned. The protective instinct that had shoved him across battlefields roared back to life.

"No," he said, sharper than he intended. His voice cracked off the cavern walls, startling even himself. "No. We're not doing that." He shifted closer to Pinky without quite realizing it, putting himself between her and the offerings. "We won't exploit her like that."

Knight didn't argue, but his attention stayed on the skinks. His eyes narrowed, not in awe but in assessment, tracking the way they held themselves, the way their gazes shifted between Pinky, the bowl, and the humans' weapons.

"They're hurt too," he said after a moment, nodding toward the scorched scales, the bandaged flank on the blue-tail, the way the brown one favored one leg. His tone was flat, measuring. "They're not surrendering. They're offering a deal. Aid, maybe shelter. Maybe more." His gaze slid to Pinky's small, sleeping form, to the faint tremor in her fingers. "In exchange for..."

He didn't finish. He didn't have to. The rest of the thought hung between them like a live wire, humming in the dim, fungal light.

The skinks' intent stare never left Pinky. Their throats pulsed with low, steady hisses that sounded almost like chanting. It wasn't the sharp threat-noise they'd heard in the fight; this was softer, rhythmic, edged with something that made the hairs on Bradley's arms stand up. The way they held themselves— heads bowed, hands open, bodies angled toward her but kept at a careful distance—felt less like wariness and more like worship.

It hit him then how far apart their worlds were. To him, she was a girl in a gifted dress, curled on cold stone, breathing too shallow after doing something that shouldn't be possible. To them, she was that woman of light—a creature that had erased half a monster in a heartbeat. A thing you knelt to. The reverence in their eyes made his gut twist. They weren't looking at a frightened survivor. They were looking at a goddess.

Questions crowded in, ugly and sharp. Were they begging for their leader's life, or was this only the first step in some ritual he could barely guess at? Was this an offering, a test, or the start of demands that would only grow heavier? Bradley couldn't tell if he was looking at future allies, fanatics, or something in between.

Behind that knot of uncertainty, another pressure throbbed—Alysha and Jorgen, lying motionless somewhere in the tunnels behind them. The thought of leaving them out there made his chest tighten. Sandstone corridors, cold fungus light drifting over two bodies no one was watching. He'd seen enough unclaimed dead in his life; he wasn't about to add his people to the list if he could help it. But dragging Pinky and Mustang deeper without knowing if Alysha and Jorgen were even alive felt just as reckless.

"Mustang and I will stay here with Pinky," he said at last, voice low but steady. He didn't take his hand off her shoulder. "Someone needs to go back for them. They won't be far."

Knight shifted his weight, one hand pressed briefly against his ribs before he straightened. The pain was still there, written in the tight lines around his eyes, but his answer came without hesitation. "I'll go," he said. The gravel in his voice made it sound like a foregone conclusion. "Karl, you're with me. I'll need help getting both of them back here."

Karl grunted once in answer, not bothering with bravado. His gaze flicked toward the tunnel mouth, then to Pinky, then to the skinks, measuring distances the way he always did. He rolled his shoulders, as if settling an invisible pack, and nodded.

Karl's sense of the stone and Knight's sheer stubbornness would have to be enough to retrace their path and haul Jorgen and Alysha back. The tunnels swallowed sound quickly; even now, Bradley could hear only the slow drip of water and the quiet rasp of his own breathing.

The skinks stayed put as Knight and Karl moved off, their tails flicking with nervous energy. They didn't reach for weapons. They didn't move to block the way. They simply watched—

eyes gleaming in the bioluminescent haze—as if the departures and returns of these soft-skinned strangers were as important as the shifting of the earth itself. Their posture wasn't friendly, but it wasn't hostile either. They were anchored here, orbiting Pinky, as though whatever future they saw for themselves rose or fell with her next breath.

Once the echo of Knight and Karl's footsteps faded down the tunnel, the cavern contracted. The fungus-glow flattened, throwing longer shadows. A slow, hollow drip somewhere in the dark ticked off the seconds, each one a reminder that their margin for error was razor-thin.

Bradley stayed close to Pinky, dropping into a crouch beside her. The stone was damp beneath his knee, cold leaching through his fatigues. He brushed a stray lock of hair back from her face with two fingers, careful not to jostle her. Her skin was warm, her pulse steady at the throat, but there was a slackness in her features he didn't like—a tension just under the surface, as if some part of her was still braced for impact.

The skinks shifted but didn't close in. Their muscles flexed and relaxed under patterned scales, restless without stepping over whatever line they'd drawn in their own heads. Their eyes, lidless and unblinking, stayed fixed on Pinky. When they glanced at Bradley or Mustang, it was quick and sideways, the way you checked on other worshippers, not rivals.

The offerings sat untouched between them: the stone bowl of faintly glowing liquid, viscous and slow to move, and the lump of pale fungus at its side, its surface pulsing with an internal light. The stuff smelled faintly of wet earth and something metallic, like old blood and crushed leaves. Bradley had the irrational sense that taking any of it would lock them into a pact he didn't understand.

Mustang paced a narrow line, boots scuffing grit across the rock. His damaged arm was bound tight against his chest, but the rest of him couldn't stay still. "Well, damn," he muttered finally. "This just keeps getting weirder. We've got lizard worshippers now." The comment landed flat, his usual edge blunted by fatigue and something close to disbelief.

Bradley didn't answer. The joke wasn't wrong, exactly. It just didn't make him feel any better. They weren't just a squad in a hole—they were on someone else's altar, and they hadn't agreed to that.

In the skinks' eyes, Pinky wasn't a casualty to protect or a kid to keep away from the front lines. She was the blast of impossible light, the thing that had unmade a monster with a word. A conduit to something these creatures had probably been whispering prayers to long before any of them fell into this place. The hope in their faces was as raw as it was unnerving; they looked at her the way starving men looked at full rations.

A rasping hiss broke through his thoughts. The blue-tailed leader took a cautious step forward, claws clicking on damp stone. Its crest flared slightly, then flattened as it stopped just short of the bowl. It pointed—first to the glowing liquid, then to Pinky, then back again. The gesture was slow, deliberate, almost pleading.

Bradley met its gaze and saw no malice there, only a desperate expectation. They weren't trying to drag Pinky away. They weren't reaching for her or for his weapon. They were asking.

He didn't like this idea of the lizard creatures worshipping her. It didn't help that they had no idea how alien their goals might be. He had no idea what they even were. They might not want Pinky for profit as they understood it—or in the clinical, weaponized way the Foundation would. All he knew was that there was an appeal from a creature who had just watched its new goddess step into the world, annihilate their nightmare, and collapse.

And every part of that request, however earnest, made his skin crawl.

Bradley's protective instinct rose like a wall. "No," he said, not raising his voice, but putting iron in it. "Let her rest."

The word sat between them like a drawn line.

For a long moment, no one moved. The skinks clustered near their offering, shoulders hunched, crests twitching, their need for salvation almost a physical pressure in the air. Bradley held his ground at Pinky's side, every muscle tight, fingers resting lightly on her shoulder as if he could keep the world off her with that one point of contact. Two different hungers faced each other—one for a miracle, the other for a child's right to be left alone—and neither was willing to give.

The leader drew in a long, slow breath, throat sacs flaring. It let the air out in a thin, drawn-out hiss, eyes moving from Pinky's sleeping form to Bradley's hand and back again. The sound wasn't a threat. It was frustration, the noise a mind made when the universe refused to follow its rules.

Mustang stepped forward before it could sharpen into something worse. "Look," he said, keeping his tone level, hands spread slightly to show he was empty. "We get it. You're

347

hurt. Scared. Same as us." He nodded toward Pinky, then back to the scorched stone where the scorpion had died. "But she's just a kid. That—" the gesture was short, precise "—isn't something she can turn on and off."

The leader watched him in silence, crest lifting a fraction. The humans' urgency was different from its own, but there was a pattern there it could recognize—creatures trying to protect their wounded, trying to live through the next hour.

It tilted its head, bioluminescent filaments woven into its crown catching and scattering the fungus-glow as it moved. For a heartbeat, Bradley thought he saw something like comprehension in those slit-pupiled eyes; or maybe it was just calculation, a weighing of what it could force and what it might lose by trying.

With a string of clicks and low hisses, it turned its back on them to address the other skink. Their earlier agitation bled away into quieter sounds, a muted rumble of argument and reluctant assent. The cavern shrank to the drip of water and the faint rasp of scaled feet as they shifted their weight, waiting.

When the leader turned back, it moved more slowly. It stepped forward until it was an arm's length from Bradley and stopped. Then it extended one hand, palm up, claws curled back, throat stilling as if it didn't dare breathe.

The meaning was plain enough. A truce. An invitation to walk alongside each other for a while, to see if survival could be shared without putting everything on Pinky's shoulders.

Bradley met its gaze and felt the weight of it settle through him. They needed an exit, food, information—and now they had two unconscious allies, a half-shattered squad, and a girl who could erase monsters. Standing alone on principle would get them all killed. He couldn't afford purity down here.

"All right," he said quietly, mostly to himself. He lifted his hand, careful not to move too fast, and set his palm against the skink's.

The skin under his fingers was rough and ridged, but warmer than he expected. For the space of a held breath, they simply stayed there—human and reptile, both tense as pulled wire. Then the leader's shoulders loosened, just a fraction, and it gave a short, sharp exhale that sounded almost like relief.

Behind it, the second skink's posture shifted. Its hisses softened, the harsh edges rounding off into something closer to conversation. The leader turned its head and answered in kind —quick exchanges of sound that carried purpose now instead of panic.

Footsteps and low voices echoed from the tunnel before that new balance could settle. Knight and Karl appeared out of the dark, silhouettes resolving into sweat-streaked faces and hunched shoulders. Jorgen and Alysha lay across the litters they dragged, limp but intact, lashed to frames of braided fungus stalks and rope.

Both men looked half-ready to drop. Dirt streaked Karl's beard; Knight's jaw was clenched, his breathing rough, one arm curled protectively around his ribs. Relief glinted under the exhaustion in their eyes all the same—they'd found them, and they'd brought them back.

Bradley pointed to a patch of relatively dry stone away from the worst of the slime. "There," he said, voice rough with more than fatigue. "Let's set up camp. We're done moving for now."

They set to work without argument. Packs came off. Bedrolls unrolled. Jorgen and Alysha were eased down onto the flattest ground they could find. The skinks moved in step with them, silent but unresisting: hauling a stalk here, bracing a litter there, their clawed hands surprisingly sure when it came to shifting weight without jarring the unconscious.

By the time something that resembled a camp took shape, the cavern felt different—smaller, but also less hostile. Human and skink—patched together by nothing more noble than shared exhaustion and the simple fact that none of them could face this place alone.

The leader straightened at last and turned away from the little circle of light and bodies. It threw back its head and loosed a sharp, piercing hiss that bounced off the stone like a signal flare. Then it jabbed one claw toward the mangled remains of the scorpion, its corpse already slick with encroaching fungus, and another toward the black mouth of the tunnels beyond.

Message given, it looked back once at its injured subordinate, now settled closer to the humans' supplies, salve drying dull on its scales. Then, without further ceremony, it slipped into the darkness. Its companion followed, tails flicking, until the fungus-glow swallowed them and their claws faded into the rhythm of the dripping stone.

Dark pressed in at the edges of the light. The cavern had shrunk to a bowl of fireglow and fungus, everything beyond it swallowed by green haze and black stone. The humans ringed the salvaged campfire, its thin flames licking at a pot that Karl kept nudging with the back of his spoon. Grease and smoke curled up together, carrying the sharp, gamey scent of rat jerky stew and the cold, wet reek of the tunnels.

The skinks had claimed the far side of the chamber. Their narrow bodies were cut into jagged silhouettes against the bioluminescent mats, scales catching and throwing back a faint, sickly shine. The injured skink hunched over the stone bowl of glowing liquid, claws hooked around it like it was the only thing holding it upright. Its hisses came out low and frayed, broken by ragged breaths, but there was still iron in its eyes—something stubborn that Bradley recognized all too well.

No one spoke. The fire snapped now and then, sending sparks up to die in the damp air. The wounded skink's breathing rasped in counterpoint. Between the two sounds lay everything they weren't saying—the memory of Pinky wrapped in light, the half-vaporized scorpion, the fact that they had just watched a child turn into something that had no place in any sane world.

Knight finally broke. His gaze drifted past the fire to the skinks standing in their halo of green. "They live down here. They know these tunnels. Can they lead us out?"

Before anyone could answer, Pinky stirred.

She let out a soft, raw sound and curled tighter for a heartbeat, then her eyes blinked open. Confusion rolled across her face as she took in the scene—the firelight, the glowing shelves of fungus, the injured skink hunched like a broken idol, the drawn faces of everyone watching her.

Bradley was already moving. He dropped into a crouch beside her bedroll, his hands careful on her shoulder and wrist, checking pulse and temp out of habit as much as concern. "Easy," he said quietly. "You're safe. We've got you."

Across the cavern, the wounded skink lifted its head. It loosed a low, rolling hiss that rose and fell in a strange cadence, almost like a lullaby dragged over broken glass. Clicks threaded through the sound. The hair on Bradley's arms lifted in spite of himself.

Pinky's expression changed. Surprise flickered there, and something like recognition.

"It's okay," she whispered, more to herself at first. Her voice shook but held. "He says he just needs to rest. They're hurt... really hurt."

Bradley stared at her, thrown off his axeis. She'd always read people well, but this wasn't body language or tone—you couldn't fake understanding of that guttural mess across the cavern. He felt Mustang's attention sharpen beside him without having to look; the tactical officer had gone very still.

"Pinky," Knight said, his usual bark sanded down by hesitation. "Did you...understand that?"

She looked from the skink to Knight, then to Bradley, eyes wide in the firelight. "Yeah," she said slowly. "But it's not words. Not like ours. It's more like...like the feelings come first, and the sounds just sit on top of them. I just...know what they mean."

Firelight and fungus-glow fought over the chamber, orange and green wrestling across stone and scale. Bradley felt that old, familiar tug-of-war inside him answer in kind—hope clawing up one side of his ribs, unease grinding down the other. If she could speak for them, if she was a bridge between species, that was an edge he'd be stupid to ignore. But it came from the same place as the light that had erased half a monster. Whatever was waking up inside her wasn't done.

The wounded skink hissed again, a longer sequence this time. Its uninjured hand spread, palm up, then pressed to its own chest, then swept in a line toward the dark tunnel mouths beyond the fire. Its stare never left Pinky.

She listened, head tilted slightly, as if straining to catch a faint radio channel. The fire popped; somewhere in the dark, water dripped steadily. When she spoke, her voice had lost its earlier wobble.

"They know a way out," she said. "But it's going to be bad. They need us to help them get there."

The words hung in the damp air, heavier than any stone. To Bradley and the others, it was just Pinky relaying what she'd "felt"—route intel, warning, plea. But on the far side of the fire, both skinks straightened. Their heads dipped in unison, hisses softening into something that skirted reverence. Their eyes fixed on her with a focus that made Bradley's skin crawl.

It struck him then: whatever passed between her and them wasn't just translation. Something in the way she spoke back, in the steadiness of her tone, had landed deep.

And she was still just a girl sitting in the dirt, blinking sleep from her eyes.

Karl let out a low whistle. "Well, ain't that somethin'..." The disbelief in his voice rode under the words, rough as gravel.

Knight met Bradley's gaze across the fire. The look that passed between them was short, sharp, and heavy—too many questions to voice, the beginnings of a plan neither of them liked, and the awareness that they were piling more and more weight onto shoulders that weren't built for it. Pinky missed the adult calculus entirely. Her attention stayed on the injured skink, her expression open, all raw concern and none of their caution.

The hurt skink hissed again, softer now, the edge of pain dulled into something more intent. Its pupils thinned as its stare drifted past Pinky, past the fire, toward the still forms of Alysha and Jorgen laid out on their bedrolls. Its chest rose and fell in shallow pulls, yet its attention sharpened, drawn toward the pair like a needle finding north.

Pinky's head tipped, as if she felt the change rather than heard it. "What is it?" she asked, staring back at the skink. Her voice came out quiet, almost wary. "What about them?"

She pushed herself to her feet and padded over to Alysha. The woman's skin looked washed-out in the mixed glow of flame and fungus, lashes resting motionless on cheeks that had gone too still. Pinky knelt, fingers light as she brushed a stray lock of hair away from Alysha's forehead. She studied her face with an intensity that seemed borrowed from someone older.

"They're...sick," she said at last, looking from Alysha to Jorgen, then back toward the skinks. "They won't wake up. I don't know why." The wobble in her voice matched the tightness that went through the circle of adults.

More hisses followed, a low back-and-forth between the two skinks. Pinky listened, her brow knitting, eyes gone distant the way they had when she'd first spoken for them. When she turned back to the humans, something like shock sat underneath her words.

"They...they want to help," she said. "They think they know what's wrong..."

Hope flared in Bradley's chest before he could stop it, a reflex he'd spent days beating down. He reined it in with an effort. "How could they possibly…?" he started, because cave-dwelling reptilians diagnosing his people was several bridges too far.

"They call it the wasting," Pinky answered.

The terminology sounded odd from her, like it didn't quite belong in her vocabulary. She pushed on anyway. "They say it's like…like their bodies are running out of energy. The kind they use to heal, to fight…it's fading." The explanation tumbled out haltingly, but the shape of it held. In this place, with everything else they'd seen, it didn't even sound impossible.

Mustang gave a low, disbelieving huff. "Well, that's a new one," he muttered. "Magic deficiency…in a gods-forsaken hole where every damn creature we meet's practically leaking the stuff."

Karl lowered himself beside Jorgen, joints popping as he went down. He studied the older man's slack face, then glanced to the injured skink, lines of curiosity cutting through his worry. "They got some way to fix it?" he asked, voice gone more careful.

Pinky turned back to the skinks, listening to the sharp trade of hisses and clicks. Their bodies angled toward Alysha and Jorgen now, heads bobbing with a focus that looked uncomfortably like professional interest. She swallowed.

"They have something," she said. Awe crept into the words, tangled with a bit of fear. "The liquid…the glowing stuff." She nodded toward the stone bowl cradled in the leader's arms.

"They say it comes from the mushrooms. It's…concentrated. Like—" she searched for a comparison "—like medicine. Only different."

Bradley felt his pulse hammer behind his eyes. On one level, it was absurd—mushroom juice and cave magic curing whatever had dropped Jorgen and Alysha. On another, it sat perfectly in line with all the other bullshit down here. That didn't make it safe. It just made it plausible.

Knight's gaze swept the cavern, taking in the glowing caps overhead, the skinks, the tunnels yawning like open mouths. "If what they say is true," he said, voice rough, "then we're sitting on a powder keg. Word gets out about some kind of 'magic medicine' down here and every thing that crawls is gonna come sniffing after it."

He wasn't wrong. Bradley could already see the knock-on effects on the surface, if this ever reached it. Black markets. Cartels. Wars built on whatever was in that bowl. But that was a future problem. The two people lying motionless on the stone at his feet were a present one.

A harder line settled into his jaw. "First things first," he said. His voice dropped, steady and clinical now, the way it went when he had to make a call no one liked. "We have to see if it works." His gaze flicked between Alysha and Jorgen, then to the skinks, then back to Pinky. "If this buys them a chance, we take it. The rest…" He exhaled slowly. "We'll figure it out as we go."

Karl carefully took the stone bowl from the skink leader. The liquid inside shifted with its own soft radiance, a viscous swirl of pale glow that painted his calloused fingers in ghost-light. Up close, it smelled faintly of damp earth and something sharper, almost metallic. With a care that surprised even him, he tipped a small measure into a cut-down ration tin, watching the thin stream cling to the metal before pooling at the bottom.

Pinky moved to Alysha's side and knelt. "Here," she murmured, holding the makeshift cup close to Alysha's lips. "They say this will help." Her voice carried more steadiness than she felt; the fear lived in her eyes, in the tight set of her shoulders. She understood enough to know they were gambling with something they didn't understand.

Bradley supported Alysha's head, guiding the liquid past slack lips. A thin trickle escaped and he wiped it away with his thumb, counting heartbeats under his fingers out of habit. Across the fire, Jorgen lay motionless, chest rising and falling in shallow, even pulls. When they finished with Alysha, they repeated the process with him, the glow of the liquid briefly catching along his beard before it vanished into his mouth.

Silence settled over the cavern like a dropped curtain. Fire crackled softly. Somewhere deeper in the tunnels, water dripped in a slow, indifferent rhythm. Alysha's face stayed slack, her breathing still shallow and uneven. Jorgen didn't twitch, didn't shift. The waiting stretched, each second dragging, grinding their fragile hope down grain by grain.

Relief guttered, then went out. Alysha lay as she had before. Jorgen remained a carved shape on the stone. The faint glow of the fungus made their stillness look almost staged, like bodies laid out for display.

Mustang blew out a breath, frustration sharpening the sound. "So much for a miracle," he muttered, the edge of his usual sarcasm blunted by sheer exhaustion.

Knight rubbed at the bridge of his nose, eyes ringed in bruised shadows. "Maybe they were wrong…" he said, voice low and rough. It wasn't an accusation so much as fatigue given shape.

A burst of urgent hissing cut across the rising despair. The skink leader leaned forward, crown of bioluminescent fungus bobbing as it gestured sharply toward Pinky, its tail twitching with agitation.

Pinky listened, head tilted, eyes narrowing in concentration. The cadence of the sounds seemed to pass through her rather than merely around her. When she turned back to the others, her voice carried an urgency that made Bradley's pulse jump.

"They say…because they were so weak, so sick, it'll take time," she said. "The medicine—it has to build up."

Bradley felt hope sink, then catch on something stubborn and refuse to drown. Maybe it was true. Maybe it was wishful thinking wrapped in alien biology. He looked to Karl, the question unspoken but clear.

"More treatments?" Karl asked, meeting his gaze. Weariness dragged at his words, but there was no flinch in them, just the flat acceptance of a hard road.

Pinky turned back to the skinks, listening through another flurry of clicks and hisses. She nodded slowly. "Yeah. Small amounts, over and over. Like food." She glanced at Alysha, then Jorgen. "They say it'll work. Just…slow."

The knowledge settled over them like added weight on an already overloaded pack. It was hope, but hope with strings attached—a chance to pull Alysha and Jorgen back, paid for with dependence on a glowing liquid none of them understood and an alliance they weren't sure they could afford.

No one spoke for a long moment. The fire popped. The skink leader clutched the half-empty bowl tighter, watching them with unblinking, reptilian focus. Around them, the cavern breathed its damp, cold breath.

Bradley drew in a slow, steadying inhale. "All right," he said at last, voice low. "We keep the doses small and spaced. We watch them closely. If there's any change—we see it first."

No one argued. They were past the point of clean choices. Pinky shifted back to Alysha's side, the weight of the unknown pressed in on all of them. The glowing liquid might save their friends. It might bind them tighter to this place and these creatures than they could yet see. Either way, they were committed now—one careful swallow at a time.

# CHAPTER EIGHTEEN

The cavern moved around them in a slow, stubborn march.

Mustang slung his rifle over his dead arm and fell in beside the crowned skink, sweat shining in the bioluminescent wash. The reptile's wounds no longer bled freely; its movements had a new steadiness, each clipped hiss and sharp gesture mapping out turns and hazards with the assurance of something born to these tunnels. Its claws tapped a steady rhythm on the wet stone, a rough counterpoint to the faint scrape of boots and dragged litters.

Knight, Bradley, Karl, and the unadorned skink rotated through the harnesses. Rope bit into shoulders and palms. Every shift of weight set the makeshift litters rasping over the uneven floor, Alysha and Jorgen swaying with each jolt. Progress came in fits and starts, a grind rather than a march, but behind the drawn faces there was a hard, burning intent: they were not leaving anyone behind.

Pinky moved between them like a fragment of misplaced color in the green wash—dress dulled by grime, hair catching stray glints of fungus-light. She adjusted blankets, straightened limbs that had shifted, murmured under her breath to Alysha and Jorgen as if they were simply sleeping through a watch change. The motions steadied her hands as much as theirs, a small, deliberate refusal to let them become just weight on the litter poles.

The tunnels pressed close. Water dripped somewhere ahead in a slow, hollow cadence. Fungal glow smeared the rock in sickly greens and blues, throwing long, twitching shadows that turned every outcrop into a half-formed threat. With each step, the same questions circled: how long would the skinks' medicine take to work, if it worked at all? Were they being led toward an exit, or deeper into someone else's territory to pay a price they hadn't been told?

Even so, stubbornness held the line where faith did not. The faint changes in Jorgen's breathing, the hint of color seeping back into Alysha's cheeks—real or imagined—were enough to keep them moving.

Without warning, the crowned skink lifted a hand, claws spread. Mustang stopped short, weight rocking on his heels. The group tightened instinctively, the litters settling with a dry scrape. For a moment there was only breath—ragged, uneven —and the soft plink of water somewhere in the black.

Knight shifted his grip on the litter poles and met Bradley's eyes across the glow. No words, just the shared calculation: if this was a bad turn, they were committed deep enough that backing out might be worse.

The skink angled its head toward the rock wall and pointed. In the fungus-light, a narrow fissure resolved—a seam in the stone barely wide enough for a man to pass, let alone a pair of laden drags. Cold air trickled from it, smelling of mineral and old, stale water. Claustrophobia crawled up Bradley's spine; that crack was either a way forward or a stone throat waiting to close.

"Well, that doesn't look promising…" Karl muttered, voice rough with fatigue. Lines of strain dug deeper into his face as he studied the gap.

The choice was simple and vicious. Try the slit in the rock and risk being pinned in a place they couldn't even swing a rifle, or turn back into a maze that had already bled them half dry. It hardly felt like a choice, where else could they go? Bradley shuddered under the weight of it, They needed help. Not only in getting out, but in the medicine promised.

Pinky's voice, small but steady, cut through the tense silence. "They say…it's the only way."

The weight of it settled on Bradley's shoulders. He met Knight's gaze and saw the same fight behind his eyes—the instinct to protect, clashing with the cold math of survival. They had dragged themselves this far through hell; every victory had bought them another impossible decision.

"We go," Bradley said. His voice came out rough, but it held. "One at a time. Those litters won't fit."

Knight's jaw flexed, but he didn't argue. Mustang gave a short, grim nod. "I'll go first," he said. "Clear the way. If something's waiting, better it hits me than all of you at once."

They lowered Alysha and Jorgen carefully onto the damp stone. The litters, lashed together from fungus and rope, were useless here. Instead they needed to break them down, they went to cutting lashings, cordage, and threading it into crude harnesses to drag instead of lift. The fissure was wider at the base; if they were lucky, it would scrape skin and gear but not trap bodies.

Mustang, guided by clipped skink hisses, approached the crack. Up close, it looked even worse—rock edges slick with condensation, the darkness beyond swallowing the weak fungal glow. He angled his shoulders and slid in, rifle hugged to his chest. Stone rasped against his clothes, a slow grind of fabric and grit. His muttered curses and the fading scuff of boots were the only proof he hadn't been swallowed whole.

Knight went next, hauling Jorgen with him. Rope bit into his palms, his breath coming in controlled grunts that bounced back off the stone. Karl followed with Alysha in tow, his curses lower, the sound of a man forcing tired muscles through one more task whether they liked it or not. The scrape and drag of their passage sawed back into the main chamber like a slow, metallic blade.

Pinky's turn came sooner than she seemed ready for. She stared at the fissure, pupils wide in the sick green light. Then nodded to herself. Without waiting for anyone to coax her, she slipped sideways into the gap. For a moment her rainbow dress caught on the rock—bright fabric smearing against wet stone—then she was gone, claimed by the dark like the rest of them.

Finally, Bradley was alone with the echo and darkness ahead. He drew in a breath that smelled of cold mineral and old water and stepped toward the fissure.

The rock closed around him at once. Rough stone scraped his shoulders and ribs, snagged at his clothes, scraped skin through fabric. His chest compressed, each breath shallow and loud in his own ears. Fungus-light died behind him in a few arm-lengths; ahead, the world was reduced to blackness and the faint, muffled sounds of the others.

Panic prowled just under his skin. The urge to shove backward, to claw his way out and run for the relative openness of their last camp, surged sharp and stupid. He forced it down, inching forward, boots feeling for uneven ground, forearms braced against the rock to keep his ribs from grinding on every protrusion.

The fissure didn't just close around his body; it closed around his thoughts. Every scrape of stone against flesh, every snag of cloth, felt like another layer of hope being pared away. His breath came rough and controlled, each exhale a reminder of how little room he had to lose his grip.

He kept moving. There was no going back, not really. Not with Alysha and Jorgen already dragged through, not with Pinky on the other side of the rock. Even if they tried to reverse, they'd rip themselves open doing it. Somewhere ahead, he could hear voices—Knight's low rumble, Mustang's sharp edge, Pinky's higher thread weaving through—and he fixed on that sound like a lifeline.

The point of no return wasn't a moment; it was this crawl. Every painful shove forward, every breath of stale, narrow air, pushed them deeper into whatever waited beyond.

The rock eased off his ribs in a sudden lurch. Bradley stumbled forward as the fissure widened, boot skidding on damp stone.

For a heartbeat he just stood there, gulping air that scraped his lungs, before the new cavern resolved around him.

Mustang and Knight held the near wall, rifles up, faces carved into hard lines. Alysha and Jorgen lay on the slick floor between them, the skinks ringed around the unconscious pair like wary sentries. Pinky crouched at their heads, one hand on each forehead, rainbow dress a shock of color against fungus-lit stone. She looked small and stubborn and wildly out of place in the middle of all that chitin and scale.

"Clear," Mustang grunted, letting his rifle dip an inch. Nothing about his stance relaxed; his eyes kept moving, cutting across every crack and shadow.

Bradley hauled himself fully out of the squeeze. His muscles shook with the sudden release of tension. He dropped to one knee without meaning to, palm braced on the cold floor as his vision pulsed at the edges. The crowned skink hissed sharply, the sound pitched high with urgency.

Bradley blinked grit from his eyes. "What is it?" he rasped.

The answer came in stone, not words.

A low tremor rolled through the cavern, vibration humming up through his hand. Dust sifted from the ceiling in a fine, gray veil. A heartbeat later the mountain roared—rock splitting somewhere behind them, a crack like distant thunder amplified in close quarters.

He spun toward the fissure.

The narrow passage shuddered, then began to fold in on itself. Chunks of rock tore free and tumbled down in a choking cascade. The sound was a physical thing, a battering ram of noise that slammed into his chest.

"Damn it!" Mustang swore, lunging sideways. He snagged Knight's harness and jerked him back as a slab the size of a man's torso crashed down where they'd been standing.

The skinks bolted in opposite directions, claws scraping frantically at the stone as shards rained around them. Their earlier reverence vanished, replaced by raw, animal panic; hisses climbed to shrieks as they darted for open ground.

Pinky screamed. She flattened herself over Jorgen's chest, fingers clawing at his vest as if she could anchor both of them in place by will alone. The sound of her fear cut through the grinding rock, sharp as shrapnel. For one sick beat Bradley saw her crushed under falling stone—dress smeared red, small limbs pinned and still.

Karl moved first. With a hoarse curse he lunged, boots skidding on the grit. One thick hand seized Jorgen's rope harness; the other hooked into the back of Pinky's dress. He heaved, hauling both clear just as the fissure let out a final groan and gave up the rest of its teeth. Rock slammed down in one last heavy cascade and then…silence.

Dust rolled out in a choking wave. It burned Bradley's throat and eyes, settled in a fresh, gritty film on sweat-slick skin. Where the narrow passage had been, there was now only a jagged wall of rubble, wedged from floor to ceiling. Whatever thin line back they'd had—real or imagined—was gone.

The collapse landed inside him as hard as the stone had landed on the floor. His heart hammered against his ribs, each beat loud and useless. Trusting the skinks had taken them through that crack. Now the way behind was sealed in solid rock, and the only thing waiting on this side was more darkness.

He forced his gaze away from the ruined passage and found Knight and Mustang. Dust streaked their faces, eyes bloodshot and hollowed by fatigue. There was no illusion of hope in their expressions, just a shared understanding of the corner they'd backed themselves into.

We're trapped, Bradley thought, and saw the same conclusion already written in their eyes.

But none of them said it. Not out loud.

The shadows seemed to swallow what resolve they had left. The weight of the collapsed rock behind them, the murk ahead, the way the air itself pressed in on their skulls—all of it gnawed at the thin shell of determination they'd been wearing since the tunnels first closed over their heads.

Mustang hitched his rifle higher over his bad arm, jaw locked tight. "Lead on, lizard-folk," he muttered, the forced humor sitting crooked on top of bone-deep exhaustion.

The skinks hissed back, urgency sharpening the sound. The crowned leader limped toward the darker cut in the wall, moving with a vigor that didn't match its injuries—driven by fear, or faith, or something in between.

They fell in behind it without a word. Knight took point at the skink's flank every step measured and wary. Karl and Bradley bracketed the litters, boots scraping careful lines as they eased Alysha and Jorgen over the worst of the stone, guarding each unconscious body as if a wrong jolt might finish what this place had started.

Pinky came last, fingers knotted in the worn hem of Karl's coat. The rainbow smear of her dress had lost any hint of playfulness; it just looked wrong down here. She no longer skipped or drifted ahead. Her steps matched theirs, small echoes of tired strides, her face drawn in a tight, watchful mask.

The air changed as the passage narrowed. The clean mineral damp of the tunnels soured into something acrid and stale—old paper left to rot in a flooded cellar, undercut with the sweet, stomach-turning edge of decay. Heat grew with it, a close, sticky warmth that clung to skin and made the stone sweat.

Mustang coughed, eyes watering. "Damn, what's that stench?" He wiped his brow with the back of his good hand, rifle still cradled but a little looser now, unease bleeding through the habit of readiness.

The skinks didn't slow. If anything, their pace increased, hisses coming faster, sharper, as the sounds around them shifted. The steady drip of water thinned, replaced by a different rhythm—a soft, irregular patter, like dry claws skimming stone just out of sight.

Pinky stumbled on a loose rock. Her sharp intake of breath knifed through the hush. Bradley's hand shot out, fingers clamping around her forearm a little harder than he meant to.

"I've got you," he said, voice low and rough. The reassurance rang thin in his own ears, but she held his gaze for a heartbeat, fear plain and honest in her eyes. It looked too much like his own.

The passage spat them into a wider chamber without warning.

The familiar green-blue wash of fungus gave way to a different light—a sickly pallor filtered through veils of webbing strung from wall to wall. It broke the glow into ragged strips and trembling patterns, shadows stretching and shrinking with every small movement. Heat rolled from the far end of the cavern, a heavy, suffocating wave that carried more than warmth. It felt inhabited.

Silence pressed down, thick and listening. Beneath it, faint and constant, came soft scuttling, the sound bouncing from rock to rock until it seemed to come from everywhere at once. The smell hit full strength here: rank decay layered over a dry, musty musk that did not belong to mammals.

Karl's fingers tightened around his climbing pick until the leather creaked. "Spiders," he whispered, barely moving his lips. The word was almost nothing in the air, but the dread inside it needed no more volume.

Every shadow seemed to twitch. Every strand of web stirred in the corner of their vision.

The skinks froze. Whatever drove them before snapped into something simpler—fear. Their hisses dropped to thin, nervous threads as they edged backward, scaled shoulders brushing human legs. They pressed in close, not as guides now but as creatures seeking the larger bodies between them and the dark. Whether they had led the humans into a lair by mistake or had hoped the humans would brave a place they themselves loathed, no one could tell.

The only certainty was this: whatever waited in the webs ahead, even the skinks wanted no part of it.

Panic surged through Bradley, cold and sharp, sweat prickling under his filthy collar. Every instinct screamed at him to bolt— run, hide, vanish—but there was nowhere left to run. Behind them, a tomb of fallen rock. Ahead, a lair that stank of old kills and silk.

Knight moved before the terror could freeze them. He shifted and squared himself between the litters and the dark. "Circle up," he ordered, voice low and hard. "Keep those litters in the middle."

They moved, not cleanly but with the frantic clumsiness of the exhausted. Boots scraped. Gear clanked. In heartbeats they'd pulled in tight, backs angled outward, weapons up. The weak cones of their lamps, mingled with the green smear of fungus-light, pushed the dark back just far enough for them to finally see what they had walked into.

Webs. Everywhere.

Thick, dust-dulled strands carpeted the floor, tugging at their soles. Curtains of silk hung from the ceiling in drooping swaths, trembling with each breath of air. Every filament caught the light with a greasy sheen, the whole cavern feeling less like open space and more like the inside of a waiting mouth.

Pinky pressed herself against Bradley's side, her small frame shaking. He wrapped an arm around her automatically, feeling every tremor. The memory of what she'd done to the scorpion was still fresh, but it didn't matter here. She was just a shaking body under his hand, a girl staring at webs.

From somewhere ahead came a sound that crawled along his spine: a dry, layered chittering, the click of hard parts meeting, the whisper of many legs brushing stone. A huge shadow peeled itself from the gloom, then another shape behind it. Eyes caught the light—two, then four, then eight cold, polished points reflecting their circle back at them.

The first spider stepped into view. It was massive, low and heavy-bodied, its jointed legs ending in barbs that bit into stone. Hair, stiff and pale, furred its carapace. Fangs the length of dagger blades jutted from its mouth, shining wet beneath the web-filtered glow. Behind it, deeper in the nest, more bulk shifted. They hadn't stumbled on a stray predator. They were inside a hive.

Mustang shifted his stance, cradling his shattered arm close. The sling did little to keep the constant throbbing from turning his stomach. Sweat filmed his brow despite the chill.

Karl leaned in beside him, shoulder to shoulder. "Here," he muttered. "Set it on me. Get a steadier shot."

Mustang glanced at him, teeth bared in something too tight to be a smile, and did as told—rifle braced against Karl's solid frame, good hand settling into its old, familiar place on the grip.

The chittering rose, a layered chorus that seemed to come from every webbed corner at once. They were boxed in, and every one of them felt it. Not scouts. Not liberators. Just meat someone else was about to collect.

A ragged, guttural cry split the sound.

The crowned skink—banded tail dragging, torso still wrapped in crude bandages—lunged past their line with a speed that stunned Bradley. It hurled itself at the lead spider, scaled bulk slamming into hairy leg. The creature reared back with a hissing shriek, fangs snapping down in reflex. The skink twisted away, claws scrambling for purchase, its own answering hiss raw and furious.

Bradley didn't waste the opening. "Now!" he shouted. "Keep 'em busy!"

Mustang drew a breath and squeezed the trigger. The rifle kicked against Karl's shoulder, a bolt of sizzling energy slamming into the spider's flank. Chitin blackened and cracked. The beast shrieked and thrashed, barbed legs gouging furrows in the stone, chunks of web tearing loose and filling the air with choking dust.

In the shadows beyond, more shapes stirred. The rest of the spiders began their advance—slow, deliberate, testing the circle.

The uninjured skink barked a staccato string of hisses. Then it darted forward—not to attack, but to weave around the leader's snapping legs, slashing at webbing and stones, its movements chaotic on purpose. Its darting form drew the nearest spiders' eyes, their attention snagging on the fast, unpredictable target.

For a few thin breaths, the humans weren't the only things on the menu.

Knight moved first. As the skinks and spiders tore at each other in the center of the cavern, he and Bradley broke from the circle in a sprint, each grabbing a litter. Webs dragged at their boots, stone bit their knees when they slipped, but they muscled Alysha and Jorgen toward the far wall, as far from chittering legs as they could get. They shoved the litters into a shallow recess, just barely out of reach of the nearest strands.

"Stay with them," Bradley rasped, more prayer than order.

Mustang swore as his grip slipped on the rifle's fore-end, his bad arm a dead weight against his chest. "We need a chokepoint," he growled, eyes raking the webbed ceiling. "Something to slow those bastards down."

Knight followed his gaze, and his mouth twisted into a humorless grin. "Can do."

He swung his blaster up—not at the spiders, but at the thickest knots of web strung high overhead. Two shots cracked the air. Blue-white bolts sizzled into silk, burning through strands that had hung there for decades. Something gave with a sharp, whip-like snap.

A curtain of webbing big as a sail tore free and dropped. It hit the cavern floor in a collapsing sheet of dust and sticky filament, smothering the lead spider mid-lunge. The creature shrieked, legs lashing. Skinks took the opening instantly, darting in with a rush of hisses, claws and crude spears hacking at limbs and tangling more of the curtain around the joints. For a few seconds it was a raw tug-of-war—scaled bodies hauling against a mass of thrashing chitin.

The advantage nearly broke as fast as it formed. The spider's barbed legs sawed through strand after strand. Smaller spiders, disturbed by the commotion, began to pour around the sagging web-wall, their bodies low, eyes glittering as they tested the edge of the humans' circle.

Sweat stung Bradley's eyes. He scrubbed his forearm across his brow, tasting dust and metal on his tongue. "We've got to buy time," he said, voice tight. "Distract them—pull them off us, anything."

Mustang's gaze swept the cavern, hunting. It snagged on a thick cluster of bioluminescent fungi clinging to a higher ledge —dense, bright, and fragile-looking. An idea snapped into place, reckless and fast.

"Knight. Karl." His tone sharpened. "I need webbing. Long pieces. Now."

They didn't argue. Knight and Karl waded back to the sagging curtain, blades flashing dull in the filtered light as they slashed off rope-thick strands. Sticky silk clung to gloves and sleeves, stretching in stubborn ropes as they dragged it free.

Bradley dropped to his knees beside Alysha and Jorgen. He yanked a strip off his already-ruined sleeve and dipped it into the skinks' glowing liquid, the stuff they'd called medicine. It clung thick to the fabric, warm and faintly sweet, pulsing with a soft inner light as it soaked in.

The seconds bled out. With a final, violent convulsion, the trapped spider tore itself from the fallen web. Shredded silk snapped free from its legs. It reared up, chittering in rage, front limbs hammering the stone.

He let out a sharp, carrying whistle and stomped hard, boot scattering pebbles into a dark corner of the cavern. The sound rattled off the walls. A wave of smaller spiders broke toward the noise, their attention snagged by motion and vibration.

At the same time, Bradley laid the glowing cloth on the floor and dragged it in a crooked line away from the litters, smearing a trail of faint phosphorescence toward the fungus cluster high on the rock. The scent of the liquid—strange, sweet and sharp —mixed with stale air and rot.

The big spider's many eyes twitched, tracking the glow. Its head lowered, mandibles flexing, attention drawn along the luminous path.

Karl and Knight finished bundling webbing around the stone spearheads the skinks still clutched. The silk wrapped thick and

375

fast, making gummy, uneven bulbs at each tip. Knight flicked open his multitool, coaxed a spark—and the webbing caught, burning in uneven, hungry tongues that spit oily smoke.

The crowned skink barked something harsh and rising. On the signal, the pair of skinks stepped forward, aimed high, and hurled their flaming, web-wrapped spears at the fungus cluster.

The spears hit with a wet thud. The webs stuck, fire licking outward. The cluster burst apart in a muffled, concussive puff —spores billowing in a thick, shimmering cloud. The blast wasn't bright enough to blind, but heat and pressure rolled through the cavern in a short, brutal wave.

The lead spider reared back, legs jerking as the hot air and spore-laden dust slammed into its face. It shrieked, scrabbling, the carefully measured hunger in its movements replaced by stumbling, disoriented fury.

For a heartbeat, the cavern opened around them—spiders off-balance, web-curtain sagging, spores still hanging in the air.

"That's it. Go!" Bradley snapped.

They lurched into motion. Knight and Karl grabbed the litters, muscles already burning, dragging Alysha and Jorgen over stone that snagged and jolted every step. Mustang backed with them, rifle up, teeth gritted, while the skinks spread out along their flanks, hissing sharp and high. It was ugly, uneven, barely controlled—but they moved, all of them pulling in the same direction.

The reprieve vanished fast. The lead spider shook off its disorientation with a violent shudder. Its mandibles clicked, as its fat body pivoted toward the fleeing group. Smaller shapes poured after it, claws whispering on stone, drawn by heat and motion and the tang of blood.

The ground fought them. Every ridge snagged a litter, every shallow depression twisted an ankle or wrenched a shoulder. The harness ropes bit into palms already rubbed raw. Breath grew ragged, harsh in their own ears, drowned beneath the rising chitter of the swarm behind them.

"Can't... keep... this up," Karl panted. His words came broken, each one punched out with effort.

Mustang scanned ahead, eyes jumping from shadow to shadow. "We need cover—" he rasped. "A choke point, anything—"

The skink leader answered with a sharp, urgent hiss. It jerked its head toward a dark seam in the cavern wall: a slit of shadow, barely more than a crack, low to the ground and tight as a coffin. Even from here Bradley could see the problem— too narrow for litters, too tight for speed—but it was a way out. Or at least, a way *away*.

Hope flared in his chest, painful and bright. He didn't trust it, but he grabbed it anyway.

"Go!" he barked. "Get them into that fissure. We'll hold the line."

Knight and Karl dropped the litters in the same motion, the frame clattering against bare rock. With curt gestures and breathless orders, they herded Pinky and the skinks toward the gap.

Pinky glanced back, eyes huge in the sickly light, then latched onto the crowned skink's good arm. Together they squeezed toward the narrow opening, Alysha's litter dragging behind, the skinks' claws scraping as they hauled her dead weight into the fissure. Guilt punched through Bradley—eyes catching Jorgen's still form unconscious, alone—but there was no time to weigh it.

He turned back to the cavern with Knight at his side.

Bradley's pistol felt small and slick in his hand. Useless or not, he brought it up, sighted on the nearest cluster of eyes, and fired. The shot cracked the air, the muzzle flash carving brief, sharp shadows across wet stone. A spider jerked, one leg buckling, but it didn't stop—just stumbled and kept coming.

Beside him, Knight shifted his weight. A barbed limb swept in low and fast, gouging stone instead of ribs as he twisted away. It still caught his side, dragging a line of fire across his torso, but he stayed upright. His blaster butt slammed down into the spider's face, driving the creature back a half-step. It wasn't elegant. It didn't need to be. It bought them another breath.

The cavern dissolved into flashes: mandibles, legs, the slap of boots on stone; the weight of the pistol jumping in his grip; the dull, wet crunch when Knight's blows caught something soft instead of chitin. He didn't aim for killing strikes in close range. He aimed at joints, eyes, anything tender in reach.

A blur moved at the edge of his vision. For an instant he thought it was another spider breaking through, but the shape resolved into scaled limbs and a bioluminescent crown.

The skinks.

They had come back, hissing through their teeth, and were now racing toward the abandoned litter. They stooped, each taking a side, small bodies bowed under the weight of Jorgen's mass and the rough frame.

They lifted—and nearly collapsed. The litter lurched, one corner bouncing hard off the ground. Even with two of them he could see the strain in their movements, the tremor in their arms, the way their legs shook under the load.

The realization struck him cold.

They had an exit. They had a sliver of time. But they didn't have enough hands—or enough strength—to carry everyone through.

"Karl, go with them!" Bradley bellowed, throat raw, never taking his pistol off the advancing mass.

One of the skinks hissed, the sound edged with something close to gratitude, and fell back. Together—Karl and the two reptiles—shouldered the litters. Rope burned into calloused palms and rough stalks bit into flesh. The frame lurched and bounced, but they moved. Inch by inch, they stole distance from the spiders.

Bradley's chest knotted as he watched their backs recede toward the crack in the rock. A child, two unconscious comrades, and three figures already pushed past their limits—it was a retreat that looked too fragile to succeed. But Mustang slid in tight on his left, rifle braced along his ruined arm, and Knight planted himself on the right, arm up as if his shield were still there, shoulders squared. For all the rot in New New York, its hard lessons had taught Bradley one thing: how to stand in the gap. Pinky would make it. She carried the same stubborn edge he'd seen in every soldier who refused to stay down, even if his own path ended here on a cave floor.

He swallowed the last of the fear clawing at his throat and forced it into something he could use. There was only the line

379

now—his line. The pistol rose and fell in a steady rhythm, each shot cracking against the cavern walls, each muzzle flash carving spiders into stark negatives of legs and fangs.

With Knight's battered frame braced beside him and Mustang's fire stitching the dark, Bradley faced the crawling tide. They weren't going to win. That had never been the point. They would bleed this swarm for every heartbeat it tried to take. Every second they clawed back with their own pain and fury was another pulse of time for the girl dragging her way through the suffocating dark with Jorgen, Alysha, and the skinks at her side—proof that, at least, she didn't have to face that darkness alone.

# CHAPTER NINETEEN

Each echoing drip of water drove another spike of pain
behind Karl's eyes. The sound had weight here, a cold tap-
tap-tap that made his skull feel hollow. He would have
given anything for the clean ring of hammer on steel, the
roar of a proper forge, even the drunken shouting of his
cousins around a hearth. Anything but this smothered quiet
and his own ragged breathing, echoing back at him from
wet rock.

He stumbled, boot skidding on a slick patch. The floor was
treacherous—natural stone, uneven and slick, not the broad,
honest flagstones of a dwarven hall. The tunnel pinched at
his shoulders, scraping leather and skin alike. He wasn't
meant for this kind of earth. He liked stone you could trust,
stone carved and shored and lit—this was stone that shifted
and leaned and seemed to resent him with every step.

The litter dragged at his arms, a steady, grinding pull in his
shoulders and spine. The crude frame had already welded
itself to his grip; his thick, calloused hands had long since

stopped feeling like separate things. Every jolt sent a faint vibration through the unconscious weight lashed to it, a reminder of what he carried and how badly one misstep could go.

Beside him, the skink pressed on, limping but relentless. It was shorter by a handspan, quarter his width, all corded muscle and sinew. Its scaled fingers clenched the other side of the frame in a death grip. For a "primitive" cave-thing, the bastard had grit. Life down here adapted or died, and this one had chosen his side.

Behind them, the fight fell away in broken echoes—muffled shouts, the distant shriek of something huge and hungry. Each fading sound was a knife between his shoulder blades. They had escaped; but he wondered if they'd just exchanged a sure, visible death for one lurking somewhere ahead. There was no comfort in that, only the iron fact that they had left friends behind.

The fissure they'd forced themselves through was a jagged wound in the cavern, barely a crack by dwarven standards. Karl turned to glance back at it and almost laughed. Too tight even for most of his kin, were it not for sheer stubbornness and the knowledge that anything wider would already be clogged with his corpse.

The skink leader jabbed its free hand toward a new break in the rock—a narrow, sloping crevice disappearing upward into black. A slit of deeper shadow in the already suffocating dark.

Karl swore, old mountain curses grinding out between his teeth. It wasn't battlefield fear—no enemy to face, no line to hold. This was the slow crush of the world itself, the knowledge that there was rock above, rock below, rock on all sides, and not a single decent arch or support beam in sight. He was a son of stone, of great halls with ceilings so high the smoke vanished into them. This was not stone you lived in. This was stone that buried you.

But the look in the skink's eyes—round, black, and burning— was the same one he'd seen in every stubborn bastard who'd ever refused to stay down. There was no going back through that fissure. Forward, or nothing.

He dragged in a breath that tasted of mineral and mold. "Right then," he muttered, mostly to himself. He hitched the litter higher, every muscle protesting, and pushed on. The scrape of stalk on stone, his hoarse breathing, and the skink's ragged hissing settled into a brutal rhythm. Step, drag, gasp. Step, drag, hiss.

The passage twisted upward, an angled choke that forced him to hunch even more. The floor was all protruding stone and hidden dips, each step a blind test of what would give under his weight. His thighs burned, his shoulders felt packed with hot sand, and each breath rasped loud in his own ears. The skink's pained wheezing rode beside his own, thinner but just as stubborn.

The litter seemed to get heavier with every meter—not just meat and bone, but the knowledge that if he dropped it, if he slipped, there was no one behind them to pick it up again. He could almost feel the spiders at their backs, feel their legs, even though the only sound now was the drip of water and the grind of their own boots.

Then, abruptly, the rock eased its grip. The walls pulled back by a handspan, then two. The ceiling rose enough that he could straighten halfway without scraping his scalp. The skink lurched to a halt, chest heaving, and jerked its snout toward a shallow cut in the rock—a narrow alcove scooped into the wall, barely big enough for the litter and their cramped bodies. But compared to the throat of the tunnel behind them, it looked like a king's chamber.

Karl eased the litter down, every joint singing in protest as the weight finally left him. The sound of wood settling on the floor was almost beautiful. He slumped with his back to the wall, feeling the rough, damp rock bite through his clothes, and let his head rest there for a moment, eyes closed.

The skink folded down beside the litter, clutching at its side, long tongue flicking once in obvious pain. The only sound between them was the steady drip…drip…drip of unseen water and their shared, uneven breathing.

For now, at least, the cavern beyond their little pocket stayed quiet. No chitter of legs on stone. No gunfire or screaming. No whisper of webbing dragged through the dark. Just the close air, the sting of sweat and fungus in his nose, and the narrow nook  as their bodies surrendered to exhaustion.

A hard, sour satisfaction settled in Karl's chest. They'd slipped the noose again, stolen one more breath from a world that kept trying to grind them flat. It wasn't victory—barely even a reprieve—but it was a moment where the world and things in it weren't actively killing them, and that counted for something.

The injured skink eased itself closer to the litter, curling its thin body around Alysha and Jorgen like a scaled shield. Its sides still trembled with fatigue. Those wide, black eyes—usually sharp and watchful—held a raw edge now, a flicker of the same bone-deep strain he felt in his own joints. This flight was eating them all.

Karl sagged back against the wall, feeling the cold seeping through worn fabric into tired muscle. A dwarven miner, he thought sourly, hiding from the rock instead of mastering it. He pictured broad caverns lit by steady lanterns, proper pillars where the load-bearing should be, a sky of cut stone arching overhead. Instead he had this: a seam in the earth that could pinch shut anytime it pleased.

Still, the old lessons were there, settled in his bones like dust in a beard. Dwarves endured. You picked your line through bad stone and you kept cutting, no matter how much the mountain complained. As long as there was breath in him, he'd keep carving, inch by ugly inch, until they found daylight or a grave.

A soft, strangled noise broke through the steady drip of water. For an instant he thought one of the unconscious had stirred, but the skink by the litter stayed still, its crown barely pulsing with light. The sound came again.

Pinky.

She was huddled tight against the litter's frame, knees drawn up, shoulders shaking in the faint glow. The skink's light carved her into a little knot of shadow and washed out color, all that rainbow cloth dulled by grit and dust. For all her strange tricks and eerie calm, for all the way she walked through this madness like it was half-familiar, she was still small. Smaller than any child had a right to be in a place like this.

Something moved under his ribs, not pity exactly, but the hard, familiar anger that came when life asked too much of the young.

"Pinky," he rumbled, his voice more gravel than sound.

Her answer was a quiet collapse, the sobs she'd been choking back since the spiders finally forced their way out muffled against her own arms. She folded in on herself, a shaking bundle in the corner of his vision.

Karl shifted, joints protesting, and eased himself down beside her. He didn't try to tell her it would be all right; that kind of lie had no place here, and she was too sharp to believe it anyway. The darkness still pressed in. The way back was buried. The way forward was a guess.

So he just stayed. Solid stone in a world that wouldn't stop moving.

Time stretched thin. The steady drip-drip-drip marked it out while her sobs wore themselves down to hiccupping breaths. At last, without looking up, a small hand groped sideways and found his. Her fingers were cold and slick with tears and grime. His palm swallowed her grip, rough and scarred, but he squeezed back all the same. A simple trade: I'm here. So are you.

"We fight on, eh?" he said at last, voice low. "Dwarves, lizards, little girls—we don't go down easy."

She gave the tiniest nod, more felt than seen, but she didn't let go of his hand. That was enough.

Across from them, the uninjured skink worked in quiet concentration. Its long fingers moved with surprising care over Alysha's and Jorgen's still forms. In one hand it held a cracked stone bowl, the thick liquid inside casting a soft, sickly glow against the rock.

With a claw tip, it dabbed a smear of light onto Alysha's brow, then tilted a few drops between her parted lips. The rest it saved for Jorgen, repeating the careful motions, its hisses dropping to a low, almost musical murmur. Not the sharp bark of warning or command, but something closer to a lullaby in a language of croaks and hisses.

In the cramped alcove, it was a strange, fragile picture: a dwarf and a girl pressed shoulder to shoulder, two unconscious humans breathing shallowly on a rough-hewn litter, and a cave-born reptile administering its glowing brew with priestlike care. Not friends but bound together by the simple, ugly fact that none of them would last long alone.

Karl watched the skink work, his thoughts caught between hope and hard habit. The stuff clearly did something—he'd seen it stop the slide, hold Jorgen and Alysha at the edge instead of letting them tumble into whatever waited beyond. But that was all it had done so far. No rally. No turn. Just... stalling.

Then Jorgen groaned.

It was small—barely more than a breath forced past a dry throat—but it cut through the alcove like a hammer blow. His eyelids twitched, then cracked open, pupils slow to catch the dim glow. His gaze found the skink first, flinched, then dragged itself over to Karl.

"Where..." The word scraped out of him, rough as uncut stone. "What..."

Karl leaned in, the answer sticking for a moment in his throat. "Safe. For now," he said at last. "Had ourselves a bit of a scrap. That's the short version."

Jorgen frowned, pain and fog knitting his features. Something in him shifted, a shard of memory struggling to settle. His hand lifted, shaky and clumsy, reaching blindly until Pinky caught it in both of hers. His fingers curled around hers, weak but there.

"Bradley…?" The name rode out on a thin breath, more plea than question.

The air went heavy. Pinky's grip tightened; fresh tears spilled down her cheeks in hot streaks. Karl felt the lie trying to form —something easy and soft—but it died quick.

"Rest," he said instead, gentling his voice as much as his gravel could manage. "You're in no shape to help. Let the medicine do its work."

He shot a look at the crowned skink. The creature met his eyes, then eased closer to Jorgen's shoulder. It let out a low, rolling hiss, soft clicks threaded through it like a chant. Jorgen's brow smoothed. Whatever he understood—or didn't—his eyes slipped shut again, the weight of exhaustion dragging him under.

Not much, Karl thought. But it was something.

It was the first time Jorgen had clawed his way back to awareness since the strange sickness had taken him. It wasn't a charge or a battle cry—just a groan, a question, a name—but in this place, where everything seemed to only move one way toward the grave, it felt like the rock had finally given a little under the pick.

The change was slow. Agonizingly so. Karl was used to knowing where he stood—steel met bone, stone met steel, and the outcome was clear. This…waiting…gnawed at him. Every hour Jorgen's chest still rose and fell, every time his fingers twitched around Pinky's hand, felt like a small win in a war he couldn't see.

Pinky clung to those small signs with a ferocity that made his chest ache. She barely left his side. When Jorgen's gaze managed to track her for a heartbeat, dull and clouded but present, she leaned in and whispered to him—comforting scraps of nonsense and made up songs that bounced softly off the stone. Between whispers, she wiped his brow with the edge of her sleeve, like this was any sickbed and not some lightless hole under a hostile world.

The skinks watched it all with an intensity that set his teeth on edge. Where they'd once hovered only around Pinky, now their eyes stuck to Jorgen as well. Their hisses had changed—less sharp, less like orders and warnings, more like something… almost formal. Karl didn't pretend to understand, but he knew the look of someone recognizing a fighter who refused to lay down.

Hours bled together, marked only by the steady drip of water and Jorgen's uneven breathing. Karl's back screamed from the stone at his spine, his eyes burned from the glow, but he refused to close them. He'd dug under mountains more forgiving than this damned place; he knew better than to look away when the ceiling was thinking about coming down.

Pinky drifted eventually. Curled against the injured skink's side, she shivered in her sleep, her rainbow dress dull with grime, her face creased with worry even in dreams. The creature curled fractionally closer, one thin arm resting near her without quite touching—a strange, instinctive shield.

A soft series of clicks drew Karl's attention. The crowned skink was on the move again, stone bowl in its hands, the liquid inside still glowing with that steady, fungal light. It shuffled to

Alysha's side and knelt, its ragged breathing loud in the cramped alcove.

With slow, deliberate care, it dipped a claw and traced a thin line of light across Alysha's brow. A few drops followed, eased between her parted lips. The stuff clung to her skin and pooled in the hollow of her throat, casting her features in a ghostly sheen. She didn't stir. She lay as still and cold as one of the carved guardians in an old dwarven hall, all sharp angles and untouched dust.

The skink didn't falter. It finished the dose, its hisses falling to that same low murmur it had used on Jorgen, as if the sound itself were part of the treatment. Karl watched, shoulders heavy, caught between the stubborn hope that this slow drip of borrowed power might be enough—and the hard knowledge that in this place, nothing came without a price they hadn't seen yet.

The skink shifted its weight and crawled to Jorgen. In the glow of the bowl, its narrow face took on an odd gentleness—hard scales and ridges softened by intent. It tipped the stone just enough for a few thick drops to slide over Jorgen's cracked lips and run down his chin in glowing tracks.

A tremor ran through Jorgen's frame. His fingers twitched against the stone. This time, when his eyes opened, they held more than fog. He coughed, the sound wet and rattling but edged with returning strength.

"What…" His voice scraped out, rough but firmer than before.

Karl leaned in, relief tightening his chest even as habit kept his tone flat. "Don't push it," he rumbled. "These lizards are patching you up."

With Karl's help he dragged himself upright until his shoulders hit the wall. The effort left him shaking, breath sawing in and out, but his gaze had focus now—sharp enough to fix on the bowl still cradled in the skink's hands.

"More," he rasped, jaw set. "Need...more."

The crowned skink seemed to understand. It angled the bowl toward him. Jorgen gripped it with unsteady hands and drank, greedily, the luminous liquid painting his face in sickly light. Another shudder rolled through him, then a long, ragged exhale. His shoulders sagged, but something in him had shifted —less corpse, more stubborn bastard too mean to stay down.

"Can talk..." he muttered, testing the words. "Where're...the others?"

Pinky edged into the narrow space between Karl and the litter, eyes bright and raw. "They're not here," she said, and some of the light went out of her face as she said it. "But you're getting better." The whisper barely disturbed the heavy air.

Jorgen's mouth twitched into a ghost of his usual grin. "Got a stubborn streak," he said, the old dry humor bleeding through the rasp. "Not going...without a fight."

Karl gave him the short version. He kept his voice low, letting the steady drip of water fill the gaps between hard facts—the wasting that had clung to Alysha and him dragging him under, the fungus-lit caverns, the scorpion and the spiders, and finally Bradley, Knight, and Mustang planting their feet and turning to face the swarm giant spiders so the rest of them could run.

Anger cut through Jorgen's fatigue like a wildfire. His fingers curled into a fist in Pinky's grip. "Asshats," he breathed, the word coming out on a frayed chuckle that turned into a cough. "Kinda hoped they'd be too stupid to die."

"Asshats they may be," Karl said, "but brave asshats." The correction landed heavy rather than sharp.

Pinky's tears spilled over again. She wrapped both hands around Jorgen's fist until his fingers slowly unfurled, gripping back with more strength than sense. Her thumb traced circles over his knuckles, as if that alone might keep him anchored.

Karl kept going. He told him about the skinks—the bowl of light, the slow drag back from whatever edge Jorgen and Alysha had been drifting toward; the fight in the spider caverns; the way Bradley had refused to fold, the way Knight had held a line that should've crushed him, how Mustang had kept firing with one good arm and nothing left in the tank but spite. He didn't dress it up. He just laid the pieces out, one by one, in the close dark.

When he finished, the alcove fell quiet again. Only the drip of water and Jorgen's breathing filled it. Jorgen sagged back against the rock, his features carved into grief and an iron resolve struggling against the limits of a body that had almost given up.

"There's a chance they're still alive," Karl said at last, barely more than a breath. "Spiders… store food." The thought hung there, foul and tempting. "But to go back now, after what they sacrificed…walk into the same web they dragged us out of… feels like spittin' on their choice. They ran toward the danger so we could get you, Pinky, and Alysha out."

"Yeah, they are the only ones that can play hero," Jorgen whispered, voice fraying. "Gotta find a way back…"

Pinky nodded, eyes blazing in the dim glow. "I want to help," she said. There was nothing childish in it, just a simple, hard decision.

Jorgen tried to shift, to pull himself away from the wall as if he could stand on anger alone. His muscles answered with a wave of shaking weakness that stole what little breath he had left. The fight in his eyes guttered, then narrowed to a banked coal.

"Rest," Karl said, more softly than Jorgen had ever heard from him. "We'll sort it. But you're no use to anyone if you snap yourself in half trying to sprint on a broken leg. Let the brew do its work. Strength first. Plans after."

The stone at their backs stayed cold and unyielding. But for the first time since they'd dragged Jorgen's limp weight onto a litter, Karl could feel the man pushing back against it. Not with fists or steel—but with the stubborn, ugly refusal to quit.

Jorgen closed his eyes. The darkness behind them matched the world he'd woken into—heavy, monstrous, pressing in from all sides. But in that dark he could imagine Bradley's last stand, Knight's square shoulders, Mustang's crooked grin as he'd turned back toward the fight. They hadn't thrown their lives away. They'd bought this—this escape and the chance for those left to get out. If he lay here and let it all slide away, their sacrifice meant nothing.

The steady drip became a drum in his ears, counting out seconds he couldn't afford to waste. He dragged his eyes open again. "More," he rasped, lifting a hand toward the cracked bowl in the skink's claws.

The creature hesitated, pupils narrowing. Its questioning hiss slid along the rock.

Karl leaned in, suspicion creasing his brow. "You don't know what this stuff does long-term," he muttered. "Could just as easy finish you as fix you."

\*\*\*

Jorgen set his jaw. The last dose still burned faintly in his veins, a thin warmth pushing back the chill that had settled in him. It tasted like ass. It had taken every scrap of will not to spit it back up. But he was sitting now. Talking. That was more than he'd managed in…however long he'd been out. "Worth the risk," he ground out. "Gotta try."

The skink studied him, then filled the bowl again. The thick liquid slid over his tongue, gag-sour and cloying, and he forced himself to swallow. Heat spread from his chest, down his arms, into his numb fingers. The exhaustion didn't vanish, but it loosened its grip, just enough.

He pushed himself higher against the wall, vision wavering. Pinky pressed in at his side, a small, solid weight, her shoulder braced against his. He let her take some of the sway without comment.

Karl grunted. "Looks like you've got a bit of fire left after all." His gaze sharpened. "Now we just gotta figure where to aim it."

Jorgen inhaled—slow, ragged—and something in him tightened into place. The idea came half-formed and reckless, but it wouldn't let go. "I know exactly where," he said. The words came easier, each syllable stronger than the last.

He shoved off the wall. His knees buckled and Pinky let out a startled noise, grabbing for him, but he caught himself on the rock and kept moving, one hand trailing for balance. Every step toward Alysha's motionless form sent a fresh wave of pins and needles through his legs.

As he walked, a faint glow bled into the edges of his vision. At first he thought it was the bowl, or some trick of the fungi—but the light moved with him. A soft halo, not the harsh green of the mushrooms or the sickly gleam of the skink's potion, but a low, warm gold, began to pulse at the crown of his head and down through his arms. It brightened as he forced each step, as if stubbornness was feeding it.

Even the skinks stilled. Their ridged heads turned to follow him, the bioluminescent crown of the lead skink dimmed beside the new light.

Jorgen sank to his knees beside Alysha. In the gold wash, her face looked carved out of wax—too still, lashes dark against skin gone almost gray. His throat tightened. "Time to wake up, baby bird," he whispered, voice rough and full.

His hands hovered over her chest. They didn't shake. Not this time.

He drew in a breath, deep as his battered lungs allowed, and let something inside him uncoil. The warmth that had been building surged out through his palms. Golden light spilled over Alysha, wavering at first, then steadier, wrapping her in a soft, humming glow. It was gentle where everything else in these tunnels had been brutal—spreading along her ribs, pooling in her recesses, soaking into the stillness of her limbs.

Karl stared, the lines in his face gone slack. The glow painted every crack and scar in soft inner fire flowing out of Jorgen. The skinks' narrow eyes widened; they leaned in despite themselves, their usual hisses and croaks replaced by a hushed, reverent clicking.

For the first time, Karl could see it—the way Jorgen's breathing synced with the rise and fall of the light, the way the potion's radiance and the man's own stubborn will tangled together. Some buried knack dragged out by need, by the glowing brew.

"Stone take me," he breathed, hardly aware he'd spoken.

Pinky edged closer, eyes wide, her breath catching as the faint luminescence bled outward from Jorgen into Alysha. The glow crawled across the stone, pooling into a shallow, shimmering ring of gold around her body.

The alcove held its breath. Only the slow drip of water and Jorgen's rough, uneven breathing broke the silence. Time thickened, every heartbeat stretching into something slow and viscous. The light rose and fell with his lungs; each faint tremor in his hands sent ripples of energy shivering over Alysha's still frame.

Sweat gathered along his brow and ran in thin lines down his temples. The power he'd dredged up burned erratic—faltering, flaring, never quite steady. It was raw effort made visible, a rough, stubborn force pressed against the waxen stillness of Alysha's chest.

Pinky stood behind him—watching. She set a hand on his shoulder, fingers tightening when his hands shook. The touch carried no magic, just a steady, human weight. A plea: keep going.

The skinks shifted their coils, claws scraping softly against the stone. The liquid in their cracked bowl glowed one color, Jorgen's light another. Even with what they'd seen their medicine do, they couldn't understand this—this quiet, golden bleeding of strength from one body into another—sat outside anything they knew.

Karl stayed where he was, back braced against the rock. Stone and steel he understood. Even the skinks' glowing brew he could wedge into some corner of sense as "alchemy." But this —the rules bending for one stubborn man's say-so—tugged at the edges of everything he trusted.

Alysha gasped.

The sound was small, but it hit like a hammer. Her eyes flew open, wide and unfocused, searching the cramped alcove. Confusion burned there—sharp, frightened, achingly familiar —and behind it, something else: a spark.

Jorgen sagged as if someone had cut his strings. The gold drained from his hands, dimmed around Alysha, and bled away into the stone. He let out a ragged breath that turned into a half-laugh, half-groan. "That…took it out of me," he managed, a crooked ghost of a smile tugging at his mouth.

Pinky threw her arms around him, small frame tightening to keep him upright. She shook, but her grip didn't.

The skinks crept closer in cautious increments, the fungal crown casting a faint halo along the rock. Their hisses held no demand—only a wary, intent curiosity.

Karl cleared his throat, the sound rough in the tight space. "Are you…better?" he asked Alysha, the last word coming out heavier than he'd meant.

She tested her arms first, then her breath. Her gaze moved from Pinky to Jorgen to Karl, taking in each weary, watching face. A thin smile cut through the grime, and a single tear edged down her cheek. "I think so," she whispered. In the hush that followed, it might as well have been a shout.

Relief hit the alcove like a warm draft. Shoulders slumped. Someone exhaled a breath they'd been holding long enough to hurt. Jorgen's gamble had actually worked. Alysha might still be weak, still be pale, but there was a person behind her eyes again, not just a shell waiting to be buried.

Jorgen's head lolled back against the stone. Whatever glow had been clinging to him was gone now, leaving his skin washed-out and his lips dry. Sweat plastered his hair to his forehead, darkening the roots.

"You did it," Pinky murmured, steadying him as he slid sideways. Her hand, braced against his chest, barely covered the span of his ribs.

Karl pushed off the wall with a grunt and crouched beside them. "Rest," he rumbled, tone softer than the word. "We've got a bit of life back in the tally thanks to you. Time you took some shut-eye before you fall over."

Jorgen forced a weak smile. "Just…need a moment." He dragged in a ragged breath and let it out slowly, as if he could push the lingering rush out of his lungs with it. "Let me be clear… that wasn't healing."

The words cut through the cramped alcove. Alysha, who'd been testing the curl of her fingers, stilled. The small movement of her hand froze halfway, her eyes snapping to his face.

Karl's shoulders tightened. "I don't understand," he said, the confusion grinding in his voice. "What do you mean that wasn't healing?"

Jorgen closed his eyes, gathering himself. His lashes trembled against skin gone too pale. "I don't have any healing powers," he rasped. "Not that I know of, anyway. What I…what I did was transfer some energy. Just trying to…jump-start your furnace."

His hand shook as he reached for her. The touch he set on her fingers was light, almost tentative, but the effort etched strain into his jaw. "Felt it…the energy flow," he murmured. "Ran me down, but—" he met her gaze, a tired spark of hope flaring there "—but it got you back."

Alysha's eyes glided from his face to the skinks and back again, taking in the cracked bowl, the faint glow, the tension lining every set of shoulders. "So…it's not a cure?" she asked quietly.

Jorgen gave a small, exhausted shake of his head. "No. It's not. More like the way a battery works," he said. "Charge moves from one place to another. But it's risky—took everything I had for that one shot."

Silence pressed in, heavier than the stone overhead. A moment ago, Alysha's first breath had felt like a breach in the darkness; now the weight of it all settled back over them, thicker than before. Jorgen's trick—whatever it was—was no answer.

CHAPTER TWENTY

Darkness.

Not the simple absence of light—the kind that lets you pretend your eyes will adjust—but something that *pressed*. It crowded his face, his ribs, the dark corners of his mind. In it, movement: a dry tick-tick of chitin, the rasp of many feet, and once, close, a wet hiss that made his stomach seize.

Adrenaline hit like a shock collar. Bradley tried to jerk upright, to snatch for a weapon, but his arms answered late, as if the signal had to travel through mud before it reached muscle.

He swung an elbow for leverage and struck something that wasn't stone.

It gave, but only a little.

Cool, damp, resistant—an awful, living *give* under a slick skin, like flesh wrapped in rubber. He pushed again, fingers splayed, and the truth slid into him.

He was wrapped.

He thrashed, and the world answered by tightening. Whatever held him flexed with his struggle—elastic, clinging—compressing his arms to his sides, pinning his legs, smearing every movement into drag. It wasn't rope.

His mind caught up in terrifying flashes: spiders. Venom. Paralysis. Wrapped up to wait.

A hiss passed his ear so near he felt the air shift. He snarled—no words, no call for help, just the sound an animal makes when the trap has already closed. He forced his hand forward inch by inch until his fingertips brushed a different texture—hard, ridged, with stiff bristles set in rows.

For half a heartbeat he thought: moss.

Then his palm mapped a curve. Plates. The edges of something jointed.

Carapace.

He was cocooned—stuck to it like meat to a slab—and surrounded.

The skittering multiplied. It circled in tight arcs, claws clicking over silk and stone. He clawed at the binding, fingers sinking into wet fibers, trying to find a seam, anything to tear. The mass stretched, but refused to give. His own struggling only seated it closer, sucking snug to his skin as if it enjoyed the fight.

A sick image rose—himself as a wrapped roast, softened by panic, made easier by his own effort.

His strength bled out fast. The first surge burned away, leaving a dull heaviness in its wake. He dragged air through his teeth. With the fatigue came the treacherous thought: stop moving. Save yourself the fear.

He was going to die here—trussed in an arachnid larder in a place no one on the surface even knew existed.

"They're leaving us alone for now."

Knight's voice cut through the dark—rough, familiar, close enough Bradley felt the sound in his chest.

Bradley swallowed and tasted metal. "Wha… Knight?" The name scraped out of him. "Where—"

"Stay still," Knight said, the same tired patience he used on rookies about to get themselves killed. "Conserve your strength. We're in a bad way, but panicking isn't going to help."

The clicks and skitters were still there, still circling in the dark. But now there was something else to hang onto—a voice he knew, cutting a thin hole in the suffocating black.

The silk clung to him in damp, fibrous layers, breathing against his ribs with every shallow inhale.

Blind panic clawed at his throat. A different instinct—learned, drilled into him—tried to cut through it.

"How?" he rasped, the word scraping out of a throat gone dry.

Knight exhaled, the sound heavy in the smothering dark. "Spiders," he cursed. "Got my legs first. Couldn't reach the damn multi-tool."

A chill ran through Bradley, cold enough to numb the ache in his bound limbs.

"We gotta…" he started, and the words died on his tongue.

There was no "gotta." No plan could save them with their current resources. Just two bodies laced up waiting their turn.

"Easy," Knight murmured. Somehow, in the middle of all this, his tone stayed almost level. "We think this through. Or at least pretend to, yeah?"

The name punched out of Bradley before he could stop it. "Pinky…" His chest clenched. "Alysha…the others…"

Knight didn't answer.

The silence that followed was worse than a no. Worse than anger. It hung between them, thick as the web.

A fresh wave of helplessness washed over him, sour on his tongue. Had they gotten clear? Or had the spiders let them run, just to catch them when they ran out of steam?

"We'll get out," Bradley rasped. He wasn't sure who he was trying to convince. "We're not—this isn't it."

Knight let out a soft snort. "Optimistic, aren't you?" he said. Under the dryness there was something else—something that sounded a lot like respect. "Tell you what. We won't die quiet, that's for damn sure. The problem is…" A pause, then a grim chuckle. "We don't have anything to swing. Even if our arms were free."

The web under his back shifted, a subtle tremor that threaded through his cocoon. Something was moving across it—light, precise, each step sending a faint vibration through the silk.

"Hear that?" Knight whispered, voice dropping low. "They're getting hungry. Coming in closer."

Bradley tried to move his arm. The silk bit in, fibers tightening with every twitch. Pain flared up his shoulder. If he could just get one hand free, claw at the cocoon, find a seam—but the stuff held, elastic and merciless. His own body had become proof of how efficient these things were.

The vibrations intensified, pulsing through the web like a heartbeat out of sync with his own. Something heavy skittered across the strands over his chest, each footfall ending in a tiny scrape. A hiss rolled over him—wet, guttural, close enough he could almost feel the humid exhale against his face.

He froze, locking every muscle.

"Spiders can pick up on chemo-signals," Knight muttered. "Especially fear."

The words slid under his skin. For a moment, they made his pulse jackhammer.

Then, slowly, he latched onto them.

If they could taste panic, maybe if he stayed calm it might buy them more time.

He dragged air into his lungs through his nose, deep as he was able. Forced himself to focus on concrete things: the clammy chill of the silk against his neck, the copper taste of blood at the back of his tongue, Knight's breathing somewhere to his right.

He pictured his fear like a valve he could turn, forcing it down, tamping it flat.

But under the weight of the web and the press of the dark, Bradley held still and clung to the only weapon left to him— his rational mind.

A guttural screech split the dark, close enough that the vibration ran straight through the silk pressed to his skin. Then the tremor stopped.

Knight swore—short, strangled. For one sick heartbeat Bradley thought they'd done it, that trying to choke down their fear had only made them stand out more.

Fabric tore. Something ripped, wet and fibrous. Then... nothing. Not the vast, suffocating silence of the cavern, but a tight, contained quiet right beside him.

"Knight?" Bradley forced the name out. It sounded wrong in this place, a human word thrown into a nest.

A rustle answered him. A ragged breath. "They're biting me," Knight growled. His voice was strained and wrecked, but steady in a way that made Bradley's stomach twist.

Horror clamped down. Knight's breaths, the flat report of his own dismantling, turned into a running commentary on how this ended. Their last stand in the webs, all that noise and blood and stubbornness—this was the payoff. Bradley hadn't seen what happened to Mustang when the spiders swarmed them; the silence now suggested either another cocoon somewhere in the dark or a lieutenant who'd refused to be taken and paid for it in pieces.

He pictured Mustang pinned like this, wisecracks smothered under silk, or already opened up as the first course. Mustang, whose sarcasm hid a spine that never bent. The thought punched through him harder than any blow.

Despair coiled in its place, slow and cold and certain. This was it. No charge, no last grenade, no miracle counter. Every struggle, every hard-won sliver of hope, led here—to becoming calories for something that shouldn't exist.

Something moved at the edge of his vision.

Light—faint and ember-red, dancing just beyond the weave of web over his face. A reddish-orange glow, like coals under ash. He blinked against the dark, eyes straining, but it danced just out of focus, a taunt his mind tried to smooth into madness.

"You see it too?" Knight gasped. His breaths were ragged now, each one dragged over glass. "Light… something's coming…"

The chittering shifted, picking up a new edge, a strange agitation Bradley hadn't heard before. As the glow swelled—brighter, more defined—the wet sounds of feeding cut off. A single, monstrous hiss rolled across the cavern, deeper than the spiders' clicks, followed by an explosion of skittering legs… moving away.

Then came the pops.

Sharp, cracking reports snapped through the dark in quick succession, followed by an unnatural shriek big enough to shake dust from the unseen ceiling.

The scuttling rose to a frantic clatter and then receded, until the only things left were Knight's labored breaths and Bradley's own heart hammering in his ears.

Light punched through the darkness—no longer the ember-smear of before, but a clear, dancing orange edged in yellow, alive in a way the fungus never was. It bobbed and swayed as it moved toward them, peeling shadow off the cocooned silk with every step.

"Fire…" Bradley breathed, the word breaking in his throat. A laugh tried to follow it and came out as a choked, disbelieving sound.

They were not creatures of the flame, these things that ruled the deep. Down here, heat was rare, light rarer, and fire was the one force that could turn these hunters into fleeing shadows. The spiders had scattered from it. That much was clear. But who in all this buried nightmare would come for them?

The ember-glow swelled, orange bleeding into yellow until it burst into a hard, stinging starburst. The dark peeled back to reveal a single, blazing torch held in a small, shaking hand.

Pinky.

Her face was smeared with soot, cheeks tracked by drying tears. She looked tiny against the cavern, but her eyes were bright with furious relief.

"Gotcha!" she called, voice cracking around the word.

Karl loomed behind her, dwarf-broad and solid in the dancing light. Sweat and grime darkened his already black beard, and the strain of the last fight etched new lines into his face, but his eyes were clear and sharp as they swept over the web-wrapped shapes.

The torchlight painted the cocoon in harsh detail. Silk glistened where fluids had soaked through; here and there, hollow spider legs and husks clung to the strands like discarded tools. For one nauseous heartbeat, Bradley saw himself as part of it.

Karl stepped in without hesitation. The torch threw his shadow long across the web as he grabbed hold and tore. The strands were tacky and resistant, but they parted more easily than Bradley had feared, snapping with wet pops at the strength of dwarven hands.

"Still with us?" Karl asked, breath rough, concern buried in gravel.

"Barely," Knight croaked somewhere to Bradley's right, voice shredded but alive.

Pinky dropped to her knees beside them, torch wobbling in her fist. With her free hand she clawed at the silk, small fingers sinking into the gummy weave. "We need to get you out," she panted. "Jorgen... Alysha..." The names came out like a prayer and a reminder in one breath.

Karl pulled a chipped knife from his belt and tossed it toward Bradley. The handle smacked into his cocoon near one numb hand. "Cut yourself the rest of the way free," Karl ordered, already reaching for another section of web. His voice rang off the stone. "Time's wasting. Won't be long before more come sniffin' for leftovers."

He wasn't wrong. The air still carried the bitter stink of scorched silk and spider ichor, smoke hanging low.

A roar split the haze—human, furious.

Mustang burst through a tangle of web-streaked rock, rifle up, firelight flashing along its scarred frame. He moved with a hitching, one-armed ferocity, eyes wild and very much alive.

He wasn't alone. The two skinks loped at his flanks, scales dulled by dust and streaked with drying blood. Bite marks pitted their limbs and flanks, but their eyes glittered, pupils thin slits of focused intent. In the torchlight they looked like something carved for a tomb wall and then set loose.

"You two alive?" Mustang rasped, chest heaving. The relief under the rasp was so raw it almost hurt to hear.

He recovered fast, slinging his rifle to one side long enough to toss their lost weapons toward the half-cut cocoons. Metal and polymer clattered against stone and sticky silk.

"Thanks to this little lady," Knight managed, nodding toward Pinky. The torch flame jumped, throwing her shadow huge across the ceiling—small in the flesh, towering in firelight.

Around them, the cavern resolved into a nightmare tableau: spider bodies sprawled in broken heaps, ragged cocoons torn open, strings of web sagging from the ceiling like old, dirty tinsel. Their own faces—smeared, hollow-eyed, soot-streaked —looked like they belonged here now.

Karl took it in with a quick, measuring glance, then jerked his chin toward the tunnel behind him. "Not a moment to waste," he said. "Jorgen, Alysha… they're this way."

The torch swung as he turned, flame guttering once before steadying.

Fear gnawed at Bradley in a steady, grinding way. The last time he'd seen Jorgen and Alysha they'd been fading, that strange magic deficiency hollowing them out from the inside. Karl's urgency dug cold fingers into his spine—if the skinks' medicine hadn't done enough…

Mustang didn't wait for orders. He pushed ahead, rifle tucked against his good shoulder. The skinks fell into step with him without being told, one on each flank, their lean bodies angling out to form a scaly screen. Karl brought up the rear with Pinky tight at his side, climbing picks hanging loose in his grip, every step a promise to bury steel in anything that came too close.

The heavy, rhythmic thumps that had guided them earlier were gone. Only the drip of unseen water and their own ragged breathing filled the cracks between their footsteps. Shadows leaned in from the edges of his light, making every jag of rock look like a waiting limb. Still, they climbed, shouldering into a narrow crevasse where the air warmed and a distant, flickering glow licked at the stone ahead—firelight, strong enough to push back the swarms.

Mustang let out a hoarse roar as they spilled from the crack into a wide cavern. Firelight flared off a lattice of webs and scattered arachnid corpses. At its center, Jorgen and Alysha stood back to back, outlined in orange. Jorgen was pale, jaw clenched, moving on a kind of shaky momentum—batting spiders aside with the stock of his air rifle, snapping off shots when he had a heartbeat to reload. Alysha moved beside him, sword work less fluid than Bradley remembered, every step careful, but with each swing something steadier kindled behind her eyes.

Mustang brought his rifle up one-handed and fired from the hip. Each crack of plasma lit the webs in stark flashes and tore a screech from the swarm. Dog-sized spiders recoiled under the barrage, bodies shining wetly where the bolts struck. The stink of burned chitin rolled across the cavern, hot and chemical, riding over a sweeter, rotting smell from torn carcasses on the floor.

Bradley's gut turned. Smaller spiders had mobbed the immense corpse of the first beast they'd brought down, tearing into its ruined abdomen. Limbs and mandibles worked in a frenzy, the swarm eating its own like a pit of starving rats.

"Damn things are cannibalizing their own," Karl spat beside him. "Hungry… means there's more coming."

"That's so gross!" Pinky yelped, her face twisting. She darted forward anyway, torch held high. Flame washed across the nearest webs, and the front rank of spiders flinched, legs tucking in as they backed from the heat.

The skinks surged with her, hissing sharp and furious. Crude spears jabbed. A tail snapped sideways with a meaty crack, sending a small spider tumbling, legs curling. For a few precious breaths the front of the swarm staggered, momentum broken.

It was enough. Bradley and Knight ran for Jorgen and Alysha, boots slipping on ichor-slick stone. "Hold fast!" Bradley shouted, pistol already barking. The weapon felt small and underpowered compared to Mustang's rifle, but every round that punched through a bulbous eye or shattered a leg bought space.

They slammed in alongside the others, turning them into a rough, human wall. Behind them, Pinky's torch and the skinks' spears worried at the edges of the swarm. It was not a battle so much as a delay—ducking under lunging fangs, hacking at jointed legs, firing into whatever came closest, then stumbling back a step to do it again. Every spider that dropped convulsing to the stone was one more heartbeat to breathe, one more yard toward the narrow cut of passage behind them.

All around them, the webbing trembled. Strands quivered overhead, the vibrations running out into the dark like a signal.

Bradley felt it in his spine as much as his boots: something heavier was moving out there, answering the call.

Mustang glanced past the press of bodies toward the choke behind them. The mouth of the tunnel was half-choked in silk and debris, but it was a way out.

"Karl!" he barked. "Timer. Now."

Karl was already there, crouched low in the webbed mess just shy of the tunnel mouth. Mustang's last plasma grenades sat bundled tight and tucked under strands like an egg sac, the timer wired into the sticky knot. Karl's thick fingers fumbled at the dial, mouth moving as he counted under his breath, eyes flicking between the countdown and the oncoming swarm.

Jorgen's knees buckled.

It looked like he was going down, but Alysha slid under his arm, taking more of his weight than her own state really allowed. Her shoulder hit his ribs; he grunted, but his hand tightened weakly on her sleeve instead of pushing her away.

"I've got you," she murmured.

"Thought I was supposed to be the one sayin' that," he rasped back. The words came rough, but there was a spark in his eyes that appreciated the moment .

Mustang slowed just enough to glance over his shoulder. The torchlight carved deep lines into his dust-caked face. "You stay upright, old man," he said. "I didn't just burn my last grenades to deliver you to a spider buffet."

"Bossy," Jorgen muttered, sucking in another painful breath.

Behind the front line, Pinky had gone quiet just a pale face smeared with soot and the stubborn, pinched line of her mouth.

Bradley's hand found hers without thinking. She clung like he was a handhold on a sheer face.

The swarm surged again, and this time it moved different—less hungry scramble, more coordinated push. Through the writhing bodies Bradley caught it: a bulk in the back ranks, forcing its way forward. A crown of legs. An abdomen like a boulder. Faceted eyes catching torchlight and throwing it back in dead glass flashes. Too big. Too sure. The matriarch was coming, and the smaller ones shifted aside for it without hesitation.

Bradley's stomach went cold. "Move," he said, and didn't wait for anyone to argue. "Back. Back to the tunnel."

They gave ground in hard inches. Knight took a hit on his crutch and nearly went down; Mustang hooked an arm under his shoulder and dragged him upright without looking. The skinks slid ahead hissing warnings to one another as they retreated.

Karl rocked back on his heels. "Set," he grunted, and slapped the pack into place like he was sealing a coffin. Then he lunged forward, shoved Pinky toward Bradley, and snarled, "Go!"

Alysha hauled Jorgen into the tunnel mouth. Bradley followed, pulling Pinky with him. Mustang held the rear, rifle spitting defiance into the oncoming black while the timer ticked down behind them.

They hit the tunnel in a staggered rush—boots skidding, shoulders scraping stone. Webbing snagged at clothes. Pinky twisted hard to look back, eyes wide, as if expecting the swarm to pour through the choke behind them.

"Eyes forward," Bradley told her, voice tight but gentle. "Focus on what's ahead, not what's behind."

414

She swallowed, still staring. "They sounded so hungry," she whispered. "Like… like the noises the big dogs made behind the cages. Only worse."

Bradley had no answer. He squeezed her hand once and kept moving.

Behind them, the cavern erupted.

A blinding white flash poured down the passage, followed by a roar that punched the air out of lungs. The floor kicked. Stone shrieked. Something slammed into Bradley's back and drove him to a knee. Dust and grit came down in choking sheets, and for a moment the world was noise and darkness and the taste of rock on the tongue.

Then the sound changed—less open cavern, more sealed tomb. The rumble died into a settling grind. When Bradley's ears stopped ringing enough to hear again, the entrance behind them was gone. Not a doorway—just rubble and snapped strands, a wall of broken stone packed tight where the tunnel had been.

They had survived. Barely.

Mustang coughed dust and spat. "We move," he snarled, wiping grime off his mouth with the back of his hand. "This tunnel keeps going. It's the only reason we aren't dead already."

Jorgen tried to straighten and failed. Alysha cinched her grip and leaned harder into him. "Keep breathing," she muttered. "Just keep moving."

The drip of water changed—less frequent, more distant. The air shifted from dust-and-chitin to something else: a faint dryness that didn't belong in these caverns. Karl sniffed, brows knitting.

"Smell that?" he grunted.

Knight, limping along with his makeshift crutch, let out a low hum. "Less rot. More… airflow. Might be a bigger chamber up ahead. Or a shaft."

"Please be a shaft," Mustang muttered. "Preferably one that doesn't open into a spider daycare."

The tunnel kinked sharply left, then climbed in a shallow, grinding slope. Every step drove protest up through their legs. Jorgen's breathing turned ragged again; Alysha's jaw clenched as she adjusted to his weight. The grit he'd shown earlier was gone, leaving only a worn-out man leaning hard on borrowed strength.

"Stop," Karl ordered suddenly.

Mustang bristled. "We don't—"

Karl cut him off. "Stop. Now."

They halted in a staggered line. Bradley felt it then too: a faint tremor under his boots, like something big moving very far away. Not spiders; the rhythm was wrong. A distant, dull, repeating thump that might have been rock settling… or something else entirely.

The crowned skink pressed its palm to the wall, head cocked, hissing low. Its subordinate echoed the sound, unease rippling through its scales.

"Pinky?" Knight asked, voice low. "You get anything from them?"

She listened, brow furrowing, then nodded once. "They say… big place ahead. Old stone. Bad place. But safe from spiders…

for a little while." She hesitated, eyes flicking up at Bradley. "They're scared of it too."

Bradley exhaled slowly. Old stone. Bad place. Safer than what was behind them.

"So," Mustang said, rolling his shoulder with a wince, "behind us, spider hell. Ahead of us, 'bad place.' Choices just keep gettin' better."

Jorgen coughed out something that might have been a laugh. "Story of our lives."

Bradley looked down the sloping throat of the tunnel, then back along the line of exhausted faces—Pinky's tight-lipped fear, Alysha's determined set, Jorgen's pallor, Knight's pain, Karl's stubborn scowl, the skinks' wary reverence.

"We keep moving," he said. "Slow, careful. First sign of something worse than spiders, we back into a defensible corner and make it regret meeting us. Until then… one foot in front of the other."

They shifted forward again, torches licking at the dark. The tunnel drew them on, deeper toward whatever waited ahead— another gamble in a long line of gambles.

A low hiss carried up the passage. One of the skinks had fallen behind, its steps dragging. Karl dropped back without a word, a stocky shadow between it and the dark. His gruff voice cut through the stillness. "Keep moving," he said, breath rough but steady. "Rest later."

Pinky edged closer to Bradley, her small face hollowed by the torchlight. "We're gonna get out," she whispered, voice shaking but stubborn. "We have to." It was hope and plea in one, a child's certainty thrown like a rope toward a future none of them could see.

The march blurred into a grind of footfalls and the steady drip of water. Muscles burned, lungs rasped, but fear drove them harder than any order. Every bend, every pocket of shadow promised disaster. Yet something had shifted in the dark: they moved as one. A slip of a boot drew a steadying hand, a falter at the rear pulled the whole line tighter. No one had strength to spare, but they spent what they had on each other.

# CHAPTER TWENTY-ONE

Once they were sure the scrape and skitter of legs had faded into the dark, they let themselves stop.

The tunnel settled around them: damp stone, the faint mineral tang of the underground, the tired hiss of their own breathing. Mustang leaned one shoulder against the wall, AR glasses hanging dead around his neck. Soiled and tattered clothing was streaked with dusty silk and spider gore. No one said it, but the way they moved—slow, careful, like old men—said enough.

They stopped to catch their breath. Packs slid from shoulders. Karl checked seams and braces on the nearest support strut with callused thumbs. Jorgen sank down with a quiet grunt, rubbing at aching joints and exhausted muscles. Alysha's hands moved automatically, smoothing a mat of cloth over the rock for Pinky to sit on. The girl folded down small beside her, eyes too wide in the torchlight.

The sound that broke the silence was not a scream.

It was a raw, tearing gasp, dragged up from a chest that had nothing left to give. Every head snapped toward it. Torchlight jolted, shadows stuttering across the tunnel as Mustang swung around.

Knight was already on the ground.

The sergeant's heavy frame—normally solid as a bulkhead—was on its side, armor scraping stone. His limbs jerked in brutal, disjointed spasms, boots drumming the packed earth. Veins stood out along his neck. His breath came in ragged, wet pulls, more animal than human.

"Knight!" Bradley was moving before the name finished leaving his mouth.

He dropped to his knees beside him, palms skidding over grit. The heat rolling off Knight hit him before he even touched skin. Bradley pressed the back of his hand to Knight's forehead, then to the side of his throat, jaw clenched.

Too hot. Furnace-hot.

Knight's eyes were slitted, unfocused, the whites veined red. Saliva foamed at the corner of his mouth, tinged faintly grey. The angry, pitted marks on leg had darkened, the flesh around them swollen and angry visible through the ribbons of his fatigues.

"Spider venom," Bradley's voice came out shaky. "Damn it."

The numbing paralysis in the cocoons had just been the opening act. His brain supplied the rest in clipped, clinical flashes: neurotoxins, tissue breakdown, systemic burn. The spiders didn't need to chase prey that collapsed on its own.

Jorgen dropped into a crouch on Knight's other side, joints popping as he had knelt too fast.

Knight spasmed again, torso arching. Bradley grabbed his shoulder, steadying him so he didn't crack his head on the rock.

"Easy, Sergeant. You're not going anywhere," Bradley murmured, useless comfort in a steady tone.

Alysha moved in beside Jorgen. She braced one hand on Knight's forearm, the other resting lightly on Jorgen's sleeve.

No med bay. No labs. No ice baths or antivenom or monitored drip. Just a roasting sergeant on cave floor, and a captain whose last proper procedure had been on a clean table topside.

Knight's hand clamped around his wrist suddenly, grip iron-hard despite the convulsions. For a second the sergeant's gaze cleared, locking onto him.

"Don't—" Knight managed, teeth chattering. "Don't...let me slow you...down."

Bradley swallowed hard. "Not happening," he said. "You're not a casualty; you're my patient. Big difference."

Knight's fingers slipped, spasms stealing the strength from his grip. His eyes rolled back.

Bradley heard his own pulse pounding in his ears. The world narrowed to heat under his hands, the stink of sweat and venom-soured skin.

Toxin. Not a curse or magic. Just a toxin.

The word cut through the mental fog.

"Wait," Bradley said, sharper than he meant. He sat back on his heels, hands hovering over Knight's chest as if afraid to lose contact. "It's venom. That's all it is—biology and chemisty."

Mustang looked over, face carved in hard lines by the torch beam. "Bradley—"

"Give me a second," Bradley snapped, then forced his tone down. "Help me out here. We can do more than watch him cook."

He pushed to his feet, then dropped into a crouch a pace away, fingers scrabbling through grit and loose stone. The tunnel floor was a patchwork of packed earth and exposed veins of minerals.

Clay. He needed alkaline clay. A buffer.

"Clay," he muttered. "And salts. Any mineral crust, anything sharp on the tongue."

Jorgen blinked. "We making a stew or a cure?"

Alysha's gaze tracked dubiously from Bradley to the walls, hope and disbelief wrestling there. Even Karl, who had been silently checking a crack in the ceiling, turned fully, one thick brow lifting.

"What?" Karl asked in confusion.

Bradley forced himself to inhale, deep and steady, dragging the habit of briefing a team over the top of panic.

"Basic chemistry," he said, rasp catching in his throat. "A lot of spider venoms run acidic. They break down tissue, blood vessels, nerves—and so on. We don't have antivenom, but we can blunt the degeneration."

He pointed at the wall, at the dark streaks and pale flakes caught in the torch's unsteady halo.

"Alkaline clay can bind acids. Mixed with salts, we can make a slurry and get it into him—hopefully enough reaches his intestines that his bloodstream can start neutralizing the venom in his veins and push any excess where it is most needed. It will not fix the damage, but it can slow the venom down." His gaze swept the tunnel again, searching for anything that looked promising. "Then we push water. As much as we can get. Flush what we can."

"We can find clay," Karl affirmed at last.

Hope moved through them in a small, fragile ripple. Shoulders straightening a fraction, eyes sharpening.

This was something Bradley understood.

It was medical science.

Pinky scrambled forward on hands and knees, the hem of her rainbow dress dragging in the dust. Torchlight caught in her eyes, wide and bright, making her look even younger.

"I'll find it," she said. Her voice shook, but the promise in it made him more sure of success than any of his knowledge or training.

Jorgen slowly lowered his hands from Knight's shoulders, as if afraid to break whatever thin thread Bradley had found. Wariness and something like respect tangled in his expression.

***

Pinky's small cry snapped their attention down the tunnel.

"Here!"

She wedged herself beside a narrow crack in the wall where the stone had split. The fissure opened into a shallow pocket, damp and cool. Under her fingers, the grey shifted to a sickly pale; when she dug in, it came away soft and slick, smearing her nails white.

Bradley was already moving toward her. He scooped a pinch, rolling it between thumb and forefinger. Cool. Faintly bitter, alkaline on the tongue when he dared the quickest taste.

"That's it."

The skinks converged, their bodies flowing around Pinky with quick, efficient movements. One scraped deep grooves in the adjacent rock, peeling away a crust of chalky flakes that glittered in the torchlight like crushed glass. When Pinky brushed some against her tongue, she made a face.

"Salty," she said thickly. "Tastes bad."

"Perfect," Bradley said. "Grab all you can."

It felt, absurdly, like the earth was handing them what they needed after everything they had already been through: nothing fancy, just a few unprocessed ingredients dropped on the floor of a burning house. But Knight's ragged cough tore that thought from his mind.

They hurried back.

Knight looked worse.

The discoloration around the bite marks had spread, swelling distorting the lines of his neck and shoulder until straps and clothing dug into angry, stretched skin. His face was puffed, eyes narrowed to fever-bright slits. Each breath rattled as if his lungs were full of gravel. Heat rolled off him in waves.

Torchlight threw hard shadows across his face and hollowed Knight's cheeks into something almost unrecognizable.

"Okay," he muttered, half to himself. "One messy, hypothetical experiment on a live subject coming up."

He dumped clay into the stone bowl the skinks offered, added a careful measure of water from a canteen Alysha had pulled from seemingly nowhere, then pinched in the scraped salt. His hands trembled—not with fear, he told himself, but with the urgency of getting this done before Knight crashed.

The clay drank the water greedily, turning into a lumpy, off-white paste. He stirred with two fingers until it loosened to a thick slurry that clung and then added more water so that it could be swallowed.

"This is going to be disgusting," he warned.

Pinky hovered nearby, gnawing her knuckle. Mustang had gone quiet, eyes tracking every movement. Karl stood over them, torch held high.

Bradley eased an arm under Knight's shoulders and lifted his head. The skin at the back of his neck was dry and burning. *Not a good sign.*

"Sergeant," Bradley said, bringing his mouth close to Knight's ear. "You with me?"

Knight's eyelids fluttered. A low sound escaped him—half groan, half growl.

"Gonna give you something," Bradley told him. "You need to help choke it down."

Whether Knight heard him or not, his jaw slackened when Bradley pressed the edge of the bowl to his lips. The first trickle of slurry slid in. It was cold against the furnace heat of his mouth, thick and gritty. Knight gagged immediately, throat convulsing.

He let out a strangled cry, a harsh, broken sound that scraped at the nerves of everyone in earshot. His hands clawed weakly at Bradley's forearm.

"I know," Bradley said, bracing him. "I know. It's going to feel worse before it feels better."

It felt like a hopeful lie.

They moved in a rhythm: Bradley tilting just enough, letting a mouthful in; Knight coughing, swallowing by reflex more than will; slurry smearing the corners of his mouth before Bradley wiped it away with the back of his wrist.

Through the fever haze, something sparked in Knight's eyes— a flash of awareness, confusion, stubbornness. He locked onto Bradley for an instant, as if pinning him.

"You've survived worse chow than this," Bradley said.

Alysha knelt beside him, her canteen cupped in both hands, water sloshing softly inside it as she moved. She waited until Bradley nodded, then edged closer.

"Ready," she whispered.

Karl ground his molars, his free hand flexing at his side. The torch bobbed as he shifted his weight, throwing the skinks' shadows huge and jagged along the walls. They had gone still now, huddled together, hissing softly to one another.

Bradley traded the bowl for the canteen. He tilted Knight's head slightly, thumb sweeping along the angle of his jaw.

"All right, Sergeant," he murmured. "Drink."

He tipped a thin stream of water past Knight's blistering lips. Every swallow was a fight. Knight's throat worked spasmodically, tremors shuddering through his frame as his body tried to reject everything at once—venom, clay, water, the whole miserable equation.

They fell into a cycle.

Slurry. Water. Rest just long enough for Knight's breathing to stop hitching on the edge of a choke, then back again. The only constant sound beyond his rough commands and Knight's broken noises was the steady drip of water somewhere deeper in the tunnel, a metronome for suffering.

Knight's fever climbed. Bradley could feel it, the heat intensifying under his hands. At one point Knight's back arched violently, muscles seizing in a brutal parody of strength. Bradley and Jorgen both had to throw weight across him to keep him from breaking his back.

"Easy, easy," Jorgen grunted, the words strained.

Then Knight jerked upright with a convulsive heave.

Bradley barely got the bowl out of the way.

Knight retched in great, tearing spasms, expelling slurry and bile onto the tunnel floor in a reeking splash. The sound of it—wet, guttural, emptying—filled the narrow space. The stench rose thick and sour, cutting through sweat and stone and torch-smoke.

Pinky turned her face away, gagging. Alysha's jaw clenched, but she held Knight's shoulder, steadying him through the convulsions.

Bradley stared at the mess for half a heartbeat, chest heaving. It was vile.

It was the body pushing back.

"Good," he breathed, almost inaudible. "That's good. Get it out."

They didn't stop. Once Knight sagged back, they gave him water again—small sips. More slurry in smaller doses. Time blurred into a series of repetitions: fever flush, purge, rinse, repeat.

Knight's retching lost its violence by degrees, the spasms shrinking to weak shudders. His breaths came rough but more regular, hiccuping instead of rattling. The furious heat in his dark skin dulled fractionally from raging furnace to small space heater.

The tunnel still reeked of vomit and salt and clay. Everyone was exhausted, shoulders slumped, eyes ringed dark.

Bradley dragged a sleeve across his forehead, smearing sweat and grime instead of clearing it. His arms felt hollowed out, his shoulders leaden, but when he looked down at Knight he caught the smallest shift.

Pinky appeared at his elbow with another bowl of water, both hands wrapped around the cracked stone as if she were carrying something sacred.

"I found more," she said, breathless.

"Good work," Bradley murmured, taking it from her. The rim of the bowl was cool against his fingertips.

Alysha eased back into place on Knight's other side. Her skin was still pale beneath the grime, but she didn't flinch at the smell or the sight; she'd most likely seen worse.

"Tell me when," she said, ready to steady Knight's head, to help tip the bowl.

The wounded skinks had pulled themselves in close, their tails curled tight around their bodies. Their eyes tracked every twitch. Little reptilian sentries.

Every rasping breath Knight managed, every sip of water that stayed down, was a victory.

Bradley eased Knight upright a little and shifted him so his back rested against a firmer section of rock. The stone was cool, which had to help, at least a little. He adjusted the angle of the ruined leg with careful hands, trying not to jostle damaged tissue more than he had to.

He lifted his gaze and found the others watching him— hovering further off in the gloom, arms folded, eyes reflecting tiny points of torchlight.

"Get some rest," Bradley said, surprised at how hoarse his own voice sounded. "I'll take first watch. Keep an eye on his breathing, check his leg again once I can feel my fingers."

Pinky opened her mouth to protest, then shut it when she caught his look. Alysha hesitated, then nodded, shifting just far enough back that she could stretch her legs but still reach Knight if he started to slide into spasms again.

The others settled where they were. No one moved far. They lay or sat within arm's reach of one another, gear pushed aside in a loose ring. Mustang stayed on the perimeter, but Bradley could see the way the man's weight was set on the balls of his feet, ready to move. Irreverent, sure. Uninvested? Not a chance.

Bradley drew in a slow breath and finally forced himself to really look at Knight's right leg.

With the adrenaline ebbing and the torch angled low, the damage laid itself out in ugly detail.

Old trauma first: the long, puckered lines where shrapnel had chewed meat away, not all of it had been removed. Some scars were roped and shiny, others ragged where the skin had torn under stress. Muscles along the thigh were uneven, knots and hollows where there should have been smooth bulk. Some of that was permanent; nothing short of a surgical suite and months of rehab would fix it.

On top of that, fresher layers: angry welts where spider legs had hooked and squeezed. Those he could live with.

The feeding bites were another story.

They ringed the calf and lower thigh in irregular clusters, deep punctures arrayed like the holes from a monstrous syringe. The flesh around them had gone mottled—black, purple, a sickly yellow-green spreading beneath the skin. Some bites oozed watery blood that smelled faintly metallic. Others had crusted over, swelling so tight the skin looked shiny.

Bradley swallowed down the urge to recoil. Infection was already sniffing around the edges. Without proper intervention, it would do what the venom hadn't managed yet.

He rinsed his hands with what little clean water he could spare, then set to work.

He lanced each puncture as gently as he could manage, squeezing until discolored seepage welled up and ran. Knight groaned even unconscious, leg muscles twitching under Bradley's grip. Bradley cleaned around each site with damp cloth, wiping away venom-tainted residue. He worked methodically, moving from one wound to the next, circling back, dredging and wiping and checking the heat of the skin under his fingers.

His vision started to blur, black creeping in and out with every blink. His hands shook more now, not from urgency but from sheer depletion.

He forced them steady. He'd had worse shifts in worse holes with less at stake. That was the lie he told himself, anyway.

The tunnel settled into a thick quiet. No skitter of distant spiders, no groan of shifting earth. Just the low, raw soundtrack of humans run past empty.

Then Knight made a sound that didn't fit the pattern.

A low groan, drawn up from somewhere deep in his chest. Not the reflexive noise of a body being manhandled. Something more deliberate.

Bradley froze, fingers still hooked under a strip of cloth. He watched as Knight's eyelids quivered, then dragged themselves open.

The sergeant's eyes were bloodshot, irises a dull, unfocused brown through a film of fever. But they moved. They tracked. They found Bradley's face and tried to lock on.

"Gonna…make it?" Knight rasped.

The words were shredded by dryness and damage, but they were words.

A laugh shot out of Bradley before he could stop it, half-bark, half-choke. It hurt his throat on the way up and left his eyes stinging.

"Damn right you are," he said, voice cracking around the edges. "You think we went through all that just to let you check out?"

Knight's mouth twitched, maybe in the direction of a smile, maybe just another grimace. His eyes slid shut again, but this time his breathing didn't spike. It settled, still heavy, but with a rhythm that didn't make Bradley want to count seconds between each one.

The fever hadn't vanished. Bradley could still feel the heat rolling off him, but it was no longer a climbing curve. It had plateaued.

Relief moved through the little knot of bodies like someone had loosened a wire around all their throats at once. Alysha let out a breath she'd been holding so long it came out as a shaky exhale. Pinky slumped onto her backside, palms braced behind her, head dropping forward as if someone had cut her strings. Jorgen scrubbed his hands over his face, leaving streaks of clay and blood.

Even the skinks seemed to sag, their heads lifting a fraction as if they'd been sharing the strain.

Exhaustion followed close behind, crashing in now that the crisis had eased its teeth. Muscles that had held tension too long began to shake. Joints complained. Adrenaline, finally allowed to bleed off, left behind a hollow ache.

Karl's stomach spoke up in the quiet with a low, disgruntled growl. He glanced down as if offended by his own body, then back at Knight, then around at the others.

"We need food," he said, voice rumbling through the stone.

A blunt statement that landed with the weight of fact. The fight with the venom had eaten through more than their reserves of nerve. Water was low. Rations and dried subterranean fish were gone.

Bradley's own gut tightened at the reminder, a dull twist under his ribs. They couldn't patch a man up just to starve him out.

Mustang shifted where he'd slumped against the stone, a low groan slipping out as he forced stiff muscles to move.

"Yeah. I'm on it," he rasped.

His gaze moved over the little circle of light: Knight propped against the wall, the others drooping around him, eyes sunk deep in exhausted faces. He turned his attention to the skinks.

"You two..." He jerked his chin at them. "Still got some fight in you?"

The crowned skink lifted its head. It hissed, the sound rough with fatigue. With a lash of its tail, it nudged its companion. The second skink answered with a weaker hiss, but it was assent all the same. Both shifted their weight forward, claws ticking on stone.

"Good," Mustang said. The word came out gruff but carried a thread of respect. "We need food. Something with meat on it."

He nodded toward the dark mouth of the tunnel stretching beyond their alcove, the look in his eyes hardening. "Hunting we go."

The skinks responded as if a switch had been thrown. The crown of the blue tailed skink brightened a notch, and they slipped into motion, movements still surprisingly fluid despite dried mud poultices and dried blood on their scales. They traded hisses and sharp little clicks back and forth, conversing in a pattern none of the humans understood, tails swaying in emphasis as they mapped a plan in sound and scent.

"They know these tunnels," Karl said quietly, watching them.

"Probably our only chance, then," Bradley answered.

He pushed himself upright. His legs went loose, knees threatening to buckle. He caught himself on the wall, fingers scraping over rough stone, then straightened, forcing his spine stiff.

"I'm good," he muttered to no one in particular.

They shared a look—a worn-out, wordless agreement that they hated this and were doing it anyway. Mustang swung his rifle up and over one shoulder, the weapon sitting a little awkwardly where his injury still nagged at his grip. He checked the charge indicator, and cursing the lack of power.

With the skinks gliding ahead, he stepped into the deeper dark with only a torch to guide them.

The alcove behind them shrank to a pocket of trembling light.

\*\*\*

Knight lay slumped against the wall, head tipped to one side, his fever-flush ebbing into an ashy pallor. The rise and fall of his chest was shallow but finally even, each breath edged with a faint rasp instead of a desperate choke.

Jorgen had slid down beside him, legs stretched out, back braced against rock. His eyes were closed, lashes clumped with sweat, but his hands still twitched now and then as if feeling echoes of power he'd already spent.

Alysha moved among them in a slow, determined orbit. She cradled a cracked bowl of water in one hand, a scrap of cloth in the other. Kneeling at Knight's side, she dabbed at the venom-darkened skin around his bites, washing away the worst of the grime and dried blood. She paused to wrap a fresh strip around her own forearm, where an ugly gash had crusted along the edges, then shifted to Jorgen, wiping at his visible scrapes. Her face was tight with focus, the motions small and careful, as if sudden movements might shatter what little calm they'd salvaged.

Karl knelt at Knight's ruined leg. The dwarf's shoulders filled the space, his bulk incongruous compared to his height. His thick fingers, usually better suited to rock and steel, worked the wrappings with unexpected care, easing a knot of cloth here, loosening a strip there so it didn't pinch. He checked for heat, for too-tight swelling, his brows drawn low.. For the moment, the best thing he could offer was support and stillness, and he respected that as another kind of craft. And the thought occurred to him that Bradley was a master of his craft.

Near the alcove mouth, Bradley and Pinky stood in silhouette against the torchlight, shapes cut out of orange and shadow.

Bradley's shoulders sagged, hands hooked into his belt to stop them from shaking. He watched the direction Mustang had gone until the tunnel swallowed them completely, the last glimmer of torch light and skink crown vanishing into black. Worry likely gnawed at the back of his thoughts, but he forced himself to stay put.

Pinky edged closer until her shoulder pressed against his hip. She didn't cling, didn't chatter. The elastic bounce she'd had in the oasis was gone. What was left was lean and quiet, the sort of steadiness born from having seen too much and kept going anyway.

He shifted just enough to make room for her, a hand resting briefly on her shoulder in acknowledgment.

***

Mustang moved through the tunnels at a careful prowl, boots rolling heel-to-toe despite the uneven rock. Each step sent a muted thud up his sore legs, but he kept the rhythm steady. The energy rifle rode across his back, weight dragging at his injured side, familiar hardware turned clumsy by a shattered arm.

The skinks flowed ahead of him, bodies hugging the walls, crown casting just enough glow to to see by after the torch had burned out. Their claws whispered over stone, tails brushing grit aside. They paused now and then, tongues tasting the air, then veered left or right without needing to speak.

Mustang's fingers brushed the frame of his AR glasses, adjusting them on the bridge of his nose. Wishing the familiar display floated in his vision—providing a faint wireframe overlay of distance and heat signatures.

In a place where the darkness felt almost physical, the glasses would have given him one simple advantage: he could see a little further than the thing that wanted to eat him.

Unfortunately, the tunnel ahead was worse than dark; it was a void, an absence of light that ate the horizon of his vision granted by the fungal crown of the blue-tail skink.

It prickled at the back of his neck.

His left arm pulsed with a steady, ugly ache, every step sending a dull jolt through damaged muscle and nerve. He could bring the rifle up, could lock his fingers around the grip if he had to, but he could feel the margin for error narrowing.

A soft hiss from the crowned skink snapped his attention forward.

It flattened against the tunnel wall, crown flaring a shade brighter. Mustang eased down into a crouch, the motion sending a spike of pain through his ribs and shoulder. He ignored it and focused all of his senses forward.

Something large was moving ahead of them.

It bobbed, slid sideways, paused, then jerked forward again, never entirely still. Not the sluggish drift of some half-frozen cave thing.

He held his breath and let his ears pick up what his eyes couldn't.

At first there was only the pressure of silence and his own blood roaring. Then, faint under it, a high-pitched chittering came through—it rose and fell in bursts, followed by a deeper, rhythmic clicking that seemed to reverberate through the tunnel.

Some kind of echo location, maybe?

As the skink leader advanced the glow from his crown outlined the thing—it reminded him, absurdly, of a star-nosed mole from some old documentary. A ridiculous little animal that felt its way through muck with a ring of fleshy fingers on its face. This thing was not little, despite its similar behavior. Same body plan. New nightmare.

He watched it weave closer, its erratic movement keying in on something it found interesting.

They couldn't just wait. Despite its stumbling gait, there was no doubt in his mind it was hunting.

A plan slid together in the back of his mind. The creature relied on sound; the clicks and chitters were its map. Disrupt the map. Give it something loud and obvious to lock onto, pull it off axeis long enough for a shot.

Which meant bait.

His gaze shot to the skinks. Smooth scales, low profiles. Harder to see, maybe, if it mattered, but not quiet—not to something that lived and killed by sound. Their claws, their hisses…they'd light up on its radar as surely as his own boots.

He looked down at his heavy soles, felt the tug of the rifle strap against his injured shoulder. Engaging it alone made tactical sense and a stupid kind of emotional sense too. If he blew it, he was the one who'd botch the shot, not them. But with one arm compromised, he was unlikely to get a second chance.

His hand slid to the rifle anyway, fingers closing around the familiar snarled polymer of the grip. A high energy blast would cook anything along the line of fire, provided he could bring the barrel up before the thing dissected him. Powering up the weapon would spike its signature whine, killing their stealth in an instant.

Stealth wasn't winning this one. Timing might.

He started forward.

The skinks hesitated, heads dipping in confusion. A beat later, understanding—or something close to it. They fanned out to either side of him, bodies low, claws whispering over rock. Their hisses died to faint breaths, their tails held just clear of the floor to cut down on drag.

They were ready.

The closer he got, the more the sight ahead of him changed.

He drew in a slow breath, then let out a string of quick, sharp chirps, trying to mimic the chitter he'd heard—close enough, he hoped, to sound like a challenge or a wounded something. The noise felt too loud bouncing back to him off the walls.

The creature stopped its seemingly lazy weaving and pivoted—appearing to lock onto his position with a precision that made his stomach drop. The sound followed a heartbeat later: skittering claws on stone, quick and purposeful, building into a harsh, staccato rattle that crawled up his spine.

If it came straight at him, he might not be fast enough.

Mustang brought his left arm up to brace the length of the weapon. His shoulder screamed. Sweat broke fresh along his brow. The second he powered it, the gun sung his position to anything with ears.

One shot, he told himself. Make it count.

Behind him, the skinks bunched, muscles coiling. Bodies melting into the edge of the walls. Even without looking, he could feel them wind tight.

*Ten steps,* he guessed.

The star-nosed thing surged.

*Five.*

The chittering climbed an octave, edges sharpening until it felt like needles in his teeth.

*Three.*

It burst into view as a boiling knot of flesh and motion— splayed sensory tendrils twitching around a blunt snout, each tipped in hooked claws, an obscene parody of the star-nosed mole from his memory. Its mouth gaped wide, ringed with needle teeth slick with slime. Short, powerful limbs hammered the stone, claws throwing up sparks as it launched down the tunnel.

He didn't aim so much as drag the barrel into position and trust muscle memory.

The bolt ripped out in a blinding lance, turning the world white-green burning the image into his mind's eye. The shot hit center skull. Heat blossomed around the creature head setting its dust coated, oily fur to cinder.

The thing screamed—a tearing bellow that shook dust from the ceiling. It twisted, slamming into the wall, claws gouging furrows in softer material as it thrashed. Chips of rock peppered Mustang's face and clothes, a few sharp enough to sting.

The skinks were already on it.

They darted in low, spears jabbing. In the cramped tunnel there was nowhere to circle, nowhere to step back. It was all close work and bad angles. One skink drove its crude spear into the thing's neck, earning a spray of dark, steaming blood. The other went for a forelimb—and caught a backhand swipe that raked claws across its flank.

Mustang staggered sideways, shoulder clipping the wall, and fired again. The second shot chewed through the creature's hindquarters, the smell of scorched meat and singed fur slamming into him on a wave of heat. It convulsed, sensory tendrils slapping blindly at the air, then sagged as the skinks stabbed and stabbed until the twitching stopped.

Silence crashed down as abruptly as the noise had come.

The rifle's whine wound down to a soft hum, then faded. The only sounds left were their breathing—ragged and too loud—and the slow drip of beasts pooling blood.

Mustang let his good shoulder hit the stone and slid down until one knee found the floor. His lungs hauled in air like he'd been running for miles. His left arm burned, a deep, hot throb that pulsed in time with his heartbeat. He flexed his fingers, just to make sure they still obeyed, then let them rest on the rifle.

They were still alive. The thing on the floor wasn't.

He'd take it.

The skinks hissed, the sound triumphant. The uninjured one stamped once, spear butt cracking against the stone. The other stood a little hunched, one side slick with fresh blood, but its crown flared all the same, eyes bright with leftover adrenaline.

Together they approached the carcass.

Up close, the resemblance to that old mole from his memory was worse. The creature's head was dominated by a ring of mangled tendrils, each lined with tiny, torn feelers, now blackened and curling where the bolt had burned through. Its claws were grotesquely oversized, built more like shovels crossed with butcher's hooks, several now snapped and bloody from the things reckless charge. Patches of coarse fur had been charred away, exposing blistered, grey-pink flesh underneath.

A wave of tiredness rolled over Mustang, heavy enough that his vision fuzzed at the edges.

 The tunnel suddenly felt narrower, the walls leaning in, the absence of the creature's chittering leaving a hollow ringing in his ears.

We win, he thought, and every time it costs more.

A nudge at his boot brought him back.

The crowned skink stood in front of him, eyes level with his chest. It bumped his shin with its head—not hard, but insistent —then turned and prodded the carcass with the butt of its spear. It looked back at him, crown tilting.

The message was clear enough.

Food.

Mustang huffed out something that might have been a laugh. It hurt all the way through.

"Yeah," he said, mouth quirking into a crooked, reluctant smile. "Fair point."

He levered himself upright again, every muscle complaining, and slung the rifle more securely across his back.

"All right," he rasped. His voice was barely audible. "Let's get this thing back to camp."

Up close, the mole-thing was even heavier than it looked—dense with muscle and whatever passed for bone in its warped body. Its limbs didn't bend the way he wanted, and the sensory mass at its head kept flopping obscenely with every tug.

The task felt absurd, dragging a dead nightmare through a maze of rock when his own legs wanted to fold with only one good arm. But he saw Knight's ashen face in his mind, Pinky's hollow eyes, heard Karl's blunt statement—We need food—and forced himself to yank and pull and push.

The skinks didn't hesitate. With a crackle of hisses and clicks, they arranged themselves around the carcass, finding purchase where flesh met limb, wedging claws under its bulk. On a shared, sharp exhale, they heaved.

Scaled bodies strained, muscles standing out under scarred hide. The carcass lurched off the floor, then settled again, a little higher. They adjusted, shifted grips, and lifted once more.

"Yeah," Mustang muttered, stepping in to grab a twisted hind leg with his good hand. "Just a long fucking way to go."

Battered, bleeding, and bone-tired, the three of them started the long drag back through the dark with their kill.

The glow of the skink's crown threw their shadows long and warped along the tunnel walls, exaggerating every limp and hitch into something monstrous. Between them, the mole-thing sagged in their grips, its dead weight turning the uneven floor into a gauntlet. They moved in fits and starts—drag, breathe, adjust, drag again. Each pull tore at Mustang's shoulder, set fire along the old wound in his arm, but he kept his hand locked around the twisted hindleg.

The carcass stank—burnt fur and cooked meat mingling with the damp, mineral reek of the caverns, catching in the back of his throat. Slime from its sensory tendrils smeared the rock where it bumped, leaving a glistening trail that gleamed in the low light.

They swapped places when one of them started to stumble: Mustang to the rear to push, then back up front to judge distance by memory; the skinks trading corners, claws scraping for purchase. No one complained. They didn't have breath to spare.

Somewhere ahead, the others were waiting—Knight propped against stone, Bradley counting breaths, Pinky pretending not to watch the tunnel mouth. Hunger sat like a stone in Mustang's gut, but the thought of their faces when they saw meat cut through the ache.

You're not just hauling a carcass, he told himself, shifting his grip as his fingers threatened to slip. You're hauling dinner.

Water dripped steadily somewhere in the dark, each drop ticking past like a metronome for their pace. Mustang's own breathing fell into step with it—ragged inhale, rough exhale. Underneath that, softer but just as persistent, came the skinks' low hisses and the occasional grunt he couldn't quite bite back. Together, it made a strange kind of music—three worn-out hunters dragging proof they were still dangerous.

Eventually, a faint smear of orange appeared ahead, barely there against the black. Firelight from the alcove.

He fixed on it, letting the sight pull him forward. With every dozen steps the glow grew, resolving into a single, wavering flame and the suggestion of shapes around it—people, gear, the outline of home for the moment.

His shoulders slumped, but his pace didn't falter. The closer they got, the more the weight in his hands felt like something he could bear.

It wasn't the end of anything. The food wouldn't last.

But right now, there was a fire ahead, silhouettes that were still standing, and enough meat on this ugly thing to buy them another day.

The meal—despite what it was—still counted.

The mole meat chewed like boot leather. It was tough and stringy, with a gamey tang. Fat popped now and then in the small fire Pinky had coaxed from spider silk she had picked out of their hair and off their clothes with the dried fungal stalks she had found, spitting sparks against the rock. They tore strips free with tired teeth, chewed, and swallowed without comment.

Huddled close, trading warmth with the flames and each other, they could almost pretend it was a proper camp.

Knight lay propped against the wall, jackets piled over him. His skin was still too ashen under the fever flush, but his eyes tracked the movement around the fire. Bradley had reduced a portion of the meat into a greasy broth, and he spooned it into Knight's mouth in careful, slow doses. The sergeant swallowed in small, pained pulls, throat working.

His natural color had begun to creep back into his face.

"My leg…" Knight rasped at last.

He didn't look down at it. He stared at Bradley instead as if bracing for the worst. The words weren't a question so much as an impact—recognition finally catching up.

Bradley held his gaze.

"Gonna take time," he said, pushing as much steadiness into his tone as he could manage. "There's a lot of damage. Nerves are…tricky. Sometimes they wake up. Sometimes they don't."

It was the cleanest version of the truth he could give. He'd seen men relearn how to move with worse. He'd also seen others go home in chairs. At least that's what he had thought at the time. The reality of Project Oroburos threw those memories into questions.

Something in Knight's jaw loosened, then set again. He gave a short, shallow nod and let his head rest back against the stone.

The fire continued the conversation for a time without their input.

Jorgen shifted, the haunted tightness in his eyes never quite leaving. Still, he dredged up a crooked half-smile.

"Gonna need to get moving soon," he rasped. "Loafing about isn't goin' to get us anywhere."

It wasn't much of a joke, but the point sat solid. Staying meant running out of food, water, and luck. Moving meant new problems and more holes they could fall into. There wasn't a good option, just less bad ones.

As they choked down the last of the meat and shifted into the slow, graceless business of packing up what little they had, the skinks slipped into their own routine.

They gathered a clutch of the faintly luminescent mushrooms growing in a crack just beyond the fire's reach. Under their claws, the caps crushed into a thick, pale paste that glowed softly, cold light pooling in the bowl they worked over. They added water a drop at a time, hissing in quiet argument over the consistency until it pleased them.

Then they smeared it over their wounds.

The paste soaked into torn scales and raw flesh, leaving veins of ghostly light tracing along their flanks and limbs. The crowned skink hissed low as it dabbed the mixture along the gouge left by the mole's claws; the sound held pain, but there was relief buried in it too. Their voices dropped into a rough, rasping purr that vibrated in their chests, the sound weirdly contented in the cramped alcove.

The crowned skink had hissed a series of sharp phrases and looked to Pinky. She'd listened, head tilted, then relayed in a small, careful voice that the fungus drank in "power"—and to humans, it could be lethal.

Bradley had backed off at once. Watching the paste sink into the skinks' wounds, light dimming where it met flesh, envy still twisted under his ribs all the same. He now understood why they had not offered it to himself and the other two soldiers, but Jorgen was human too. Wasn't he?

They were torn up, bleeding, limping—and still, given a handful of mushrooms and a few drops of water, their bodies started stitching themselves back together in ways his training had no language for. Knight's mangled leg and the damage to Mustang's arm had no such shortcuts.

"We'll get out," Bradley said quietly, more to the rock in front of him than to anyone in particular.

"Damn right we will," Jorgen answered, firm enough to almost convince him—almost.

The fire painted them all into warped silhouettes on the walls, stretching human shapes into long, jittering phantoms. Exhaustion had carved deep lines around mouths and eyes, pulled shoulders forward. Even at rest their hands twitched, still half-waiting for the next thing to come out of the dark.

Despite the brief warmth and the full bellies, worry coiled under it all, tight and constant.

Pinky sat with her knees drawn up, arms wrapped around them. The firelight hollowed her cheeks and made the shadows under her eyes look bruised. She watched the skinks for a long time, lips pressed together, before finally speaking.

"Their city," she whispered. "They say it's not safe."

Her voice shook on the last word. She glanced at the skinks, who still hissed and clicked about paths and dangers in a tongue only she could fully understand.

They had bled together. That had to count for something.

But they'd come from somewhere deeper still—and whatever waited there scared them.

"Not safe?" Jorgen repeated. The words came out rough, threaded with a tired skepticism. "The city? Thought they were taking us there."

Hope and dread sat side by side in his tone. A place with walls, supplies, maybe light—that fantasy had been dragging them forward as much as the skinks had. The idea of a haven turning into another death trap turned his expression sour.

The skinks exchanged a flurry of low hisses. Whatever they said, the uncertainty in it was clear.

Mustang leaned forward, his good forearm braced on his knee, eyes narrowed over the fire's glow. "How dangerous?" he rasped. "We walked into a spider nest blind. Not doing that again."

His gaze locked on the skinks, the question sharp though the words didn't carry across the language barrier.

Bradley felt his own stomach knot. They'd been so focused on what was right in front of them that the city had become a vague promise postponed until later. Pinky's warning snapped it into focus.

The crowned skink stepped into the firelight, scales still faintly veined with the glow of the mushroom paste. It hissed, a longer, deliberate string of sounds, eyes locking on each human face.

Pinky listened, brow furrowing, then translated in a small voice. "Many tunnels. Many skinks," she said. "Many... clans."

The phrasing sat oddly in Bradley's ear.

The injured skink added a rasping comment, one claw tracing a circle on the stone as it spoke.

Pinky swallowed. "He says...others want to sit on the stone of leadership. Don't want him there. Wouldn't want you there either."

So—power struggle. A city full of armed reptiles, and they'd already picked a side.

Knight's voice cut through the quiet, stronger than it had been since the fever broke. "Means we're a problem for whoever doesn't want our skink friend on that rock," he said. His mouth twitched in a crooked almost-smile. "Politics. Same mess, different species."

A few low, humorless snorts circled the fire. It wasn't funny, not really, but the shape of it was familiar in a way that made Bradley smile at the absurdity. Earth or sky, it always came back to politics.

Under the laugh, the truth: walking into that city meant stepping into someone else's fight.

"So what do we do?" Bradley asked, looking around at the ring of faces, all hollow-eyed in the restless light. "Turn around? Stay lost in the dark?"

There was no conviction in it, no mockery. Just the options laid bare.

Jorgen snorted, coughed, then forced the words out. "City means supplies," he said. "Food. Water. Maybe a way up. Don't like the sound of it, but I don't hear any better ideas."

Mustang watched the flames for a long moment, expression hard to read behind the grime and fatigue. The fire painted red in his eyes; the rest of him was shadow and sharp angles.

Finally, he looked up at Bradley.

"We go," he said. No drama, just decision. "These lizard-folk pulled us out of the fire more than once. We owe them. Plus, everything the old man said."

Bradley held his stare for a beat, then nodded. The city—dangerous or not—was at least a direction.

"Yeah, we go," he echoed. "We walk in knowing it's a hornet's nest, not a sanctuary, and maybe we can avoid getting stung."

Alysha shifted closer to the fire. She rubbed her thumb over the rim of the empty bowl in her hands, then lifted her gaze.

"Maybe…we can make a deal," she said, words careful but steady. "Our help, in their mess…for their help."

Jorgen huffed out a humorless chuckle. "Pretty sure that's what they've already been doing," he rasped. "We're in their world now. Their tunnels, their rules. And their rules sound a hell of a lot like knives in the dark. But like Mustang said, we owe 'em. And then there's that whole 'devil you know' thing."

The words burrowed under Bradley's skin. Jorgen wasn't wrong. No matter where you were, every favor had a catch.

A different memory rose unbidden: the scorpion's armored bulk thrashing under their combined assault, its stinger hammering the stone as the skinks fought shoulder to shoulder with them. They could've left the humans to be pincushions. They hadn't.

"They helped us," Bradley said, looking at the two reptilian warriors across the fire. Their scales caught the flame, throwing back copper and green. "Didn't have to. But they did."

The crowned skink answered with a measured hiss, shoulders lifting. Pinky leaned in, listening, lips moving silently to catch the cadence. She swallowed, then translated.

"He says…it was a debt," she murmured. "You saved them too. From the dark claw."

Her eyes met Bradley's. There was a child's awe there, but something older too, something that made the fine hairs on his arms stand up.

She hesitated, then added, a small spark of mischief lighting her tired face, "He also says the Serene Rae blesses us—with her favor."

The name hit the air like a blast wave. It didn't belong in the cramped alcove with its soot-black ceiling and stolen meat, and yet it settled there anyway.

Mustang snorted softly. "Serene who?"

Jorgen didn't laugh this time. His eyes widened, a flicker of something almost like reverence surfacing through all the grime and fatigue.

"The Serene Rae," he repeated under his breath. "Haven't heard that one in a long time." He shook his head, as if clearing it. "Theirs is an old faith, boy. Not just monsters and bad dreams. There's…stories."

Mustang cut through the rising weight of it with his own rasp.

"Goddesses and politics aside," he said, leaning back on his good hand, "fact is, we're all in the same boat. They bleed, we bleed. "

The fire cracked, sending a small shower of sparks up toward the low ceiling.

Karl stirred, joints protesting as he shifted from his crouch. He fixed the skinks with a steady look, eyes dark under his heavy brows.

"Don't put stock in your goddesses," he rumbled. "Or ours, for that matter. But we should keep helping each other. It's the only reason we are all still alive."

The skinks exchanged a quick hissed exchange, crowns brightening a fraction. The crowned one looked to Pinky and spoke again, the sound softer this time.

"They understand," Pinky said.. "But they say…the Serene Rae guides our steps, even in the dark. That it is good fortune, not chance, that we found each other."

Jorgen let out a snort that was half laugh, half curse. "Good fortune?" he echoed. "Doesn't feel like it, since we dropped into this pit."

Mustang grunted, a sound somewhere between reluctant agreement and unwilling resignation.

The fire shrank a little, fungal stalks giving up their last vestiges of heat. Shadows climbed higher on the walls.

Human doubt and reptilian faith sat across from each other around the same small flame. Between them, in the cramped space where their needs overlapped—food, shelter, a way forward—something that wasn't quite trust, but wasn't hostility either, began to cement.

"Let's get some rest while we can," he said, voice low but carrying.

Jorgen stretched out, joints popping like small stones under pressure. "Been a long time since I slept in a bed that wasn't the ground," he grumbled, easing his back against the wall. A hint of something like anticipation edged the complaint. "Bit of civilization, even if it's skink-made…could be a nice change."

Alysha managed a weary smile. "Just hope they don't serve spider as a delicacy," she muttered, a shiver running through her at the thought. Her eyes slid to Knight, taking in the steady rise and fall of his chest. "However, if they do, Knight could have his revenge…"

The joke was as much for herself as anyone else, but it seemed as if everyone was simply too tired. Except for Jorgen, who got a good chuckle out of it.

Bradley watched as Pinky edged over and curled against Jorgen's side, small body tucking into the curve of his arm. The old bounty hunter didn't hesitate; he shifted to make room, one rough hand resting light on her shoulder. For all his scars and gruffness, the gesture was easy, familiar.

"Tomorrow," Bradley said, eyes on the ring of black beyond their little alcove, "we walk out of this patch of darkness into whatever's next. Together."

The embers dwindled, painting the alcove in a soft, rust-red glow. Bodies sagged where they sat or lay, pulled down at last by exhaustion.

Jorgen had taken first watch, propping himself against the wall with his air rifle upright at his side. As the others dozed, he'd leaned down to mutter to her, voice pitched low so it wouldn't carry.

"Look, kid," he'd said, rough tone softened around the edges, "I know you don't actually sleep. But you gotta pretend. Folk don't like waking up to you just…starin'. Creeps 'em out."

Pinky had nodded solemnly, as if he'd handed her a rule of physics. Now she lay curled against him, breathing slow and even, eyes half-lidded. To anyone glancing over, she looked out cold. Only the slight tension in her shoulders and the way her gaze tracked toward movement gave her away.

She listened to the scrape of grit under Jorgen's boot, the faint rasp of his breathing, the drip of water beyond the fire's reach. Every change in rhythm was a warning sign filed away.

The skinks lay near the center of the alcove, close enough to share the humans' meager warmth but with their heads angled toward the exits. Their scaled hides gleamed dully in the emberlight, patches still faintly lit from the mushroom paste. They radiated a strange calm even in rest, the stillness of creatures born to hard places.

Now and then the crowned skink twitched, claws flexing, brow creasing as if some buried part of him still stalked through tunnels in his sleep.

Alysha dozed in fits, her body curled, soft whimpers leaking out when sleep dragged her too deep. Every sound pricked Pinky's ears. Knight lay farther back, his ruined leg propped on a folded jacket and spare cloth. In the ember glow his face looked carved from wax, but his chest rose and fell in a slow, stubborn rhythm.

Pinky watched them all.

\*\*\*

Jorgen was the last to pry himself off the ground, but the first to shrug into his gear. He yawned, jaw cracking, then scraped a hand over his face.

"Time to get moving, folks," he rumbled. His eyes were already sharp, the wariness there settled in like an old tenant.

Bradley knelt beside Knight. Sweat had dried to salt on his skin. Bradley checked his pulse, the heat of his forehead, then the color of his lips before speaking.

At least his fever has broken.

"We got you," he said quietly. "But it's slow and steady from here, Sergeant."

He glanced toward the skinks. They watched, unreadable, pupils narrow in the dim light.

Pinky posture made it seem as if she could feel the tension running under it like a hidden stream as she helped gather what little they had not already stowed in case Knight needed attention—bowls, strips of cloth, the last of their water—and Bradley tried not to think about how little time their supplies bought. Her hands moved faster than her thoughts, folding, tying. When her gaze snagged on the injured skink's stiff gait, an idea nudged its way forward.

"Maybe…" she began, then pushed on. "Maybe they have a way to carry him? Since we had to use the litters for fire food."

She looked straight at the wounded skink as she spoke, hoping they would be able to offer a solution. It hissed low, eyes narrowing, then traded a rapid burst of clicks with its crowned companion.

Without further discussion, the wounded one moved to the center of the alcove. It dropped to all fours and braced itself, spreading its limbs to lower its center of gravity. Its broad back, scarred and scaled, would make a crude but serviceable platform when coupled with tie downs.

Knight eyed the offered transport, one brow inching up despite the pain etched in the rest of his face. "Well, I'll be damned," he muttered. "First time a beast offers me a ride without trying to eat me first."

Alysha stepped in. "We should show them more respect than calling them beasts," she said, managing a small smile. "But we'll have Pinky tell them to be gentle if they get peckish."

Pinky snorted, the sound too quick and sharp to be a laugh, but close.

They moved with care. Karl planted himself nearby, grim-faced, being in the deep caves had seemed to sour his disposition more than the undercity of New New York. Jorgen hovered on Knight's other side, leaning heavily on a dried fungal stalk, refusing to acknowledge the tremor in his own legs.

They eased Knight up and onto the reptile's back. He grunted and tensed against the obvious pain, but met Bradley's eye with a hard look. Whatever his leg could or couldn't do, he didn't want to lay there and let them drag him like cargo.

"Easy," Bradley warned, one hand still on Knight's shoulder until he was sure the sergeant had found his balance. "Let's get him strapped on."

Another torch was prepared and lit, flame licking at the stale air, painting everything in harsh orange as they filed out: skinks first, as a precaution against their kin; Karl and Bradley on either flank of Knight and his living mount; Mustang just behind, rifle slung and eyes half-lidded but awake; Jorgen and Alysha closing the line, Pinky ghosting between them.

The tunnel swallowed them quickly. Each bend looked like the last. The world narrowed to the patch of light in front of their boots, the scrape of soles and claws, the soft grunt when someone misjudged a step. Water dripped from somewhere out of sight in a slow, steady rhythm.

Their legs burned, then went numb as they marched. Shoulders ached from the weight of packs and weapons and promises. Fear didn't scream; it settled in as a dull pressure that walked with them.

"So, old-timer," Mustang called back to Jorgen in an attempt to banish the silence, "how many years you got stacked up, anyway? Bet you've seen some things."

Jorgen snorted, a wry grin tugging at his weathered features. "Seen enough," he said. "More than my share, I reckon. But a number? That's just time passin'. Don't always make a man wiser, just more run down."

Up ahead, Karl trudged on one side of the passage, keeping half an eye on the shifting shadows. After a while, Pinky drifted up from the rear of their column to walk beside him, a tiny figure next to his squat bulk.

Karl's gaze stayed on the dark ahead, but his voice softened. "So, little one," he rumbled, "where were you before all this? Got folk topside wonderin' where you've wandered off to?"

He realized what he had just asked and who it was directed to before his mind had time to know better.

Pinky's gait faltered slightly. "I...I don't remember," she said, honestly. "Just...dark. For as long as I can remember." Her eyes slid to Jorgen, catching on the way he leaned a little heavier on stalk than he'd ever admit. "Jorgen found me. Led me to you. I don't think I could ask for a better family. Even if I had one before."

Alysha, walking light but steady, eased up to take the spot opposite Bradley at the front. The tired lines on her face matched his; they shared a look that said as much as words.

"Why do you think…" she began, then faltered. Her fingers brushed the tunnel wall, trailing along damp stone. "Why did you trust me so fast? Knowing I'm…not like you."

Bradley let the question hang for a few beats. He could hear the hollow echo of their footsteps ahead of them. There wasn't a neat answer, just instincts and a loneliness he didn't care to inspect too closely.

"Maybe," he said slowly, "it's because you had a dozen chances to run. Or cut our throats. Jorgen called you out, and you stayed. You didn't have to lift a finger, much less help us into K-94." He shrugged, the motion tight. "And I always tried to believe—even before figuring out how broken everything is —that not all of the unforeseen are monsters. Some people are just…lost or scared."

He glanced over and caught the ghosts in her eyes—pain or guilt, maybe both—and let it drop. They kept walking.

Back in the line, Mustang refused to leave Jorgen's earlier answer alone. "Don't be shy now, old man," he rasped, a faint grin tugging at his mouth. "You've probably been around since the Ice Age, surely you have some wisdom to impart."

Jorgen chuckled, the sound bouncing off the stone. "Wisdom's just scars that learned to talk to you," he said. "World doesn't care how many years you got. It'll chew you up either way. Best you can do is keep your eyes sharp and your aim sharper."

He hesitated, then added, softer, "And if you're lucky, find someone who'll watch your back when you miss somethin'."

"I hope… when we get out," she interrupted, small but clear, "we can see the sun." She swallowed. "I feel like I know what it is. I just don't remember ever seeing it."

Alysha's expression softened, the hard edges of fatigue easing. "Well then," she said, voice warm with something like big-sister affection, "that gives us double the reason to keep moving. One for us…and one for a girl who deserves more than shadows and monsters."

Bradley felt something tighten in his chest at that—pity, maybe, but threaded through with respect. Pinky matched them step for step, awake when they slept, standing guard over people twice her size and ten times her history as far as she knew. He didn't know if he'd see the sky again, but even if he didn't he wanted her to.

# CHAPTER
# TWENTY-THREE

"Wait," Bradley said, pitching his voice low. "You said... many tunnels go to the city, right? Are there other ways in? Smaller tunnels. Less...obvious."

The skink tilted its head, pupils narrowing. It hissed a thoughtful string of sounds, clicks peppered through.

Pinky listened, cheeks hollowed with concentration. "It says...yes," she breathed. "Tunnels for...workers. For bringing things. Smaller. Hidden. But..." She glanced up at Bradley. "Not made for...big ones like you."

Jorgen scratched at his beard, mouth twisting. "Old bones ain't meant for knife-fights in trenches," he muttered. "But they crawl better than they rot."

Alysha's hand settled on the hilt at her hip, fingers ghosting over tooled leather. "And if they find us in those cramped tunnels?" she asked, voice hardly louder than that constant drip of water that seemed to follow them.

Bradley turned back to the skinks. "Show us," he said. "Take us to these tunnels. We'll go slow and quiet. And hope they don't catch us."

The two skinks hissed back and forth, the exchange quick and sharp. At last the crowned one gave a small, resigned wave of its hand and motioned them forward. The subordinate, brown skink adjusting the rigging to drag Knight, rather than carry him.

Karl pinched out the torch.

Darkness fell in a single breath. The world shrank to sound, touch, and Pinky's whisper as she repeated the skinks' hushed directions: "Down. Left. Careful stone. Low roof."

They moved by feel and followed the dim glow of the fungal crown. The air grew thicker, carrying the wet, mineral tang of deep earth and an undercurrent of musky reptile scent. Every breath sounded too loud. Every scuff of a sole, every bump of pack against stone, seemed to echo down the passage like a shout.

The new route twisted and dropped with no pattern. They stooped, then hunched, then were forced to hands and knees as the ceiling dipped. Knight, strapping and stubborn as ever, let out muffled grunts when the injured skink bearing him had to squeeze through a sharper bend, scraping his boot or jarring his leg. He didn't complain; the sound was mostly teeth grinding and breath hissing between them.

Without light or landmarks, there was no good way to tell if they'd been at it ten minutes or an hour. The only measures were the burn in thighs and shoulders, the rawness of palms, and the way Bradley's eyes ached from straining at a darkness that never lifted.

Sweat beaded along his hairline. It wasn't the effort; his lungs had plenty of capacity left. It was the weight of the rock overhead, layers and layers of it, pressing down. His fingers twitched toward his weapon as if the solid weight of it could carve him some breathing room.

There was nowhere to swing it, nowhere to go if panic got a foothold.

He forced his hand back to the task at hand, nails scraping grit as he kept moving.

Jorgen kept his breathing steady, but the crawl was wearing on him. Every time he had to twist or push, a hot wire of pain shot up his spine and flared behind his eyes. No bounty at the end, no payout waiting at some dusty bar, and the gnawing fact that he'd been out of coffee for far too long made Bradley worry about the mental state of the old man.

Karl took to the cramped stone like he'd been born to it— which, in a way, he had been.

Pinky moved between them and Alysha, one small hand wrapped around the woman's fingers whenever possible. She'd known darkness that didn't end, trapped inside her own mind. This wasn't that. She had people that cared about her now.

Bradley was the one who'd asked for the worker tunnels, who'd traded a straight walk into the lions' den for this blind crawl through someone else's back door. His stomach rolled, fear for the others tangling with the sour edge of nausea. He wanted light. Even a pinprick. Something to tell him they weren't just burrowing deeper into their own graves.

The skink in front of Knight slowed, nostrils flaring. It let out a low, uneasy hiss.

Pinky stiffened. "It...smells others," she whispered, voice shaking. "Ahead. Many."

The word drifted in the cramped space and everyone. Bradley's spine went cold. He saw them spilling headfirst out of this crawlspace into a crowd—no cover, no plan, just a line of targets in a tunnel.

Metal clicked softly as Jorgen shifted. The old hunter eased his air rifle into a more workable grip, thumb brushing the safety, the movement economical and silent. First thing that stepped into his line and meant harm was going to learn what a steel ball at close range felt like.

The crowned skink hissed sharply, the sound carrying a command even the humans could hear. It gestured in jerky, urgent motions, then veered hard right into a slit in the wall that barely deserved to be called a passage.

The new tunnel was worse.

It was no longer a walkway but a crawlspace gouged for bodies slimmer and lower to the ground. Stone scraped along shoulders and backs. Knees and palms took the brunt, skin shredding against damp grit. The rock was cold and clammy where it brushed faces; the air tasted fetid and sour.

Every instinct screamed to back up, to widen out, to find space enough to turn around and fight. But ahead, the skinks kept moving. And under the fear, there was that thin, stubborn thread of hope: if the "others" were on the main path, maybe this tight, miserable detour would slide them past notice.

Their progress slowed to a painful crawl. Breath grew harsh and loud in the confined air. The drip of unseen water kept time with their dragging limbs.

Then the dark changed.

It happened gradually at first, a suggestion more than a sight—the sense that the black wasn't quite as total. A faint smear of color seeped ahead, thin as fog under a door. Bradley squinted into it, unsure if his eyes were playing tricks.

The glow strengthened with each shuffle forward. Sickly greens and blues bled into the edges of the rock, turning the skinks' scales into dark silhouettes rimmed in ghost light. The crowned guide pushed faster, slipping through a jagged crack with a fluid twist of spine and limb.

One by one, the humans followed, squeezing through the narrow opening sideways. Stone hugged ribs and hips; jackets snagged, gear scraped. Then, all at once, there was space.

They spilled out onto solid ground and straightened, dragging in lungfuls of air that at least felt bigger. For a heartbeat, disorientation spun the chamber around them.

They were on a ledge—no, a precipice. One wrong step and the rock would take them.

Below, the world opened.

For a long moment, no one spoke. The first hit was terror—at nearly stumbling into a city of "others," at the drop, at the sheer scale of what lay beneath. Then the fear thinned, reshaped itself into something heavier. Awe wasn't a word Bradley had used much since falling into this nightmare, but it was the only one that fit.

The cavern revealed itself in layers the longer they stared.

High overhead, crude fissures and shaft-cuts bit into the stone, leaking down thin teeth of daylight. The beams were weak and dust-choked—tiny reminders that somewhere far above this buried bowl, there was still a sky.

Down near the floor, a subterranean lake cupped the city in a broad crescent. Bioluminescent growths laced the banks and spillways, their glow sliding across the water until the surface looked skinned in green and blue. Near the lake's center, a colossal stalagmite punched up from the depths, its bulk disappearing into the gloom above as if it held the roof up by stubbornness alone.

And around all of it—every slope, every shelf—the skink city lived.

It sprawled across the cavern floor and climbed the walls in a chaotic mass of burrows, buildings, dangling walkways, and fungal spires. Some structures looked grown, swollen and organic; others were carved straight from native stone, mouths ringed with tool marks. Slab lean-to's wedged in wherever there was purchase. Bridges and rope-lattices swayed between platforms, stitching the whole tangle together.

From this height the movement made it feel alive in a different way—scaled bodies flowing along the web of walkways and ledges, some hugging the walls, others threading between the fungal towers. Glowing arteries of fungus ran through the city like veins. The sight was unsettling and undeniably, brutally beautiful.

Bradley leaned just far enough over the ledge to get a better look, fingers biting into the rough stone. A low whistle slipped out before he could stop it.

"I'll be damned," he said. There was no hiding the note of respect. He'd expected burrows. This really was a city.

Jorgen narrowed his eyes, blinking against the strange glow, trying to make sense of the levels and paths and places guards might stand. "Best keep our heads down," he rasped.

The reminder took some of the shine off the view, but it was needed.

Alysha's attention kept drifting to the lake. The water shifted gently under unseen currents, throwing ripples of light across the central column. It was almost beautiful. Even so, a knot of unease sat in her gut.

Mustang's mind went somewhere else entirely. From this perspective, the city wasn't just a marvel; it was a layout. Lines of approach, choke points, places where light pooled and places where shadows would swallow a man.

"I can see ways in from here," he said, voice low. "Walkways, side tunnels. Maybe a few ways out, if we don't piss off everyone at once."

For a while they were content just to look, listening to the distant murmur of the city—a blend of hisses, clacks, and the faint thud of many feet on wood and stone. The tension didn't go anywhere, but it shifted, turning into a taut, focused wait instead of blind dread.

Then Alysha sucked in a sharp breath.

Pinky, hovering just at the edge of the sunlight, stepped forward without thinking. The beam caught her fully.

She was outlined in gold.

The grime and dust clinging to her skin and dress shimmered, then simply…lifted. It didn't flake off so much as dissolve, fading into the air like smoke. Faint smears of dried blood vanished. Her hair, matted a moment before, gleamed where the light touched it. In the span of a few breaths, she looked like she'd been freshly groomed—her dress even mended before their astounded eyes.

Pinky let out a startled little giggle and stared down at her own hands, turning them as if they belonged to someone else.

Mustang clamped a hand over his mouth, good hand tightening on his rifle strap.

Karl answered with nothing more than a grunt. For a dwarf raised on tales of things buried deep and old, it was hard to pretend nothing had just happened. He didn't buy into god-talk easily, but something strange was definitely going on.

The crowned skink hissed again, more excited than before. Its crown flared, casting harsh little shadows over its face—both of the skink prostrating themselves before the girl.

Alysha shook her head slowly, thoughts knotting. Was this the power the Godspear experiments had been trying to strangle? The same light human scientists had tried to kill? It made sense —a terrible kind of sense.

Looking past the girl to Jorgen, it seemed as if the light was reacting to him as well. Bending at odd angles to highlight the old man's exposed skin. What in all this was he?

Unease rippled through the group. The way the skinks looked at Pinky now—cautious, reverent, afraid to meet her eyes for too long.

"Well, ain't this a fine mess," Jorgen murmured. Dark humor curled around his words, but it didn't soften them much. "Seems our Pinky's got more tricks than came on the label."

Alysha's hand found the girl's shoulder, squeezing gently. "The skinks," she said, keeping her voice low and careful, "they think you're…"

She faltered, and Karl finished for her, his deep rumble edged with concern.

"More than a child," he said.

Jorgen snorted, one corner of his mouth twitching. "A goddess, huh?" he said. "Well, she sure cleans up prettier than the rest of us."

No one smiled for long. Their gazes kept drifting back to the city, to the skink movements below, to the way the crowned warrior at their side couldn't seem to decide whether to bow or lay flat on the ground before her.

Bradley felt fear sink its hooks in again. Pinky's sudden promotion—from scared kid and favored of this Serene Rae to walking myth—wasn't a blessing. It was tinder. Their alliance with the skinks had been exotic enough when it was just debts and shared enemies. Now they were tangled in belief they didn't understand. That was the kind of thing people killed over.

The crowned skink began to hiss in clipped, urgent bursts, crown brightening. Its body language shifted: less scout, more zealot. Even through Pinky's halting translation, the meaning was clear enough. They were to descend. To be shown. To be brought before others—leaders, elders, whoever sat on that "stone of leadership."

Bradley met the others' eyes, reading the same calculus there. Refuse, and they'd be hunted. Comply, and they'd be walking into a hall full of strangers already convinced their little mascot was divine or dangerous or both.

He turned back to the skink, something hardening in him.

"Ask him who he kneels to," Bradley said quietly. "the Serene Rae, or some skink sitting on a rock?"

He held Pinky's gaze as he said it, making sure she understood the weight of the question.

Pinky relayed the words. Surprise flitted across the skink's features; its head tilted, crown dimming as it considered. After a long breath, it hissed back a simple, firm answer.

"He says...he serves the goddess of light," Pinky translated.

The words trembled as they left her mouth.

Her knees did, too. Pinky's eyes filled, the shine of tears catching the strange light. "I don't want to be..." she whispered, voice cracking. "I don't want to be a goddess."

The cavern threw her words back at them in distorted echoes.

Alysha pulled her close, wrapping an arm around her small frame. Pinky pressed her face into Alysha's side, shoulders shaking. Alysha's own heart thudded hard, caught between fierce protectiveness and cold understanding.

Whether they liked it or not, the skink believed they were bringing a goddess home.

\*\*\*

The descent into the city became a slow, grinding affair.

The crowned skink led them along paths chipped into the rock, spiraling down. Bioluminescent fungi clung to the walls in scattered patches, washing everything in sickly greens and blues. Moisture beaded on the stone and on their skin. The air thickened as they went, warm and wet, carrying the sour musk and the faint tang of stagnant water.

Pinky's hand stayed locked around Alysha's, her fingers small but unyielding. Fear still sat bright in her eyes, but beneath it something else had taken root—excitement, the quick, guilty thrill of a child dragged along on grown-up business. Every new twist of tunnel made her crane her neck, watching and listening.

Bradley walked point beside the crowned skink, pistol holstered but ready, eyes narrowed against the shifting light. He mapped as he moved: side passages, choke points, overhangs that might hide an ambush, platforms that might serve as firing positions. Half of what he saw wouldn't matter once the chaos started, but running the calculations anyway kept his hands from shaking.

Mustang fell in behind him, scowl carved deep. The joke ratio had dropped to zero. Pinky being a goodwill token was one thing. Pinky being a living banner for someone else's religion was another. He kept his gaze moving, measuring distance and angles, but he'd never liked fighting on other people's terms, and that was all he could see ahead.

Karl walked on the other side of Pinky, close enough that a sidestep would put him between her and anything sharp. The stone itself reassured him, but the way it had been coaxed and warped into this organic maze made his teeth grind. This wasn't the clean geometry of halls carved by dwarf hands.

Fungus towers, rope bridges, living walls; it all felt like walking through a salad.

Jorgen brought up the rear. His gait was easier than it had been in days, the old ache in his bad everything dulled to a memory. He said nothing about the sunlight or the way it had soaked into him; he just kept his rifle handy and his eyes moving.

Knight's progress dictated the pace. Perched on the brown skink's back, he gritted his teeth against every jolt. The skink bore him with stubborn steadiness, but they had to slow at tight turns, at steep drops, at each new "ritual" the crowned leader insisted on.

Those pauses came more often as they descended.

At one pause, the crowned skink hissed a command. From the shadows of a side passage, others emerged—half a dozen at least. They approached, then dropped to their knees, foreheads pressing to the damp stone in front of Pinky. Their hisses rose and fell in a rough, layered chant that vibrated the air.

Alysha felt the hair rise on her arms.

Bradley watched their posture, their numbers, the way the crowned skink positioned itself slightly ahead of Pinky, as if curating the view. Faith, sure—but also staging. *Look how many kneel.* It was the kind of soft power play he'd seen wrapped in flags and uniforms topside.

They were being displayed.

With each level they dropped, the tunnels widened and the ceiling lifted. The sense of being crushed under a mountain eased, replaced by something worse: scale. The hollow echo of their footsteps faded into a low, constant murmur—the sound of many bodies moving, many voices hissing and clicking.

The heart of the city approached far faster than any of them were comfortable with. They could feel it in the faint vibration underfoot, in the way the air hummed with unseen presence.

Then the light changed.

The scattered glow of wall-fungus gave way to a steady radiance ahead, bright enough that their pupils pinched to pinpricks. Bioluminescent clusters thickened along the passage, smearing the world into a blur of pale color. They shielded their eyes, stumbling the last few steps.

The glare faded. Sound rose in layered hisses and clacks; water lapped at stone; movement tugged at the bridges overhead like a nervous pulse.

Across the lake, the far wall lifted into shadow—and that shadow held a single shape that took the whole group by the throat.

A palace.

Its façade had been carved straight out of the rock face, broad and uneven, as if the mountain itself had been coaxed into the shape of a fortress. Pillars formed from stalactites and stalagmites framed a series of deep-set entrances. Intricate carvings—scales and coiling shapes Bradley's mind didn't want to name—ran in bands along the stone. Clusters of glowing fungus had been encouraged to bloom in deliberate patterns, tracing borders and symbols in pale fire. The structure radiated a heavy, unspoken authority that made the surrounding warrens look like outbuildings.

The crowned skink hissed beside them, chest swelling. Pinky flinched at the sound, then forced herself to listen.

"The…palace," she said, voice shaking. "Home of…our leader."

Bradley's stomach knotted. He'd expected a village power struggle—a warband chief and rivals, something small enough to navigate. But this was a capital: a throne cut into a mountain, plugged into every walkway and tunnel in sight.

He glanced sideways at Alysha. Her eyes fixed on the palace as if she were trying to see through its walls. Pinky was being marched toward whoever sat at the center.

Jorgen gave a low whistle. "Never thought I'd see anything out-ugly a human city," he muttered.

Under the grumble was something grudgingly impressed.

Pinky shrank closer to Alysha's side, the sheer size of it all pressing down on her. The palace loomed. "I…I don't want to go there," she whispered, the words nearly drowned by the constant hum of the city.

"I don't think that's an option anymore," Alysha said. She squeezed Pinky's hand, voice steady in a way her eyes weren't. Unrecognized script was carved across the palace face, the layers of hierarchy implied by the architecture—it all reminded her of other powers and other courts she'd known back home. Different scales, same danger.

Around them, hisses rose and fell in something like cadence, not quite song, not quite command. Hands and claws gestured them forward. The tone held too much ritual to be called simple escort; they were being swept along as part of a procession.

Bradley took one last look over the crescent of the lake and the glowing maze of dwellings, committing as many paths and vantage points to memory as he could. Then he shifted his grip on his weapon and fell into step.

Together—pulled by faith they didn't share and politics they didn't understand—they started down the final pathways toward the palace of the reptilian city.

# CHAPTER TWENTY-FOUR

The crowned skink led them straight into the city's pulse.

The cavern floor had been worn to a dull sheen by generations of scaled feet. Paths braided and crossed, curving around squat buildings of rough-cut stone and fungus gardens. Bioluminescent moss and mushroom clusters crawled up their walls and dripped from balconies, painting everything in shifting bands of green and blue. The air was warm, thick with humidity and layered smells— some pleasant, some not so much.

They moved in dense currents—small, quick-bodied workers, broader warriors with scarred hides, elders with faded scales and slow steps. Tails flashed in the perpetual twilight: dull browns, deep blues, mottled greens, streaked reds and oranges, a living tapestry that rippled and re-formed around them.

Silence spread outward like a wave.

Reactions varied. Some simply stepped back, eyes wide and unblinking. Others went to their knees, then flat on their bellies, pressing their faces to the stone. A few bowed so low they might as well have been lying down. Everywhere—open awe or outright fear—punctuated by startled hisses and quick, whispered exchanges.

Pinky's fingers dug into Alysha's hand. Heat rose in her cheeks under all that staring. Every bow, every flattened body made her want to shrink into Alysha's side. But somewhere under the fear, deep in a place she didn't have words for, something stirred.

Karl's gaze moved over the crowds with a different kind of focus. The tails caught his attention: bands of color, bright tips, dull bases. Some matched, some didn't. His mind filed away possibilities—caste, clan, region. He nudged Bradley once with an elbow, then tipped his chin at a knot of red-tailed skinks flanking a side passage.

Bradley caught the look and gave the smallest shrug: later. Right now, Pinky was both shield and target. Anyone inclined to harm them had to think twice with half the city on their knees, but it also meant every ambitious lizard in this hole now knew exactly where they were.

Jorgen moved quieter than usual, the warmth from the earlier sunlight still tingling his skin. The reverence crawling over them itched at him, but even he couldn't deny the spectacle. A street full of potential enemies, all holding still because a scared girl walked past? There were worse ways to enter hostile territory.

Mustang snorted under his breath as yet another line of skinks folded flat. "Groveling looks pathetic no matter what species is doing it," he muttered, keeping his voice low.

Alysha's heart hammered against her ribs. She kept her expression smooth for Pinky's sake, squeezing the girl's hand whenever she felt it tremble.

"It'll be over soon," she murmured, leaning close. "Keep walking. One step at a time."

"If these lizards could blush," Mustang added dryly from just behind them, "we'd be wading through a sea of red right about now."

The sound of their boots and the skinks' claws echoed strangely in the open space.

Karl couldn't let the tail question go. "Curious, those colors," he rumbled, mostly to himself but loud enough for the front rank to hear. "Ranks, maybe. Or bloodlines. Clans."

"If I had to guess?" Bradley said, eyes still scanning. "You're probably looking at subspecies mixing back in over time. Same reason some animals have different melanin in their fur. Or people have different skin and hair."

He let his gaze slide over the bowed forms, the too-eager eyes.

"I'm more worried about how they're acting," he added quietly. "Last time I saw folks this eager to please was in the megacity. And those people were being chemically leashed."

"They could just be true believers in the myths," Mustang murmured.

Alysha shook her head, her attention on Pinky's tense grip. "Fear," she whispered back. "Feels more like fear than faith." Her voice thinned. "Fear can be hard to predict."

Bradley nodded. "Yeah. That's what worries me. For now, we ride it out. Hopefully, the crowd gets bored and finds something better to do."

A ripple ran through the crowd—a hiss cut short here, a tail twitch there. It passed over the gathered bodies like wind through long grass.

Out of the corner of his eye, Bradley caught Mustang's subtle hand-sign—a quick jut of two fingers toward a side passage. He followed the line of the gesture and saw a single skink slip away from the main thoroughfare. Its tail, banded in vivid purple, stood out against the muddier colors around it. The skink moved fast, disappearing into a narrow alley without a backward glance.

Runner. Message. Of course word was going ahead.

At first it was just a handful of skinks, shuffling closer with wide eyes and hesitant steps. Then a handful more. Within minutes, a loose tail of followers trailed behind—dozens of them, mostly unadorned, scales dulled by grime and work.

All of it centered on Pinky.

The nearer they drew to the looming palace, the more extravagant the gestures became. Skinks emerged from doorways and balconies carrying offerings: bowls carved from polished stone, bundles of glowing fungus plaited into wreaths, crude statuettes with tiny raised crowns. They laid them along the path, stacking gifts in haphazard piles as the procession passed, glancing nervously up to see if "the goddess" would so much as look their way. Vendors and artisans eyed each other sidelong, each trying to leave something grander than the last.

The palace grew with every step, its façade swallowing more of the cavern wall. The air cooled a fraction, shadows pooling deeper near its carved entrances.

That was when the current shifted.

The crowned skink at their head hissed abruptly, the guiding rhythm of its steps faltering. Movement ahead thickened as the crowd drew back. A wedge opened in the press of bodies, not for them this time, but to admit someone coming the other way.

Another crowned skink strode through the gap.

Its tail a vivid emerald that caught every stray glimmer of light. It was larger than their guide, shoulders thicker, movements smooth and assured. Where their ally's hide carried the rough, scattered scars of old battles, this one's marks were few and deliberate—lines that looked displayed rather than earned.

Flanking it came two more skinks, both broad-shouldered and heavy in the chest, tails a deep, dark crimson that almost drank in the glow around them. They moved with guard precision, eyes sweeping, bodies taking up space without effort.

The air tightened. The hum of the crowd fell into a wary silence.

The two crowned skinks faced one another, stopping just short of contact. Their eyes locked. Hisses snapped between them, harsh and clipped, too fast and layered for Pinky to follow. No weapons were drawn; none needed to be. Challenge and refusal threaded the sounds.

Around them, skinks murmured, gasped, tails twitching. The tone of the reverence shifted—still there, still focused on Pinky, but now wrapped in tension. Some of the nearest eyes drifted from the humans to the two leaders and back, measuring, calculating.

Bradley felt the fine hairs on his arms stand up.

This was a fault line opening in plain sight, reptilian politics drawn sharp—and they were standing right in the crack.

Alysha tightened her grip on Pinky's hand. She could feel the tremor running through the girl. A child realizing that stories about goddesses and chosen ones didn't keep claws and teeth from meeting flesh.

Bradley's thoughts spun as he watched the gathered skinks. Postures shifted; tails flicked with different rhythms. Some bodies leaned forward, hungry for spectacle; others edged back, ready to bolt. Factions, he thought. Lines that had always been there were suddenly lit up.

Jorgen shifted his weight, the faintest curve pulling at one corner of his mouth. "Well, damn," he rasped, breaking the silence. "Walk just got a whole lot more interestin'." His fingers drifted toward his rifle stock on instinct, not quite gripping, but close.

Mustang's lips twisted into something that wanted to be a grin and didn't quite make it. "Place your bets," he added. "Big green looks mean, but ours has a habit of picking on things larger than himself. He's bound to win one eventually."

Karl was less interested in the duel than in the crowd around it. Reverent eyes still clung to Pinky, but more and more were noticing the two crowned skinks with an intent gleam that had nothing to do with faith. Opportunity. He could taste it in the air. Back home, in the forge-city, that kind of crack in the order never got this public—not without steel and law bringing it to heel. Here, it was simply… happening… on the street. His hands tightened on the hafts of his climbing picks.

The tension snapped.

Their crowned skink hissed, shoulders bunching, fungal crown flaring brighter. The emerald-tailed newcomer answered with a deep, guttural hiss of its own and coiled forward.

They hit like two thrown knives.

Claws tore across scales, bright lines of blood welling where strikes landed. They grappled and broke apart, lunging and twisting, jaws snapping inches from exposed throats. The bioluminescent glow caught on flying droplets of red, turning them liquid glitter.

The crimson-tailed guards spread out in a loose ring, bodies low, eyes slit and sharp. They paced the edge of the fight, ready to close in but not yet moving, gauging which way the balance tilted.

The crowd surged and dipped, hisses rising like a rough chorus. Some skinks recoiled, pressing back against walls and doorframes. Others leaned in, pupils blown wide, breath coming fast through parted jaws.

For all the emerald leader's size, the clash wasn't the easy rout it might have been. Their scarred guide moved with quick, economical fury, slipping under heavier swings, twisting away from crushing bites. Where the larger skink relied on weight and punishing blows, the smaller one fought like something that had been outclassed more often than not—using angles, timing, ugly little strikes that landed in softer places. Thin cuts opened on emerald scales; more red joined the glow in the air.

Bradley's heart hammered, but part of him couldn't stop watching it like a problem to be solved. Strength versus speed. Form versus grit. It felt like two different philosophies slamming together—a polished, dominant caste and a lean, battle-scarred survivor. Whichever one walked away would drag the city a step in their direction.

Jorgen watched with a grim sort of fascination, knuckles whitening where they wrapped around his weapon.

"Ol' Scarface ain't doin' too bad," he rasped at last, grudging respect roughening his tone. "Smaller, but he's got the grit."

Mustang's usual crooked smirk tugged up, then faltered. "Yeah, but grit doesn't always win," he commented, barely audible under the rasp of claws and the crowd's growing roar.

Alysha held on to Pinky, feeling the girl shake against her side. Pinky's face had gone bloodless, eyes wide and glassy. Whatever scraps of story she'd held about goddesses returning to put things right cracked under the sound of flesh hitting flesh. This wasn't righteous judgment or fairy-tale justice—just two animals trying to tear each other apart, and one of them doing it for dominance alone.

Around them, the crowd split in its loyalties. Many skinks bowed their heads toward the emerald-tailed leader, their eyes bright with hungry admiration for his size and strength. Others stayed upright, watching the smaller, scarred skink with a different light in their gaze. Their hisses turned sharper, clustering into murmurs that rolled back through the throng. The words meant nothing to human ears, but the tone—tight, urgent—felt too close to a rallying chant.

The emerald-tailed skink drove forward on a burst of raw force, claws and shoulder slamming into its rival. The smaller one skidded across the packed earth, leaving a smear of blood in its wake. The bigger skink followed, jaws yawning wide, tooth ridges gleaming wet in the bioluminescent glow.

At the last instant, the scarred skink twisted. It rolled, scales rasping against dirt, and its claws whipped up in a desperate rake. There was a wet ripping sound and a spray of blood that caught the glow and flared sickly bright before spattering the ground.

The larger skink jerked back with a guttural cry, chest heaving. It staggered a step, then another, eyes narrowed in pain and fury. The smaller one lay on its side, body shuddering, but it had left its mark. The sudden hush that dropped over the gathered skinks said the blow had landed deeper than flesh.

For a heartbeat, it looked like it might end there—two fighters bloodied, neither willing to give ground.

Then the emerald-tail's expression hollowed into something uglier.

Fueled by humiliation and pain, it abandoned any pretense of measured fighting. A roar tore from its throat. It launched itself forward, slamming into the wounded rival with all its weight.

The smaller skink didn't have time to roll. It hit the dirt hard and stayed down, pinned under the other's bulk. Claws dug into its shoulders. The crowd's sounds sharpened—gasps, panicked hisses, a wave of noise pressing in.

The emerald-tailed leader lifted its head, jaws spreading. A low, rumbling growl built in its chest, the kind of sound meant to carry over an arena and sink into the bones of everyone listening. A statement: this is what happens when you step out of line.

Pinky choked on a sob and squeezed her eyes shut. Alysha wrapped both arms around her, turning the child's face into her chest, trying to block the view if not the sound.

Karl's grip on his climbing picks turned his knuckles pale against his deep-toned skin. Every bit of his upbringing screamed that a fallen foe deserved a cleaner end than this. But a dwarf alone starting trouble in the center of a foreign city? That was just suicide with extra steps.

Mustang's eyes roamed the ring of faces instead of the fight. He saw anxiety in some—pupils blown wide, bodies held taut and ready to bolt. In others, anger tightened jaws and flared nostrils. More than a few looked less like worshippers and more like bystanders waiting to see which way the wind shifted before they chose a side.

This had slipped past spectacle. It was a match dropped into dry brush.

The emerald-tailed skink's head dipped, jaws angling for the exposed throat—

A sharp crack split the air, louder than any hiss or roar. It snapped off the cavern walls and knifed through the tension.

The emerald leader howled, not in triumph but in shock and pain. Its whole body jolted. It lurched sideways, balance suddenly skewed, then thrashed, tail stump jerking and spraying blood.

The crowd broke apart in a rush. Skinks recoiled, shoving and stumbling, hisses spiking into full-throated cries. The pinned, scarred skink seized the moment. It tore itself free with a desperate heave and scrambled away on unsteady limbs, leaving a slick trail of crimson on the trampled earth.

Silence dropped after the initial surge of noise, heavy and stunned.

Jorgen stood where he had been, air rifle braced against his shoulder, barrel still tracking the larger skink.

On the ground before the emerald leader, its severed tail lay in the dust, still twitching, bright scales already dulling under a film of dirt.

The big skink writhed, claws gouging furrows in the earth, guttural whimpers tearing out of it—too raw to be mistaken for anything but pain. Around it, the city seemed to hold its breath, the quiet broken only by those low sounds and the faint drip of blood onto stone.

Jorgen lowered the rifle, and let a hard line settle across his features. "Anyone else wanna take a shot?" he drawled, the words bouncing off stone and scale.

Sound broke loose.

It wasn't a single roar of outrage—it fractured. One section of the crowd erupted, hissing and stamping, a raw, jubilant noise that rolled up the walls. Their cries had a sharp, desperate edge, like hope catching for the first time in a long while. Another pocket of skinks—the ones who'd bowed deepest to the emerald-tailed leader—shrank back or clustered tight, muttering darkly. Their eyes gleamed with fear and confusion.

The crimson-tailed guards snapped out of their shock and rushed to their master. They hauled him upright with careful hands, their movements stiff. Blood slicked his side and the stump of his tail; his hissed orders came out warped by pain.

He jerked his snout toward the palace, insisting on forward motion even as his legs trembled.

The procession lurched back into motion.

The maimed emerald leader and his red-tailed guards went ahead now, stride stripped of its earlier swagger. Their crowned ally—the scarred guide who had led them down into the city— fell back, walking behind the humans instead of before them, breathing hard, one arm pressed to a bleeding flank.

As they started forward, the humans traded looks over Pinky's head and Knight's slumped form.

"Damn," Mustang rasped at last, a grudging respect roughening his tone. "Where'd you learn to shoot like that?"

Alysha didn't so much as twitch a smile. She rounded on Jorgen, her voice tight with leftover fear. "That was impulsive. Reckless. We're surrounded—" she hissed.

Karl's rumble cut in. "You've made enemies," he said. "Not just him. Half that crowd saw you cut their champion down to size."

Bradley's pulse was still racing, but he forced his tone level. "And maybe made us allies, too," he countered quietly, eyes darting over the skinks now shadowing their steps. Some watched them with open approval; others refused to look their way at all. "Whatever side we land on doesn't matter, they existed before Jorgen pulled the trigger. He just tore the curtain down."

Jorgen kept his gaze on the maimed leader up ahead, lips pressed thin. "Just evening the odds," he muttered. "Didn't fancy watchin' our friend get his head bitten off to make a point." He shrugged one shoulder. "World's short on sacred things. A clean shot's about as close as I've ever seen."

Alysha opened her mouth to fire back, but Bradley stepped in, urgency cutting across the argument.

"There's a problem," he said. "Knight."

He glanced to where the soldier lay draped over the skink's back. Knight's skin had taken on a waxy cast again, sweat beading along his forehead. Each jolt of the reptile's gait drew a faint, bitten-off sound from him.

"With things this volatile," Bradley went on, "keeping him in the middle of a political parade isn't smart. If things break down, he's dead weight in the worst way."

Pinky had already followed his look. She tugged lightly at Alysha's sleeve, voice small but steady. "Can we…ask the skink to help him?"

The crowned skink—still breathing hard from the fight, still bristling from Jorgen's interference—turned a wary eye on them. Bradley stepped up alongside Pinky, keeping his hands open and visible, and spoke low. Pinky translated in stumbling hisses, gesturing toward Knight, then miming rest.

Understanding clicked behind the skink's eyes. Pride warred with practicality for a beat, then it gave a short, sharp nod. It hissed a command over its shoulder.

From the edge of the crowd, a smaller skink with dull gray scales detached itself and approached, head bowed. Their scarred ally added a rough rasp of his own—an endorsement that seemed to carry weight. Whatever the gray one was, it wasn't just a random volunteer.

The gray skink turned without a word and started back through the press, carving a quieter path. The skink bearing Knight fell in behind the gray guide, carrying the injured soldier away from the main procession and into the churning mass of bodies that was the skink city.

"They'll take Knight somewhere safer," Bradley said, dropping into a crouch so he was eye level with Pinky. His knees protested, but he ignored it. "Maybe they can find a quiet place for him to rest till this…settles down."

The girl's eyes tracked Knight as the gray-scaled skink and his bearer slipped deeper into the crowd. She nodded once, swallowing hard.

Alysha hated the idea of leaving a half-conscious soldier in the middle of a brewing street wars. Whatever else Knight was, he was still an asset they couldn't afford to lose.

"Karl," Bradley said, straightening. His tone sharpened. "Mustang. Go with them. Stay with Knight. Protect him."

Recognition clicked behind Karl's deep-set eyes. He gave a short, firm nod. "Aye," he rumbled, the word like distant stonefall.

Mustang snorted, rolling one shoulder as if shaking off an invisible hand. "Babysittin' duty, huh?" he muttered. But Alysha caught the way his gaze lingered on Knight's slack face, the tightness at the corners of his mouth. He jerked his chin toward the gray guide. "Come on, then. Let's not lose our charge."

They peeled away from the main procession—Karl's compact bulk and Mustang's lean frame falling in behind the gray skink and the one bearing Knight. In moments, they were swallowed by a branching side tunnel, the glow of the main thoroughfare dimming around them.

Bradley turned back to their scarred, blue-tailed guide. The crowned skink's chest still rose and fell a little too fast, blood darkening patches of its scales.

"All right," Bradley muttered under his breath, steel edging his voice. "Let's see what fresh hell your palace has lined up."

The blue-tailed skink dipped its head and moved off, following the road the limping emerald leader and his crimson-tailed guards had taken. Alysha and Jorgen traded a look over Pinky's head—a mix of wariness and grim acceptance.

Jorgen shifted the air rifle against his shoulder, the ghost of a sheepish grin tugging at his mouth. One shot, and they owed a debt now—to a battered skink with more grit than sense, and to whatever order kept this city from tearing itself apart.

They fell back into formation: Bradley and the crowned guide at the front, Pinky tucked close to Alysha, Jorgen watching their rear. Ahead, the tailless brute and his red-marked guards trudged toward the looming palace, leaving faint streaks of blood on the worn stone.

The hum of the crowd thinned behind them, replaced by the heavy quiet of power. Hearts beat a little faster, breaths came a little shorter as they walked toward whatever waited inside.

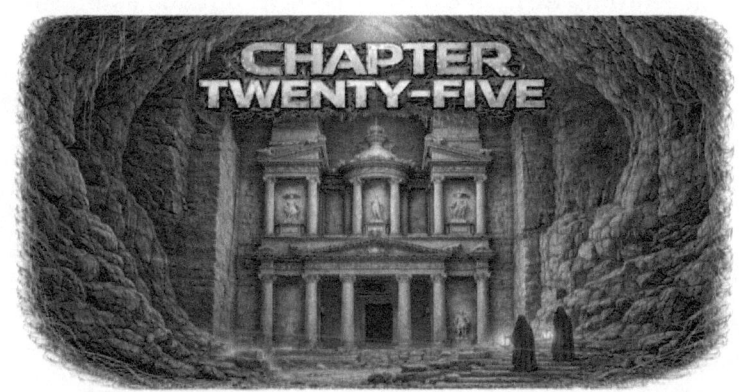

## CHAPTER TWENTY-FIVE

Here the bioluminescence clung in smears along the walls, enough to sketch jagged stone and leave the rest to darkness. The sparse fungal clusters that did grow in the corners and transitions pulsed faintly, throwing out sickly halos that made shadows jump and stretch across the rough rock.

The air carried a low, electric hum—not the buzz of a crowd, but the tight, coiled tension of a trap waiting to spring. Somewhere out of sight, claws scraped on stone and something skittered away, the sound doubling back on itself in the twisting corridors. Alysha felt eyes she couldn't see tracking their progress, weighing them: threat, tool, sacrifice.

Bradley's stride hitched as the passage opened into a vast chamber.

Torchlight hit his eyes like a slap—real fire, licking up from stone sconces, brighter and harsher than any fungus-glow. It painted the chamber in hard-edged bands of orange and black, burning away the soft illusion of a hidden warren and showing him exactly what they'd walked into.

Reptilian warriors ringed the room in disciplined rows. Scales caught the firelight and turned it into a shifting mosaic of greens, browns, and muted golds. Crude plates of hammered metal and hardened carapace strapped across chests and shoulders gleamed dully. Long spears, barbed and wicked, stood at the ready. Their slitted eyes tracked the humans with unblinking focus—cool, measuring, utterly prepared to kill.

Jorgen let out a low whistle. "Wouldn't have minded not being on the guest list for this party," he muttered.

The words were dry, but Bradley heard the edge beneath them. Since he had recovered from the wasting, Jorgen had been moving like a man half underwater. The sunlight in the cavern above had burned some of that fog out of him. Down here, with weapons drawn and odds stacked, Bradley was seeing the other side of the old hunter again—the one who didn't flinch from a bad fight if it felt honest.

Alysha's pulse hammered in her ears. She drew Pinky closer until the girl's shoulder pressed tight against her hip. Pinky's face had gone bloodless, eyes huge, hands shaking despite the death grip she had on Alysha's sleeve. Whatever the skinks called her in their hymns, this was the reality those stories never showed.

The wounded crowned skink limped on until the far end of the chamber loomed.

A raised dais jutted out of the rock, carved straight from the cavern wall. Upon it sat a throne big enough to dwarf even the largest skink they'd seen. The stone had been worked and reworked over centuries, edges worn soft by claws and time, every surface crawling with carvings—crowns, coiling shapes, stylized jaws. A single, concentrated shaft of light from a funnel in the ceiling speared down to bathe it, turning the seat into a pillar of brightness in an otherwise shifting world.

Bradley felt something cold settle into him. This wasn't some improvised council seat or gang leader's chair. This was old. Rooted. It broadcast the simple fact that others had stood where they were standing now and had their fates decided for them.

As they stopped before the dais, surrounded by torchlit scales and leveled spears, a different kind of fear took hold. Not the creeping dread of monsters in the dark, but the sharp knowledge that they had crossed a line. They weren't travelers passing through; they were inside the circle of someone else's law, in a place where decisions were carved in blood long before they were born.

A low, guttural voice rolled through the chamber, vibrating up through the stone into their boots. It seemed to come from everywhere at once until the shadows behind the throne shifted and resolved into a figure.

Another skink stepped into the light—older and far larger than any they'd seen. Its scales were dulled, edges chipped and cracked, bright colors worn to a faded patina. Joints moved with slow, deliberate care, but there was nothing frail in the way it held itself. Its eyes, sunk deep in the ridges of its face, burned with a cold, focused intelligence and something that felt like calcified memory.

It let out a single, clipped hiss.

Around the chamber, the warriors responded as one. Spearpoints raised a fraction, just enough to ease the threat from imminent kill to controlled menace. No one relaxed; the tension in the air stayed taut. But for the moment, at least, the message was clear:

They would be judged before they were torn apart.

The ancient skink came down from the dais with the slow confidence of something that had never once needed to hurry.

Up close, its scales had gone chalky gray-green, edges chipped and cracked—it's tail had faded to an almost white making it impossible to determine the elder's original clan. Thin scars latticed its muzzle and throat. Each step set a faint rasp of claw on rock whispering through the chamber. It passed the crowned emerald-tail without a glance, its gaze moving over the humans one by one.

It lingered on Jorgen.

For a heartbeat those hooded eyes sharpened, something like recognition resolving there—unwelcome and irritated. Then they slid on, settling at last on Pinky.

The girl shrank back a fraction, her fingers digging into Alysha's sleeve. The ancient skink's pupils narrowed, a strange, measuring light in its gaze that made it impossible to read whether it was seeing a child or a something else.

"So—" its voice rasped, layered and dry, as if dragged up from deep in its chest, and in English "—the goddess returns."

It wasn't welcome, and it wasn't joy. It was a statement, edged and unsettling.

Bradley's mind spun, but his mouth found words before panic could. He stepped forward, palms open, throat dry. "We don't claim divinity," he said. His voice came out steadier than he felt. "The child... she's..."

He looked at Pinky—small, pale, shaking—and the rest of the sentence snagged.

"She is what?" the ancient skink prodded. Its head tilted, birdlike, a slow, deliberate angle. The hiss underneath the words had teeth.

Alysha swallowed, then forced herself to speak. "We don't understand your beliefs," she said, voice tight but clear. "But Pinky is just a child. A lost child who wants to go back to the world of light."

Silence dropped over the chamber. Torches crackled; somewhere above, a slow drip of water pattered onto stone. The ancient skink's gaze went distant, as if it were listening to something only it could hear.

"Return?" it hissed softly. "Where is this 'world of light'?" Its clawed hand lifted, tracing a vague circle in the air above them. "Under the burning eye?" A faint sneer touched its mouth. "Such tales are myths. Whispers told by those who cannot bear the stone and shadow. They dream of a sky and call their dreaming 'truth.'"

A chill walked up Bradley's spine. For him, daylight was memory: hot wind on concrete, the glare off megacity glass. For this thing, those memories were fairy stories—blasphemy, even. It wasn't just ignorance; there was conviction there, weight given by centuries of never seeing otherwise.

He opened his mouth, not even sure what he meant to say.

A harsh hiss cut across the silence.

The tailless crowned skink limped forward, flanked by its crimson guards. Its breath still came fast, pain tightening the edges of its mouth, but its eyes burned. It launched into a rapid stream of language, all harsh hisses and click-snap syllables. The tone left little doubt: accusation, defense, pride.

The ancient one answered in the same tongue, voice lower but no less sharp. The exchange came fast, too fast for Pinky to catch more than fragments. Bodies shifted around them; some warriors leaned in, others went very still. Loyalty and resentment rippled through the rank-and-file in the flick of tails and the angle of spears.

"Change—" the ancient skink said at last, the word dragged out on a sigh. Its voice carried the tired weight of rock that had survived many storms. "Change is upon us. Whether borne by false goddess…" Its eyes slid briefly to Pinky. "…or by reckless engelken, it is here."

Jorgen's jaw tightened at the word. *Engelken.* Whatever the exact translation, he didn't need a dictionary to know it meant him.

The patriarch turned to their blue-tailed companion. A short, clipped command followed. Their crowned ally straightened despite the blood soaking his side, then moved forward on shaking legs. He sank to one knee at the base of the dais and drew something from his belt.

The severed scorpion stinger looked even uglier in the torchlight. Chitin faded to a dead matte, barbed edges jagged. He held it out with both hands, head bowed, shoulders trembling—not from fear, Bradley realized, but from the effort of staying upright.

The ancient skink leaned down to study it.

For a long moment, nothing moved. The torchlight popped and hissed. The smell of old smoke and damp stone pressed in. The patriarch's gaze traced the serrated edges, the dried venom channels, the evidence of a kill that shouldn't have been possible for something his size.

The humans held their breath. Bradley's lungs burned. Jorgen's fingers twitched toward a knife that wasn't there, lost to gnawing sewer vermin half a world and few nightmares ago.

At last, the old skink's eyes shifted from the trophy back to their crowned companion. Whatever glimmer had been there earlier hardened into something like decision.

Pinky's voice came out only loud enough for her friends. "He says…'accepted,'" she translated. She let out a tiny, shaky breath. "He has earned his place. The ritual will start when the moons turn."

The words dropped like stones.

Alysha's eyes widened. Ritual meant knives and circles and power, in every story she knew. Jorgen's hand found empty air again where his knife used to ride, and his lip curled in irritation and unease. Bradley forced his thoughts to slow, to line up, to not run screaming down every path at once.

He managed to get one question past the knot in his throat.

"Ritual?" he asked, watching the ancient skink, Pinky, and their bleeding guide. "What kind of ritual?"

The ancient skink flicked its clawed hand in a gesture that was almost casual, as if dismissing a question that had been answered long ago.

"The old way," it rasped. "A test of strength, of cunning, of worth. Only my successor may rule."

The tailless crowned skink hissed, pain and outrage bleeding together. He jabbed his remaining arm toward Pinky as she listened, the gesture sharp enough to make her flinch.

"This…creature!" he spat in his own tongue. "It fouls our traditions, it brings—"

He didn't finish.

The ancient one's tail snapped out in a blur, thick and heavy as a club. It caught the maimed skink square in the chest and sent him skidding across the stone, claws scraping, air driven out of him in a sharp, shocked yelp. He hit the floor and stayed there, wheezing, eyes wide.

The old skink's gaze swept the humans again, finally settling on Pinky. "And so the goddess shall bear witness," it said, voice gone quieter—and colder. "Witness the turning of the tides. Blessing or curse, it changes nothing. The ritual will decide."

Unease tightened the air. Bradley felt it settle in his gut. Alysha drew Pinky closer. Jorgen shifted half a step, sliding his solid frame a little more between the girl and the throne. The movement didn't escape the patriarch.

For a heartbeat, something like amusement creased the old reptile's cracked features. "Do not fret, engelken," it hissed. "Your child-goddess will be safe. For now."

The pause after those two words scraped along Bradley's nerves.

A series of hissed commands followed, snapping through the ranks of crimson-helmed guards. Before the humans could read the tone, the nearest warriors surged forward. Scaled hands like bands of iron clamped down on arms and shoulders.

Bradley staggered as a spear haft slammed into his chest and shoved him to his knees. Alysha cried out, reaching for her blade—only for her wrist to be seized and twisted until her fingers popped open. Jorgen threw his weight against the claws on his arms, muscles knotting, but three skinks bore down on him at once. Their strength was immense—dense, crushing. He managed half a curse before they shoved him face-first into cold stone.

Any pretense of ceremony vanished.

Rough hands stripped them of anything remotely dangerous: Alysha's blade was yanked from its sheath with a ringing scrape; Bradley felt his energy pistol torn from its holster; Jorgen's air rifle was wrestled from his grip and passed back through the ranks. Pouches and belts were rifled with efficient speed. When the guards were done, they were bare of anything that felt like leverage.

Spears prodded them into motion, forcing them toward a low, dark archway in the chamber wall.

As they were herded away, Bradley risked a look back. For an instant he caught Pinky standing small and alone before the throne, torches painting her in jittering bands of gold and shadow. Her eyes met his—wide, wet, terrified. He tried to put every promise he couldn't voice into his look: hold on. We're not done.

The tailless skink had found his feet again. He moved with a new, brittle purpose, dragging his injury behind him like an insult he meant to repay. He hissed something low and sharp down at Pinky, the syllables too quick and warped for the humans—but the intent was clear in the tilt of his head, the hard line of his jaw. Wounded pride. Humiliation. A ruler-in-waiting who'd been knocked into the dust in front of half his people.

They were forced down a number of corridors until roughly shoved into a dark room. A heavy stone door swung shut behind the humans with a wet, resonant thud. The sound boomed in the tight space, then died.

Darkness fell.

It wasn't the soft dim of the city's glow, but a thick, tactile dark that wrapped around their faces and crawled down their throats.

For a moment, no one spoke.

"What now?" Alysha whispered at last. Her eyes were only a suggestion in the black, but Bradley could hear the ragged edge to her breath, feel the anger coiled under the words.

Jorgen paced as far as the cramped cell allowed, boots scuffing stone. His fists opened and closed, useless without a weapon. "When we get out of here," he growled, "I'm turnin' lizards inside out like I'm pairin' socks."

The grim promise hung in the close air, half threat, half coping mechanism.

Bradley let his back find the wall and slid down until he hit the floor. The stone was cold through his clothes, leeching heat from his bones. The dark pressed in on all sides, no cracks, no glow, no hint of direction—just a solid, smothering weight.

For the first time since the sewers, he felt the shape of true impossibility settle around them, as real and heavy as the rock itself.

"Don't waste your energy," Bradley rasped, his throat dry. "We need to conserve our strength."

"Don't tell me to conserve my energy," Alysha snapped back. Her voice cut through the dark, sharp and bright with rage. In the cramped cell, Jorgen's pacing picked up, boots scuffing over damp stone in an erratic rhythm that scraped at the silence.

"We can't just sit here," she hissed, breath coming fast. "They took my blade. They're going to pay for that."

Bradley let out a slow, frayed sigh. The sound seemed to vanish into the heavy air. "Alysha, I know," he said. "But anger's not going to magic us out of here. We need to think. Find a weakness. Anything we can use."

"What weakness?" Jorgen snarled. He stopped pacing and planted a hand against the slick wall as if he could shove through it. "We're blind mice in a viper pit. "

In the dark, Bradley could hear Alysha's breathing—uneven, ragged—as she fought with more than just the room. Her blade had been more than metal; it had been a piece of the world she'd come from, a thread back to a life that made sense. Having it ripped away felt like someone had reached inside her and taken something they had no right to touch.

"We wait," Bradley said at last. He forced his voice to stay level, not rising to the bait. They weren't angry at him; they were angry at the stone, the skinks, the whole damned situation. "There's movement outside. Footsteps. Voices. Guards changing places. We listen. We pay attention. When something shifts, when we hear something we can use…"

He let the sentence trail off. No one needed him to finish it. In the stale dark, with the stink of reptile musk and wet rock pressing in, they all knew what "when" meant.

When the moment came, it wouldn't be clean. It would be teeth and claws and fists and whatever they could turn into a weapon. And whatever future the skinks had planned for them, they would have to carve out their own instead.

***

The hovel was as close to a sanctuary as the skink city had to offer—a shallow stone hollow cut off from the main tunnels and streets, lit only by a few faint patches of fungus smeared along the ceiling. The light was dim and greenish, casting everything in sickly tones.

Knight lay on a low pallet of woven roots and dried fungus. His leg didn't look like it belonged to a living man. Swollen and mottled in ugly greens and bruise-deep purples, it was pocked with puncture wounds where spider fangs had gone in. Heat radiated off it in waves.

The lithe skink with the blue markings knelt by Knight's side. A damp cloth moved in precise, looping strokes over torn flesh, wiping away dried blood and seepage. Each motion was careful, almost ceremonial. The stockier, brown-scaled skink

stood at Mustang's shoulder like a silent guard, its bulk
between them and the doorway, eyes half-lidded but alert.

Silence filled the space. No crowd noise, no city hum—just
Knight's shallow breaths and the faint slap of cloth on skin.
The language barrier sat between them like another wall.

The brown-scaled skink stepped forward and pressed
something into Mustang's hand—a gourd stoppered with a
dried mushroom. It tipped it toward its own mouth, miming an
exaggerated swallow, then pointed at Mustang with a small,
insistent nod.

Mustang lifted the gourd, sniffed, and grimaced. The liquid
inside smelled smoky and sharp, with a bitter, herbal edge.
"What is it?" he asked anyway, already knowing he wouldn't
get an answer.

The skink rolled one shoulder in a strangely human shrug, then
went through a clumsy little pantomime: eyes squeezed shut,
body shuddering as if under strain, then a hand smoothing
slowly down its own chest, breath evening out.

For a second Mustang just stared. Then the shape of it clicked
—tension spiking, tension easing.

"Yeah," he muttered, mostly to himself. "Okay."

He took a cautious sip. The brew hit his tongue earthy and
strong, with a burnt aftertaste that should've been awful but
wasn't. Warmth spread down his chest a moment later,
loosening something between his ribs. It reminded him of the
thick, bitter coffee Bradley had coaxed out of Jorgen's beans
back in the oasis—too strong, too strange, but exactly what
he'd needed at the time.

The brown-scaled skink twitched at the sound of his voice, picking up the tone if not the words. It jabbed a claw toward the doorway, then mimed shoving something away, head shaking so hard its throat frill fluttered. The urgency in the movement crawled under Mustang's skin.

"You want us to leave?" he guessed, frowning. He shook his head, jaw tightening. "Not happening. We don't walk out on him."

The blue-marked healer finished wiping Knight's leg and rose, joints popping faintly. It joined them by the pallet, eyes moving between Mustang, Karl, and the unconscious man. Carefully, it pointed at the ruined limb, hissed a low, pained sound, then traced a circle around the worst of the swelling with one claw.

Its gestures shifted: it pointed to the narrow doorway, then out, as if toward the wider maze of tunnels beyond. One hand moved in a slow, searching motion, parting invisible undergrowth.

"Medicine?" Mustang asked, hope jumping sharp in his chest.

Both skinks bobbed their heads quickly, blue markings flaring as the healer nodded. Then the blue-marked one's expression turned grave. It pointed at Knight again, held up three fingers, then folded them in with its other hand and let its body sag, a soft croak slipping out—close enough to death that no one needed a dictionary.

Cold washed through Mustang's gut. "Three days?" he whispered. He looked down at Knight's slack face, the sheen of sweat on his brow. "No. I won't let that happen. You do what you need to do…" His voice roughened. "…but we're staying right here."

Karl let out a low whistle, the sound small in the cramped room. He rubbed a hand through his beard, braids clinking softly. "Three days," he echoed. "That's not much. You really think they can do somethin' for him we can't?"

Mustang watched the two skinks a moment longer. Their faces were hard to read, built for a different kind of expression, but the tension in their bodies, the way their eyes kept cutting back to Knight, was clear enough.

"I don't know," he said honestly. "But this place isn't home. Bradley's good…but maybe they've got things down here we've never seen. Herbs or whatever passes for medicine in a hole like this."

He glanced back at Knight's leg—a mess of stitches, swelling, and spreading color.

"If there's even a chance," Mustang said quietly, fingers tightening around the gourd, "we're not walking away from it."

He turned to the brown-scaled skink and met its gaze head-on. "If you can help Knight… please," Mustang said. "You have to try."

The skink inclined its head in a slow, deliberate nod, throat-sacs pulsing. It motioned with a clawed hand for Mustang and Karl to follow, its movements clipped and purposeful.

"Whoa. Hold up," Karl rumbled, a line of caution creasing his brow. "We go wandering out there, we'll stand out like broken thumbs."

The two skinks traded a brief look. The blue-marked healer ducked under a heap of ragged bedding and dragged out two cloaks, rough-spun and stiff, dyed a dull mud-brown. They smelled faintly of smoke and lizard oil.

Karl shrugged into his cloak. On a dwarf's frame it hung a little short and sat cattywampus across his shoulders, but it broke up his outline well enough. Mustang took the other, the coarse fabric rasping against the scars on his forearms as he pulled it on. The weight of it, unfamiliar and scratchy, was a reminder that he did not belong down here.

He glanced back at Knight. The sergeant's chest rose and fell in shallow pulls, each breath a soft rasp. The leg looked worse in the greenish gloom.

"We'll be back," Mustang said, more oath than promise. "You just hang in there, buddy."

The skinks led them out through a low side passage that climbed away from the hovel, then dipped, angling down beneath the main arteries of the city. The hum of reptilian life faded behind them. Ahead, the tunnels narrowed into a twisting warren of rough-hewn stone, hacked and clawed through the earth.

The blue-marked skink took the lead, moving with a soundless, fluid gait that belied its bulk. The brown-scaled one brought up the rear, close enough that Mustang thought he could feel its breath stir his borrowed cloak.

Bioluminescent fungi clung to cracks and corners, their glow smeared like ghostly paint along the walls. The light came in patches—bright, then dark, then a faint smear underfoot. Mustang's boots slipped once on a slick patch of moss, he caught himself with a string of curses.

From far above and behind came the softened echoes of the city: distant hissing speech, the steady thud of something being hammered, an occasional high shriek that spider-climbed down Mustang's spine.

He edged closer to Karl and kept his voice to a whisper. "So," he murmured, eyes tracking the healer's tail ahead, "what do you think they're gonna do about Knight's leg?"

Karl scratched thoughtfully at his beard. His eyes gleamed with a nervous curiosity. "Honestly? No earthly idea," he admitted. "Maybe they've got some miracle root, or fungus that eats poison. Wouldn't be the strangest thing I've seen."

Their guide in back let out a low hiss and lifted a hand in warning. They halted.

The brown-scaled skink pointed toward a dark break in the tunnel wall. A curtain of woven reeds, frayed and stained, hung across the opening. Behind it, light danced—warmer and more constant than the scattered fungi-glow.

The blue-marked skink slipped through the curtain without a sound.

From where they stood, Mustang could see glimpses of the room beyond: bundles of dried herbs and knotted roots hanging in dense clusters from the ceiling; shelves carved into the rock, crowded with jars of cloudy liquid and coiled things he couldn't name; piles of chipped stones sorted by color and size along the floor. The air that leaked out carried a thick, bitter herbal scent. It was a welcome reprieve from the constant smell of rock, mud, and musk.

"You ever think about how crazy all this is?" Karl muttered at last, voice cracking just a little. "One minute we're runnin' for our lives, next thing you know we're skulkin' around a lizard city, tryin' to find who knows what…"

Mustang couldn't help a grim chuckle. "You know," he muttered, "the more I think about it, the less crazy it seems. We... adapt. That's what people do."

The blue-marked skink slipped back through the reed curtain and jerked its head for them to follow.

Inside, heat rolled over them in a sudden wave. The chamber was low and wide, its air thick with a cloying sweetness that tickled the sinuses. Dozens of small stone braziers ringed the room, their coals glowing dull orange, each feeding a thin ribbon of smoke into the air. The strange scent—floral, with a sharp medicinal bite underneath—overwhelmed Mustang.

Crude tables squatted in the center, their surfaces crowded with chaos. Bundles of dried leaves tied in knotted string. Bowls of shimmering powder that caught the light like ground metal. Roots twisted into shapes that looked uncomfortably like fingers. The brown-scaled skink waited there, methodically sorting herbs into neat piles with the patience of someone who had done this a thousand times.

It set to work without ceremony. Leaves went into a stone mortar and were ground to paste under a heavy pestle. Powders were pinched out and tipped into chipped bowls. Liquids from unmarked jars—viscous, cloudy, some faintly luminescent— were added drop by careful drop. With each new mixture, the scent in the room shifted, layers of bitter, sour, and smoke stacking over the sweetness until Mustang's eyes watered.

The blue-marked skink never broke its focus.It ground and sifted, its claws moving with a precise rhythm. The things it made didn't look like any medicine Mustang had ever seen: a thin, bubbling green liquid in a cracked ceramic bowl that hissed when a leaf fell into it; a powder so dark it seemed to swallow the light around it; a pale paste that quivered as though there were something alive trying to push free.

Whatever this was, it wasn't guesswork. There was too much method in it.

At last, the healer wiped its hands on a strip of woven fiber and crossed to a narrow shelf cut into the rock. From it, it drew a book.

The cover was long gone. The pages were dark and warped, corners flaked away, the spine bowed from damp and age. Mustang would've sworn it was nothing but a lump of ruined paper—until the skink held it out and he saw faint lines and shapes still clinging to the pages.

He took it gingerly. The leatherless spine flexed dangerously under his fingers. In the wavering light he could just make out diagrams, circles crowded with symbols, rough sketches of plants and twisted things that might once have been animals.

The blue-marked skink stood close, gesturing as it spoke in a rapid stream of hisses and clicks. The meaning washed over Mustang in tone more than words: insistence, urgency, expectation.

Karl leaned in, squinting at the pages. "Looks like we're goin' on another adventure," he breathed, awe and dread wrestling in his voice. "My guess? He's got some of what we need in here already, but the rest…" He trailed off, eyes tracking the skink's gestures. "We gotta go find it ourselves. Book's the guide."

The healer nodded sharply, seeming to understand the meaning behind Karl's words, then launched into a series of pantomimes. It mimicked climbing, claws scrabbling at invisible stone. It crouched low, hands raking through imaginary soil. It pointed toward different corners of the chamber as if marking directions on a map only it could see.

Mustang's heart sank. "How are we supposed to do that?" he muttered. "We can't just wander around." His voice dropped even lower. "And what if that three-day guess was wrong? What if Knight's got less?"

The thought hit like a punch. He gripped the book tighter than he meant to, the brittle pages crackling in protest.

The blue-marked skink's frill twitched. Even without the words, it seemed to catch the raw edge of his fear. It moved quickly back to the tables, scooping up small amounts of herbs and shavings and tucking them into woven pouches. Each packet was tied off and laid out in a neat line.

Then the lesson began.

With slow, deliberate motions, the healer showed them how to crush a certain root—lengthwise, not crosswise, to keep the sap from turning black. How to dry a leaf pressed between flat stones instead of hanging it, how much powder to pinch between thumb and forefinger before the mixture went bitter instead of helpful. It repeated the motions until even Karl could mimic them, big hands moving clumsily through the air.

No words they shared, no way to ask if any of this would be enough. But in the flick and twist of the skink's claws, in the care it took to show every step, Mustang felt something like a promise:

It would give them everything it knew.

The rest would be up to them—and the time Knight had left.

"He's tellin' us to hurry," Karl said, watching the healer's rapid gestures. Urgency roughened his voice. "But something doesn't sit right with me, Mustang. Got a bad feeling about this."

Mustang drew a slow breath, lungs full of smoke and damp herb scent. "Yeah," he murmured. "Same here." The blue-marked skink's stare was steady, unblinking, all expectation and no guarantees.

His gaze dropped to his sling.

The cloth was sweat-stained and grimy, the knot biting into the back of his neck. His shoulder still ached with a deep, pulsing throb. They didn't have the luxury of waiting for it to finish knitting itself back together. He slipped the sling off and let his arm hang for a second, feeling the weight drag against sore muscle. Then he flexed his fingers, rolled his shoulder. Pain flared, sharp and hot, but it worked.

A firefight would undo most of the healing. He knew it. Karl knew he knew it. The dwarf just watched, saying nothing as Mustang folded the sling and stuffed it into one of his many pockets. They'd been through enough together that there was no point wasting breath on the obvious.

He turned back to the healer.

Gratitude and dread tangled behind his eyes as he dipped his head in a small, deliberate nod. "Thank you," he rasped.

For a moment he let himself look around the chamber one last time—the hanging bundles, the jars of cloudy liquid, the neat lines of pouches on the table. He squared his shoulders and turned toward the tunnel mouth.

The air beyond was cooler, darker, smelling of earth and stone instead of burnt herbs. *More of the same.* Mustang stepped into it, the book and pouches heavy in his hands, Karl's boots thudding steadily at his heels as they followed their skink guide into the maze.

Alysha's eyes burned faintly in the gloom, anger crackling even if it had nowhere to go. It was heat against a cold that kept creeping in. Bradley sat with his back to the wall, knees drawn up, mind running ragged and coming back with nothing but tighter circles. Every time he glanced at the others, he saw the same thing—exhaustion, barely leashed fear, that slow bleed of hope.

Jorgen leaned against the rough rock near the door, arms folded. To anyone who didn't know him, he might have looked worn out, ready to sag. Bradley could hear the tightness in his breathing, though—the coiled, waiting energy.

"Y'know," Jorgen rasped at last, breaking the quiet, "this ain't the first time I've been locked up like some animal."

His hand scraped down his stubbled jaw, nails catching on old scars. A ghost of a grin tugged at his mouth. "Back when I was greener, I got myself mixed up with a real piece of work."

Alysha's head turned, a sliver of interest slipping through the anger. "One of the syndicate heads?" she asked. "I don't know much about the Rockies, but I heard the New New York crowd say it's all run by one syndicate or another."

Jorgen snorted softly. "Oh, it is. But this one wasn't top shelf. Small-timer. Thought he was hot shit with his shiny suits and handful of goons. Tried to build himself an empire in the bones of old Denver. Called himself 'The Duke.'"

He paused, eyes unfocusing for a moment, seeing something that was well removed from their cell. "Caught me snoopin' around. Thought I was some rival's muscle. He wasn't wrong, exactly—one of his own underbosses had hired me, got sick of his bullshit. Duke's boys jumped me before I could finish the job. Locked me up in his penthouse, waited for me to crack."

"So what happened, bounty hunter?" Alysha asked. She wanted the end of the story.

Jorgen's grin widened, showing a chipped tooth. "I played his game," he said. "Sat there day after day, starin' him down, talkin' like I was scared of him. Truth is, I really was scared shitless."

Bradley listened, filing away the details. Behind the rough humor there was always some kind of moral with Jorgen—a pattern, some ugly lesson paid for in blood.

"Let me guess," Bradley said quietly. "He started believing it. Got lazy."

"You got it, boy." Jorgen chuckled, the sound low and humorless. "Duke started struttin' in just to gloat. Show off.

Figured I was broken… or maybe, just crazy. Third week in, he slips. Let his boys start slackin' while he monologued." He flexed his fingers, knuckles popping loud in the cramped space. "Left me an openin' big enough to drive a freight hauler through."

"And you busted out?" Alysha asked, eyes glinting.

"Busted his head too," Jorgen replied with a shrug. The cold glint in his gaze undercut the casual tone. "Point is, sometimes you play dumb. Play weak. Let 'em think they got the leash. They get cocky, they make mistakes. That's when you move."

He tipped his chin toward the heavy fungal door. "We ain't beat yet, not by a long shot. This ain't no penthouse, and these lizards aren't geniuses. They're just used to everyone bowin'."

Bradley huffed out a breath that was almost a laugh. "Yeah," he said, rubbing a hand over his face. "I know. That's what I've been saying since they threw us in here—we wait, we watch, we let them think we're just…stuck."

His hand dropped to his side. In the dark, they could hear water drip somewhere beyond the wall, a slow, patient rhythm.

"We just have to be ready," he finished.

Jorgen's wolfish grin spread wider. "Yeah, I know," he said. "But I figured you could use a little remindin'. Plus—" he chuckled "—I said it better."

A sharp flash of irritation went through Bradley, quick and clean as a paper cut. Just as quickly, it dulled into something closer to reluctant amusement. That was Jorgen through and through—loud, stubborn, handing out lessons nobody asked for. Underneath it, though, was the same thing that had kept them all alive more than once: he refused to let anyone roll over and quit.

Alysha cut in before the banter could spool out. "All right, enough about patience," she said, voice low but edged in steel. "What's the plan?"

Bradley exhaled, breath rough in the chill. The question had been sitting on his chest since they'd first heard the door slam shut. He'd already run his hands along every seam of the walls, pressed his shoulder into the door to test its give, counted guard steps and tried to pin meaning to their hisses.

Nothing.

"The plan," he said at last, the words sour in his mouth, "is to wait for their next move."

"We listen," he went on, forcing himself to keep eye contact with both of them. "Watch for patterns. This power struggle out there? It's the only thing that might crack this open. Somebody overreaches, somebody gets sloppy—that's our moment. Until then, we don't give them an excuse to make us disappear early."

Jorgen gave a low rumble that might have been agreement. "Patience is overrated," he muttered. "But it buys us time to plan a proper breakout. Somethin' worth tellin' stories about if we live long enough."

The cell stayed the same; everything else came in waves. Their voices rose and fell. They took turns lying on the clammy floor, stretching cramped legs, rubbing circulation back into numb fingers. Ideas bounced around the cell like loose rounds—overpowering a guard when food came, faking a seizure to drag someone inside, Alysha squeezing through a gap that probably didn't exist. Half of it was nonsense and they knew it. Saying it out loud still felt better than sitting in silence and listening to their hope erode grain by grain.

The skinks, at least, weren't starving them.

A scrape sounded at the base of the door, followed by the wet slap of something heavy sliding forward. A shallow tray pushed through the low slot and bumped Bradley's boot. He dragged it in.

Three stone bowls of pale soup steamed faintly in the chill. Thin slices of raw mushroom were piled off to one side, their gills a bruised gray-purple. Nestled beside them sat a squat brown tuber, skin knotted and rough, like a fist of packed roots.

"Beats starving, I guess," Bradley said. His stomach answered with a hollow twist. He lifted his bowl, sniffed. The broth smelled earthy, but not spoiled—like clean soil after rain. He sipped.

It was better than he'd expected. Watery, but savory, an almost meaty depth under the mushroom tang.

"It's not half bad," Jorgen announced, already halfway through his portion, slurping loud enough to echo. Some of his old swagger crept back into his tone. "Could use salt, sure, but it beats some of the shit we've choked down since we dropped in this hole. Bless that boy, Karl does his best, but it's hard to make ice cream outta chicken shit."

Alysha snorted, a tiny spark of humor breaking through. "At least the food proves they want us alive," she said, spooning soup with more precision than appetite. "For now."

They ate. The bowls warmed their hands, if not much else. For a few minutes, chewing and swallowing pushed the what-ifs to the edges of their minds. Hunger was simple. Hunger made sense.

When the bowls sat empty, scraped as clean as they could manage, the tuber remained. Jorgen cut it in uneven chunks with a jagged edge of broken stone they'd pried from the wall. The flesh inside was pale and fibrous, smelling faintly sweet and odd.

"I'll try it," he offered.

Alysha caught his wrist. "We don't know what it is," she said. "Could be fine. Could be slow poison."

He raised a brow. "If they wanted us dead, they could've done it quicker," he pointed out. "Or just…not fed us."

"Exactly," she replied. "That's why it's not poison." She let go and sat back, eyes hard. "They're obsessed with this 'ascension ritual.' They need us alive until then. Killing us slow makes no sense if they want a show."

Jorgen shrugged, popped a small slice into his mouth, chewed, grimaced. "Starchy," he muttered. "Like somebody forgot what a potato was and tried to reinvent it from memory."

Bradley watched Alysha as she spoke, the way her anger kept coalescing into focus instead of just burning out impressed him. Even now, she refused to fold.

If she was right, the ritual bought them a window. How wide, he didn't know.

Somewhere beyond the door, a guard hissed to another. Footsteps shifted. Voices faded.

"There's a flaw in there somewhere," Bradley murmured, half to them, half to the stone. "A missed step. We just have to be ready when they take it."

The sound came first—shrill and insistent.

Not dripping water, not the soft thud of skink feet beyond the door, not Jorgen's restless pacing. A crisp little buzz that didn't belong in stone and stale air. Bradley froze, every muscle going tight. He thought he'd imagined it, just his brain inventing noise to fill the dark.

Then it came again. A short, electronic chirp.

His hand was already moving before he fully understood why. He fumbled at his jacket, fingers numb from cold, until they closed around the hard edge of the little case. He eased it free, heart beating faster than it had any right to in that cramped cell.

The thin glow leaking in under the cell door painted everything in a sickly stripe across the floor. It caught on the AR glasses as he opened the case, turning the lenses into two dull rectangles in his palm.

The earpiece sat beside them, a tiny, familiar curve of metal and plastic. Its indicator light pulsed weakly, each flash paired with a soft burst of static that barely rose above a whisper. In the quiet of the cell, it seemed deafening.

Hope hit him so hard it almost hurt.

The glasses should've been dead—out of range, out of power, out of luck. It could be a glitch, a dying battery cycling through its last confused spasms. But the little stutter of sound cut straight through the sludge in his chest, and he couldn't ignore it.

His fingers felt clumsy as he slid the glasses on. The frame was gritty against his temples, cold from disuse. He found the power switch by muscle memory and flicked it.

The faint startup hum seemed loud enough to wake the whole city.

Across from him, Alysha pushed off the wall, eyes narrowing in the gloom. Jorgen straightened, the lazy slump gone from his shoulders.

"Bradley, what…?" Alysha whispered, voice rasped thin by the damp air.

"I don't know," he breathed. And he didn't—not yet.

For a moment nothing happened. Then the lenses flared to life.

The sudden overlay of pale blue light stabbed at his dark-adjusted eyes. He blinked hard, tears stinging, as the familiar interface stuttered into existence—jagged, flickering. Error messages stacked up in the corner of his vision: LOW POWER. NETWORK FAILURE. LOCATION UNKNOWN.

He almost tore them off.

Then he saw it.

Nestled in the top-right corner of the display, so faint it was nearly lost in the static: a signal icon. One narrow bar, flashing in and out, but there.

"There's… there's a signal," Bradley said. His voice shook despite him. "My glasses… they're picking something up."

Jorgen was at his side in three strides, peering at the ghostly glow. "What kind of signal?" he demanded. "Can you trace it? Figure where it's comin' from?"

Bradley forced himself to breathe, to focus. His thumb swept through menu layers by habit, fighting the lag as the processor struggled. Half the usual functions were grayed out, but buried deeper—a service menu he almost never touched—sat the diagnostics.

He opened it.

The glasses began to scan, a thin progress bar crawling across his vision. Each tiny increment felt like a lifetime. The only sounds in the cell were the faint electronic beeps, the soft crackle of the earpiece at his collar, and the rough, uneven pull of their breathing.

Ninety-one percent. Ninety-six. Ninety-nine.

The bar ticked over, and the interface cleared.

A new line of text blinked onto the display, sharp and unreal against the film of grime on the lenses.

Signal Source: Lt. Sebastian Mustang.

\*\*\*

Both Mustang and Karl carried crude woven baskets that rasped against their palms with every step. The coverless book rode under Mustang's arm, wrapped in a strip of cloth as if that might shield it from the clammy air. It seemed to drag at him with more than its weight would suggest.

The skink apothecary had placed it in his hands with almost reverent care, but the work itself was grunt work. The looping English script curled across each page in faded ink, neat as any text Mustang had ever pulled off a terminal. The contrast between that careful handwriting and the guttural hisses of the skinks gnawed at his nerves.

"Who wrote this?" Karl asked, genuinely confused on how the skink got their hands on a book written by humans. He reached out, running a blunt fingertip along a washed-out illustration of a bulbous root, its tendrils drawn like a tangle of veins.

"Who cares?" Mustang grunted. Sweat beaded along his brow despite the chill. "Whoever it was is dust by now. I'm just glad they left us a map."

The book did spell out a path, of sorts—if you could call it that.

He'd memorized the list until the words floated in his head every time he blinked: a luminous crimson fungus clinging near geothermal vents; a root that anchored itself to the undersides of massive cave beetles; a moss that thrived in absolute dark.

They had the fungus. The root, too. One ingredient left, the most absurd of the three, and each step felt like it was ticking down whatever time Knight had been given.

Something screamed.

The sound ripped through the tunnel—a guttural, shuddering screech that bounced off the stone and came at them from all sides. Mustang flinched, every muscle clenching, as the noise fractured into a rising wave of chittering and hard, skittering impacts.

"What in the—" Karl hissed.

Beetles, centipedes, and some unidentifiable crawlies—a carpet of them—poured down the tunnel. They sized from as small as a thumbnail to as large as an urban recon drone, plated in overlapping slabs of chitin that shimmered a rainbow of colors where they caught the fungus-light. Their jointed legs scraped and clattered on the rock, a thousand tiny blades raking the floor as they swarmed.

Mustang's hand shot out, fingers clamping around Karl's arm. "Hide," he breathed. "Now."

They ducked behind a curtain of thick, gnarled fungi, the fleshy stalks cool and moist against their backs. Mustang pressed himself into the rock, the basket digging into his ribs, the book trapped hard against his chest. Karl's breath gusted hot against his neck as the swarm thundered past.

The volume of cacophonous sound rose—chittering, frantic scrapes, the hollow drum of armored bodies colliding with each other. The smell hit next: a sharp, acrid tang of insect musk and crushed shell that burned the eyes.

He held his breath until his lungs burned.

One beetle veered, clattering close enough that he caught every seam in its armor, the sheen of slime along its mandibles. It paused, antennae twitching, then jerked away, following the flow of the swarm. The last rank vanished into the dark, the sound of their passing fading into distant, disjointed echoes.

Only when the tunnel fell quiet again did Mustang dare exhale. It left him light-headed.

Karl let out a breath that turned into a shaky chuckle. "Did you feel that?"

"Feel what?" Mustang kept his voice low, though his heart still hammered loud in his ears.

"They were afraid." Karl swallowed. "Not of us. Something else. I could damn near smell it rolling off them. Those big bastards were running from something."

Mustang frowned, the unease that had been riding under his urgency rising a notch. Beetles that size didn't run from much. "Guess we aren't alone," he said.

The silence after the swarm felt wrong—too abrupt, like a song cut mid-note. The light from the fungi seemed dimmer, their colors sickened. Tunnels that had already felt hostile now seemed actively watchful.

"We gotta keep moving," Mustang said. The words came out flat, but he forced his legs to work. "The moss likes the deep dark. Maybe whatever spooked them likes it there too."

He shifted the baskets, readjusted the book under his arm, then stepped back into the main tunnel. The ambient light painted the beetles' passing in streaks of scuffed stone and broken shell fragments ground underfoot.

They went on.

A chill began to creep along Mustang's spine that had nothing to do with temperature.

The deeper they went, the more the air congealed around them. The bio luminescence guttered as if pushing through water, and every hair along their arms and necks prickled as that oppressive, waiting stillness settled over their skin.

The light felt thinner, washed out, as if something in the air was drinking it.

In the dying ambient light, Karl took out a torch made from dried fungus. Mustang quickly used his multi-tool to light it.

Shadows on the walls began to move in ways that didn't match the flicker of the torch—stretching, twisting, lagging behind like reflections in thick oil.

Mustang stopped. So did Karl. The tunnel around them breathed darkness.

"What in God's name…" Karl's voice cracked, the words scraped raw.

Ahead, the passage hooked sharply to the left. Around the bend, something pulsed—faint at first, then stronger—a low, throbbing glow the color of bruised violet. It wasn't light so much as an inversion of it. The closer it got, the more the torch seemed to retreat, its flame less a source and more a pale outline around empty air.

Then the smell hit them.

Rot. Sweet and cloying, like fruit left too long in the sun, tangled with a bitter, chemical sting that burned the sinuses. Karl gagged, a strangled sound ripping out of him as he clamped a hand over his mouth.

"We gotta get out of here," Mustang hissed. He grabbed a fistful of Karl's cloak and yanked him half around, turning to retreat—

—and froze.

Something slid into the edge of what was left of the torchlight.

At first, it was just an absence, a cutout where the light refused to land. Then it moved, and the dark took shape: a serpent, thick enough to block half of the tunnel. Its scales were a flawless, glossy black, each plate swallowing the torchlight instead of reflecting it, as if it was made of carved void.

Its head lifted as much as it could. Where its eyes—two voids, blacker than the deepest space, like a pair of miniature black holes devouring nearby stars, ringed with that same amaranthine radiance he'd glimpsed around the bend. Looking at them felt like looking down a well that never ended. Tiny motes of the torch's orange glow seemed to bend toward them and vanish.

A chill crawled up Mustang's spine and clamped at the base of his skull.

"Oh… God," Karl breathed. The sound was barely more than air.

The tunnel pinched around them in an instant. Behind: the strange glow and the reeking air that seemed to peel the breath from their lungs. Ahead: the snake, coiling, each movement slow enough to be deliberate and fast enough to be hopeless.

The book slipped from its cloth sling. It hit the damp stone with a soft, indecently small thud.

The serpent's head tilted at the sound. Its forked tongue slid out, tasting the air with a faint, wet flick. The darkness around its eyes pulsed in time with its slow, steady breath.

Karl's composure snapped. A raw scream tore out of him—a sound of sheer, animal terror that bounced off the stone and seemed to go on and on.

The snake reacted like someone had driven a spike into it.

Its head whipped toward Karl, body bunching in one sinuous motion. Its mouth opened in a wide, silent gape that showed rows of hooked, glassy teeth and a throat that was just deeper blackness.

Mustang's fear didn't go away. It was just overwhelmed by instinct and training.

Move. Aim. Shoot.

His rifle came up in one smooth motion. The weight tugged at the half-healed muscles of his bad arm; pain lanced from shoulder to wrist, bright enough to blur his vision. He rode it out, jaw clenched, letting muscle memory do what it could.

"Run, Karl!" he snapped, voice snapping like a shot in the cramped space.

Karl didn't argue. The torch jerked backward as he turned and bolted, light strobing wildly across the walls as he stumbled deeper into the passage, away from the serpent and toward whatever waited in the dark.

The snake didn't so much as glance after him.

All its attention funneled into Mustang. Those all-consuming eyes locked on the barrel of his rifle, on the heat of his body, on the tiny island of human defiance standing alone in the failing light.

The violet glow in its sockets brightened, shadows creeping across the floor like spilled ink.

Mustang's finger tightened.

The rifle spat a bolt of focused energy that turned the air white between them. The smell of scorched ozone slapped his face. The shot hit along the creature's side, drawing a blazing gouge across its scales. Black shell flashed silver as it burned, an ugly, jagged trench carved into the perfect darkness.

The serpent reared back, a convulsion rippling its length. Its jaws snapped shut and a sound tore free—a low, vibrating hiss that rumbled in Mustang's ribs more than his ears. The pools of void where its eyes should have been flared, ringed with furious violet.

Mustang's hand dropped to his belt on reflex. Cold metal met his fingers. The flashbang was up and away before he'd fully registered the motion—pin torn free with a sharp metallic snap, cylinder bouncing down the tunnel in a series of hollow clinks.

"Eyes!" he barked, though Karl was already looking away.

White swallowed the world.

The detonation hit like a hammer. Light punched through his eyelids, a solid slab of brilliance, followed by a roar that turned the tunnel into a vibrating drum. Pressure slammed into his chest. For a heartbeat there was nothing—no sound, no sense of direction, just pain and static and a skull full of afterimages.

The serpent convulsed in the glare. For a brief, searing moment Mustang saw it: the coiled bulk, the glossy scales turned chalk-grey by overexposure, the black eyes bleaching to ghostly discs before the darkness rushed back in.

He didn't wait.

The heavier shape at his belt came free next—the plasma grenade. His finger thumbed the activator, arm cocked. He aimed not at the snake, but past it—at the heart of the darkness, the place where light itself seemed to die.

The grenade rang off the tunnel wall rebounding into the edge of that unnatural depth.

The serpent's head snapped toward the sound.

"Move," Mustang breathed, already throwing himself backward.

He hit the floor shoulder-first and rolled. The blast hit an instant later. Heat and force slammed through the passage, a solid, invisible wall that lifted grit and shards of rock into the air. The thunder of it swallowed even the tinnitus already screaming in his ears. The world became a smear of green-white light and stinging dust.

When the ringing settled into something his brain could process, he forced his eyes open.

The tunnel was a wreck. Stone was blackened and cracked, chunks blasted out of the walls. The amaranthine glow was dimmer now, its greedy pull on the torchlight weakened. Smoke hung low, carrying the acrid stink of burned rock and scorched flesh.

The serpent lay amid the debris, coils heaped and twisted. Smoke oozed from scorched patches along its length where scales had bubbled and split. It hissed, a ragged, broken sound. Those void-black eyes narrowed, the violet ring around them guttering, but the easy, fluid threat was gone. Its movements were jerky now, hesitant.

Injured—not dead.

Mustang staggered to his feet and ran.

His boots slid on loose stone and smeared black blood. Every breath rasped hot in his throat, lungs scraping against the lingering heat in the air. Behind him, over the ringing in his skull, came the crunch and thud of something massive forcing its body through the ruined tunnel.

He risked a glance back.

The snake was coming.

It poured after him with a brutal, uncoiled fury. Scales, still slick with whatever passed for its blood, gleamed where the plasma had chewed through the black. Its eyes burned brighter, twin pits of violet-rimmed void. Each lunge punched fresh cracks into the stone.

Ahead, the tunnel pinched down into a narrow seam, a slit of deeper dark and a hint—just a hint—of cleaner air. Mustang threw himself at it, twisting sideways. Rock tore at his shoulder through the cloak. He forced himself through, ribs grinding against unyielding stone.

The serpent's bulk slammed against the bottleneck behind him, the impact booming through the rock. Dust rained down in a gritty curtain.

"No!" Karl's shout ripped through the cacophony, back along the tunnel they'd come from—a sound full of panic.

Mustang braced for the inevitable: the hot punch of fangs, the crush of jaws, the end.

It didn't come.

Instead he heard a strangled screech, the rush of dislodged air, and the meaty *thunk* of something solid striking flesh.

The torch hit the ground nearby, flame hissing as it rolled through spilled blood. The world went almost black, just the pulse of the snake's eyes and the faint, hateful violet down the passage.

Mustang clawed for the fallen torch, fingers closing around the rough stalk. He dragged it up, shielding the flame with his body. The weak circle of light flared, wobbling, and the scene snapped into focus.

The serpent was reared up the cavern wall, its body whipping in savage arcs. On its back, near the base of its skull, clung a stocky shape in a mud-colored cloak.

Karl.

He straddled the serpent's spine, legs locked tight, his black beard matted and glistening. One of his climbing picks was already buried deep between the plates at the base of the skull, haft being used as an anchor to keep the dwarf seated. The other rose and fell in his fist in brutal, unmeasured strokes.

Steel flashed in the torchlight. Each swing drove the pick down again with raw, stubborn force. The sound was wet and ugly—metal punching through shell into softer matter beneath. Black blood, thick and glossy as tar, sprayed in ragged fans, spattering Karl's face and cloak.

The snake bucked, slamming its head into the rock. The impact sent a shudder through its whole length. Karl was nearly flung loose, nearly crushed—fingers wrap around his buried pick, boots skidding. He roared—a hoarse, wordless sound—and drove the pick down again.

Again and again.

The serpent's hisses broke into wet, gargling noises. Its coils lost coherence, slumping against the stone as if something had cut the string that held it upright. The violet glow in its eyes wavered, then guttered.

With one last convulsion, it crashed to the floor, nearly tearing Karl free. The dwarf rode it down in a spray of black ichor, both picks buried to the hilt at the base of the skull.

Then it was still.

The void-black eyes stared at nothing, surface filmed over, the unnatural light gone. The tunnel, robbed of that hungry darkness, felt suddenly smaller, less infinite.

Mustang let the torch dip, his arm trembling with the comedown of adrenaline and the dull throb of abused muscles. "You…idiot," he managed, voice raw.

Karl, still sitting astride the dead serpent, spat a mouthful of black blood to the side and wiped a forearm across his face. His chest heaved. "I think… I think it's dead," he croaked.

Up close, with the torch shaking in Mustang's hand, the thing looked less like a serpent and more like a toppled piece of nightmare architecture—coils sagging, head twisted at an ugly angle, black ichor still leaking in slow, syrupy ropes.

He slid down the wall until his backside hit stone, legs trembling. Mustang stayed upright a beat longer, lungs sawing, then the adrenaline snapped loose.

"Why… does… everything… in this shitty… underground… hell… have… to be… so… fucking… big?!" he rasped, each broken word punctuated with a boot heel driving into the serpent's slack jaw, its side, the ruined base of its skull. Wet thuds answered him. The pick wounds gaped, weeping luminous rivulets that smeared under his sole.

The fury bled out of him as quickly as it had come. He let himself drop beside Karl, spine sliding down damp rock, the torchlight wobbling in his hand. The exhaustion hit like a collapsing ceiling—bone-deep and absolute. They were still breathing. Bruised, ringing, soaked in alien blood, but breathing.

Out of sheer spite, Mustang levered his rifle up over his knee. The stock settled against his shoulder. He sighted on those dead, black eyes and squeezed twice.

Two clean lances of energy cracked the confined air. The serpent's sockets burst in twin blossoms of boiling ichor, spattering the far wall in a sizzling spray that filled the tunnel with the acrid stink.

"Stay dead," he muttered, lowering the rifle with a hand that wouldn't stop shaking. The muzzle smoked faintly. His ears still rang from the grenades. Burnt flesh, hot metal, and coppery blood made a cloying stew in the air that turned his stomach.

Karl let out a shuddering breath, then a rough, incredulous chuckle. "Damn, Mustang," he wheezed. "Never took you for the sort to kick a corpse while they are down." There was no real reproach in it—just a tired amazement that they were still here to say anything at all.

Then Karl made another sound—half laugh, half gasp.

"Well, I'll be damned…" he breathed. He pushed off the wall, swayed, caught himself with a hand against stone. "Look, Mustang. Look around us."

Mustang frowned, forcing his eyes past the mess they'd made. Beyond the bulk of the dead snake, where the crevice widened by a handspan, the torchlight finally reached something other than rock and blood.

A low carpet spread out from the base of the wall, hugging every damp surface in a soft, uneven mat. It glowed—not harshly, but like the amaranthine light from before, but with a muted, steady radiance.

Moss. Thick, spongy, thriving in the deepest shadows.

The moss they'd been risking their necks to find.

It had been under their boots, just beyond the choke point, when the snake came.

For a second, Mustang could only stare. Then the absurdity of it twisted through his exhaustion, a bitter taste in the back of his throat.

"Son of a..." he rasped, the rest of the curse lost against his clenched fist as he pressed it to his mouth, somewhere between a laugh and a sob.

Karl's laughter spilled over, edged with hysteria. "Never been so happy to be covered in snake guts in my life," he choked out, stumbling forward. He dropped to a crouch and began scraping the glowing mat into his basket with both hands, careful and frantic at the same time. "Come on, help me— before something bigger comes lookin' for dinner."

Mustang pushed himself upright, legs protesting. He knelt beside Karl, the moss cool and damp under his fingers, its faint light catching in the black spatters on his skin. Together they worked in efficient motions, filling the woven baskets with as much of the living carpet as they dared strip away.

The tunnel stayed quiet. No more skittering beetles, no new shapes moving in the dark—just the drip of ichor, their own ragged breathing, and the soft tear of moss coming free.

When the baskets were heavy and his knees felt like ground glass, Mustang straightened. His rifle strap bit into his shoulder as he hoisted it back into place. His hand brushed the pouch at his side where they'd stowed the other ingredients.

The book was gone, lost somewhere back in the chaos: buried under rubble, or lying in the serpent's wake. But the important pieces weren't ink anymore. They were in his head, and Karl's —the list of plants, the proportions, the rough order of steps the skink had mimed out with patient claws.

Knowledge survived, even when paper didn't.

He drew a slow breath, lungs burning on the exhale. Knight's face rose unbidden in his mind—ashen, sweating, leg a ruined mess. Three days, the skinks had said. Maybe less.

Mustang tightened the flap on the pouch, felt the reassuring weight of the gathered plants and the faint, living glow of the moss in the basket at his hip.

"All right," he muttered to the dark, to the corpse, to himself. "We got what we came for."

He turned toward the way back, every step already aching, and started walking.

# CHAPTER TWENTY-SEVEN

The stink of crushed herbs hung thick in the chamber, sharp and green over the low animal reek of skink and damp stone. Each heavy *thock* of the mortar against the bowl set a faint tremor through the packed-earth floor, a slow, steady heartbeat under the crackle of the brazier.

Mustang and Karl hunched close to the shallow fire, rough bandages tugging at torn skin with every shift. Heat licked their faces but couldn't quite chase the chill out of their bones. The flames threw warped shadows up the fungal-plastered walls—brief, jerking echoes of tunnels, of teeth, of slick black scales rearing out of the dark.

The healer's presence helped in a way Mustang didn't like to examine too closely. The skink moved with an unnervingly grace, claws and long fingers working the mishmash of roots, ragged fungus, and their hard-won moss with ritual certainty. Vials and chipped bowls ringed it like offerings. Its slit-pupiled gaze never left the mixture as it ground, sifted, and steeped, the movements smooth and practiced.

"That snake…" Karl muttered, gaze fixed on the skink but seeing something else. "Never seen anything like it. Scales black as the void. Eyes like… like dying stars."

Mustang grunted without looking up. The gutted pieces of his energy rifle lay across his lap, innards exposed: cabling, coils, a scorched power coupling he'd already repaired twice. Field repairs without a bench or tools felt like working surgery with a spoon, but he'd worked with worse. His thumb traced a cable clamp while his mind replayed that amaranthine glow swallowing the light.

"Didn't feel right," he said, more to the rifle than to Karl. "Like it didn't belong to this place, just… got dropped here and everything around it learned to be afraid."

The skink ignored them, or pretended to. It tipped a viscous liquid into a clay bowl. A nose-stinging scent rolled through the room and tangled with the earthy musk of the other ingredients, making Mustang's eyes water.

"You ever seen one of those before?" Karl pressed, voice low, as if the dead serpent might somehow still be listening.

"Definitely not," Mustang answered, fingers already teasing a warped contact back into line. "Was kinda hopin' you'd have a story tucked away. You're the cave-rat. I've spent my whole life topside. You're from a forge city—figured if anyone'd heard a rumor…"

Karl snorted and shoved a hand through his dark hair, leaving a smear of dried blood. "We had cave-ins and bad air back home. Sick rock, sure. But not that. If somethin' like that had ever been down in our shafts, the whole range would've been telling ghost stories until the end of days."

Mustang let that settle and kept working. One eye stayed on his hands; the other wandered the room, cataloging exits, angles, and tools he could turn into weapons if things went sideways. Shelves sagged under bundles of dried plants. Every piece of the healer's craft was strange—but none of it *felt* out of place the way the serpent had. But a lot of it creeped him out.

The idea came to him the way good ones usually did—late, obvious, and annoying.

The rifle devoured matter and turned it into charge, stored in layered capacitors. If he could bleed a controlled trickle off one of those banks, step the voltage down, he could siphon enough to power his AR unit without cooking it. He had enough scraps to cobble a crude converter if he didn't mind the risk of it blowing in his face.

He stripped a cable, twisted leads,modified a capacitor. It wasn't pretty, but it didn't have to be. It just had to work.

Mustang slipped on his AR glasses, the familiar weight settling against the bridge of his nose, and jacked the charging lead into the port. He powered them up and pulled up diagnostics. The interface blinked alive over his vision in a faint, ghostly overlay. Battery percentage crawled upward by single digits. The signal bar in the corner stayed stubbornly empty.

No connection, but the unit was charging.

"You really think this is gonna work?" Karl asked, doubt and hope wrestling in his voice.

Mustang didn't look away from the faint numbers ticking higher in his HUD. "Damned if I know," he said. "But sitting here waitin' for the next bad surprise isn't a plan either."

He snapped the rifle's casing shut with a practiced click. The solid weight of it across his thighs grounded him, a small sliver of the familiar in a world that had gone sideways.

They watched in taut silence as the skink lifted the clay bowl in both clawed hands. Its movements slowed, taking on a ceremonial weight. Each tilt of its narrow head, each low, breathy hiss sounded like a prayer whispered into the dirt— words meant for something older than the tunnels or the city above them.

Knight's life now hung on that alien knowledge. A week ago, Mustang would've pegged this thing as just another trap waiting to close. Now it was their surgeon, their shaman, their last shot at keeping the sergeant among the living after a bad toss with a colony of giant *fucking* spiders.

The healer knelt at Knight's side and tipped the bowl. Thick, bitter-smelling liquid slid into Knight's slack mouth. The scent —sharp metal and rot and crushed greenery—burned Mustang's nose. Knight gagged at once, chest hitching in a violent spasm. His breath turned to a wet rattle, choking on the viscous brew.

The skink moved faster than Mustang expected. It cupped Knight's jaw in long fingers, rolled his head to the side, and worked his throat with firm, practiced taps. The choking stuttered, then eased. Air rasped in and out again.

"Think… think it's working?" Karl's voice was barely more than a scratch in the little hovel.

Mustang crouched closer until his knees complained, bracing one hand against the packed earth and the other against Knight's hot cheek. The skin was still fever-warm, tacky with sweat. "I don't know," he said, voice gone rough. "But what else have we got?"

The skink stayed folded beside Knight like a carved idol, eyes unblinking. It clicked, head tilting a fraction with each rise of Knight's chest. Even without knowing a word of its speech, Mustang could read the posture: waiting. Expecting *something*.

Time stretched. Knight's breaths stayed ragged, but Mustang felt the pattern shift under his hand—less frantic snatching, more steady drag. The pauses between each inhale shortened. The rattle at the top of his lungs smoothed out by a hair.

Karl let go of a breath that barely counted as a laugh. "Is it… is he gettin' better?"

"I think so," Mustang murmured. The words felt brittle. "He's not fighting to get air as hard. That's something."

The healer broke its own stillness with a sudden, bright chirp—a sound several octaves above its usual rasp. It gestured toward Knight's leg with the tip of one claw. The flesh around the seeping punctures was still angry and swollen, but no longer looked ready to split. Red had faded to a darker bruise-purple. The worst of the gloss had dulled. Less heat. Less shine.

Relief sluiced through Mustang. It didn't erase the unease—that this was all being done with tools and brews he didn't understand—but it outweighed it for the first in three days.

His muscles gave out the moment his mind let them. He eased back until his shoulders hit the wall. The rough-packed dirt felt almost soft against his spine. The room tilted then steadied.

Across from him, Karl slid down to the floor with a grunt, then barked a soft, incredulous laugh.

The skink puffed its throat sac, pleased with itself, and rattled out another string of chirps and hisses. It pointed to a woven sack tucked near the wall—the same bundle it had dragged back from its own, more elaborate den. From inside it drew more dried roots, curled leaves, and twist-knotted stems, laying them out with the care of a jeweler sorting gems.

This time the smell that rose as it worked was less harsh metal and more damp forest floor: loam, old bark, something bitter and green. Mustang watched the healer crush and knead until a thick, dark paste formed—glossy and wet, clinging to its stone pestle.

"A poultice," Mustang realized aloud. Not just a drink to pull Knight back from the edge, but something to keep the poison from taking the leg.

The skink produced a strip of leather from its sack—surprisingly smooth, oiled to keep it supple. It held the strip up, then touched the paste, then Knight's leg, then the leather again, its gaze gliding between the humans with pointed insistence.

Mustang met that look and nodded, the motion slow but firm. Message received. Responsibility accepted. "We've got this," he said quietly. It was as much for the healer's sake as his own.

Together, he and Karl set to work. Their hands felt huge and clumsy compared to the skink's deft claws. They unwound the old bandages, the cloth sticking to dried blood in tacky patches. The scent of old infection—sour and faintly sweet—rose with the peeling fabric.

Underneath, the leg looked bad, much worse than the exposed bites. The flesh around them was necrotic and blackening. Human and dwarf worked together to scour the wounds. It took time and effort, but where blackish pus had oozed earlier, only a thin sheen of clear fluid now seeped from shallow holes—a tiny, universal sign that the body had stopped losing ground and started to fight back.

The skink pressed the new poultice against Knight's ruined leg with careful, steady hands. The paste seeping into the raw flesh. Knight groaned, a low sound dragged up from somewhere deep in his chest, but his breathing didn't spike into panic. If anything, each inhale came a fraction deeper, a fraction steadier.

Mustang and Karl wound the leather strips around the limb, fingers clumsy next to the healer's precise touch. The leather pulled snug. Crude, sure—but tight, clean, and holding.

When they tied off the last strip, the skink leaned in, gaze evaluating their work. It gave a soft, approving hiss and clicked once, then padded back to a shadowed corner of the hovel. There it folded in on itself, tail curling over its toes, lids sinking shut. Not asleep—Mustang could feel those eyes still ticking open now and then—but resting, waiting.

He and Karl traded a look—tired, frayed, but undeniably relieved.

Exhaustion did what fire couldn't. Karl stretched out beside Knight, his bulk a barrier between the sergeant and whatever might decide to poke its head through the reed curtain. Mustang slid down with his back near the door, rifle within arm's reach, boots braced against the dirt floor.

Sleep came in broken snatches. Mustang dropped off only to jerk awake again, heart racing, throat raw as if he'd been shouting. A grenade's flash behind his eyes; a tunnel full of devoured light; the serpent's black, starless scales swallowing his rifle's muzzle flare. Each time he surfaced, the hovel reassembled around him: the ember-glow, Karl's snoring, Knight's harsh, wet breaths.

Karl didn't fare much better. The normally unflappable dwarf mumbled in his sleep, shoulders twitching, legs kicking as if he were still scrambling over rock. Even out cold, his hand kept drifting toward the handle of a climbing pick.

The change, when it came, was small.

Mustang woke to silence—not the suffocating, ringing kind, but a softer quiet. Something in the rhythm of the room had shifted. He blinked sleep from his eyes and focused on Knight.

The sergeant's breathing rolled in slow, even waves, like someone deep in natural sleep instead of drowning an inch at a time.

Relief hit Mustang so hard his vision blurred. He blew out a shaky breath and nudged Karl's shoulder with his boot.

Karl came awake with a snort, hand scrabbling for a weapon on instinct before his eyes found Knight. Mustang didn't say anything. The difference was right there, plain as the moss glow.

Karl's jaw worked, a rough sound catching in his throat. "He's actually…" He didn't finish the sentence, just let the air leave him in a low whistle.

The skink had already uncoiled. It glided back to Knight's side, head bobbing as it inspected the bandaged leg. Clawed fingers pressed lightly along the edge of the poultice. A stream of quick hisses and bright chirps spilled out—sharper, higher-pitched than before. Mustang couldn't parse the words, but he could read the loose shoulders, still tail, and proud flare of the throat sac.

The wound itself was still ugly when they peeled back a corner of the leather to look but the worst of the swelling had gone down. The redness had softened at the edges, the heat leached out. No smell of rot, just damp skin and herbs.

Knight groaned. Not the mindless, poisoned sound from before, but something more human: annoyed, pained, stubborn. His eyelids fluttered, squeezed shut, then fluttered again as though against bright light that wasn't there.

"There he is," Karl breathed, voice rough with something halfway between laughter and a sob.

Mustang's mouth tugged into a tired half-smile. "Looks like it," he said. He met the healer's gaze and gave a single nod. No shared words, but the meaning crossed anyway: *You did good. We know it.*

The skink dipped its head in return and stepped back, leaving them room.

Beneath the gratitude, other worries coiled tight. Knight might live. That didn't change the fact that they were buried in a city of armed lizard zealots, cut off from Bradley, Alysha, Jorgen, and the kid... and that the last time he'd seen the others, Jorgen had just shot the tail off what passed for local royalty in front of a packed crowd.

He glanced at Knight, watching the steady rise and fall of his chest, then looked to Karl. The dwarf was still staring at their friend.

"Soon as he's stable, we need to figure out how to reach Bradley. Find out what kind of mess they stirred up after Jorgen clipped that lizard's tail."

Karl snorted, the corner of his mouth twitching despite everything. "Yeah," he said. "Feels like the kind of stunt you don't just walk away from."

"Exactly." Mustang leaned his head back against the wall, staring up at the rough ceiling.

In Mustang's hand, the rifle hummed faintly, his AR unit drinking in power one slow percentage point at a time. It wasn't much, but it was a line—however thin—back toward Bradley and the others.

Karl rolled his shoulders, joints popping in the close, earthy dark, then pushed himself to his feet with a low grunt. Mustang followed, feeling the drag of bruises and half-healed burns as he slung his rifle and checked Knight one last time. The sergeant slept on, chest rising steady and sure beneath the fresh leather wraps.

"Ready?" Karl asked.

"Yeah," Mustang rasped. The brazier's smoke stung his eyes as he turned toward the reed-hung doorway, the tunnels beyond breathing cold air in his face. With Knight on the mend and a flicker of tech-lit hope in his pocket, he and Karl squared their shoulders and stepped toward the dark again, ready to trade the cramped safety of the hovel for whatever waited in the winding black.

\*\*\*

Bradley's mind went blank, then hope and dread crashed into each other in his chest so hard it hurt.

Jorgen's bark tore the silence apart. "Mustang! That means—"

Alysha was already moving. Her hand shot out, snatching the glasses off Bradley's face. The faint AR glow painted her features in blue, sharpening the hunger in her eyes. "Where?" she demanded, breath hitching. "Where is he?"

Bradley's hand went up reflexively, then he forced his fingers to unclench. "You're not gonna see him in there," he said, keeping his tone as steady as he could. "Let me—Alysha, I need to try to connect to the signal."

Static. A faint, insistent crackle from the earpiece.

Icons wavered, error codes faded in angry red. In the top corner, a tiny bar twitched—one, maybe two segments of signal. *Was he getting closer?*

"Come on," he breathed.

The crackle sharpened, stuttered, then broke open into a voice —ragged, strained, and so familiar Bradley felt his knees almost give out.

"…Karl, calm down. Yes, it connected. Bradley, do you read?"

Mustang.

Alysha slapped a hand over her mouth to smother a gasp. Jorgen let out a roar that bounced hard off the slick stone, a laugh mixed with a battle cry. Bradley just stared at the wavering HUD, the little signal bar fluttering like a pulse.

"Mustang!" he choked. His own heartbeat thundered in his ears. "Mustang, it's Bradley!" He fumbled the menu open and toggled the mic function on. "We're here—we're alive—stuck in a cell, the skinks have us, but we're alive! Can you hear us?"

Static swelled, swallowed the words. For a moment there was only the hum of the AR unit and their own ragged breathing, ghosting white in the cold, stale air.

Then: "Bradley." Mustang's voice came back distorted, but solid enough to grab onto. "What's your status?"

The signal dipped, the bar dropping, then bumping back up. Each hitch made Bradley's stomach lurch.

Alysha tore the glasses from his hands again, pressing them tight against her ear as if sheer force could pull Mustang closer. "Mustang, it's Alysha," she said, the words rushing out. "Is Knight with you? Is he okay?"

The reply came in broken shards, words chewed.

"...Knight... alive... skink healer... leg's bad but... not dead yet..."

Another burst of static, then fragments of a story slotted between the noise: a tunnel that ate light, a serpent, grenades, Karl killing something.

Bradley reached carefully this time, and Alysha forced herself to let go, passing the glasses back. He slid them on, focusing through the jittering interface.

"Mustang," he said, forcing his voice into the same briefing cadence he'd used topside. "Listen carefully. We're in the palace. Some kind of…king—or elder—has us locked in a cell. There's a ritual coming. They called it an ascension. Power struggle between crowned skinks. They took our weapons. We've got guards, but I don't think they are worried about us escaping."

Static hissed, then Mustang's voice pushed through, strained but intent. "…ascension… figures. We're in a side warren. Knight's stable—for now. Skinks helped. I've rigged the rifle to trickle-charge my AR. Signal's crap." A crackle, then: "… need metal. Antenna. Something we can run up closer to you— boost this."

Bradley's mind spun, already mapping imaginary corridors over the blank stone around him. Antenna. Conductive metal. Guards. Ritual.

"They're using Pinky—think she's a goddess. It's volatile as hell. We need to get out before the ritual. Before they decide what to do with us."

The signal fluttered low, almost vanished, then surged weakly back.

"…Copy… We're not far…"

The rest dissolved into a wash of static.

Bradley stared at the empty signal bar as it blinked, then held at a single faint line. The sudden quiet felt heavier than the dark.

"He's alive," Alysha whispered, eyes bright in the dim. "Knight's alive."

Jorgen let out a breath that turned into a rough chuckle. "Hell of a thing," he muttered. "Mustang fightin' snakes in the basement while we rot in the royal suite."

Bradley swallowed.

"We're not alone," he said, more to himself than to them. "He's close enough to reach us. That means we've got a line. However bad this gets…we've got a line."

Mustang's voice crackled once more in Bradley's ear, thin as a ghost. "…you get out? Any way to…?" The last word dissolved into static, then nothing. The tiny signal icon on the HUD winked out, leaving only the dim interface glow.

Silence crashed back in.

Jorgen let out a long breath and sagged against the spongy fungal wall. The pale growth dimpled under his shoulder, weeping a slow bead of moisture that ran down his jacket. "Well," he rasped, a wild light in his eyes, "Couldn't ask for much better." He scrubbed a hand over his face, grin not quite hiding the tightness in his jaw. "Still gotta get outta this hole before they decide we're dessert."

Across from him, Alysha's hands shook, fingers flexing and closing as if they needed something to break. Elation warred with fury in her expression, making her look feral. "How?" she demanded. "They've got us locked up like animals, and Mustang and Karl are…somewhere." Her voice thinned, frustration scalding the edges. "We don't even know where."

Bradley pulled off the glasses and stared at the dead display for a heartbeat, then forced himself to move. Sitting still felt like drowning. "Think," he muttered, more at himself than at them. "Come on, think."

He paced the narrow length of the cell, soles whispering over cold stone. The soft, steady glow leaking around the edges of the door was their only light, a reminder that things were happening outside this box while they sat and stewed.

"They're obsessed with that ceremony," he said, words coming faster as he forced his mind into order. "The 'ascension'— whoever gets to sit on that throne next. That's our window."

He jabbed a finger toward the door. He looked between them, eyes hardening. "They're not a unified machine. They're disorganized. That's our edge. If we can kick the right piece out from under them—cause a distraction when they pull us out for the ascension—we might be able to slip out while they're busy tripping over their own tails."

Alysha's eyes flashed, the hopeless slump gone from her shoulders. "And then what?" she shot back. "We bolt into a maze and hope we literally run into Mustang? He could be on the other side of the cavern."

Bradley opened his mouth, then stopped. His mind snagged on something Jorgen had said earlier—about the Duke in Denver, about playing weak in a cage until the man with the keys got sloppy.

He turned, really looking at Jorgen. The old bounty hunter was a hunched shape in the corner, but his eyes were sharp, watching Bradley over folded arms.

"That was your plan this whole time?" Bradley said quietly.

Jorgen pushed off the wall, bones cracking as he straightened. The grin that spread across his weathered face was all teeth and trouble. "You're startin' to get it…" he rasped, that coiled energy back in his stance as if the cell were suddenly too small to hold him.

\*\*\*

The interruption hit like a kicked door.

One moment the cell was all damp stone and ragged breathing. The next, the stone door shuddered and peeled aside, letting in a rush of cooler air and a glow from the corridor. Harsh hissing spilled in after it.

Bradley flinched before he could stop himself. Alysha was already on her feet, spine straight, eyes gone hard. Even Jorgen, half sprawled in the corner, came alive—pushing off the wall with that loose, predatory readiness Bradley had learned to recognize. There was nothing tired in him now.

Two skinks filled the doorway. The front one was thicker through the shoulders, scar tissue puckering the scales along its throat and jaw like melted wax. It jerked its muzzle toward Bradley, then Alysha, the clawed hand making sharp, economical gestures as it hissed and clicked.

"What now?" Alysha snapped, the words leaking out before she could swallow them back.

Jorgen stepped forward before the guards could. The motion looked slow, resigned—Bradley knew better. "Guess it's our turn for the show," he rumbled, letting the skinks grab him by the arms without a fight. "Time to break a leg, or more…"

Bradley's heart hammered in his throat. Too soon. Every instinct screamed it. Mustang wasn't ready, wherever he was; they didn't have a plan in place. They needed more time.

They weren't getting it.

He forced his shoulders to sag, let his knees soften, made his gaze go dull. Let them see a tired man, not one counting steps and doors.

Out of the corner of his eye, he saw Alysha catch on. Her chin dipped, fiery hair sliding like a curtain to hide the blaze in her green eyes. Her fists unclenched. She let the nearest skink push her, stumbling just enough to look convincing.

Jorgen grunted as the scarred one shoved him into the corridor, but he glanced back. Bradley read the message: play along. Wait for the crack.

They were driven through the bowels of the palace, the soft floor squelching under their bare feet where fungus had overgrown stone. The tunnels stank. Bioluminescent growths clung to the walls and ceiling.

More skinks than before crowded the passageways. They clogged intersections and balconies, tails knocking together, claws clicking on stone as they jostled for vantage. Hisses overlapped in a constant, feverish murmur that made Bradley's skin prickle. Some bowed low as the scarred guard passed with his human prizes; others only stared, their slit eyes bright with curiosity.

His gut tightened. Whatever was about to happen wasn't routine. The whole city felt drawn toward a single point.

They were funneled toward the broad tunnel he recognized. The closer they came, the more the sound grew: layered hissing, low rumbles, the faint clatter of spear hafts. Bradley's stomach knotted when the massive doors of hardened fungus and carved rock loomed ahead.

The throne chamber.

Memory rose unbidden: the tailless crowned skink's stare, flat and cold; the old patriarch's voice rasping about change; the first glimpse of just how deep this power struggle ran. Bradley swallowed hard. That tailless brute and his wounded pride were somewhere beyond those doors. He doubted the lizard had forgotten Jorgen's shot.

The doors parted with a grinding groan. Heat and light rolled out to meet them.

Inside, the space opened up into a vast bowl of stone. Bioluminescent clusters smeared the walls, layered over by the harsher orange of torchfire jammed into crude iron brackets. The light bled together into a restless, dirty glare that left no corner truly dark.

Every ledge and balcony was packed. Skinks lined the walls and ringed the central floor, scales glinting, spears and jagged blades catching the firelight. Their hisses rolled over one another in a dissonant, living chorus that bounced off the slick rock.

They had brought them into the heart of it.

At the chamber's heart lay the thing that froze Bradley's blood.

It wasn't a throne, or some solemn altar of stone. It was a hole —a rough, open pit dug out of the rocky earth, its rim stained dark. A fighting cage without bars. The floor of it had been scraped flat and gouged again and again. In its center, a circle of some luminous mineral had been poured and traced, a sigil that pulsed faintly, breathing sick light up into the haze of torch smoke.

The smell hit next. Blood, iron-thick and gone sour, layered over fresher copper and the reek of scaled bodies packed too close. This wasn't pageantry. This was slaughter dressed up as tradition. A place where rulership was beaten out of whoever survived the longest.

After they were lowered into the pit, the guards shoved them forward until they stood just behind the blue-tailed skink that had brought them this far. From here, the picture snapped into focus. The factions arranged around the pit. The circle meant to mark the "right" to rule. The chosen fighters.

Them.

Bradley didn't need translation to read the expectation in the crowd. They weren't honored guests. They were part of the show—foreign champions lashed to their blue-tailed ally, meat and spectacle for the "ascension."

Then he saw the dais.

The ancient king sat slumped upon his carved stone chair, withered claws wrapped around a crude scepter studded with bits of glass and bone. His eyes were half-lidded, but the torchlight picked a cold, reptilian awareness from the cracks of his face.

It wasn't the king that yanked the breath from Bradley's lungs. It was the small figure standing beside him.

"Pinky," Alysha whispered, but the name was swallowed by the rising roar of the crowd.

The girl stood in a white dress with rainbow trim, the one that had belonged to Alysha's sister. It looked impossibly fragile, a scrap of color and memory dropped into a butcher's yard. Pink hair combed, bare feet on stone, she stared out over the sea of scales with violet eyes far too wide for her small face.

Her gaze swept the chamber, searching. When it found them—Bradley, Alysha, Jorgen at the blue-tail's back—her expression changed. Her expression shifted, just a little. Her shoulders straightened, she gave the tiniest nod, and ghosted a smile in their direction.

Bradley felt Alysha's breath catch beside him. Jorgen's posture changed entirely.

The old bounty hunter's slump was gone. His spine lengthened, weight settling into his heels. The loose, lazy affect fell away like a coat. He didn't snarl or lunge, but something hard and quiet lit behind his eyes. Bradley had seen that look.

Whatever game of "broken prisoner" they'd been playing was done.

Across the pit, four other crowned skinks took their places along the rim. Each stood flanked by scarred warriors whose armor looked more like old wounds hammered into plates. Blue faced orange, purple, red—and at the far side, hulking over the others, the tailless monstrosity Jorgen had shamed. Its trunk-thick body rippled with muscle, the stump of its tail wrapped in stained leather. Even from here, Bradley could see how it leaned forward, eyes locked on them, hatred as bright as the torches.

The king raised a desiccated hand.

Noise died. Only the drip of water and the distant howl of the deep earth remained.

When he spoke, his voice raked across the chamber, amplified by the bowl of stone.

No surrender. The pit stayed open and the fight went on until there was one ruler left.

560

The king's gaze crawled over the assembled skinks, lingering with an almost hungry malice on the tailless brute.

The crowd exploded.

Hisses and roars slammed into one another, ricocheting off the vaulted ceiling. Warriors along the walls hammered spear hafts against shields. The five factions spread along the edge of the glowing circle, each cluster scooping up weapons from a pile of crude offerings—stone axes, hooked bone blades, lengths of sharpened chitin.

A guard shoved something against Bradley's chest. He looked down.

Spiked mitts. Thick leather that buckled around his forearms, each knuckle capped with a dull metal stud. Cestus, his history sims supplied, absurdly calm in the middle of all this. Gladiator gear. Close work. No distance.

He slid his hands in and cinched the straps, flexing his fingers. The weight felt wrong and right at the same time. He'd done some boxing, years ago. Officer school hadn't just been lectures and field dressings.

"Interestin' choice, kid," Jorgen muttered, accepting a flint dagger with obvious disappointment but no hesitation. The chipped edge caught the light in jagged flashes. "Never figured you for a brawler."

Bradley let out a tight breath that wanted to be a laugh.. "If we are really doing this, maybe I finally show you a thing or two."

Jorgen's mouth crooked. "That'll be the day," he said, but there was approval in the rasp. "Still... I like the spirit."

Bradley rolled his shoulders, feeling the unfamiliar drag of the mitts. The circle below them pulsed again, throwing sick light up over the snarling faces and lifted weapons.

This was lunacy.

Chaos bred gaps. Gaps meant options.

He scanned the pit rim, counting blue marks, orange stripes, the flash of purple tail, the emerald green mass that hated them. And beside him, he had Jorgen—rested, angry, and more dangerous than these lizards understood.

Insane or not, this might be the only window they'd get.

If they lived through the opening act.

The pit detonated.

Five factions hit at once, a tangle of claws and teeth and crude weapons. Flint spearheads punched through scales with wet pops. axes slammed into bone and stuck there. Knives flashed and vanished in the press, only to reappear buried to the hilt in someone's ribs. The air turned hot and wet with breath and blood, a sour stew of reptile musk, smoke, and human sweat.

Bradley and Jorgen were shoved down into it, funneled toward the glowing circle at the center with their blue-tailed patron.

A shape loomed—orange tail, plated shoulders. Bradley barely got his guard up before a scaled fist drove into his diaphragm. Pain cracked through his chest. He staggered, tasted copper, then forced his feet to plant on the slick stone.

Hit back. Don't think.

He drove a cestus-clad fist into the skink's throat. The studs bit; cartilage crunched under his knuckles. The orange warrior reeled, claws scrabbling at its neck. It recovered fast, launching into him with a shoulder like a battering ram. They went down together, sliding through warm blood. Talons raked at his side, tearing cloth and skin. Bradley trapped one wrist, rolled his weight, let old memory take over. Short, brutal arcs—temple, jaw, temple—his fists thudded against bone until his arms burned and the orange tail's strikes turned to spasms.

He peeled himself free, chest heaving, cestus slick.

Jorgen was harder to follow.

The old hunter moved through the chaos like he'd been waiting for this room his entire life. No wasted motion—just sharp pivots, sudden lunges. A spear jabbed for his gut; he stepped inside it, broke the shaft against his forearm, and turned the jagged half into a spike he slammed up under a skink's jaw. Another came at his flank with a stone club; Jorgen slipped past and let the blow glance off his shoulder, then drove his chipped flint dagger into the attacker's armpit, ripping down until the arm stopped working.

He fought like gravity didn't quite apply to him, like every collision had been rehearsed.

Across the pit, the tailless brute finally saw a path.

It crashed forward, shoulders rolling, two crimson-tailed guards glued to its sides. Jorgen answered with a roar that cut through the noise, more challenge than fear. Then they were on each other—muscle against muscle, scarred fists and stone blades caught in a vicious knot of motion that dragged nearby fighters into its orbit and spat them out broken.

Bradley ducked as a spear whistled over his head, the shaft close enough to rattle him. He smashed an elbow into the wielder's face, felt something give. Around him the skink in the blue-tail's retinue was dying fast. One took a blow that split its skull open, another went down clutching a belly wound that spilled dark coils over the circle's glowing lines. Loyalty didn't mean much when your insides were on the floor; more than one skink turned tail, trying to drag their wounded away from the worst of it.

A flash of red hair cut across his vision.

Alysha moved along the ring of combat like she'd found the one thing this world couldn't take from her—the right to stab back. Her flint daggers were crude compared to her lost blade, but in her hands they seemed to know where to go. A purple-tailed warrior lunged with a spear aimed straight for her heart. She dropped low, felt the wind of it shear past her ear, and stepped inside the reach. One knife punched up under its ribs, the other carved across the tendons at the back of its knee. The skink half-turned, gurgled, and went down hard, blood spreading in a bright fan over the already soupy mud.

Up above, the king barely moved.

He sat hunched on his throne of carved rock, clawed hand resting on his scepter, eyes dull but intent, taking everything in. To him it didn't look like chaos at all. Bradley could see it in the stillness of his shoulders: this was a tally. Who was strong enough. Who was desperate enough. Who could be broken, who had to be killed.

The mob ringing the pit didn't bother with that kind of calculation. They surged and swayed as one heaving mass, hissing and shrilling, tails whipping the air. Every kill drew a fresh wave of sound that rolled around the chamber like thunder in a cave.

The floor of the pit had become a butcher's slab. Bodies lay where they'd fallen, some twitching, some already still. The luminous circle was smeared and broken, its lines lost beneath bright blood and shattered chitin. The blue-tailed leader fought on, but an ugly gash in its side oozed steadily; each step dragged, each swing of its weapon just a fraction too slow.

Jorgen, relentless, had hammered through enough bodies to get where he wanted—right back in the tailless skink's face. The two collided again and again, the big reptile's raw strength meeting Jorgen's grinding refusal to go down. The brute's claws opened bloody furrows along Jorgen's ribs; in return Jorgen slammed fist and steel into every vulnerable joint he could find. His breaths came in ragged bursts, his knuckles were split and dripping, but his eyes were bright, fixed with one simple intent: finish it.

On the far side of the circle, a crimson-tailed warrior stumbled into Alysha's path. A sloppy bandage sagged across its torso, already soaked through. Its spear drooped. She didn't hesitate. One quick, clean stroke took its throat, another buried a blade to the hilt under its jaw. It folded with a wet sigh.

Instinct dragged her gaze toward Jorgen, to where he traded blows with the creature that he had humiliated and that would gladly tear Pinky apart out of spite. Every part of her wanted to help the old man remove the threat.

But her eyes slid higher, to the dais.

To the withered king, and to the small girl at his side in a rainbow-trimmed dress.

The old thing on the throne had taken Pinky like a toy, like a prop, the same way it'd turned this pit into a stage. The tailless skink, the orange tails, the purple and red—none of them were the true problem. They were pieces being burned down for spectacle.

The real power sat in shadowed stone, watching its world tear itself apart for the right to kneel closer to it.

Jorgen and the tailless skink crashed into each other like two things that had spent their whole lives learning how to hate.

Every strike between them landed with the weight of that history. The air around them buzzed, charged by the feral focus of the crowd and the hot stink of blood. Jorgen's breath came rough through clenched teeth, but his gray eyes were clear, cold. Rage drove him forward; it didn't blind him. It sharpened him.

The tailless skink moved on pure fury. Its remaining claws tore at the air, its chest heaving, eyes fever-bright. Both broke apart long enough to pick up a discarded weapon from the ground. It lunged again, reckless, swinging a jagged spear haft in a two-handed arc meant to cave in Jorgen's skull.

Jorgen slipped half a step to the side. The blow skimmed his shoulder instead of his head, force enough to send a jolt down his spine. He rode it, turning with the impact, using it. The flint axe in his hand feinted high, then cut low, forcing the skink to twist and bring its forearm up to block.

Bone met stone.

The axe bit into the limb with a crunch that turned a few nearby skinks away, hissing. A guttural roar ripped out of the tailless would-be king—not pain so much as raw, wild outrage.

It jerked back, tearing itself free. Where a hand had been there was now a mangled, bloody club of bone and hanging flesh.

It did not stop.

It came again, staggering, but still big, still strong, still furious. It hurled itself at Jorgen with its remaining arm outstretched, claws grasping for his throat, teeth ridges bared for his face. For a human, it would've been suicide. For the skink, it was devotion—to its own wounded pride.

Jorgen met it like he'd met a hundred bad decisions in his life.

He caught the lunging wrist, boots skidding in the blood-slick mud. Muscles bunched in his forearms. The skink's weight drove him back a step, two, but he dug in, shoulders locked. The axe, still in his right hand, rose high.

Alysha saw the whole thing through the red haze of her own fight.

Her daggers dripped, her lungs burned, but her mind stayed cold. Jorgen could hold that monster—for a little while. It wasn't the duel that worried her. It was the way the tailless one's guards were closing in, circling like sharks that smelled blood in the water. If they piled in, Jorgen would be buried under scale before he finished the job.

She scanned the pit. Bodies. Flint. Blood. No clear path to him that didn't run straight through a half-dozen armed skinks.

Her gaze snagged on a fallen warrior near the edge of the circle. A flint spear still jutted from its slack fingers, shaft sticky with drying blood, its crude point intact.

That would throw.

Alysha moved.

She slipped between two locked fighters as they grappled, boots splashing through pooled blood, shoulder brushing scaled backs. Someone snarled and swung at where she'd been a heartbeat before. She didn't look back. She vaulted over a limp orange tail, snatched the spear from the corpse's hand, feeling the rough fungus-wood rasp against her hands.

If she went for the guards, she'd pull some off Jorgen. For a moment.

She looked up at Pinky in her rainbow-trimmed dress.

The thought struck her. The king owned this room. The pit, the rules, the "goddess," all of it. As long as he sat there, this farce would go on.

Fine.

She planted her feet, drew in a breath that tasted of iron and smoke, and let the fury of a hundred small losses—the stolen blade, the stolen child, the ruined life—coil into her.

Her yell cut across the pit as she hurled the spear.

The shaft flexed in flight, a dark blur rocketing toward the dais. The king jerked, too slow. The flint head ripped through his shoulder, tearing open his rough garment and carving a bloody line along his scaled chest before slamming into the carved stone behind him with a hard, ringing crack.

Not a killing blow—but it didn't have to be.

The reaction was instant.

Silence rippled outward in a shockwave. Blades stopped mid-swing. Every skink eye in the chamber jerked upward, drawn to the sight of their ancient ruler flinching away from a human, blood welling bright against faded scales.

Then he shrieked.

The old skink's voice tore out of him, higher and fiercer than it had any right to be, shredding the hush. He snapped his scepter toward Alysha, spitting hisses and barks that even the humans could read as pure, incandescent rage.

Skinks peeled away from their duels. Warriors abandoned half-finished kills, turning their backs on rivals to swarm toward the human who had dared attack their king. Only the blue-tailed ally held position, stubbornly locked in a desperate knot of combat. The rest spilled across the pit like a living tide, weapons raised.

Alysha found herself suddenly alone in a widening ring of hostility. Flint axes, spears, and jagged knives leveled at her chest and throat from every direction. She could feel the heat of their breath, smell the musk and copper on their scales. There was no path out, no clever trick here.

Her pulse hammered, but her eyes were steady.

She'd done what she came for. Every gaze in the chamber, from the lowest gutter-skink to the king himself, was fixed on her—on the engelken who'd just torn up their sacred script. The ritual was broken. The rules were gone.

On the far side of the arena, Jorgen felt that shift like the click of a set trigger.

The tailless skink faltered for a fraction of a heartbeat, its attention dragged toward the screaming king. It was enough. Jorgen wrenched its arm aside and drove forward, bringing the axe down with everything left in him.

Stone edge met skull with a wet, cracking thud.

The blow split scales and bone alike, cleaving deep. The tailless aspirant sagged under him, legs folding, body crumpling to the floor like a dropped puppet. Its eyes rolled, then went dull, the long shudder of its body ending in stillness.

For the first time since the fight began, Jorgen straightened fully.

He looked across the pit. Alysha, a single human figure ringed in blades, stared back at him. For a heartbeat, through the roar and clash and the king's shrill commands, they shared a wordless understanding.

Then the scaled bodies and flashing weapons crashed in from all sides.

\*\*\*

Mustang squeezed the trigger. The rifle bucked against his shoulder, the familiar thrum of discharged energy rattling up his arm, syncing with the hammering in his chest. The first blast punched through the skull of the guard looming over Alysha—one heartbeat there, the next a burst of light and red mist that painted the stone in a wet halo.

The arena lurched.

Skinks reeled back, hisses snapping into a jagged chorus of confusion. Another guard snapped its head toward the sound— Mustang lined the sight, exhaled, and turned half its face into vapor. A third dropped an instant later, spine charred black where the shot had carved through its neck.

From his perch on the rough lip of stone above the royal chamber, Mustang was a phantom at altitude. Old muscle memory slid into place: control the breath, ride the recoil, let the world shrink until there was only target and trigger. Years of sniper work came roaring back, clearing the fog of underground insanity.

Every squeeze of the trigger added a new scorch mark, a new ruined corpse. Ozone bit at his nostrils. It wasn't enough. There were still too many blades, too many bodies, and they were beginning to understand that death was coming from above.

In the pit, Jorgen's snarl cut through the chaos.

He spun, shoulders squared, recognizing the crisp brutality of Mustang's work. A grin ghosted over his blood-smeared face. "Bradley!" he bellowed, voice breaking against the cavern's roar. "Get to the girl! I'll draw 'em off!"

The words snapped Bradley out of his stunned trance. He saw it now—the break in the guards' formation, the hesitation as some skinks turned toward the screaming spectators, others toward Alysha, others looking up for the unseen shooter.

There. That sliver of opening.

He ran.

The blue-tailed skink lay crumpled near the edge of the circle, its side a slick dark mess. Bradley lowered his head and drove into the nearest warrior, leather-wrapped fists crashing into scaled ribs. His form was sloppy, every strike dictated by urgency, but momentum and desperation made up for it.

The skink staggered, caught off-guard by the human's sudden ferocity. Others turned, dragged by the commotion, and the pressure around Alysha loosened.

She felt it—the gap, a breath in the crush trying to cut her down.

Her knives flashed, more instinct than thought. She stepped into a clumsy spear thrust, steel kissing tendon, then rolled past, leaving a warrior clutching a ruined arm instead of gutting her. Mustang's shots carved ragged holes in the ring closing around her; Bradley slammed into another defender from the flank; and beyond them, Jorgen became a moving wall of violence, his axe hacking down any skink dumb enough to stand between him and the humans.

She answered their efforts with a roar of her own and drove forward.

Her blades wove a brutal geometry, carving open exposed bellies, hamstrings, throats. Each kill punched another hole in the ring around her. The guards wavered—panic overtook the ritual.

Mustang watched all of it through a sniper's tunnel vision.

Targets were thinning. Too many skinks were bolting for cover, peeling away from the pit lip, scrambling along the ledges. The formation around Alysha collapsed entirely as the remaining guards realized the ritual was over in every way that mattered.

He rolled his shoulder, shifting along the ledge until he had a clearer view.

And there, framed in the torchlight on his grotesque fungi-and-stone throne, the ancient king was suddenly alone.

The attendants who'd clung to his sides had scattered, pressed back by their own panicking warriors. The old skink clutched his crude scepter in one withered hand, the fabric at his shoulder torn where Alysha's spear had grazed him. Blood seeped between faded scales. His beady eyes—once cold, amused—were wide now, bright with a feral, cornered terror.

It was a long shot. Too far, bad angle.

But the king was leaning forward, screeching commands that no one was listening to anymore, silhouette exposed against the dim glow behind the throne. Mustang breathed, slow and even.

"C'mon," he muttered under his breath, his attention pouring through the scope. "Hold still for me."

He squeezed the trigger, sending one more lance of white-hot energy screaming across the cavern toward the ancient reptilian tyrant.

Mustang hissed a curse through his teeth. The distance had been too much. The shot hit—he saw the impact, saw the ancient king jerk sideways and pitch off the throne—but it wasn't the clean kill he'd wanted. The old reptile's scream cut through the chamber, a knot of attendants flung themselves over him, scales flashing as they dragged his body away from the chaos.

The guards closest to the elder felt it. Whatever leash had kept them focused on the pit snapped taut.

They surged toward the throne in a hard, scaly wave, spears lifted to form a living wall around their wounded king. Others broke off, angling along the rim preparing to launch spears in his direction—if they could find him.

"Shit," Mustang muttered, already shifting his aim.

Jorgen had become the brutal center of gravity in the churn, axe rising and falling, his leathers soaked and slick, skink bodies slipping under his boots. Alysha flashed nearby, all red hair and flint daggers, cutting down anything she could dance into.

New shapes dropped into the pit—spectators, whipped past fear and into frenzy. They hit the mud swinging crudely chipped blades and stolen spears, more fanatics than fighters. Individually they were nothing. Together, they would be a tide.

Mustang changed tactics.

He stopped hunting single heads and started carving lanes. Each energy burst gouged through clustered bodies, searing through ribs and spines, turning tight lines of skinks into collapsing piles of meat. Heat shimmered around the barrel.

And still it wasn't enough.

For every cluster he blew apart, more skinks poured in, clambering over their own dead to reach the humans and the disgraced blue-tailed claimant. His rifle was no longer a path to victory—just a shield made of light and terror, buying seconds at a time. And probably not for much longer.

Jorgen felt the shift on the ground first.

Between one heartbeat and the next, the rhythm of the fight changed. It wasn't just the number of blades. It was the direction of the push. Before, the factions had hacked at each other as much as at the humans. Now the press moved in one direction, toward them.

Their escape had been close enough to taste, a raw possibility hanging in the air.

Now the window narrowed with every step of every lizard charging the pit.

"Bradley! Alysha!" a voice bellowed, cutting through the chaos.

Karl. The sound came from above—a ladder of rope and reed hanging in view. His broad shape loomed there, waving them up. "Come on! Now!"

Bradley staggered, a fresh tear of pain running down his side where something sharp had found soft flesh. The soaked patch on his shredded uniform clung cold and tacky against his ribs. Karl's shout snapped into place. This was as good as it was going to get. Run now or die here.

Alysha heard him, too.

Her shoulders burned, forearms numb from the constant jar of impacts. Her knives felt heavier with every swing. She backed away from another snap of skink jaws, buried a dagger under a jaw hinge on reflex snapping the brittle flint blade, and kicked the corpse clear before it had even finished twitching.

She lifted her head and saw Karl. Saw the press of bodies between them. Saw Mustang's shots ripping holes that closed just as quickly. If they stayed, the numbers alone would swallow them.

Jorgen saw it all and hesitated.

His gold-ringed gray eyes tracked the path Bradley and Alysha would have to take. Too many spears. Too many knives. No cover unless someone stood in the gap and turned himself into a wall.

He made his choice.

"I'll hold the door!" he roared, chopping the nearest skink down with an overhand blow that sent bone shards skittering across the blood-slick stone. "Move your asses!"

Bradley didn't argue. He grabbed Alysha's arm, yanked her free of a stumbling corpse, and they ran. Their boots skidded on the slick floor; skink blood smeared up their legs in dark streaks as they pushed for the ladder. A spear nicked Bradley's shoulder, spinning him sideways, but Alysha's hand was there, hauling him upright before he lost speed.

Behind them, Jorgen became a dam.

He planted his feet at the narrowest pinch of bodies near the edge of the pit and met the oncoming tide head-on. The axe rose and fell in a brutal rhythm—hacking and turning away weapons as they came. He didn't fall back. He bit out a hoarse laugh and drove forward, ramming his shoulder into a skink's chest hard enough to send it tumbling into the circle of its kin.

Mustang saw them break.

From his ledge he caught a glimpse of red hair and Bradley's battered frame clearing the lip of the pit and darting toward a shadow that resolved into Karl's broad silhouette. Relief flared —before frustration burned over it.

He dragged the rifle's sight off the fleeing pair and back to Jorgen. The old bastard was being swallowed, shapes piling on him from every side. Mustang fired, shot after shot, burning corridors into the mass. Bodies jerked and dropped, tails whipping in reflex before going limp. The heat from the rifle seared his gloved hands.

Skinks flinched from the bursts, hesitating just long enough for Jorgen to tear another one open. Light and blood made a stuttering curtain around him, a flashing barrier that slowed the horde without ever stopping it.

It was all Mustang could give them: seconds bought in energy and recoil and cooking flesh of his hands. Seconds for Bradley to dive into the tunnel. Seconds for Alysha to scramble after him, Karl hauling them inside.

Seconds, Mustang knew, that Jorgen was paying for in blood.

A shadow fell across him.

Mustang rolled onto one shoulder, rifle coming up in a smooth, automatic line—and stopped, finger easing a hair off the trigger.

Not a crimson-guard or some frothing fanatic. The skink healer loomed over him, its scales catching stray light. Its eyes, round and unblinking, held only a flat, focused resolve. Both arms were wrapped around a wicker frame loaded with squat clay pots, each stoppered with something waxy and black. An oily, chemical stink seeped from the seams, cutting through the reek of the devastation below.

In the pit, Jorgen had carved himself a pocket of space. He stepped through another a spear thrust, chopped down with his axe, kicked the dying skink clear so the next one would trip over it. But the pit's lip was a living conveyor belt of bodies; more combatants dropped in with every passing second, the sound of their hissing building back toward a roar.

On the far side, Bradley and Alysha hit the tunnel. Karl's big hand caught Bradley by the back of his jacket, hurling him into the darkness. Alysha scrambled after them.

The healer hissed—and heaved one of the pots out over the void.

Mustang slid flat onto his stomach, cheek against the heated frame of the rifle. He tracked the clay arc as it cleared the rim, tumbling toward a knot of skinks piling in around Jorgen. Somewhere under the ringing in his ears, he could hear Jorgen still roaring.

His mouth twisted into a smile.

*Mad as hell,* he thought.

He exhaled, squeezed.

The energy bolt caught the pot on its descent into the fighting pit. It bloomed white—

The explosion was a hard, concussive hammer blow. Heat rolled up the wall in a greasy wave. Skinks nearest the blast were flatted to the ground like broken toys. The roar swallowed the arena's noise, left nothing in Mustang's ears but a solid wall of high, whining static.

When his vision stopped strobing, the scene below had been redrawn.

Jorgen lay on his back near the blast radius, dust and blood smeared across his face, axe still gripped in one hand. Around him, the skinks closest to the explosion were either motionless or crawling in blind, stunned circles. Beyond that ring of ruin, others hesitated, their charge broken by shock and the roar of thunder.

A jagged, imperfect corridor torn open between Jorgen and the ladder. Not safe, but open.

Beside Mustang, the healer had dropped to one knee, clawed hands scrabbling for another pot. Its throat clicked, eyes fixed on the pit with the same cold purpose it'd worn over Knight's wounds. It thrust the next pot up toward Mustang, sinewy arms trembling under the weight.

He took it, heart still pounding out of rhythm against his ribs. The clay was slick with oil; the smell leaking from the stopper was like rancid pitch and sulfur.

"Guess we're committed," he sighed with a smile.

He tossed the pot out, felt the strain in still healing muscles as it left his hand. The healer's gaze tracked it, and gave a tiny jerk of its snout—an alien nod.

Mustang rolled his shoulder, lined up the shot, and fired again.

The second blast lit the chamber in another brutal, colorless glare. He saw every detail burned into his retinas: Jorgen curling into a ball by instinct, skinks further out raising their arms too late, a few scrambling for the walls like insects from boiling water. The boom hit a heartbeat later, slamming into the air.

Yellow-white afterimages swam in front of his eyes. The atmosphere crackled with leftover energy. Burnt sulfur rode over the coppery stink of vaporized blood.

Down below, the pit was a churning, smoking crater of half-moving forms. Skinks tried to regroup, but now every step sent them slipping in puddled gore. Somewhere in that mess, Jorgen would be clawing his way toward the ladder, using every heartbeat Mustang bought him.

The healer was already fumbling for another pot.

Mustang blinked hard, trying to clear the burn from his vision. He was starting to lose feeling in his blistered hands.

The consequences would have to wait.

He settled in behind the sight again, shoulders braced, the familiar weight of the weapon anchoring him. His finger found the trigger, steady now.

# CHAPTER TWENTY-NINE

Pinky stumbled after the retreating king, her steps swallowed by the thudding march of claws and armored feet. The palace tunnels shook with distant roars and booming explosions, chaos from the grand chamber chasing them like a stormfront. Smoke crawled along the ceiling in smudged gray veins. Her stomach rolled; she swallowed hard and kept moving.

The king loomed ahead of her, a hunched mountain of faded scales. It leaned so heavily on its attendants that each step was a lurch. Around them, the wall of guards never broke. Shields and spears hemmed her in, tails lashing, claws tapping the rock in a constant nervous rattle. Every time she glanced back, all she saw was more scale and leather and alien light—no glimpse of Bradley, Alysha, or Jorgen.

A sob clawed up her throat and stuck there. She had thought—just for a moment, when the arena exploded into chaos and streaks of plasma carved through the dark—that something would change. That the fighting would pull the guards away. That she could slip out and run to them. She had watched them stand in that horrible pit, outnumbered and outmatched, and the sight of it had burned a hard little coal of guilt in her chest. They were here because of her.

Instead she was being pulled farther from them with every turn. A pretty piece to wave in front of allies and enemies alike. A thing to trade.

Her fingers knotted in the rainbow hem, the material whispering against her shaking hands. It felt like a lie on her skin—too soft, too bright, a costume. Not armor. Not anything that could help. She was no goddess or princess, just a scared girl who needed people to save her.

The panic crept back in. The tunnels seemed to tighten, pressing in on her. Old memories—faces she couldn't quite see, hands reaching, the smell of antiseptic and burning metal —crowded the edges of her mind. She was back in a cage. Back in a lab. Back on a table. Trapped.

Something inside her uncurled.

It rose slow, like something waking at the bottom of a deep lake. It pressed against her conscious thoughts, whispering that these creatures—all of them—should be on their knees. That the skinks should be screaming at her feet, not steering her through their halls. Words that weren't quite hers brushed across her thoughts, cold and hungry: kneel, bleed, obey.

She flinched and shook her head, breaths stuttering. The feeling didn't leave. It simply…shifted, sinking its claws in deeper.

She thought of Alysha instead—Alysha's blade flashing, the way she stepped between her and danger. Bradley's stubborn, tired eyes, the way he kept thinking even when everything was falling apart. Jorgen's laugh, rough as gravel, and the way he never backed down from anything. Mustang's ferocity, and how he never missed a shot.

They were still fighting. Still alive. Every blast and scream echoing faintly down the stone said so. She wanted them safe. She wanted out of the tunnels. But threaded through all of that, bright as lightning, was another want entirely:

Show them. Show these crawling things what they are attempting to hold. Show them what it means to try to chain—

Anaku'tawa.

The name slid through her mind with the bitter-sweetness of poison on the tongue. The walls seemed to come alive, not closing in but flexing, pulsing with some slow heartbeat she could feel pulsing through her body. Everything in her vision smeared and doubled.

Pinpricks of light sparked on the backs of her hands.

She stared, wide-eyed, as tiny points of radiance pushed up through her skin, bright as stars under shallow water. A faint glow spread along her arms, pale and soft at first, then stronger. Power thrummed under throughout her body—hot and wild, slipping away like water when you tried to reach for it. It hurt, a little, but in the way a deep breath hurts sometimes. It also felt...right.

A small sound escaped her—strangled laugh—that wasn't her own.

The procession stuttered to a stop. Hisses rippled through the ranks of guards as they twisted to look. Torchlight jumped as spears lifted, tails stiffening. The king's carriers hissed sharp questions; the narrow tunnel filled with the dry rustle of scales against stone.

Ahead of them, the passage narrowed around a single hulking shape that hadn't been there before.

It blocked the tunnel, wrapped head to toe in a cloak the color of wet mud. Soot streaked the fabric. It didn't move. It just stood there, planted in the king's path.

Pinky blinked hard, dragged out of the sliding, tilting fog in her head. The lights only she could see, died on her skin, vanishing into a residual warmth, like she'd been holding her hands too close to a fire. Her fingers ached with the need to curl into fists; she forced them to unclench from the hem of her dress.

Confusion tangled with an icy thread of fear as she peered past the wall of guards at the cloaked figure. Something about the set of its shoulders, the way it occupied the space, tugged at her. Familiar.

Then a voice boomed through the hissing and the clatter of spears.

"Pinky."

Her head snapped up. For a breathless second her mind refused to believe it, but her chest knew—hope slammed into her so hard her knees nearly buckled.

The cloaked figure stepped forward. Mud-stained fabric slipped from its shoulders, and torchlight caught on a freshly shaven head.

Knight.

His face was thinner, the skin around his eyes sunken and dark —darker than the rest of him, but he stood planted, barring the skink king's escape. One leg braced, one shoulder dipped, blaster leveled over the heads of the guard wall and straight at the limping king.

"Pinky," he said again, louder. "Come here."

The skinks reacted on reflex. Hisses flared, bodies bunched, spears and crude shields angling toward him in a ragged line. Tails lashed the stone, claws scraped as they shifted, a living barricade tightening around the king.

Knight didn't flinch.

Pinky was already moving. The press of bodies broke for a heartbeat as the guards glanced between their wounded ruler and the strange human blocking the passage. She slipped through a gap at knee height, bare feet slapping wet stone, dress hem whispering around her ankles. By the time Knight's free hand came up with something metallic, cold and egg-sized, she had both arms locked around his thigh, burying her face in the smoke-stained cloth.

He yanked a pin free with a sharp twist and threw the device low, skipping it off the rock at the front rank of guards. It bounced once, twice. The hiss of a fuse cut through the hissing voices, thin and deadly.

The skinks hesitated, backing away a step despite themselves. The king, half-supported between its carriers, spat a harsh command, forcing them forward. Spears came up again, their points trembling.

The grenade went off in a choking blossom of gray.

Noxious fumes roared down the narrow tunnel, swallowing torchlight in a rolling wall of smoke. The air turned thick and bitter in an instant, reeking of burnt resin and chemicals that clawed at eyes and lungs. Flames guttered behind the veil, throwing warped shadows that writhed in the roil.

Out of the chaos, Knight was there. Beside her, she hugged him overjoyed at seeing one of her friends, at being rescued.

Pinky coughed, the sound muffled against Knight's leg. The world narrowed to the drumbeat of his heart under her ear, the forest of bodies and tails vanishing into shifting gray.

Caught between suffocating smoke and the unknown human threat, the skinks surged in a messy, instinct-driven rush instead of a drilled formation. Some lunged blindly toward Knight. Others flailed sideways, crashing into their own line, hissing in anger and confusion. Somewhere, the king's voice coughed out more orders, but the words shattered against the echoing chaos.

***

Knight's vision vanished as he waded into the first wave. Smoke burned his eyes, turning everything into a smear of orange and black. But he didn't need to see to know where they were. He could smell the reptile filth in front of him. He could hear claws skittering, armor scraping, ragged breaths growing closer.

His leg throbbed, venom damage aching deep in the meat despite the skink healer's work. Running wasn't an option. Standing had always been his specialty.

"Hold on," he grated.

He shifted his weight, dragging Pinky a fraction behind his hip, and dropped his stance. The blaster tracked by sound, not sight. He fired in short bursts, sweeping the tunnel where the noise was loudest.

Stabs of white heat lanced into the murk. Each shot carved a brief, unbearable hole in the smoke—enough to silhouette open jaws, raised spears, and startled eyes—before the darkness rushed back in. Screams followed. Hot droplets hit his hand and forearm, spattering his knuckles as one skink pitched forward at his feet, its hissing ending in a boiling gargle.

He pivoted, putting his shoulder to the rock wall to narrow the angle they could reach him from, letting the stone take some of the crashing weight of the next body that barreled through the fog. Scales scraped his sleeve. He drove the muzzle up under where he guessed the chin would be and fired.

Anger burned away the ache and the exhaustion. It roared in him like a furnace, feeding every decision. They had dragged this child in front of a throne and presented her like an offering. They had put hands on her, called her goddess or tool—it didn't matter which. They had taken his people.

They would pay. *They would die.*

Another shape lunged out of the gray, too close for comfort. Knight braced his bad leg, hooked an elbow around Pinky to keep her from being torn loose, and slammed his fist into the oncoming chest. Something cracked; the body crumpled, claws scrabbling uselessly.

Super-heated blood splashed his fingers as he angled the blaster down and fired point-blank. The tunnel stank of it now, copper over musk, layered with the acrid tang of ozone from each shot.

Somewhere, the king was still *talking* in that vile hissing language. The sound that had carried so easily in the throne room now sounded weak and pathetic. It sounded less like a sovereign and more like a coward begging for strangers to save him.

The smoke began to dissipate, dragged along the tunnel by a sluggish draft. Shapes emerged—first suggestions, then bodies. One skink sprawled on its back, chest punched open. Another lay draped over a fallen spear, limbs twitching. Still other littered the ground with cauterized, fist-sized holes in them from his blaster.

The tunnel had gone quiet, except for the ragged breathing and the wet, weak sounds of things trying to stay alive and too stupid to understand they were already dead. His lungs felt like they'd been scraped with sand, but he was working. He ignored the discomfort.

Beside him, Pinky let out a strangled sob.

He glanced down. Her face was streaked with soot and tears, hair clumped in damp pink strands against her cheeks. She clung to his leg hard enough to make his already abused muscles protest.

"It's okay," he said, or tried to. The words came out hoarse. "You're safe now. I won't let them hurt you anymore."

He tightened his grip on the blaster until his knuckles blanched under the grime. He could feel every tremor running through her, each small shudder traveling up through his leg. He wanted to promise her more than a temporary reprieve in a corridor full of corpses. Wanted to say it would all end, that he could drag them back to sky and sun and something like normal. Whatever that might be.

He wasn't sure that was true. He'd bleed making it as close to true as he could. He would make all the skink bleed for it if her had to.

A scrap of sound carried from deeper in the tunnel—a scuff on stone, a strained whimper trying not to be heard and failing. Old, cracked, bitter. The king.

Knight's jaw clenched. Of course the bastard hadn't died yet.

"Stay here," he told Pinky, voice dropping into the clipped tone of an order. "Don't move."

Her fingers dug into his cloak, a mute refusal. He paused, torn between keeping her with him and shielding her from what he was about to do. He looked down again.

Her eyes were huge in the half-light, but there was something else in them now besides fear—that strange, deep gleam he'd seen before, like light shining through stained glass from the wrong direction. Innocent face, not-so-innocent edges. Whatever she was, "helpless" wasn't the right word.

"Fine," he muttered. "Stay close. Watch my back. But don't get under my feet."

She nodded quickly and shifted behind him, one hand still locked on the back of his cloak.

He moved forward with a careful, dragging gait, bad leg reminding him of every second he'd spent fighting to keep it. His boots carved channels through cooling blood and slid on loose scales. Charred fragments of clay crunched under his

591

heel. Every step set little shocks up his spine, but the sound ahead pulled him on.

The king came into view a few yards on, outlined against the darker smear of stone. The once-imposing reptile lay on its side, shoulder and hip ruined, thick tail twitching uselessly. It clawed at the rock, trying to drag itself away, one leg trailing limp and dead behind it, talons leaving weak scrapes in the damp grit.

It looked smaller now. More fragile. Stripped of the throne and the crowd and the presence, it was just another animal.

Knight leveled the blaster, sight settling between its hunched shoulder blades. The movement felt simple, right even. One squeeze, and this part would be over.

"Nowhere left to run, lizard," he rasped.

The king froze. Its head turned, until one milky, hate-clouded eye fixed on him. The other lid drooped, burned and swollen. It gazed past Knight's shoulder, searching the smoke behind him for rescue that wasn't coming.

It hissed—short, pained, full of venom it no longer had the strength to spit through action or words.

Knight stepped closer. The tunnel floor popped under his boots as he crushed brittle flakes of scale. Each step made the old reptile flinch, its body curling in on itself as far as its broken frame allowed. Its fear was a physical thing.

Heat rose behind Knight's eyes, the heat of rage, of wrath, of retribution. The moment they'd told him she was gone, that they'd lost her. The nights he'd lain awake listening for a child's voice that never came.

All of that fury found its focus in the terrified face in front of him.

"You and I," he said, "we've got unfinished business."

The king hissed again, softer this time, a threadbare edge of defiance over a deep well of fear. Knight could have ended it with a trigger pull. Clean. Efficient. The way he'd been trained.

He lowered the muzzle a fraction instead, letting the barrel hover just above the creature's spine.

"It isn't really justice unless you have to scrub it off of your hands," he went on, almost conversational, though his grip shook. "It's slow. It sticks. Leaves a mark that lingers."

The words tasted ugly in his mouth, but they were honest.

He slung the blaster up onto his shoulder in one smooth motion, freeing his hands. The king's body jerked at the gesture, as if some part of it understood that this was going to be worse. Knight's boots whispered over stone as he closed the last of the distance.

Behind him, Pinky didn't speak. The link between them stretched taut—her small shadow sliding with his, the tunnel holding its breath as the old tyrant cowered on the floor and the human who had come for him kept coming.

"We should go find the others," she whispered, voice thin and frayed.

Knight didn't look at her.

His thumb found the activation stud on the multi-tool. The plasma blade hissed to life with a hungry hum, bathing the tunnel in a hard blue-white glare.

"We will, Pinky," he said, the words pushed through clenched teeth. His voice didn't sound like his own. "I'm almost done here."

He stepped in.

One brutal, downward stomp took the elder skink's ruined leg at the knee.

The cutting tool met flesh with almost no resistance. There was a flash, the harsh crackle of vaporized tissue, the stink of cooked meat. The king's scream ripped down the passage, a ragged, animal sound that bounced off the slick stone and came back at them from every direction.

Blood burst out in a brief, violent arc before the wound seared over, hot crimson splattering the floor in a wide fan.

Knight's lips peeled back in something too sinister to be a smile. The sound hit some pleasurable place inside him and he kept going.

"That's for getting my attention," he rasped.

The king tried to drag itself away, claws scrabbling uselessly. Knight followed, step for step. The super-heated blade whispered across its back in a diagonal line. Scales split, black-red fluid welled up and ran. The reptile bucked and screamed again, voice breaking.

Pinky watched, rooted to the stone. Her fingers had slipped from his cloak but still twitched, as if they wanted to grab him again. Her face was pale under the grime, eyes wide and dark, yet there was no flinching in them—only a tight, intent focus, as if a part of her was taking notes.

Knight didn't see it. He moved in a tight circle around the king, breathing hard, the plasma's harsh glow cutting stuttering arcs over the walls. Each cut came easier than the last, hatred finding new places to land now that it had a body to abuse.

"And that," he said, voice dropping into something almost calm, "is for taking someone I care about."

The king had stopped trying to fight back. Its limbs shook, long body smeared with its own blood. Wet, rattling breaths rasped in and out of its chest, each one a struggle.

Knight stood over it, shoulders rising and falling. His hand steadied on the grip.

He sank the plasma blade slowly down into the chest, just off center, through bone and cartilage softened by age a fraction of an inch at a time. There was resistance, then a sudden, sick little give. The king's last sound was a strangled gurgle. Its body arched once, a full-body spasm, then sagged. The light in its eyes clouded and went out.

He left the blade in long enough to be sure. When he thumbed it off and pulled back, the tool felt heavier in his hand than it had any right to.

For a moment he just stood there, breathing hard. Blood soaked the hem of his cloak, speckled his boots, dried in tacky streaks along his hands and forearms. The manic edge in his gaze ebbed, leaving a hollow flatness behind it, like someone had thrown a switch and cut all the feed.

Pinky stumbled back a step. Her face was a knot of things— concern, relief, and something darker that didn't belong on a child's features. The tunnel swallowed the king's absence quietly. Only Knight's ragged breaths and the slow drip of blood broke the silence.

He shoved the multi-tool away. The haunted look was already creeping into his expression, as if the weight of what he'd done was catching up to him now that there was no one left to swing at.

"Let's go," he said, voice down to a scrape. "We still have to find the others."

\*\*\*

Alysha's legs went out from under her. She hit the tunnel wall hard, cold stone biting through sweat and bruises. Beside her, Bradley slid down in a graceless heap, breath sawing in and out like broken glass.

Karl's hands came into view, big and calloused, offering them the gear the skink had taken from them.

"How...?" Bradley managed, voice shredded.

Karl cut him off with a lopsided smile that didn't reach his eyes. "We'll unpack that particular miracle later," he said. "Right now, we need to—"

The rest vanished under a thunderclap as an explosion hit like a collapsing wall. Air slammed through the tunnel. Dust and grit cascaded from the ceiling, stinging Alysha's eyes, coating her tongue in chalk. The rock under her boots shivered.

Bradley went corpse-pale. "Jorgen..." The name crawled out of him, barely more than breath.

Alysha's heart lurched. For a moment she was back in the pit—blood everywhere, Jorgen's roar, the tailless skink's skull opening under his axe. Her body moved before the rest of her caught up. She shoved herself upright, every muscle howling protest. The returned pistol vanished into Bradley's hand; her own fingers closed around the familiar weight of her blade. The grip sat against her palm like something that had been missing, a small, solid piece of herself.

"I'm going back for him," she said.

Karl stepped in front of her, shaking his head. "Not the best of ideas," he said quietly. "Mustang's doing his thing, and buying us time. Jorgen…" He swallowed, jaw working. "Jorgen'll probably be okay. Right now, best way to help is get as far from that cage fight as we can. Let them find us instead of us running back into a cave-in."

The words hit like a bucket of cold water. Alysha's grip tightened on the hilt until her knuckles ached. Every instinct clawed at her—turn around, dive back in, put her blade between Jorgen and the world. Walking away felt like cowardice, like abandoning him to bleed out alone.

Karl must've seen it all on her face. His tone softened, took on the weight of someone who'd buried more than one friend under rock and bad timing. "We get to a spot that isn't about to come down on our heads," he said. "Somewhere we can think. Then we figure out the next move. Right now, going back doesn't help anyone."

The tunnel thrummed with distant echoes—muffled roars, faint hissing, the aftershock of explosives rattling through earth. Over it all, Alysha could hear her own pulse, a hard, frantic pounding in her ears.

*He's right,* some grim corner of her admitted. *Charging back in means Jorgen has to worry about you too.*

Jorgen would never hesitate. He'd barrel straight into hell for her, for any of them, without a second thought. The thought twisted something sharp in her chest.

Bradley had pushed himself up to one knee, pistol clutched tight. Dust streaked his face, his eyes too wide in the dim fungal glow. He looked from her to Karl and back again, caught on the same knife edge she was. The line of his jaw screamed that he wanted to go back—that leaving anyone behind felt like one more betrayal he couldn't live with—but he would reason it out too.

Common sense. Or survival instinct. Or both.

He shut his eyes for a moment, pulled one breath, then another, and stayed where he was.

"We can't just leave him," Bradley said at last. They echoed down the tunnel, hollow against the distant booms of Mustang's handiwork.

"We're not," Karl replied. There was no softness in it, only iron. "But we need to be smart about it. Find a place to regroup, then maybe—maybe—we circle back and actually make a difference." He jerked his chin toward the way they'd come, where the air still shivered with aftershocks. "Right now, though…" He gave a lopsided shrug and cocked an eyebrow at Bradley.

Alysha drew a slow breath and forced her fingers to unclench around the hilt of her blade. The weight at her hip seemed to double, dragging at her exhaustion. "Lead on," she said. It came out a ragged whisper, but it held.

Karl turned without another word and pushed deeper into the maze. They followed.

Ahead, Karl moved with a miner's certainty, picking slits in the stone no sane surface-dweller would've called a path. Side passages took them one by one, swallowing the worst of the roar behind.

Vibrations rolled through the earth in dull waves, rattling pebbles from the ceiling. Each distant boom drew an involuntary flinch from Alysha, her mind painting Jorgen's silhouette at the center of every shockwave—ax raised and laughing as the skink tried to bury him.

That same laugh felt like a ghost trailing them through the dark rather than a promise he'd walk out behind them.

After what felt like an hour and could've been ten minutes, Karl lifted a hand. "Here," he murmured.

They'd squeezed into a narrow fissure, little more than a crack in the mountain's ribs. The rock pressed close on both sides, slick with condensation. Here, the thunder of the arena was reduced to a low, constant rumble—distant weather instead of the sky falling.

"We rest," Karl said, exhaling hard. The word carried a frayed thread of relief. "Catch our breath, then we head for the rendezvous point."

Bradley let his shoulders sag into the damp wall. The stone leached heat out of him, but his legs were done arguing. He shut his eyes for a moment, then opened them again, gaze unfocused on the cramped stretch of floor. "Mustang," he said quietly. "He saved us…"

"Yeah," Karl replied, a short huff of air that almost qualified as a laugh. "And you're probably never gonna hear the end of it."

\*\*\*

The sight of his friends vanishing up the ladder was a strange kind of mercy. One heartbeat they were trapped in the pit with him, the next Karl was waving them off and hauling them away from this mess. They were alive. Getting out. That was enough to shave the edge off the panic gnawing at him.

Hope. Damn nuisance, that.

Jorgen's world narrowed to steel and scale. The flint axe sat just right in his hand, rough haft biting his palm, every swing sending a jolt up through old bones that suddenly didn't feel so old. He hacked through a skink's guard, the blade splitting collar and ribs. Hot blood splashed his forearm, slick and coppery, stinging when it hit an open cut. He barely registered it.

He had managed to get up the ladder. Would've been nice if the fighting had been contained to the pit. However, once over the edge he could see that it was lizard on lizard violence as far as the eye could see.

Fuck it. Let them kill each other.

There—beyond the press of bodies, beyond the churned mud and smeared gore—was the prize. Next to a tunnel entrance: his rifle's familiar profile, the sag of his gunna sack. Everything they'd stolen. Everything he wanted back.

Another clay pot sailed overhead, wobbling through the smoke. Jorgen's eyes tracked it on instinct. Follow the arc—back to the ledge, to Mustang lining up the shot like some lesser god of overkill. Jorgen didn't think, he just moved—dropping the axe and throwing himself sideways, hands slapping over his ears.

The blast hit like a hammer made of air. Sound punched through his chest, rattled his teeth, turned the world into white light and a rushing roar. Gravel and lizard bits pattered over his back.

He rolled to a knee, scooped up the axe, and kept going. No time to pat himself down. Nothing felt broken that wasn't already.

A spear jabbed in from the side, clumsy, desperate. He twisted, felt the rough stone scrape his shoulder instead of the point going in, then answered with a backhand swing. Flint met skull with a meaty crack that vibrated up his arm. The skink folded, eyes empty before it hit the floor.

More adrenaline flooded him. Limbs that had been lead in the cell now felt light. Every breath burned but fed the fire in his chest. Another warrior lunged, claws spread wide. Jorgen stepped into it, drove the axe down in a brutal chop. Bone parted; the reptile split open from shoulder to gut, hot viscera slapping the ground.

He grinned—broad, feral, blood-slick teeth bared. The nearest skinks faltered. He saw it: the stutter in their advance, the flare of their pupils, tails twitching in uncertainty. Rage alone they understood. Something that enjoyed this? That rattled them.

Behind it all, another roar rolled through the arena, deeper than the rest. Another of Mustang's blasts slammed into the far side of the pit, tossing skinks and chunks of stone skyward. Dust and smoke washed over Jorgen, tasting of burned meat and sulfur.

Beautiful. Distraction and deterrent, packaged in fire.

The distance to the gear pile shrank—three bodies, two, one. His fingers tingled, itching for the cool, familiar grip of his rifle, the simple pleasure of a weapon that didn't rely on getting close enough to smell his enemy's breath. The melee had its charm, but he preferred to keep his blood on the inside.

A skink stepped out of the press—a little taller, plates thicker, crude armor strapped tight over its shoulders and chest. A cruel spear rested easy in its claws, not gripped in panic but balanced, practiced. Its eyes swept the field, found Jorgen, and fixed there with cold recognition.

Not another soldier, he realized as his grin stretched his face. A handler. A champion.

Jorgen shifted his stance, weight settling, axe rising in a lazy guard that wasn't lazy at all.

"Come on, then," he muttered under his breath, throat raw, ears still ringing. "Let's see what you got, bigg'un."

Frustration flared, then settled into a familiar, gnawing weight. Now that the adrenaline was dying, every cut and abrasion he'd ignored coming back with interest. His ribs burned every time he drew breath. His arms felt packed with wet sand. The air was so thick it felt like something you had to chew before you could breathe. Retreat wasn't an option. Leave this one standing and the rest would find their courage again.

The skink moved with a cold, reptilian grace that made his skin crawl. It circled him, spear held low, barbed head tracking his chest. Not a thug. A hunter. It hissed a challenge, tail cutting a slow arc over the smeared stone as it tested his footing, his timing, the sag in his shoulders. In those slit-pupiled eyes he saw it—anticipation. It had been waiting for someone who could hit back.

Jorgen shifted his grip on the axe, bringing it up into a tighter guard. Sweat slid into one eye, salt burning. He blinked it away and met the skink's gaze, letting it see the same thing. I'm tired. I'm hurt. Come find out what that buys you.

They came together in a rush of motion and sound. Flint rang off stone, haft against shaft, the spear a streak of pale barbs in the torchlight. The skink was fast—too fast for a man his age to be trading blows with—but speed wasn't everything. Jorgen's body moved on old wiring, reflex more than thought: twist, catch, shove, step inside and take away his space.

Pain lanced across his side. The spear's tip pierced through leather and skin stealing his breath. He grunted, tasting iron as his teeth clicked together. The smell of his own blood rose under the heavier reek of skink musk— a reminder of how quickly this could all go sideways. Another inch and that thrust would've opened him like a sack.

The skink pressed in, sensing the hit. Jabs came in flurries now, the barbed point nipping at his ribs, his throat, his legs. Jorgen gave ground because he had to, boots skidding on stone slick with gore. Each impact of spear on axe jarred through his forearms, leaving his hands buzzing. His shoulders screamed protest. His lungs burned. Somewhere behind the ringing in his ears he could still hear the crowd, the distant crack of Mustang's rifle, but here, in the tight circle, there was only footwork and not dying.

Anger rose, cutting through the exhaustion where no second wind remained. This wasn't how he went. Not after everything. He was Jorgen, stubborn old bastard who'd outlived syndicate bosses, cult nuts, wild-eyed raiders, and one self-proclaimed "Duke" of ruined Denver. He'd bled in worse places than this.

But even as he forced the spear aside with a desperate parry that rattled his teeth, the truth dug its claws in. His arms were slower. His feet heavier. The skink was fresh enough, smart enough to see it. One slip—one bad step—one heartbeat late, and that little toothpick wasn't going to graze him.

It was going to finish the job.

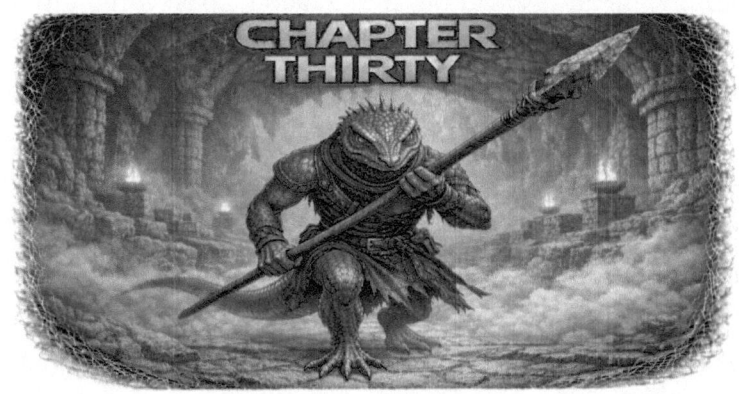

# CHAPTER THIRTY

Mustang's climb down from the perch was controlled, hands and boots finding holds by muscle memory, but there was no caution left in him. Every explosion he'd called down into that pit had wound him tighter, pulled him closer to the darker place of his mind.

The arena had come apart.

Through gaps in the rock and the thinning smoke, he caught flashes of skinks turning on each other—axes rising and falling, spears jabbing at their own kind. Torches guttered in the haze, throwing ragged light over scales slick with blood. He couldn't hear their hisses anymore; the rush in his ears drowned everything else out. He didn't need the sound to read it. He recognized panic, recognized the way this hierarchy cracked when they kicked hard enough at the base.

The skink healer followed him along the narrow shelf, claws clicking quietly on the stone. Its eyes were blown wide in the torchglow, but there was no fear in its posture. Just that strange, intent fascination. It clutched its basket tight to its chest like relics it refused to drop, the pungent reek of oils and charred herbs threading under the sharper smells of singed skink and ozone.

The rifle throbbed against his palm, hot enough that the polymer burned through his gloves. He noted that this overheating problem was likely the reason the Telluric Foundation had mothballed this technology. He could feel the numbed parts of his hand where the meat had been cooked.

He lost track of how many shots he'd fired. How long he'd ridden the rifle past sane. The counter in the back of his skull— the one that usually ticked off energy expenditure and ammunition—had gone fuzzy somewhere between the third blast and the first airburst. Something had rooted itself in him during that barrage, a bright seed of sadistic joy. Every trigger pull had been one more step off the safe edge, and he'd liked it far too much.

Part of him wanted the noise to stop. Wanted the smoke to clear, the screaming to die down, the rifle to cool in his hands so he could think again. Underneath that, buried deeper, another part grinned at the ruin and wanted to see how far he could push before he finally snapped.

He hit the tunnel lip where he'd stashed his gear and pulled himself up onto the ledge. The stone here was cooler, the air less choked with ash. He turned.

The healer had dropped to a crouch just inside the mouth of the passage, watching him. Its throat fluttered once. Those lidless eyes, for all their alien slant, held something he recognized—

gratitude, curiosity, and the taut, bitter satisfaction of someone who had just kicked a corrupt society in the teeth.

Mustang gave it a tired smile. "Hell of a house call," he muttered.

It couldn't understand the words, but it seemed to catch the tone. With a low hiss it ducked its head in a short, deliberate bow. Turning on its heel, it slipped back toward the smoke and screaming, tail lashing as it vanished into the shadows.

He watched it go. Maybe he'd just delivered a wound grave enough to the established order for the right skink to begin healing his people. Then again, maybe he'd just blown holes in the wrong load-bearing walls. Revolution, civil war, quiet collapse—whatever came next, it was going to be ugly. The weight of it brushed his shoulders.

Then he shrugged it off. He had enough of his own problems to deal with.

His pack waited where he'd left it, wedged behind a shelf of dead fungus. When his fingers brushed along the interior, they rattled over slim pickings—couple of grenades, a shaped charge, not nearly enough, if the road ahead was anything like the one behind.

"It'll have to do," he muttered under his breath, clicking the last clasp home and slinging the pack over one shoulder.

The adrenaline high that had carried him through ebbed in fits. His head pounded with each heartbeat, a dull hammer blow behind his eyes. A tremor ran through his fingers when he checked the rifle's status panel; the numbers swam for a second; the still living flesh of his hands began to register their injury. Heat warnings, power draw spiking, barrel stress ticking toward red.

He forced his hand still despite the growing pain, and forced his breathing slow. In through the nose. Hold. Out through the mouth. Again. The old drills rose up unbidden, cutting across the jagged urge to run back and fire until the rifle tore itself apart.

Find the others. Get out.

The words settled into a rhythm in his mind, something solid to march behind. Not burn it all. Not see how many more he could drop. Just: find them, get clear.

He stepped back to the lip of the ledge and risked one last look out over the arena. Skinks were still moving down there, but in knots and clumps, shoving, breaking, reforming. Whatever order they'd strutted when this started was gone.

Turning away, Mustang set his shoulders and headed into the tunnels in the direction Karl had taken Alysha and Bradley. The route was etched in his memory from hurried planning—two rights, follow the incline, then a narrow cut that stank of stagnant water and bat guano. Away from the pit. Away from the king's seat. Away from the center of the storm he'd helped kick loose.

The echoes of distant explosions chased him down the passage like ghosts on his heels.

The rifle rode heavy on his shoulder, more than just metal, polymer, and overheated coils. Every step made the strap bite a little deeper, each jolt a reminder of what he'd just done with it. Tool or crutch. Lifeline or habit. Soldier, or just a man who'd learned to solve every problem with a trigger pull. The question nagged at him in the quiet, dogging his heels as faithfully as any shadow.

*Had they made it out? Had Karl actually gotten them clear, or was he walking toward a pile of bodies cooling?* Fear for himself became background noise; fear for them rose like a tide of bile.

He slowed his pace without meaning to, trading speed for silence. No more grand entrances, no more explosions for the hell of it—one wrong noise in the wrong tunnel could bring a clutch of angry, confused skink down on him. He kept to the edges where the rock broke in jagged shelves, one hand brushing the wall now and then to steady himself, fingers coming away gritty and damp. Every bend of the passage hid a pocket of deeper shadow, each cross-tunnel a question mark.

So he walked, alone with the drip of unseen water and the soft rasp of cloth and webbing against his gear. When the doubt tried to crawl back in—images of Jorgen buried under skinks, of Alysha's blade going still—he shoved it aside and focused on a single, stubborn thought: they were alive until he saw proof otherwise. Karl was too careful. Bradley was too careful. Alysha was too skilled. And Jorgen was just too damned ornery.

They were alive. They had to be.

\*\*\*

The world tipped sideways, then narrowed to the jagged point of the spear. Chipped flint caught the torchlight as it drove for Jorgen's chest. He saw the intent in the skink's eyes—that cold, greedy flash that said it knew he was too slow, too tired, too old to get out of the way.

He knew it too. His legs felt thick, joints screaming as he tried to twist clear. Not fast enough. Not anymore.

A blur of blue scales slammed in from the side with a hiss that split the air. The impact knocked the spear off line—just enough for the world to become noise and motion.

When his mind caught up, he found himself staring at something that made his gut lurch.

The blue-tailed skink lay sprawled at his feet, chest heaving in short, wet breaths. The spear that had been meant for his heart jutted from its ribcage instead, blood spilling in a dark, slick sheet across the stone. Its fingers twitched, then stilled.

A sound tore out of Jorgen that he didn't recognize—a strangled curse of denial. This was the stubborn bastard who had led them to the city, who had fought with them, for them— more than once. Who had just stepped in front of a killing blow meant for him.

His knees almost went out. His hands, slick with skink blood and his own, tightened on the rough haft of the axe.

Heat answered.

It started in his chest—a hard, sudden bloom that shoved against his ribs—and rushed down his arms. The axe shuddered in his grip. Golden light seeped from the cracks in the fungus-bound head, then surged, pouring along the grain like molten metal. It brightened, throbbing in time with his hammering pulse until the crude weapon glowed as if it had been dragged fresh from a forge.

The hair on his forearms lifted. His teeth buzzed. A pressure built behind his eyes, sharp enough to make him wince. The light swelled, catching in the blood slick on his fingers, painting his battered knuckles in molten gold.

Something else answered too, deeper than his own anger—a slow, grinding weight he didn't recognize.

The stone around him drank the light and threw it back. He caught the reflection in a patch of wet rock—his own face ringed by a brilliant corona that hovered just above his tangled hair, a band of gold that pulsed with each ragged breath.

Across from him, the armored skink had gone utterly still. Its spear dipped. Wide, lidless eyes darted from the dying blue-tail to the glowing axe to the ring of light over the human's head. Horror and something that looked a lot like reverence warred in its stare.

Jorgen swallowed, throat raw. Grief, fury, and that alien heat knotted together in his chest until there was nowhere for any of it to go but out.

He lifted the glowing axe in both hands, shoulders screaming, and let the roar tear free—broken, jagged, and loud enough to shake dust from the ceiling as it slammed through the cavernous room.

All he saw was his target.

The armored skink, spear still slick with the blood of others, stood framed in the wrathful glow. The rage in Jorgen flared, ready to drive the axe straight through its skull.

Then he really looked at it.

Not at the armor or the weapon, but at the way its fingers shook on the haft, at the twitch in its jaw, at the way its gaze kept flicking past him—toward the fallen blue-tail, toward the shattered arena, toward the tunnels where its world was coming apart. Not a monster. Just another bastard trapped under a rotten throne, same as he'd been in Denver, same as half the people he'd hunted for credits.

He saw fear.

The heat in his chest stuttered. The halo above his head winked out, like a dying bulb. Golden light bled away from the axe, leaving nothing but flint edge, crusted skink blood, and his own shaking hands.

Jorgen lowered the weapon. His shoulders sagged under a weight that had nothing to do with years.

"Go," he rasped. His voice sounded foreign to his own ears, hollow and doubled, like it was coming from down a different tunnel. He swallowed and forced the words out again, clearer. "Take your wounded. Get out."

The skink stared at him, spear half-lowered, its throat pulsing. Disbelief sat plain on its reptilian face. For a second he thought it might come anyway, might take the gamble and try to finish what it started.

Instead, it bent—slowly, like a man moving through a bad dream—and scooped up the broken blue-tail's body. Its eyes never left Jorgen. A ragged hiss rasped out of its chest, more exhausted than defiant. It jerked its chin, and the handful of survivors limped to obey: dragging the injured, hoisting the dead, stumbling past without meeting Jorgen's eyes.

They gave him a wide berth, as if the space around him burned.

When the last scaled back vanished into the smoke-hazed tunnels, his legs stopped pretending. He dropped to his knees like someone had cut his strings.

The golden glow was gone. Just the stink of death, the fading ring of screams from deeper in the city, and the ringing in his ears. The only proof anything had happened was the axe beside him, still tacky with gore, and the echo of that impossible heat crawling around in his ribs.

He'd always been able to call the halo, as long as he could remember—cheap parlor trick, never more than light above his head when he needed to scare someone straight or bluff his way past a superstitious drunk. This was the first time it had done anything like that. The first time it had seemed to have its own will.

The loss of his friend—and that's what he had been, in the end—it hit him harder than he wanted to admit. *Stupid*, he thought. *Stupid to feel anything for a lizard*. But the way the limbs had sprawled—the way all the life had just left him—that was familiar. Too familiar.

*Danny...*

Jorgen's hands shook as he stared at them.

A bitter taste climbed the back of his throat. What the hell was he now? Killer, sure. He'd made peace with that a long time ago. But this—glowing like some cheap saint in a charlatan's cathedral, sparing commanders, mourning lizards.

Mavis wouldn't recognize him. He could hear her laugh in the back of his skull, low and warm, asking what fool mess he'd wandered into this time. Gods, he missed that sound. Missed her. Missed the man he'd been when she still believed he was decent.

He pushed himself upright. Pain flared down his side, and his vision swam. The world tilted.

He caught himself on the damp wall, palm scraping over cold, sweating stone. Around him, the arena had changed while he'd been lost in himself. The big fight was done. Now the skinks were turning on each other in pick up factions, snapping and hissing as all semblance of order crumbled. New lines being redrawn in real time.

*Good.*

His gaze snagged on familiar as he turned to the tunnel: the worn stock of his rifle, the scuffed canvas of his gunna right where Karl had dumped them earlier. He staggered toward them, boots slipping in blood and offal. Every step sent a fresh jolt through his nerves. His lungs wheezed like bad bellows.

He stooped with a grunt that ripped at his bruised ribs and scooped up the rifle, the weight settling into his shoulder like it belonged there. The strap of the gunna bit into a sore collarbone as he dragged it over his head.

The fight in this chamber didn't want him anymore. That was fine. Bradley was out there somewhere, and Alysha, and the rest of the idiots he'd somehow let turn into his people.

*His people*, he thought, shaking his head.

Jorgen started walking, each footfall a negotiation with his battered body. The air down the passage was cooler, carried faint echoes of distant shouting. Somewhere ahead, his companions were either cutting their way free or bleeding out in the dark.

## A LIGHT FOR THE LOST

\*\*\*

The lake's black surface kissing the shore in small, patient laps. The sound should have been soothing. It only made Knight's skin crawl. Every gentle splash felt like time slipping away.

He shifted his weight, biting back a curse as his bad leg throbbed. The skink poultice had neutralized the venom, but the limb still pulsed with a bone-deep ache, hot under the tight wrap. Sitting was awful; standing made it worse. There was no position that didn't remind him what he couldn't do.

Which was most anything that required endurance.

Pinky crouched beside him at the edge of the rock shelf, her toes almost brushing the dark water. Her gaze never left the massive stalagmite rising from the middle of the lake.

The thing looked like a tooth driven up through the cavern floor. A spiraling path had been carved into it, winding up and around out of sight..

"Is that where we need to go?" she asked, voice soft.

Knight followed her line of sight and gave a curt nod. The motion tugged something in his neck, another small ache to join the chorus.

"Yeah," he muttered. "That's our way out."

Between them and that spiraling path stretched a broad, flat pane of water, black as engine oil, broken only by slow ripples and the pale smear of reflections. No walkways. No boats. No conveniently abandoned skiff waiting with their names on it.

Just cold depth and the flat certainty that if he went under with that leg, he wasn't coming back up.

"Can you swim?" he asked, glancing sideways at her.

"I don't ever remember trying," she said after a moment, as if she was testing the thought from all angles. The bioluminescent glow painted blue-green hollows under her eyes, catching on faint, pearly flecks that sometimes lit beneath her skin when she was upset. Right now they were dark, but he didn't trust that to last.

Silence settled between them. Somewhere farther around the cavern, a drop fell from the ceiling, the plink echoing like a clock tick.

"Well," Knight grunted, forcing the words out if only to cut through the tightening in his chest, "today might be a good day to learn."

The joke went nowhere. Pinky just blinked, then tilted her head slightly, studying him like she was trying to decide—something.

He sighed inwardly. Gallows humor, despite his enjoyment and appreciation of it, he had never developed the proper timing.

Up close, the changes in her were impossible to ignore. He'd been trying not to look straight at her, as if ignoring it might force reality to behave. But there was no pretending in the slow churn of the moment.

She'd shot up. Not much, a few inches, but on her frame it made a world of difference. Limbs that had been all gangly pre-teen angles now had length and line, the first shadows of adult muscle and curve. Her jaw was a touch sharper. Fingers longer. The dress she wore was tighter in places and shorter in others, fabric filling out where it used to hang loose.

Eleven, maybe twelve, in the sewers. The girl beside him looked fifteen, maybe sixteen.

The eyes hadn't aged in any way that made sense. They'd gone a different direction—deeper, more aware, like someone older had taken up more space behind them.

He dragged his gaze back to the water.

"Look," he said, this time picking his words like his bootsteps, careful and deliberate, "worst comes to worst, I'll carry you. I've got enough in me for that."

The sentence tasted like a lie even as he said it. His leg burned at the thought of kicking against unseen currents with her weight on his back. Drowning in some subterranean sump wasn't how he'd pictured going out. But if that's what it took to get her across…

His tone betrayed him anyway. A quaver on the last word, a roughness he couldn't blame entirely on smoke and exertion.

Pinky didn't answer. She brought her knees up to her chest and hugged them, watching the central spire as if it might turn and look back at her.

"We'll figure it out," Knight said, attempting to shore up his flimsy promise. "Mustang's got that overclocked brain. And Bradley comes through when it counts. Between the two of them, somebody'll come up with a better idea than 'jump in and hope for the best.'"

A frown creased his brow as the words left his mouth. Saying the names out loud made their absence feel sharper. The last hours had been all smoke and screams and tunnel mazes; now that he'd finally stopped moving, the cracks in hope were easier to see.

He forced himself not to follow that thought.

Something else nagged at him, quieter but more persistent. He shifted, studying Pinky out of the corner of his eye. Not the height, not the altered lines of her face—he could acclimate to that. But, there was something off with the way she held herself now. No fidgeting. No balling her hands in her skirt. No unfocused glance darting around.

She sat still. Very still.

"Pinky…" He let the name hang for a second. Saying the other one—the one he had heard from her own lips—felt like inviting it in. "You feel okay?"

It was the kind of question you asked a kid after a nightmare, not after allowing her watch you torture someone, something. Ridiculous on its face. But the unease crawling along his spine didn't care.

Her head turned, slowly. Violet eyes met his, reflecting pinpricks of light. He thought he saw that other glimmer again, the one that had flared in the tunnels—points of light under the skin, stars caught in flesh—but then it was gone, leaving only that too-calm gaze.

"I'm… here," she said after a heartbeat, the answer simple and not simple at all.

Knight held her stare, listening past the words—to the steadiness of her breathing, the way her hands relaxed on her knees instead of tightening. He was right. There was a different weight behind her eyes.

Like something inside her had finally started to wake.

Pinky's gaze stayed on him. Not blank, not dazed—focused. Too focused. Then she smiled. It was small and bright in a way that made his skin crawl.

"I feel… better than I ever remember feeling," she said at last.

Her tone was light. Bubbly, almost. The kind of voice you used coming back from a festival, not after weeks of captivity and a fresh trail of corpses.

He tamped down the urge to grab her by the shoulders and shake the unsettling weirdness out of her. That wouldn't fix anything. And if something else really was sitting behind those violet eyes, shaking her might just wake it up faster.

So he did what soldiers did when the rules stopped making sense: he watched. Catalogued. Filed it away for later.

Footsteps. Not the light, skittering drag of skink claws, but heavier boots, stumbling a little, echoing in a rhythm he knew. Adrenaline cut through his unease like a fresh blade.

"Stay here," he murmured, leaning toward her, keeping his voice just above the water's sigh. "Stay low. Stay quiet."

He didn't know why the instinct hit so hard—only that some part of him didn't want her standing in the open.

She opened her mouth as if to argue, then closed it. Something unreadable passed across her face. She slid back into the shadows near a sagging fungus-encrusted pillar, folding herself up small.

Knight gave her one last look, then pushed himself upright with a low grunt. His leg throbbed all the way to his hip.

He kept low as he moved, using hunched fungal huts and broken stone outcroppings for cover. His blaster felt right in his hand, weight and balance familiar as his own heartbeat. He thumbed the safety off but kept his finger outside the trigger guard.

Shapes resolved out of the dim—three of them. One squat and broad, one tall and spare, one with fiery red locks not even the blue wash could tame.

He stepped out from behind a half-collapsed fungal wall, blaster up but angled just off-center.

"Hold it," he barked.

The trio froze. For an instant the cavern was nothing but silhouettes and the heavy rasp of overworked lungs.

Karl's blocky outline. Bradley's wiry frame, shoulders sagging. Alysha, weight balanced even while exhausted, hand twitching toward a weapon that wasn't there, then settling as she caught sight of him.

Knight lowered the blaster, though he didn't sling it. The ache in his chest had nothing to do with his leg.

"What took you so long?" he growled. It came out sharper than he'd meant, frayed nerves instead of humor.

Up close, they looked worse than he'd imagined. Karl's beard was matted with grime and flecks of dried blood, his shirt torn at the shoulder. Bradley's uniform was shredded, stiff with sweat and ichor, dark circles carved deep under his eyes. Alysha's hair was loose, streaked with skink blood and soot, a faint tremor in the fingers wrapped around the hilt of her blade.

"Long story," Karl said, letting out a breath that was more groan than anything. "Chaos broke loose. Thought we might not all make it."

Bradley only nodded, jaw working. The usual restless energy in his eyes was tamped down to a dull, brittle focus.

Alysha stepped forward a pace, her gaze skimming over Knight's leg, his roughed-up gear, then looking past him as if she could see through rock. "Mustang? Jorgen?" she asked. "Have either of them made it?"

"No," he answered. "Not yet."

Alysha's fingers clenched a little tighter around her weapon. "They'll make it." The words sounded like she was throwing them at the darkness, daring it to argue.

Knight wanted her certainty. All he had was a creeping, hollow ache that those two should have been in front of him by now, trading insults and complaining as if it was an Olympic sport. The quiet pressed in.

"You know what they say," a voice rumbled out of the gloom behind them, dry and amused. "Speak of the devil, and he'll come strolling out of the dark."

Jorgen stepped into the light with a grin that nearly split his battered face. Mustang loomed at his shoulder, clothes scorched and torn, eyes burning with a tired, wired brightness.

Relief hit Knight like an impact. His grip loosened on the blaster without him telling it to. His lungs remembered how to breathe.

"Took your damn time," he muttered, the corner of his mouth ticking up.

Jorgen snorted. "You try wading through a lizard riot at my age and see how quick you move."

Mustang didn't bother with a quip. Up close, Knight could see the fine tremor in his fingers where they rested near the rifle sling, the faint scorch marks along the weapon's casing. The man looked like he'd been chewed up and spat out by half the tunnels in the city—but he was still standing.

Knight gave them both a short, sharp nod. They were together again. Not safe. Not by a long shot. But together.

"Don't start," Mustang rasped, the words catching on a throat still raw from acrid smoke. A crooked smile tugged at his mouth anyway. "Good to see you too, Knight."

Alysha was on him and Jorgen in a heartbeat, boots splashing through the slick film along the shore. Up close, the damage was worse—Mustang's clothes scorched and torn, Jorgen's leathers stiff with dried blood, both of them reeking of smoke, sweat, and skink musk. Her hand hovered uselessly between them for a moment before she settled for a quick, rough squeeze to Mustang's shoulder, fingers digging in as if to test he was real. Relief softened the tight line of her jaw, even as her eyes tracked every bruise and burn.

Bradley came in slower, like his legs weren't entirely convinced this wasn't some hallucination conjured by exhaustion. He bumped his knuckles against Jorgen's, the contact a dull tap through bandages and grime. "You crazy old bastard," he muttered, voice hoarse but steady. "Glad you made it."

Jorgen huffed a laugh that sounded more like a cough. "Takes more than a lizard riot to punch my ticket," he said, though the way he leaned on his rifle to stay upright took some shine off the bravado.

Knight followed the spiral cut into the central stalagmite with his eyes, the stone path climbing out of sight into gloom. The lake between them and that route might as well have been an ocean. The damp chill off the water crept through his clothes, settling into the bad leg until it throbbed in time with his pulse. Swimming still sounded like madness…but with Mustang and Jorgen here, with Karl steady as bedrock and Bradley thinking three moves ahead, the impossible felt a shade less impossible.

# CHAPTER THIRTY-ONE

Cold hit him first.

Knight broke the surface with a ragged inhale, the lake's chill clawing at him. Water sluiced off his jacket and ruined trousers as he stumbled into the shallows, every step sending a white-hot spike through his bad leg. When he reached the stone shelf and solid rock rose under his boots, he let out a breath that was little more than a relieved curse.

"Well," he grumbled, more to his own rattled nerves than to anyone else, "that wasn't so bad."

Jorgen snorted beside him, soaked to the bone, scars and gray-streaked hair plastered dark against his skull. Bradley was there too, teeth chattering, but his hands were steady as he slipped Knight's arm across his shoulders. Together they hauled him upright. The stalagmite towered over them—an immense spine of stone rising out of the black lake, its base slick with moss and old spray.

Ground. Treacherous, algae-slick, and cold, but ground all the same. He'd take it.

Karl was already at the base of the formation, one broad hand running along the carved ledge that spiraled upward. His fingertips traced the gouged path with the casual familiarity of a man who'd spent a lifetime reading stone.

"Old," he barked, knuckles rapping once against the rock. "Very old. But she'll hold. See there?" He jerked his chin toward the dark shapes higher up—shallow hollows cut into the curve of the stalagmite. "Waystations."

"Shelters," Bradley breathed, the word escaping on a hopeful exhale. His breath steamed in the cool air, face streaked with droplets he hadn't bothered to wipe away.

"Assumin' they ain't full of nasty surprises," Jorgen muttered. He rolled one shoulder and winced, a flash of pain tightening before stubbornness buried it again. His gold-ringed gray eyes never left the niches above, weighing distance against how much fight was left in his limbs.

Mustang trailed in last, moving as if the weight of the cavern hung from his shoulders. He leaned his back against the stalagmite, one hand braced flat against the damp stone. His breath came in shallow pulls.

Alysha stepped in beside him, water-dark hair hanging in heavy ropes against her shouders. "You alright?" she asked quietly, the sharp edges smoothed from her voice by concern.

He managed a nod that looked more like a slow sway. "Just need…a minute," he rasped. His fingers twitched, as if still feeling the phantom recoil of his rifle.

Knight watched them. Every one of them carried a new limp. The price of not dying. It never came cheap.

"We can't stay down here," he said, forcing the gravel back into his voice. The ache in his leg flared as if to argue, but he pushed through it. "Those shelters'll do for a breather, but I don't want a pack of skinks trying to squeeze past us on that path. We move before they think to follow."

They started up.

The carved ledge hugged the stalagmite, no more than two bodies wide in places. The stone was worn smooth by long use, edges rounded, the faint grit underfoot slick with moisture. The air cooled as they climbed, the damp crawling into Knight's clothes and settling in his tired muscles. Bioluminescent fungi thinned with every upward turn, their soft blue and green glow giving way to gloom. Shadows thickened, swallowing the lake below until it vanished, leaving only the muffled memory of water lapping somewhere far beneath them.

Each step was work. Sweat trickled cold down his spine, salt stinging the raw places spider venom and skink claws had left behind.

The first waystation emerged from the curve of the stone almost without warning—a shallow hollow scooped into the stalagmite's flank, just deep enough to cram them in out of the open path. No doors or carvings. Just rough-hewn rock, damp and uneven.

It looked like heaven.

Knight made it three steps inside before his leg quit arguing and simply folded. He hit the floor in an awkward sprawl, the breath punching out of him in a short, startled grunt. The cold of the stone seeped through his soaked clothes, but he didn't care.

"Damned... scenic route," he muttered, more air than voice.

Jorgen followed a heartbeat later. He eased himself down with considerably less grace, back sliding against the rough wall until he found a spot that didn't jab directly into a bruise. His face screwed up as he settled, teeth bared for a second in a silent snarl at his own protesting muscles, then smoothing out into something like weary satisfaction.

Alysha and Bradley moved with a kind of brittle urgency, motion running ahead of what their bodies actually had left.

Mustang sank down nearer the mouth of the hollow. His chest lifted and fell a little too fast, as if the climb hadn't quite let go of him. Even sitting, there was a coil in him, a wired restlessness that made his fingers tap, then still, then tap again against his thigh.

Karl did what Karl always did—he made himself useful.

He shrugged off the apothecary's pack and set it between his boots, big hands careful as he worked the bindings loose. Inside, everything was wrapped tight in woven fiber. Karl peeled one open and snorted.

"Not exactly a gourmet feast," he said, fishing out pale curls of dried mushroom and tough, dark strips that might once have been meat. "But it's got sustenance."

He tipped the lot into a dented metal pot, that seemed to have accumulated more dents and dings since the last time he had seen it. Then jerked his chin toward a thin sheet of water seeping from a crack in the wall. It chimed faintly as it dripped into a shallow divot in the floor. He scooped from there, the water shockingly cold as it splashed into the pot.

Bradley crouched beside him with his multi-tool. A quick twist and a bright tongue of flame sputtered to life, licking at the bottom of the metal. The smell of hot metal gave way to something better as the water warmed—earthy mushroom, a faint tang of smoke from the dried meat, and the sharper nose-prickle of crushed herbs Karl added with a miser's care.

Soon the pot was murmuring, steam curling up to soften the chill that clung to the hollow. The scent seeped into everything —into wet cloth, into the stone, into noses that had known nothing but dust and blood and reptile musk for too long.

They passed around rough metal bowls, ladling the stew in small portions. It was thin, but the broth was rich, the meat chewy and salty, the mushrooms soft and almost sweet. Heat spread from tongue to gut to stiff fingers around the bowls. For the first few minutes, conversation was limited to slurps and low, satisfied sounds.

Somewhere in there, the knot in Knight's shoulders eased by a notch.

When the pot was scraped clean, they shifted into the practical business of hurt bodies. Knight sat with his back braced against a protruding ridge of stone. Bradley knelt at his leg, peeling back bandages smelling faintly of skink poultice and old blood.

Cool air hit the swollen flesh and Knight hissed through his teeth.

"We need to take it easy once we start out again," Bradley said, voice low but firm. His fingers were gentle, but there was no doubt in his tone. "Push this too hard, you'll lose the progress you've made."

Knight grimaced. He hated the truth in it almost as much as he hated the weakness in his own limb. Still, he gave a short nod. "Not planning on sprinting any marathons," he muttered.

He looked over Bradley's shoulder. "Mustang. Let's rig a charging cable to my blaster. Be nice to have more than one working AR unit."

Mustang eased himself over, movements stiff, and dug into his own pack. The cable he needed came out in a coil of scavenged insulation and mismatched connectors. His fingers, though tired, knew what they were doing. He snapped one end into Bradley's pistol, then clipped the leads to connectors on the unit's housing.

The AR unit booted to life, startup sequences crawling across the interior of its lenses. Soft status lights pulsed in the dimness, beating a slow, steady rhythm against the walls of the waystation.

"Keep your pistol fed, and it will have you at a hundred percent soon enough," Mustang said.

Bradley's gaze snagged on the lieutenant's arm as Mustang started to push away. The shoulder was rounded in wrong places, the muscles around it tightening every time he shifted.

"Sit," Bradley said, that same command tone he used training in emergency wards. "Since you're here."

Mustang scowled on reflex, but he obeyed, lowering himself without argument. Bradley loosened the sling, checked the set of bone and scar, and prodded gently along the healing tissue. Mustang's jaw clenched, a muscle ticking, but he stayed still.

"It's mended better than it has any right to," Bradley said, re-tightening the sling with brisk efficiency, "but climbing and swimming on it didn't do you any favors."

"I can shoot one-handed if I need to," Mustang muttered.

"I didn't say you couldn't," Bradley replied. "Just go easy on it."

For once, Mustang let it go. When Bradley moved on to Alysha's bruised ribs and the cut along Karl's forearm, Mustang accepted another small bowl's worth of stew from Karl and drank it quietly, staring at the wall just beyond the circle of light. When he finished, he set the bowl aside with careful fingers and drifted back to his earlier spot near the entrance—close enough to hear breathing, far enough that the shadows could hide the worst of what was written on his face.

Jorgen lowered himself down beside Knight with all the grace of a man much older than he looked. Every motion betrayed the stiffness in his tired body. He exhaled as his back hit the rock, letting his head rest against the wall. For a moment his eyes tracked the others—the way Alysha's hands shook just slightly as she rewound her own bandage, the slump in Karl's shoulders now that work was done, the way Mustang stared into the dark.

The only sounds were the quiet tick of cooling metal, the faint whine of the charging rig, and the slow drip of water in the dark beyond the hollow.

Jorgen cleared his throat at last, the sound rough, dragging over old scars.

"I ever tell y'all about a job I had…" Jorgen asked the stone more than anyone, his voice rasping out of him like it had been mangled in an industrial accident. A crooked smile tugged at his lips. "Tracking down a three-legged dog for some syndicate boss's kid?"

Alysha glanced up from her blade. She'd been working the scrap of cloth along its edge in small, precise strokes, letting the familiar rhythm settle her nerves. At Jorgen's words, the motion slowed. The corner of her mouth twitched. Only he could go from arena bloodbath to lame-dog story without missing a beat.

Pinky lay curled at Alysha's feet, bare toes tucked into the warmth of Alysha's calf. She giggled, the sound small but bright in the cramped hollow. The glow from the AR units limned her changed features, but the delight in her eyes looked achingly familiar.

Karl, mid-sip, snorted. The laugh caught him off guard and a spray of stew shot from his nose. He choked and wheezed, beating a fist against his chest while Bradley muttered something about manners and handed him a rag. Jorgen, sitting sprawled out and propped on his arm heavy with exhaustion, obligingly mimed a lopsided sprint, one knee jerking up like he was chasing something that kept drifting out of reach.

"Took me three days in the slums," he went on, that far-off grin creasing the weathered lines of his face. "Bribin' sewer urchins, sleepin' next to trash fires…the whole shebang. Finally find the mutt, mangy thing, missin' a leg and an ear, stinkin' like old socks left in a corpse." He shook his head, amused even now. "And there's this lace-head, high as a kite, on his knees prayin' to it. Candle stubs, little offerings of canned beans and cheap booze. Swear to you, looked me dead in the eye and told me I was offendin' the holy spirit."

A low ripple of laughter rolled around the waystation. Even Mustang huffed out a breath that might have been a chuckle, his head tipped back against the rock, eyes half-closed. Karl wheezed out the last of his cough and chuckled helplessly, shaking his head. Bradley's begrudging smile was lit strange by the pulsing green of the charging AR units.

The tunnel below and the memories that went with them felt further away. The world narrowed to clinking metal, soft laughter, and Pinky's quiet snicker when Jorgen added, "The kid cried less for that dog than his dead did over the bill I passed him."

***

The climb dragged on in a dull, punishing rhythm. No one wasted words—each of them had run out of easy ones a long time ago.

Mustang hung a few paces behind the main cluster, his rifle slung, his bad arm cradled in the sling Bradley had bullied him back into. It freed his good hand for balance and left his eyes to do what they did best—take stock, measure angles, tally threats.

Pinky climbed near the middle of the line, between Alysha and Karl. On the surface, it was almost normal: small frame, bare feet walking with sure, quick steps; pink hair still defiantly bright against the gloom. But everything else about her was wrong. She moved with too much poise. There was a composure in the set of her shoulders, in the way she paused to check the drop, that clashed with her general persona.

Every now and then she'd glance back down the path. Her eyes caught the dim glow from the fungi and AR units and threw it back sharper, as if something—or someone—were looking out from her eyes. Mustang felt the hairs on his neck stand up each time. The part of him trained to categorize threats filed her in a strange new drawer—*friendly*, for now, but stamped with a question mark.

The path narrowed.

Karl raised a hand and the line shuddered to a halt. His voice came back thin and hollow in the high space. "Slow and steady," he barked. "One at a time past this bend. You slip here, you aren't getting a second chance."

Wind breathed up from below, damp and cold. The path underfoot felt narrower by the second, the rough grit of it grinding through boot soles.

They edged around a bulge of rock, pressed close to the wall. Mustang forced himself to keep moving, to not look down, to not think about how far they'd climbed. He tracked Pinky's progress, watched Alysha keep an arm ready near the girl without being obvious about it, watched Knight bring up the rear of the lead cluster, leg dragging a little more with every step.

Jorgen was ahead of Knight, shoulders hunched, one hand trailing along the stone for balance. The old man's usual swagger had bled into a stiff, careful shuffle. His boots slid on a patch of damp lichen, just enough to throw off his rhythm.

"Watch your—" Karl started.

Jorgen's foot skated out. His weight tipped sideways, toward the empty air.

634

Knight moved before he could think about the pain. His bad leg shrieked as he lunged, but his hands were already reaching. Fingers snagged leather—Jorgen's long coat—right as the old man's center of gravity went past the edge.

The momentum yanked Knight forward. The edge of the path crumbled under his boot, stone skittering away into the dark. For a sick second they were both hanging, Jorgen flailing, Knight's shoulders stretched to tearing.

Knight dug the heel of his good foot into the rock and hauled. Tendons burned. Something in his thigh gave a hot, tearing protest. With a hoarse shout, he leaned back with everything he had.

They crashed back in a tangle, Knight slammed the wall of the path, Jorgen's weight driving the air out of the big man's lungs in a wheeze that sounded more like a dying bellows than a man.

The world snapped back in a rush of noise.

Knight's vision pulsed black at the edges. Pain roared up from his leg, white-hot and dizzying, but when he forced his eyes open, Jorgen bracing him against the wall, not tumbling into the void. The old man's fingers were buried in tattered riot gear, knuckles white.

Mustang stayed where he was, a few steps back—close enough to cover, far enough not to crowd the narrow ledge. His eyes moved over the group, counting: Jorgen, Knight, Alysha, Bradley, Karl, Pinky. For a second his gaze snagged on Pinky; she was staring down into the darkness where Jorgen might've fallen, her expression—almost thoughtful, a curious tilt to her head before she looked away.

Jorgen's breathing rasped as the adrenaline bled out of him. He dropped to his knees on the stone path, bracing one hand on the wall, the other pressed to his ribs. The skin beneath his beard had gone a lighter shade of pale.

"Damn close, that was," he coughed at last. The gold-ringed gray of his eyes looked washed out, exhaustion etched deep around them, but the raw spike of terror was gone, replaced by the dogged stubbornness they all knew too well.

Karl crouched beside him, one big hand hovering near Jorgen's shoulder in case he listed. "Easy, old man," he said gruffly. "You scare us like that again, I'm throwin' you over myself. You need to rest."

Jorgen huffed, trying for a grin and almost managing it. "No," he rasped, shaking his head. "We need to make it to that cave at the top. Can't be more'n an hour, if that. I just…" He exhaled hard, a shudder running through him. "Just need a few minutes to get my soul back inside my skin."

Karl studied him, weighing stubborn pride against the grim reality of the drop inches away. The stone under them was too narrow for a real argument.

"A few minutes," Karl conceded with a nod. "Catch your breath."

Despite their desire to continue on, they stopped at the next and likely last waystation. After the near miss, it felt much smaller than the others they had stopped at.

They packed into the hollowed niche in the rock, backs to rough stone, the memory of Jorgen's boots skidding toward the drop replaying. It should've been a refuge, but everyone's nerves were simply too frayed.

Knight slid down the wall until he hit the floor, jaw tight as his bad leg flared with each inch he dropped. The ache had settled into a constant, throbbing burn. Sweat beaded along his hairline despite the chill.

Mustang eased down beside him, the sling cradling his arm a grim reminder of his own limits. He uncapped his canteen and held it out.

"Drink," he said. His voice was low, stripped of bravado. "You did good. Not many would've been able to catch him. Fewer still would have tried."

Knight took the canteen, the metal cool against his fingers. The water was chilled and metallic, but it cleared the dust from his throat. He wasn't sure if Mustang meant it as praise or simple observation, but he took it as the former.

Across the niche, Bradley worked in silence over Jorgen's cuts and scrapes. His hands moved with practiced care, brow furrowed in a concentration that looked a lot like guilt.

"This one's shallow," Bradley mumbled, dabbing away dried blood, more to himself than to Jorgen. "You'll be fine. Try not to fall off any more mountains."

"I'll pencil that in," Jorgen rasped. He hissed when Bradley pressed a tender rib, but stayed still.

Alysha hummed a near tuneless scrap of sound.

Pinky had curled up against the far wall, knees hugged to her chest, bare toes pressed to the cold stone. Her wide violet eyes tracked each of them in turn, calm where they should've been shaken. Mustang noticed every glance. His own gaze kept returning to her.

Karl stood near the mouth of the niche. He scanned the spiral below and above, hearing only the deep wind.

They dozed in shifts, boots never unlaced, weapons always within reach. The rock leached heat from their bodies; muscles that had carried them through grudgingly gave up some of their exhaustion.

The respite was short.

When they moved again, it was with straps cinched tight and bleary eyes. Jorgen rose slowly, one hand still braced on the wall until his knees stopped shaking. His shoulders squared, and he took his place in the line with the stubborn set of a man who refused to owe death a second favor.

The path coiled ever upward, tighter now, more exposed. The air lost the humid weight of the lower caverns. With each step, a faint, almost imagined freshness appeared—a whisper of wind that hadn't been filtered through mold and deep stone. The thought of sunlight—a real sky—hung somewhere above them like bait on a hook.

Near the final stretch, Karl led, feeling his way around the bends, hand sweeping the stone before each step. Knight ended up wedged between Karl and Jorgen, carefully leaning on both men more than he cared to admit. Their shared grunts and harsh breaths became a rough, ragged rhythm, a three-part chorus of effort.

Behind them came Alysha and Bradley, then Pinky, light on her feet and disturbingly sure near the edge. Mustang brought up the rear, his eyes working as hard as his legs, counting heads every few seconds.

The spiral tightened one last time—and then opened.

The cave mouth yawned ahead, a dark arch punched into the bottom of the vaulted cavern's ceiling.

"Well folks, welcome to the asshole of the world," Jorgen laughed through heavy breaths.

Knight let himself imagine blue sky beyond it. Wind. Sunlight. Aboveground air that didn't taste like rot.

Instead, as they crossed the threshold, composition of the flooring changed under their boots.

The scrape of limestone became the hollow clank of perforated metal decking underfoot. The sound echoed up into the dark. The air shifted as well—much drier, carrying the ghost of mineral spirits and stale air.

They had climbed out of a living cave and stepped into something constructed.

Harsh lines replaced natural curves. Support beams jutted from the walls at precise intervals. Incandescent lights—long dead— ran along the ceiling, their metal casings rusted, their bulbs clouded with dust. The distant outline of doors broke the tunnel ahead into segments. On the walls, signs with blocky, unfamiliar symbols and faded hazard icons pointed deeper inside.

Knight's stomach dropped.

"Another damn maze," he muttered. His step thunked against the grating, the vibration traveling up his bad leg. He had traded one labyrinth for another.

The question burned in all of them: had they clawed their way out of the skink's barbaric pit just to walk into another of the

Foundation's buried toys? Or were they about to trespass into some other long-forgotten tomb?

"Look on the bright side," Mustang chittered. "At least this was made by people."

Alysha and Bradley moved ahead a few paces, weapons drawn. Their shoulders stayed tight, eyes sweeping every doorway, every corner. Bradley thumbed his AR unit's light to life, a spear of pale glow cutting a narrow channel through the dark. Alysha's blade caught the beam, its edge flashing before she lowered it again.

Behind them, Pinky stepped onto the steel as if it were nothing more than a different kind of stone. No flinch at the hollow clang under her bare feet, no widening of the eyes at the oppressive geometry of the place. She walked with a strange, distant calm, fingertips trailing briefly along a metal rail as though confirming it was real, but generally unconcerned.

Mustang watched her profile as she continued forward, that same unease creeping cold fingers up his spine. The girl who'd once clung to every adult in reach was now moving through the world like it couldn't touch her.

*Is she even just a girl anymore?* The thought came unbidden, and he didn't like it. *But what kid ages four years in a day?*

He shifted his rifle on his shoulder as he followed the others into the man-made dark, the sense of victory from their escape already guttering under the weight of the new unknown waiting ahead.

"How far up does this go?" Karl whispered. "And what in hell are we gonna find at the top?"

His breath puffed white in the cooler air, vanishing into the dark.

Jorgen, leaning heavily on the railing, managed a crooked grin that didn't quite reach his eyes. "If we are lucky…" he panted, "a shower and a hot meal."

No one laughed. The thought of hot water and real food hurt more than it comforted.

Mustang moved past them, scanning as he went. The steel grating creaked under his boots, the sound too sharp after months little more than echoes and dripping water.

"I don't think that's in the cards, old man," he grunted, not looking back.

Grim and silent, they pushed deeper into the guts of the structure. Their weapon lights carved thin lanes through the dark—pale beams sweeping over flaking paint, rusted conduit, and faded walls. Every step set up hollow echoes that chased them down the corridors.

The architecture was definitely human in design. No curves, no organic growth—just bulkheads, crossbeams, and doors inset with heavy locks. Function over form, the sort of place designed for efficiency and control, not comfort.

Jorgen dragged his fingertips along a wall, over a long black streak where heat had kissed steel. The scorched metal flaked under his calloused hand. He stopped at a side corridor marked by a faded yellow-and-black emblem, the biohazard symbol barely visible under grime.

"A research lab," he growled. "Likely built centuries ago. Old world military, maybe."

Mustang angled his light toward a cracked glass frame bolted to the wall—an emergency map, its ink faded but not yet gone. He stepped closer, wiping dust away with the back of his hand causing a crack to force on the brittle face from the pressure. Ghost-blue lines and numbers emerged, along with a stamp at the bottom: a worn eagle and block letters.

"He's right," Mustang said quietly. "United States Army." His brow furrowed as he tracked the schematic layout. "Deep-site research facility. Classified. A little over six hundred years, if these dates are real."

"I wonder what they were doing down here?" he asked, mostly to himself.

No one answered.

Alysha moved point on their loose formation, blade sheathed but her hand never far from the hilt. Her eyes checked each doorway, each t-intersection, each shadow their lights didn't quite burn away. Once, she flinched and pivoted at the faint slap of something far off. The sound came again, softer, bouncing oddly in the metal throat of the corridor before fading.

They weren't alone. Whether that meant skinks, rats, or something the Army had cooked up and left behind, no one said.

Pinky walked just ahead of Mustang. The AR light caught the side of her face now and then, washing her features in stark white. There was no tension in her shoulders, no tightness at the corners of her mouth. The claustrophobic hallways, the weight of history pressing from all sides—none of it seemed to bother her. Her violet eyes slid over hazard signs and rusted doors as if this were just another cave, another skin the world had pulled on.

Mustang filed that away with everything else about her that now refused to fit.

With each turn, the walls carried a kind of echo that wasn't quite sound—a sense that people had moved here once with purpose. Orders barked. Laughter. Arguments in incandescent-lit corridors. All of it long gone, leaving only an impression stamped into metal and concrete. Under that, something emptier still: the hollow of abandonment.

They passed shattered lights, a security station with its glass punched out and chairs scattered as if by a hasty retreat. Alysha drew her sword and swept its light over a doorway welded shut from this side, bead lines of old weld catching faintly.

Then the hallway opened.

They stepped into a broad chamber that had to be the mess hall. The space swallowed their lights, high ceiling lost in shadow. Long metal tables lay overturned, some twisted as if something massive had rolled through. Wooden and metal chairs were broken in piles against one wall in a chaotic drift. A serving line sat behind a low barrier, trays scattered on the floor like dropped shields.

On the far side, shelves that once held rations stood bare. A long-dead smell haunted the room—mold, stale grease, and the bitter scent of whatever preservative had outlived the food it was meant to protect.

Bradley toed a crumbled bit of foil. "People ate here," he said quietly. "Every day. Until they didn't."

His voice disappeared into the empty room.

Jorgen drifted toward a side passage marked by peeling paint and a strip of stenciled letters worn past legibility. He couldn't have said why that corridor pulled at him—only that something in his gut tugged in that direction, the same stubborn instinct that had kept him alive longer than he had any right to expect. Karl fell in behind him without comment, Alysha at his shoulder, eyes hard. Pinky trailed them with that same unsettling composure, her bright presence muffled now, as if something dark had been drawn over the girl she'd been.

For Knight, Bradley, and Mustang, the sign for BARRACKS— flaking white paint on a rust-browned plate—decided things. None of them truly believed there'd be anything useful here, but soldiers went to barracks the way pilgrims went to shrines. If there were ghosts here, they deserved someone to look in on them. To remember. To bury what needed burying.

The mess hall doors boomed shut behind the departing group, the echo a hollow clap that chased itself down the corridor.

Knight limped harder now, leaning more of his weight onto Bradley's wiry frame. "You sure about this?" he rasped, voice stripped down to gravel. "Feels like walking into a grave."

Bradley huffed a breath that was almost a laugh. "Welcome to the last few months of our lives," he said. "We've been buried for how long? This one just smells a little… mustier."

Mustang moved a few paces ahead, rifle low but ready, his beam sweeping vents, doorframes, the seams of the floor.

"Can't be much farther, can it?" Bradley whispered, more hope than question.

No one answered.

The first door they reached was a slab of metal with a handle furred in rust. Mustang wrapped his fingers around it and gave a practiced twist. For a moment it resisted, then the hinges surrendered with a long, complaining groan that crawled up Knight's spine.

Their lights spilled into the room.

Rusted metal cots lined the walls in double rows, some collapsed in on themselves, others still standing like bare ribs. Where mattresses remained, they were little more than rotted husks, dark with mold. Footlockers sat at attention at the ends of the beds, most of them gaping open, lids warped and empty.

The air had a taste to it—old sweat sunk into fabric, iron from rust, dry dust. Underneath it all was a faint, stale human smell that time hadn't quite managed to wash away.

They stepped inside.

Even here, decay hadn't erased everything. A few dog-eared magazines lay scattered on the floor, their covers bleached almost to ghosts. A deck of cards fanned across a crate, half the suit faces gone to mildew. Above one bunk, a faded photograph still clung to the wall, corners curled, the faces within blurred into smudges by age and moisture. All that remained clear was the outline of bodies crowding together, shoulders pressed, heads tipped close in the universal shape of squad photos.

Knight's throat tightened. Different century, different army— but still the same.

They moved on, room after room, each one a variation on the same quiet ruin. Uniforms hung in moth-eaten tatters from wall hooks. Boots collapsed into themselves at the slightest touch, leather gone powder-soft with dry rot. Name tapes peeled off drawers, unreadable. Time had worked through this place methodically, breaking everything down to the same dull palette of brown, gray, and red rust.

Knight's leg finally forced a halt. He eased himself down onto the edge of a cot frame in one of the single run away from the enlisted barracks, the metal shrieking in thin protest beneath his weight. The jolt sent a spike of pain through his limb; he rode it out in silence, breathing slow.

His hand slipped down to steady himself on the nearest footlocker. The lid, warped but not fully open, shifted under his palm. Something solid pressed back against his fingers, not the soft crumble of cloth or paper gone to mush, but leather—dry, cracked, still whole.

He dragged the locker open the rest of the way. Dust puffed up in a fine gray sheet, catching in his nose and making his eyes water. Nestled at the bottom lay a small book, about the size of his hand. The cover was scarred and faded, but the stamped letters were still legible.

He brushed a thumb over them, clearing away the dust.

A journal. A soldier's journal.

Knight hesitated, thumb resting on the cracked leather. Opening it felt like walking into someone's head without knocking. But the weight of the place, the cots, the rust, the quiet—everything, whispered that whoever had owned this journal deserved at least one person to know he'd existed.

He eased the book open. The spine crackled. Faded ink ghosted across the yellowed pages in a cramped, hurried scrawl. On the inside cover, just above a smeared unit stamp, was a name:

Private First Class Harold Miller.

Knight ran a calloused thumb under the line, jaw tightening. Six hundred years and change, and the handwriting looked like most grunts he'd worked with. Same rushed letters. Same little hooks at the ends of words. Same need to put something down so you didn't come apart.

He let out a slow breath, then turned the first page.

\*\*\*

Jorgen chose the corridor with the worst promises.

The hazard paint had peeled into curls, but he could still make out the ghosts of warning symbols beneath it. He snorted under his breath and pushed on anyway. Known trouble didn't scare him half as much as the kind that stayed quiet.

Alysha fell in behind him without a word. Her shoulders were squared, the steady focus she wore when she'd accepted the odds and trudged forward anyway.

Pinky drifted along at the rear, eyes catching and holding the weak aura from Alysha's sword. The glow made her irises look almost luminous. She didn't pant, didn't stumble, didn't fidget with the strain of the climb. She moved like she was watching a play, not living it.

The passage constricted into concrete throat. Alysha's blade flame painted the walls in an orange veil, picking out flaking paint and rust streaks. Underneath the old warnings, the concrete was mottled brown, gray, and sweat-stained.

"Something bad went down here a long time ago," Karl muttered, voice gravel-deep.

Jorgen coughed, the sound dry and raw. "Maybe that's what the skinks were hidin' from," he rasped.

The tunnel widened suddenly and spat them out into an underground garage.

Rows of rusting vehicles crouched in the dark—buses, canvas-covered troop carriers, trucks with rotted tires sagging off cracked rims, something that might once have been a tank under its blanket of dust and corrosion.

The silence wasn't complete. Faint, muffled birdsong filtered in from somewhere, thread-thin and uncanny in the stale air. An insect buzzed furiously in the long grass poking up through a crack near the far wall.

Alysha led, sword held low. The light of the blade throwing their shadows long and monstrous across the walls and the hulks of dead machines. Jorgen and Karl followed with weapons ready.

The absence of opposition made their nerves hum like live wire.

Pinky padded close to Alysha's heel, gaze unfocused, as if the vehicular mausoleum were no more interesting than another hallway. Her violet eyes slid past gnarled tow chains and hanging cables without blinking. Fear didn't seem to find purchase in her at all—and that chilled Alysha more than any lurking monster might have.

At the far end of the garage, their lights caught on something that shouldn't have been there.

One of the massive bay doors—thick corrugated steel scored with ancient blast marks—stood slightly ajar. Through the uneven wedge of space spilled light so bright it hurt.

Sunlight.

Jorgen squinted, hand lifting reflexively to shade his eyes. Rows of dust motes swam in the beam like tiny, lazy comets. Outside the gap, they could just glimpse rough stone, wild growth, the faint suggestion of sky.

"What the…" Jorgen's voice broke off, roughened by awe and confusion.

Karl stepped closer, careful of the twisted rebar jutting from the floor. He ran his fingers along the edge where the door met rock. The stone hadn't been cut to frame the steel; it swelled and flowed around it, swallowing it like a tree swallowing a fencepost.

"This place didn't get built into the rock of the mountain," he said quietly. "The mountain grew around it."

However strange that might be, hope—dangerous and impossible—swelled in their chests.

After so long buried beneath earth and stone—with only fungus and fire for light, a miracle born of this tomb of buried machinery, the strip of daylight knifing through the bay door torn from its tracks looked unreal. Alysha's eyes burned. She'd forgotten how sharp real light could be.

She stepped toward it, sword lifted by habit. The little flame along the blade was pathetic against that gold, a guttering candle trying to stand up to a literal star. With a small, decisive motion, she slid the weapon home. The sudden loss of its glow plunged the garage into deeper shadow; the only brightness was that wedge of sun ahead, too bright to look at full-on.

Then Pinky became a blur of motion.

The girl darted past them in an after image of bare feet and pink hair, faster than Alysha would've believed her body could manage. She slipped sideways through the gap where steel had been torn away from living rock, shoulders scraping rust and stone, and was gone. A heartbeat later a sharp, startled sound carried back through the opening.

Jorgen swore under his breath and pushed after her, one big hand braced on the cold edge of the door. Light slammed into him as he squinted through. Alysha came at his heel, eyes narrowing against the glare.

Outside, the world exploded into color.

They stepped out into a carpet of waist high green. Wind whipped the tall grass in rolling sweeps, warm and clean, carrying the scents of sap and flowers and baked earth. Above, sky stretched out forever in a hard, impossible blue.

Pinky stood in the middle of a mess of wildflowers like a princess out of some fairy story. Sunlight poured over her, turning her hair into a riot of pink.

The girl twirled, holding a fist full of flowers aloft. Laughter spilled out of her, bright and clear, ringing off the hillsides like birdsong. There was nothing in her face but delight. No haunted shadows, no strange distance, no hint of the name that had slithered through Pinky's lips in the dark.

Only joy.

Alysha watched in awe. Jorgen's cracked lips tugged into a crooked smile, though his eyes stayed wary as they tracked the hills and mountains beyond.